# the brightest light of sunshine

# the brightest light of sunshine

## LISINA CONEY

PAGE
&
VINE

Page & Vine
An Imprint of Meredith Wild LLC

## Content Notes

This story contains themes of sexual assault (there are no scenes depicting an explicit sexual assault), profanity, explicit sexual content, and topics that may be sensitive to some readers. Reader discretion is advised.

*To the ones that bloomed*
*when the world expected them to wither*

# part one: seed

# chapter 1

## GRACE

I'm usually not one to make spur-of-the-moment decisions. If anything, I ruminate for weeks about whether this choice or the other will lead to disastrous consequences that will eventually ruin my life.

Like that one time I spent five full days pondering if I really needed those shoes only to find out they were forever out of stock when I finally decided I wanted them.

But this is different because I *know* I want this. Damn it, I do.

I've been thinking about it for literal months—my dads gave me a thumbs up when I Facetimed them about it, and so did my cousin Aaron and my best friend Emily, the only people whose opinion I fully trust. They didn't call me crazy or try to wipe the idea from my mind, which I assume is a good indicator that this is a rational thing to do.

So why am I hesitating now? At the very front of the tattoo parlor, of all places?

There's a guy inside. As much as he's trying to look engrossed in whatever is on his laptop screen, I know he's spotted my awkward nearby presence and is now wondering why the hell I'm standing still in front of the shop.

To be fair, I'm wondering the same thing.

I decide that taking a few seconds to scan him from head to

toe and calm my nerves in the process won't hurt— or head to waist, since the counter hides everything else.

Mysterious Tattoo Guy has got the whole bad boy look going on, which I guess is fitting for someone who tattoos people for a living. What do I know? This isn't my kind of place, and maybe that's why I feel so itchy everywhere.

A black t-shirt with the logo of the shop hugs his chest and does nothing to hide how ripped he looks. As I continue my perusal of Tattoo Guy, a question pops into my head—is it possible for arms to be bigger than a human head?

Well, I might just have my answer right there.

Both of his bulging arms are thoroughly covered in ink down to his knuckles. I spy a couple of tattoos on his neck, too. His short, dark hair with a wave is tossed backwards carelessly, but a loose strand falls over his forehead. Is it brown? Black? I can't tell from here.

What I can tell is that his orbs are as dark as night, because suddenly he lifts his head, and our eyes lock. *Great.* Without giving myself another second to think, I push the glass door open. I've had enough time to mull this over, and I've made my decision.

I think. I hope.

"Hi," I greet him with a small, nervous smile.

"Hey, there." He gives me a much easier grin, like he's used to skittish weirdos walking into his workplace on a daily basis. "What can I do for you?"

I clear my throat and look around quickly. The place looks and smells clean, which I guess is everything I could ask for from a tattoo parlor. The shop seemed smaller from the outside, but now I notice the narrow, well-lit hallway at the back leading to a wider space full of a few stations mostly hidden from view by large screens. The buzzing of a tattoo machine echoes in the walls, so the place mustn't be empty.

It's the best-reviewed tattoo parlor in town, so I expected to see a whole queue at the door when I got here. But that's not how this whole thing works, I suppose.

"So... I, um..." Nope. No hesitating now. I'm already here, aren't I? "I'd like to book a tattoo appointment, please."

"Sure. Got any designs in mind?"

His gaze doesn't move away from mine. He doesn't look down at the short hem of my summer dress or at my exposed arms. Nothing. But still, the fact that I have his undivided attention, that he's noticed me at all, makes my blood rush to every corner of my body.

Hot waves of nervous tension pulse through me until they trigger my usual response—a rapid heartbeat, uneven breathing, and a dry mouth.

*Calm down. Jeez. He's being perfectly civil.*

"Just a short quote." That I'm now too self-conscious to say out loud. "And it would have to go on my ribs."

"It would *have* to go on your ribs?" he asks in an amused voice.

My cheeks flush and I suspect I look like a tomato salad right now, but I ignore my body's natural response for my own sake.

"I can't get it in any visible places. I'm a ballerina," I explain.

"I see." The glee isn't gone from his eyes, and for some reason it makes me feel nervous. I take a step back, hoping he won't notice.

He does.

"I have a free slot at ten in the morning on Friday. That work for you?" He sobers up at once, not lifting his gaze from the laptop screen. I almost feel bad about it. I shouldn't be on edge like this, damn it. It's been four years. It's been four years and three days ago, actually, which is why I'm about to subject myself to the torture of painful needles and unremovable ink. Even though I can still hear his rough voice and his dark laugh in my head, the memory comes a lot less frequently.

And now it's as bad a time as any other to allow it back into my system.

Thanks to years of intensive therapy, I know the walls aren't closing in on me right now. I know my head is playing tricks on me, and that I'm not in some imminent danger. I'm aware of all this, and yet my lungs still close, sweat still clings to my skin, and my breathing is still labored.

Clarity hits me then. This is a terrible idea.

"I'm sorry," I manage to let out among the growing panic rising in my throat. "I... I don't think I'm ready yet."

"Okay." To his credit, he doesn't pressure me into making the appointment anyway nor does he try to convince me that my nerves will go away the moment I sit on the chair.

A beat of silence in which my feet can't move and my words don't come out passes before he speaks again. "Are you all right?"

The unexpected concern in his voice pulls me out of whatever place I was being dragged into, like an anchor at the bottom of the darkest sea.

I can't believe I've lowered my guard like this again. "Yeah, all good." I give him an awkward smile that doesn't reach my eyes. "Right. Okay. I'm... I'm sorry for wasting your time."

Curiosity fills his gaze, but he doesn't press. "No worries, sunshine."

Funny choice for a nickname, because my head feels like a raging thunderstorm right now.

Without saying another word, I turn around and exit the tattoo parlor. Only when I leave the block do I manage to breathe easily again.

Yep, totally a mistake.

I don't care what happened to me four years ago, how far I've come, or how strong it made me—I'm not going back there to ink the reminder in my poor skin forever.

# CAL

"Yo, Cal. Who was that?" Trey, my guy at the shop and my closest friend since high school, comes up to me with a scowl on his face. He's been tattooing our friend Oscar for two hours straight, and what better way to clear his head than to bug me at the front?

"Some girl wanted a tattoo but chickened out," I tell him without taking my eyes off the huge windows at the front. It's pointless—I know she's not coming back.

I could tell tattoos weren't her thing the second I spotted her standing outside with that indecisive look on her face. But hey, I'm all for trying new things, especially if my business profits from it.

"Ah, classic." He sits his hipster glasses higher on his nose. He insists they're normal-looking glasses, but I'm not buying it. Trey is a goddamn trend-follower if I've ever seen one. "Did you know her?"

"Didn't ring a bell."

Trey shrugs. "Weird. This place is small."

Warlington isn't a small town at all, but I get what he means. Warlington University's campus is only ten minutes away, and the guys and I know everyone who strolls by. The fact that our parlor is the most popular and best reviewed in town helps. Frequenting Danny's, the most crowded bar in the area, also does.

Everyone, college kids or not, can be found at the bar on a Friday night. And on Saturdays. And on Sundays. And well, pretty much every other day of the week.

Everyone but tattoo-on-my-ribs girl, apparently.

I really shouldn't call her that. Having worked this job for a decade, I know people have different opinions about tattoos. I never judge, as long as they don't judge me. Someone has yet to call me a criminal or some shit to my face because of my—

perhaps—excessive amount of ink, but I guess my six-foot-three wall of muscles makes them think twice. Good.

"Is Monica still coming at five?" Trey asks.

I check our schedule on the laptop. "Yeah, she hasn't canceled. She's all yours. I've got Aaron in—"

The words die in my throat as the door opens. *Speaking of the devil.* Aaron greets both of us with a fist bump when he reaches the front desk.

"Yo." Trey grins. "Wasn't your ass here last month?"

Aaron puts his hands up in fake surrender. "Guilty as charged, man. I saw that skull with the snake coming out of its eyes Cal posted last week and I had to get it on me."

Trey snorts.

I break out in a small grin. "Come on, Big A. Let's get it over with."

Aaron follows me to my station and instantly removes his t-shirt, messing his short brown hair in the process. He's here so alarmingly often that he already knows the drill.

As I prepare his skin, he rambles about whatever the hell happened at the gym yesterday. I have no clue who any of his gym buddies are or why this Maddox dude getting a new car is such a big deal, but he's one of my closest friends, so I listen politely.

Aaron Allen used to be a business major at Warlington University four years ago before he graduated with honors. Now, he owns a tapas restaurant near campus that is filled to the brim every single night. And he doesn't even work there—he simply comes up with all the business strategies and deals with the finances.

I've gone to him for business advice on occasion, which is why I give him a little discount on all his tattoos and why he's here every few months, probably. Quid pro quo, or so they say.

It's not until I've got the first half of the tattoo done that he changes topics. "Hey, quick question. Did a girl with shortish blonde hair come by earlier?"

I don't lift my gaze from his forearm as I tell him, "Stop pestering women around town."

"Gross." I can't see him, but he's definitely making a face right now. "I was asking because she's my cousin, you fucker."

At that, I look at him. Only one girl came by the shop today, and she did have shortish blond hair that reached past her shoulders. "Why are you asking?"

He relaxes back on the chair. "She told me she was going to make an appointment today. Did she?"

A non-committal sound escapes my throat. "She backed out at the last second."

"Called it." He sighs and throws his head back. "I knew she wouldn't go through with it. I love her to death, man, but she's got this annoying habit of overthinking everything way too hard."

I remove the excess ink from Aaron's skin. "You mean she's a sensible woman who doesn't jump into shit like you do?"

He snorts. "Right. That's because you haven't known her for twenty-two years."

So, she's eight years younger than me. Not that her age is any of my business, but it's still a piece of information I consciously bury in my head. What for, I'm not sure.

"Is she in college?" I ask, because for some reason it intrigues me. Probably because she looked so freaked out when she walked in and hurried out like that.

"English major." He smiles sheepishly. "She's so badass. Moved here four years ago all on her own for college. I thought you knew her?"

I shake my head. "I don't even know her name, man."

"Right. It's Grace."

*Grace.* She looks like a Grace, all right.

"You coming to Paulson's party Friday night?" If I didn't know him, I would be surprised by Aaron's sudden change of topics. But because I do, I don't even bat an eyelid.

"Don't know." I haven't given it much thought. "I might have to stay home with my sister."

*If my mother is drunk off her ass*, I want to add, but I don't.

"Shit. Can't you bring her with you?"

I stop the needle and give him a funny look. "She's four."

Aaron's torso shakes with laughter. "Fuck, dude. I can't believe I forgot. I've met her! Definitely *don't* bring her over or she'll be scarred for life."

"You don't have to tell me twice," I mutter.

As if I'd ever let my princess get within two feet of Paulson and his friends. I have nothing against the guys except that they can't keep the words "fuck," "shit," "cock," and "pussy" out of their mouths for more than five seconds. Which are the last words I want Maddie to incorporate into her ever-growing vocabulary.

And yeah, all right, I'm a foul-mouthed bastard too (sometimes), but at least I can control myself around innocent ears.

I finish Aaron's tattoo in silence, at least on my part. He keeps chatting about god-knows-what, but my mind is too distracted to pay any more attention.

It's not that I'm dying to go to Paulson's on Friday, but I hope for the life of me I don't have to stay at home for the wrong reasons. My mother's last sobriety record lasted a total of eight days, and it's only getting worse as the anniversary of her brother's death rolls around.

It's been fifteen years.

To be fair, my mother already had a few issues with alcohol way before Uncle Rob passed away, but it's gotten worse ever since Maddie was born.

Even though I was living on my own and in another city, I had to move back here when my sister was born because my mother was "too exhausted" to take proper care of her—not like she would ever admit that out loud—and my poor excuse of a stepfather didn't seem to realize he had a kid to provide for. So it was either I moved back, or I let social services take Maddie away. And that was not going to fucking happen.

Since then, my mom has gotten slightly better at parenting. I still visit my sister every day, drive her to and from school, and sometimes she sleeps over at my apartment, but it's nothing like the hell I went through when she was born.

Despite living alone, I made sure to rent a place that was big enough for two, with two rooms and two bathrooms, because I knew it would come to this. I knew the time would come when my sister needed a safe haven away from our mother and her dad, Pete.

I really don't want to take my sister away from her home, but if I don't, someone else will, eventually. And then everything will go to hell.

Maddie isn't unsafe with our mother by any means, or else I would've taken her out of that house years ago. My mom isn't abusive, and Maddie isn't unhappy with her. No, she's just... neglected.

I was once a neglected kid without an older sibling to look after me, and I turned out fine. Mostly. But I don't want that life for her. The moment my mother crosses the line, which I suspect will be soon, I'm taking my baby sister with me for good.

Hell will freeze over before I let my princess have the same miserable childhood I did.

# chapter 2

## GRACE

"On a scale of one to ten, how badly do you want me to smack you across the face with this shoe right now?" I ask Emily, because I'm pretty sure my best friend has a death wish I wasn't privy to.

She crosses her arms like she's outraged by my response and frowns at me. "On a scale of one to ten, I'm two seconds away from dragging you across campus with me whether you like it or not."

I glare at her. She glares back.

And I sigh, defeated.

Emily is dressed to kill tonight, looking as stunning as ever, and I wish I could get that kind of confidence back. The kind of confidence that was stolen from me all those years ago.

Because it's still warm outside, she's wearing a short, emerald green dress that hugs each and every one of her generous curves, paired with some nude sandals I've stolen from her wardrobe once or twice. Her black hair is up on a tight ponytail and her manicured fingers are tapping on her arms impatiently.

"Do I need to remind you—"

"No, you don't." I know exactly what I said to her three years ago, and I curse that moment every day of my— sometimes— agonizing existence.

Okay, maybe that's an exaggeration.

Emily is one of the very few people who knows about the

assault. It happened the summer before I moved here from my hometown in Canada, and I almost didn't come to Warlington because of it. Luckily, I had a solid support system—a.k.a. Aaron and my dads—who reminded me how badly I'd wanted to come here, since I decided I was going to be an English major when I was fifteen.

Warlington University is a pioneer campus in English and Literature, and somehow, I was smart enough to be accepted into their exclusive program. I wasn't going to throw this once-in-a-lifetime opportunity away because some asshole didn't know that no means no.

Years of therapy have led me to the good place I'm in today. Or okay-ish, rather. The fact that I never once blamed myself for what happened helped me move on faster, I think.

Not that you truly move on, not really.

Every day I live with the reminder that he took my freedom and my choice away from me, crushing them in the span of a few short, horrifying moments. But at least I'm here to talk about it, and I'm thankful for it.

"So repeat what you promised me the year we started rooming together," she says, narrowing her impossibly gray eyes at me. Honestly, I've never seen such a fascinating eye color.

I let out the loudest sigh imaginable and lower my gaze to the ground, because I can't stand the intensity of hers. And I recite word by word what I promised her three years ago, when the administration office assigned Emily as my new roommate and unknowingly gifted me the best friend I've ever had.

"I, Grace Allen, bravest and strongest woman alive, promise my best friend and future hottest and smartest teacher, Emily Laura Danes, that I will attend at least one party each semester and that I will step out of my comfort zone more often because I'm surrounded by people who love me and have got my back at all times."

There. I haven't forgotten a single word.

She nods, a satisfactory gleam in her eyes. "And how many parties have you been to in the last semester?"

I sulk. "None."

"And the semester before that?"

"None."

"And what is this?" She gestures at nothing in particular, but I know what she means.

"The first semester of our last year at Warlington."

"Exactly." She kneels in front of me and rests her hands on top of my thighs for support as she searches my eyes. For what, I don't even want to know. "This is just a house party, walking distance from campus and all. Aaron will be there. I will be there glued to your side all the time. But most importantly, I'm pushing you to come because deep down I know you want to. It's that little troublesome head of yours that won't let you take this step."

I still can't look at her because I hate that she's right. I hate that my traitorous brain refuses to stop messing with what my heart desires. I've let fear control my life for years, but Emily's right—I'm not planning to fail my courses, and neither is she, so this is our last year at Warlington University. Am I really going to let my past keep me from making the most of my future?

"Plus," she adds in a wicked voice that I know all too well. "I didn't want to pull the Dax card, but..."

My eyes widen. "Shut—"

"Uh-huh. We're not doing this, darling. I know you have a crush on him, so don't even bother." She smirks like she knows the depths of my secrets. She does. "I heard from Amber that he'll be at Paulson's tonight. So... Do with that information what you will."

Now she's just dangling the piece of juicy meat in front of the chained beast for funsies.

"You're being unfair." I glare at her, but I can't hide the small twitch in my lips.

Emily eyes me knowingly. "Is it a yes, then? Will you get dressed and come with me?"

To be fair, I was going to accept before she threw Dax into the mix. It's not that I'm against parties, although I do tend to get nervous around large crowds. Especially drunk crowds. And we all know that a party isn't the ideal place to be if you want sobriety.

It's been almost a year since I went to my last one, and I kind of miss the feeling of getting all dressed up and dancing for a few hours, having fun with my girls.

Surely, it can't be that bad.

Right?

* * *

Wrong.

This is terrible.

We arrive at Paulson's quite fashionably late, since I hadn't even showered before Emily ambushed me with the idea. By the time we are both dolled up and ready, and after a ten-minute walk to the brick house Paulson shares with two of his teammates, I already regret saying yes to this.

Everybody is drunk out of their minds, which is to be expected from a party thrown by none other than a professional athlete and quite the celebrity at Warlington, but jeez. Even Aaron is already four beers deep into oblivion, which leaves me with one less buffer.

Emily links her arm through mine as we make our way to the living room, where our friends said they were going to be. As I run a quick scan of the room, I spot a few Warlington graduates and other people who know Paulson one way or another.

*Great, more drunk people to deal with.*

Our friend Amber has been a friend of Paulson's for years,

which gets her invites to all his parties—that means we get to come, too.

But no Dax so far.

"Em! Gracie! You came!" Amber's cheery voice greets us the moment we reach the living room. Her wavy blond hair falls in loose waves, and she's wearing a red top that looks amazing on her. "Céline was just about to tell me all about her hookup with Stella this summer. Come on! If I miss even a second of this, heads will roll."

My mood shifts instantly. *This* is the crowd I want to be around, no matter if we are surrounded by people who make my skin crawl.

I met Céline and Amber through Emily in my second year at Warlington University, and although I'm not as close to them as I am to Em, I couldn't imagine my college experience without them.

Céline is Canadian, like me, and we share some classes since she's all about Linguistics Anthropology. She's also the tallest girl I've ever met, with the most impressive red hair, and freckles for days. And she's finally built up the courage to make a move on Stella. Seriously, she's been crushing on the girl for like, what? A year? It was about damn time she acted on it.

Amber, on the other hand, looks like a pixie standing next to her. She's clad in that to-die-for red top that hugs all her curves. She's one of the sharpest people I know, and she's going to law school next year. Which is fitting, since Amber can win arguments with her mouth closed and persuade you into doing whatever she wants, even if you hate the idea altogether.

"So, get this," Céline starts as she makes room for us on the couch. Some couple is making out on the other end, so I end up standing. "I'm in Montreal with my parents for the summer, helping my sister with the shop, yada, yada, yada. You know the drill. And one day—"

"Oh my god!" Amber squeals, even though Céline has revealed literally nothing.

"Shut it, woman. Let me finish," Céline shushes her, but she's smiling. "Okay, so one day I'm closing the shop and guess what? Stella texts me. Says she's in town with some friends and wants to hang out with me." A pause. "*Alone*."

Amber squeals even louder, drawing the attention of a few people around us.

"Did you hook up with her?" I ask eagerly because I've been waiting a whole lifetime for this ship to sail.

"I'm getting there." Céline smirks. She knows she has us on the edge of our seats. "Naturally I say yes, and she picks me up for dinner. We have an *amazing* time, honestly. We've talked before, but she's actually like, super fun and smart and—"

"Cut to the part where you shove your tongue down her throat, honey," Emily says.

"So impatient," Céline rolls her eyes at us. "She takes me back to her rental and we hook up in her room. I stay all night. Best sex of my life. The end. Is that summed up enough for you?"

Now we are all squealing. "Is she here tonight?" Amber asks.

"Well, duh," she answers with a smug smirk. "She's over there playing beer pong with Aaron, Brian, and Maxwell."

Sure enough, I turn around and spot Stella with my cousin and two other guys I don't recognize. Aaron catches my eye and waves for me to come over. I grab Emily's arm and give it a squeeze. "I'm going to hang out with Aaron for a bit."

"Okay, hon. We'll be here," she assures me, and just like that I leave my friends behind and make a ten-second walk to my cousin that almost makes me gag.

*Nothing is going to happen to you. Aaron is right there. Emily is behind you, watching.*

The most reasonable part of me knows this, but the poor little thing isn't strong enough to prevent my mind from spiraling.

Once I reach my cousin, he wraps a long, muscular arm around my shoulders and pulls me against his sweaty chest.

"Ugh, how can you be so stinky already?" I try to push him away, but he doesn't let go and plants a loud kiss on top of my head instead.

"I'm so glad you came, G," he says, ignoring my pleas.

"Uh-huh." I love him, but right now I would rather be anywhere else than right under his stinky armpit. Perks of being five-two. Yay.

He releases his monster grip on me when I push him again. That's when I notice Stella beside him. "Hey, Stella. Long time no see."

"Grace, hi." She gives me her signature white-teethed smile that shines against her dark skin. With her long, thick braids and her chiseled jaw and nose, I don't think I've ever come across a more beautiful woman. No wonder Céline is into her. She's one of the kindest people I've ever met, too. "It's been way too long. Aaron and I here are giving the guys a run for their money."

"You tell them, baby." Aaron high-fives her. He might be twenty-six, but he still acts like a college kid. I don't blame him, though—adulthood is a pain in the ass. If he's not ready to say goodbye to this lifestyle, I'm not going to be the one who judges him for it.

I shake my head in amusement as the two guys on the opposite end of the table, Brian and Maxwell, start reassuring me that *they* are the indisputable leaders of this beer pong table. But I'm barely listening, because suddenly a flash of white catches my eye.

Not a flash of white—Dax Wilson himself.

An alarm goes off in my head. He greets a couple of guys as he enters the living room, right across from where we are standing by the dining table, and I'm *not* ready for him to see me like this.

Granted, I don't look too bad—I'm wearing a loose baby

blue dress that isn't short enough to make me uncomfortable, and my hair is having a good day, but unlike most girls here I'm not wearing heels (I love heels, but between them and pointe shoes, my feet can never catch a break). I also didn't go overboard on the make-up, because it makes me panicky when men look at me and see a piece of meat instead of a woman they can have a civil conversation with.

So, yes, maybe I'm a tad underdressed, but at least I'm here at all, and that's a big enough milestone for me.

Now, however, I regret not having dolled up a bit more thoroughly. Just a little.

Sure enough, Maxwell shouts Dax's name and he comes over to the makeshift beer pong table.

*Oh, my god.*

"Dude." Dax shakes his head as he approaches his friend. "Almost didn't make it. That chick Megan threw herself at me the second I stepped on the porch. Said something about coming to the next game." He says something else I can't make out over the loud music, and they laugh.

My stomach plummets, but I mask it well. Arguably, Dax is one of the most handsome, sexiest, most attractive (you get it) guys on campus. Plus, he's on the hockey team. What kind of girl in her right state of mind wouldn't throw herself at him? Jeez, I would do it myself if I weren't so self-conscious and such a chicken.

Dax is an English major too, so we share some classes. He transferred from Boston last year, which is why we haven't talked much. I rarely ever go out, and he goes out a lot, so there's your answer as to why he doesn't even know I exist.

Well, that's a lie—he knows I exist because he's smiled at me a couple of times in class and even asked me for a pencil once. The chances of him remembering my name are slim to none, though, but it doesn't bother me.

Their conversation goes on, and I zone out until Dax calls my cousin's name. "Hey, Aaron! Went to your tapas place the other day. It's solid."

"Thanks, man," my cousin replies, but there's an edge to his voice. His arm goes back around my shoulders as he turns to Stella. "Mind if I go outside for a minute? We've pretty much won this thing already."

"Sure," she assures him quickly. "I'll call in a replacement."

"Come on," Aaron whispers in my ear and leads me away from Dax.

"Where are we going?" I'm only mildly pissed that he didn't ask me if I wanted to leave. As we make our way past the living room, we pass his beer pong replacement—a very smiley Céline.

"I've just said it. We are going outside." He presses me closer to his side when we pass by a group of drunk football players who are nudging each other. Aaron's still not smiling, and the fact that he looks surprisingly sober is freaking me out.

"You wanted to go outside all of a sudden?" I raise a suspicious eyebrow even if he can't see me.

"Yup."

I'm not buying it, but I also don't have the energy to argue with him about it. Aaron is a closed book. In all the time we've been close, which is forever, we haven't had an honest conversation about his feelings ever. Not even when his high school girlfriend dumped him on prom night and, despite being so clearly upset, he kept shrugging it off and got drunk instead.

The thing is, every emotion shows on his expressive face nonetheless, so it's not like he can hide how he really feels. That's why every time I sense something is bothering him, like right now, I have to suck it up and pretend everything is fine because he won't tell me a thing. Asking is pointless. That's Aaron Allen for you.

Once outside, he takes out a cigarette from the back pocket

of his jeans and lights it up. If my aunt found out that he smokes despite having promised her he would quit a year ago, she would make him swallow the whole package in one gulp. But because I'm a great cousin and he's a grown man, I won't say a thing about this.

"Didn't expect you to come tonight." He blows out the smoke.

I move to his other side so the air doesn't carry it directly to my face. "It wasn't in my plans," I confess. "Em convinced me."

"Ah, that one." His lips curve around the cigarette in an affectionate smile. "Always getting you into trouble."

I don't tell him about my promise to her three years ago, or about Dax. I'm not ready to admit out loud that I might be interested in a guy again after all these years because I absolutely don't want to have *that* conversation with Aaron of all people. He's like a brother to me.

"It's always trouble I can manage." He knows this, but I still feel the urge to remind him.

He puffs out another cloud of smoke. "I like Emily for you. She's a tad crazy, but still sensible enough to know when she's toeing the line."

And that's why our friendship works so well, I think to myself. She reminds me to live a little, while I remind her to relax a little.

"How are those ballet lessons going? Kiddies giving you too much trouble?" He steps on his cigarette to put it out and an easy smile draws on his lips.

It's no secret that Aaron would trade his job for mine in a heartbeat—well, maybe not the ballet part because he can't dance for shit, but my cousin loves kids. He jokes he'll have an army of children one day, but I see it.

"They're amazing." My spirits lift instantly when I speak about the little girls I teach. "We had our first class of the semester last Tuesday. Oh, Aaron, you had to see their little faces when I told them they were going to perform at the Christmas recital. They were so excited."

"Duh, of course they were excited if you're their teacher." He looks at me in the same way my dads have always looked at me— like I'm the single most important person in the entire world. "I'm super proud of you, G. Like, stupidly fucking proud of you."

My heart swoons at his words. "I know. You keep telling me."

"And I'm never gonna shut up about it." He grins. He's about to say something else when his phone rings. He looks at the caller ID and frowns. "It's the restaurant. I have to take this."

"Go ahead," I tell him when he throws me an apologetic look.

Aaron walks away towards the empty road where the noise of the party isn't so bad, and while my eyes are glued on him, I keep reminding myself that I'm fine. I'm safe, and he's right there.

I really did this tonight, didn't I? Despite my initial doubts and insecurities, I choked my fears to death, listened to my heart, and tagged along with my friends. All things considered, the night isn't going too badly. I've gossiped with my girls, saw Aaron (which I barely do these days because we're both too busy), and I even was in the same room as Dax outside of class. Talk about improvement.

A sudden boost of pride rushes through me. I did it. I put on this cute dress and went out to a party. And look— I'm safe and sound. I can't wait to tell my dads about it in the morning.

Not even two minutes later, Aaron jogs back to me with a scowl on his face. "Gotta go to The Spoon. A customer refuses to pay for some fucking reason I don't get."

"They *refuse* to pay? People can do that?"

"Don't even ask. I really don't need to get worked up or I'll punch them in the face. Come on, I'll walk you inside."

"I'm fine." I grab his arm to stop him. He looks down at me, confusion all over his features. "I know where to find my friends.

Plus, you're in a rush right now. I'll be okay."

"Don't be silly, it'll only take me five seconds to walk you in."

"Aaron." I stop him once more. When I talk again, my voice sounds so steady I surprise myself. "I already came here tonight. Baby steps, remember? Well, I'm also ready to go back inside and find my friends. *On my own.* If I don't find them in five minutes, I promise to call an Uber and leave."

Aaron sighs. For a moment I think he's going to drag me inside despite my protests, but then he says, "Text me whether you find them or not, all right? I'm never too busy for you."

"I know." I give him a smile. "Now go. Hurry. And don't punch your customers in the face. It's not a smart business move."

"I'll try." His lips are on my forehead for a second, and then he's already jogging towards the tapas bar. It's only a ten-minute walk from here, but he'll get there sooner with those athletic long legs of his. "Text me!"

I dismiss him with a nonchalant wave. When he disappears down the dark street, realization hits me—I'm on my own, exactly like I wanted. I'm not allowed to complain now, am I?

*Okay, Grace, breathe.*

Breathing? I can do that. I've been doing that all my life, actually.

I know what I have to do. Turn around. Go inside. Find my friends. Stay with them. Text Aaron.

It couldn't be simpler, really.

So why does it go to hell the second I move?

"Hey, Gina? No—Grace! You're Grace, right?" A male voice I don't recognize asks behind me.

I could pretend I didn't hear him, but I'm suddenly alone in front of Paulson's front porch, so I don't think it would work.

Really? Two seconds ago there was a freaking herd out here.

"Hey. Do I know you?" I force a smile as I turn around, because I've learned the hard way that a man who feels rejected is a dangerous specimen. And I'm not feeling particularly brave tonight.

When I look at him, his face still doesn't ring a bell. He's tall, broad shoulders, short brown hair, and the clearest shade of blue eyes I've ever seen.

"Um, I think you do. We take creative writing together," he says in a casual tone, hands in his jean pockets and all. He would look approachable enough if I was any other girl, carrying a different set of trauma. But I'm not.

"I'm sorry." I grimace. "I don't remember you."

"I'm Wes." He holds out his hand for me to shake, but I don't take it. Awkwardly, he puts it back in his pocket. "So, you came here with anybody?"

"With some friends." I point towards the house. "I was on my way to find them, actually."

"Ah, that's too bad." He takes a step closer, and I take a step back. He's not being particularly creepy or anything, just your standard college guy behavior, but I'm not in the mood. "I was wondering if maybe you'd want to grab a drink with me?"

Absolutely not.

"Um." I shift clumsily on my feet. "It's just that they're *really* waiting for me."

Have I forgotten how to say 'no'? Is that it?

"I'm sure they won't mind if you bail on them to have a good time with me." He smiles, and now I'm freaking out.

A good time? A good fucking time? No, no, no—

"Sorry, but I really need to go—"

Wes takes a step closer and my breath hitches. "Come on, doll. Just one drink. I promise to keep it PG."

I shake my head and start walking backwards. "Sorry, but no."

I hate how small my voice sounds. I hate that I'm apologizing. I hate that I was feeling so confident and now it's all gone to hell.

"All right. Let me at least walk you inside and—"

"She said no."

A sharp, deep voice cuts through the anxiety in my chest. For a moment, I think Aaron is back and my breathing relaxes. But then Wes moves a little to the left, and I see exactly who that piercing voice belongs to.

It's the guy from the tattoo parlor.

# chapter 3

## CAL

Surprisingly, my mother isn't drinking when I drop my sister off on Friday afternoon. Once I park in front of her one-story house, I barely have time to react before Maddie unbuckles herself from the backseat and sprints to the front door, yelling for my mother in a happy voice.

My selfish ass can't help but think it would be much, much easier if my sister didn't like it here. It wouldn't hurt this damn bad to think about the possibility of taking her with me for the long run. But she loves our mother—which I'm grateful for—and she enjoys playing with the neighbor's kids, and all her favorite toys are in her room here.

She has a life in this place—a life she enjoys, and a life I don't want to strip away from her.

Sadly, there's not much I can do but hope that my mother behaves so I won't have to burst my sister's happy bubble any time soon.

"Mommy! Mommy!" I follow Maddie's excited chants to the kitchen, where my mother is making dinner. A cheese omelet, by the smell of it. "Sammy took me for ice cream!"

"Did he, now?" My mother throws her a loving smile before she plants an affectionate kiss on top of her head. She might not know how to show it in the healthiest way, but our mother loves us. And that's all I could ask for, really. Other folks have it way worse than we do. "What flavor did you choose?"

"Strawberry," she answers, beaming, "because it's pink."

"Duh," I say with a knowing smirk. My sister loves everything pink, therefore *princess*. It's not the most original in the broad history of nicknames, but she loves it because it makes her feel like her favorite one, Rapunzel. She's even trying to grow out her hair to look more like her, even if I always insist that she's a lot prettier than any princess.

My mother glances at me over her shoulder before going back to her omelet. "Are you staying for dinner, Samuel?"

"Can't. I've got an appointment in," I check the time on my phone, "thirty minutes."

"Nooooo, Sammy," my sister whines as she hugs my legs with an impressively strong grip. "Don't go. I'll miss you."

My heart swells with all sorts of emotions when her big brown eyes look up at me, and she pouts. She can't do this to me, damn.

"Tell you what." I kneel until we're at eye level. "I don't work tomorrow afternoon, so how about I pick you up and we go on a picnic by the lake?"

Her eyes widen with excitement. "The lake with the sand playground?"

"The one and only." I hug her tiny frame to my chest and plant a loud kiss on her forehead. "No more ice cream, though. You've already had two this week."

She nods and tucks her head under my chin. "Okay."

I kiss her again. "See you tomorrow then, princess."

Maddie takes off towards her room, her dark hair flying everywhere. Before I've even stood straight again, my mother's voice startles me. "You're good with her."

A sharp pang of annoyance hits me right in the chest.

"Didn't you expect me to be?"

I eye her carefully as I wait for a response. My mother is a tall woman, and so is my dad, hence my six-foot-three frame. She used to be on the slim side once, athletic, but now her stomach is bloated due to all the alcohol she chugs like there's no tomorrow. Her long brown hair looks damp, oily, her face tired.

Now that I think about it, I can't recall the last time Larissa Callaghan walked into a room and just...shone with happiness.

"I already told you, Sam. I didn't know how you were going to take the news about having a little sister." She finishes up the omelet and sets it on a plate. "Maddie! Dinner's ready!"

Learning that my mother was pregnant when I was twenty-six had been a shock, all right, but mainly because I didn't expect her and fucking rat-ass Pete Stevens to last longer than a week. The fucker still refuses to remember he has a daughter.

I run a quick scan of the living room, where Maddie's father tends to spend the entirety of his days since he lost his job at the car shop two months ago. Every time I come by, the slug is perched on the couch as if he got paid for it. "It was an adjustment," I tell her honestly as I hear my sister's little footsteps running down the narrow hall. "But I love her more than anything. You know this."

"Who do you love more than anything, Sammy?" Maddie asks with a mischievous gleam in her eyes. "You have a girlfriend? Can I meet her?"

I chuckle softly. "I was talking about you, peanut."

"Oh." She only looks mildly disappointed. "No girlfriend?"

"No girlfriend." And I doubt there will be one for a long, long time.

I'm still trying to process the hell I went through the last time I attempted to have a serious relationship, not to mention that distractions aren't welcomed right now. Not when my family life could go to hell in an instant.

A heavy, dark cloud of uncertainty has been looming over my head for years—a warning of sorts. About what, I'm too scared to know.

But my four-year-old sister and my gossipy mother don't need to know that.

"A girlfriend would be good for you," my mother chimes in, because of course she does. "You work too much. It's practically all you do."

"That's not true." I shift uncomfortably on my feet while my sister sits down to eat her omelet. Talking about my feelings has never been my forte, let alone with my parents. Well, with my mom—it's not like my poor excuse of a father has ever been around to talk to him at all. "I'm going out tonight, actually."

"With the guys at the tattoo shop?" She arches a skeptical eyebrow, and I know what she's thinking.

"No. I'm dropping by at Paulson's. I have other friends, you know."

"Sure you do," she teases.

"Sure you do," Maddie repeats with her mouth full.

Hey, it's not my fault I'm barely a social person as it is, and on top of that everyone in this damn town is either getting laid or getting hammered at random parties. I don't mind the occasional gathering, although staying at home has always been more appealing to me.

"Whatever. I didn't come here for a roasting." I smirk as I make my way towards Maddie to give her another kiss. "Be ready tomorrow at three, all right? I'll pick you up."

My mom comes up behind me and rubs my back with affection that is so rare between us these days. "Thanks, honey. I'll see you tomorrow."

Taking one last look at the kitchen before I close the front door behind me, I catch a glimpse of my mother opening the fridge and reaching for a cold beer.

And so, it begins.

* * *

House parties aren't my thing, but somewhere in the back of my head my mother's words ring true—I work too much. When was the last time I met my friends outside the parlor or at Danny's? Guilt is, perhaps, what leads me to Paulson's brick house two hours after I finish my last appointment of the day. He's been a client of mine for years, and he's a solid dude, mostly, which is why I agreed to come tonight.

Except that I don't even make it inside.

"Come on, doll. Just one drink. I promise to keep it PG."

I have no clue who this dipshit is, but something in my chest tightens when I recognize who he's talking to.

Grace. Aaron's cousin.

And she looks fucking terrified.

Her shoulders are tight with tension, she's walking backwards towards the house, and her expression mirrors that of a deer caught in headlights. I know uneasiness when I see it, and right now there's not another emotion on her face.

"Sorry, but no," she tells the guy in a small voice.

But Dipshit can't take a hint. "All right. Let me at least walk you inside and—"

"She said no."

I surprise myself with the deep, authoritative voice that leaves my mouth. See, I'm usually a chill guy. I don't care enough about anyone else's business to get involved in any kind of drama.

But this? This boils my fucking blood, and I don't even give myself enough time to understand why before I make my way towards the guy.

"Didn't you hear?" I stand so close to him that the pungent smell of his wannabe-playboy cologne invades my poor nostrils. "Get back inside and stop bothering her."

The dude has the audacity to give me a smug smile. "Or what?"

Pointless, really, given how I tower over him, and he looks

like a stick figure next to my muscled frame. I'm not one to brag, but years of hitting the gym, playing all kinds of sports and great genetics will do this to you. This, meaning looking "fucking terrifying." In Trey's words, not mine.

From the corner of my eye, I see Grace gaping at us, unmoving. I don't look her way as I lower my head to Dipshit's ear and whisper, "Or I'll break your fucking legs and shove them into your idiotic mouth, since you refuse to shut it."

Color drains from his face, and he swallows thickly.

"Hey, dude, I was—"

"About to go inside? Leave Grace alone? Learn to take a fucking hint?" I snarl. "For your own sake, I hope it's all three."

He gulps, and without saying another word, he keeps his head down as he passes by Grace before disappearing inside Paulson's house. I'll have a word or two with him later about the kind of assholes he invites to his parties, but right now that's not my focus.

My priority is Grace, who has yet to move from her spot in the middle of the driveway and is shaking like a leaf in the wind.

I take a tentative step forward and speak in the softest voice I can manage, the one I use with my sister when she's just woken up from a bad dream and every noise startles her. "Hey. Are you all right?"

Her eyes snap towards me. They're of a beautiful light hazel color, and they look scared as fuck. When she speaks, even her voice trembles. "How do you know my name?"

"I'm friends with your cousin Aaron," I answer, taking another slow step towards her but giving her enough time to retreat. When she doesn't, I add, "I'm Callaghan."

That's what my friends call me, anyway—well, more like Cal since it's not so much of a mouthful. My mom is the only one who refuses to give up Samuel, my first name, and Maddie calls me Sammy because she thinks it's funny.

Grace nods, although I don't think she knew my name. "From the tattoo parlor?"

I can't help a small smile. "You remember me."

She averts her gaze and wraps her arms around her petite frame as she keeps shaking, even if less violently now. I'm still too far away to tell, but I don't think the top of her head would even reach my neck. She's hilariously small, like one of those fairies Maddie loves so much. Her blond hair falls loosely over her shoulders, and her smooth, pale skin is peppered with goosebumps despite being warm outside.

But I know she's not shaking from the cold.

"I...I want to go home," she mutters, more to herself than to me.

"All right," I say carefully. "Do you want me to call a cab? Aaron?"

"Don't call him." Her eyes widen with even more panic, making me regret the suggestion and wonder why that would freak her out so much. "I'll walk."

I frown. "You're not doing that. It's late and you're all shaken up."

She glares at me. "I'm perfectly capable of taking care of myself."

"I know." I really don't, but the determination in her eyes takes me aback. I take a deep breath and hope this doesn't come out creepy. "Listen, I didn't even want to come here anyway. Parties aren't my thing. Let me walk you home, or at least call a cab for you. You can keep your finger on the SOS button of your phone if it'll make you feel safer, but I refuse to let you leave alone."

Her breath hitches, and for a moment I think she's going to call me out on my toxic alpha tendencies or something, but she simply says, "I'll take an Uber."

With shaky fingers, she takes her phone out and starts

typing. A couple of minutes later, she looks up and takes a hesitant step towards me. "They'll be here in five. You don't have to wait with me."

I don't answer. Instead, I keep my distance as she approaches the edge of the curb and pretend all my focus isn't on her.

I know a panic attack when I see one, and I also happen to know how to proceed— keep your distance, don't say a word, don't freak her out even more. All those steps vary from person to person, but Grace and I don't know each other, and something tells me she wouldn't appreciate any more male attention tonight, so I stay away.

Five minutes roll by, and her ride isn't here yet. Grace keeps glancing at the time on her phone, as if doing so would summon the car, but another five minutes pass and there's still no sign of her Uber. I'm about to break the silence and offer to walk her home again, but she beats me to it.

"Thank you for earlier," she half-whispers without even looking at me.

"It was nothing." Stealing a glance in her direction, I notice that at least she's not shaking anymore. "You knew that guy?"

Grace shakes her head. "He said we take a class together, but I haven't seen him in my life."

He probably made the whole thing up, anyway. Dudes these days would do anything to get a woman's attention— and into their pants, if they're lucky enough. It only makes me want to punch Dipshit harder.

"So, you're a student at Warlington?" I subtly change topics, hoping it eases her nerves a bit.

"English major." I already knew this, but I nod in acknowledgment anyway. To my surprise, she doesn't end the conversation there. "It's my last year."

"That's exciting. Any plans after graduation?"

She shifts on her feet. It's only then that I notice she's wearing sneakers, which is probably why she looks so short.

"Still unclear." She checks the time on her phone again. A beat of silence passes between us, and then, "Callaghan, right? So, you work at the tattoo parlor?"

I'm half-shocked that she hasn't ended our conversation yet, given how shaken up she still looks, but I don't comment on it. Instead, I say, "I own it, actually." Because for some stupid reason I want her to know this.

"Really?" Her eyes widen in surprise. "That's... That's great."

I snort. "Why do you sound so surprised?"

"You look...young, I guess." She gives a brief, almost discreet look that I catch anyway. There's no lust in her gaze, only muted curiosity, and yet my stomach still somersaults.

"How old do you think I am?" I smirk.

She gives me a quick once-over, and I don't think I'm imagining the way her lips curve upwards—only slightly, but it's there. It's something, and I'll take it. I'll take anything over a panic attack.

"I'm not answering that," she says.

"Why not?"

"What if I say like, forty, and you're nineteen or something?"

I choke. "You think I'm *forty*?"

"Obviously not." She rolls her eyes with the faintest hint of amusement. "It was just a figure of speech."

"Well, take a guess. I promise you won't hurt my ego."

Was that a laugh? I think she laughed.

"Mm-hmm... Twenty-eight?"

"I'm thirty." Close enough. "Impressive."

A shy smile touches her plump lips. "You don't look *that* old."

Right on cue, a white car slides on the side of the road.

Grace looks at me one last time and says, "Thank you."

I don't have enough time to tell her that it's nothing, or that she should text me when she gets home safe even though I don't have her number, because she gets in the backseat and the car drives away.

But the funny feeling in my chest stays right there.

# chapter 4

# GRACE

"Hand on our hips." I check the reflection in the mirror to see if the girls are following. "All right, now wave with your hand like this. That's it, well done! Wave at the mirror, yes. Point those feet."

I do as I say, the classical music mixing with the girls' giggles.

"Miss Grace, like this?" Taylor asks as she waves at her reflection and shifts from one little leg to the other.

"Yes, Taylor. Well done!" I beam. "Now, girls. Watch this. Arms out." They copy my movements. "Relevé and turn."

The girls giggle as they spin around the classroom, and I laugh with them. The Christmas recital is still months away, but even so, I don't think we'll get very far with the choreography. Grabbing the attention of four-year-old girls for a whole hour is as stressful and difficult as it sounds, but I wouldn't trade my job for anything. Plus, the parents don't care about perfect movements or synchronized dancers—all they want is to see their little ones having fun on stage, and I can assure them that will definitely happen.

"Good, well done," I praise the class as I glance at the clock. Only five minutes left. "You did beautifully today, girls. Now's time for some free dancing, yes? I'll play some music and you can do any moves you want."

The girls cheer and get ready in the center of the class. Despite only being our third lesson of the semester, the ten girls

40

are already very tight friends. I press play on some Offenbach, because they don't care about the music. I love his pieces and watch as the parents gather on the outside of the classroom, ready to take their children home.

Adelaide—my boss and the owner of The Dance Palace—had to leave early to take her son to a birthday party, which means I'm closing the studio today. This is my last class of the day, and I can't wait to go back to the dorms and take a much-needed shower.

I've been practicing ballet for the last seventeen years, and at some point I thought I would become a professional dancer. My plans changed when I discovered my love for literature, and now I want to be a writer if the stars align, but I refuse to give up on ballet when it's given me so much over the years.

It gave me confidence when I lacked it, friends when they were scarce, and a purpose when I was all but lost. And now, it provides me with a job I love and a stable income.

The first thing I did when I moved to Warlington was find a good ballet studio. Adelaide offered me a try-out lesson four years ago, and the rest is history. On top of teaching the younger kids on Tuesdays and Thursdays, as well as some older girls, I also take lessons with Adelaide's most advanced class.

Sometimes it's a struggle to balance it all with school, but I'm not willing to give up on ballet for anything in the world. It keeps my body and my head in check, and I need the latter more than my next breath.

Once I announce that the class is over, the girls and I do a round of applause before they sprint outside to meet their awaiting parents.

"Goodbye, Miss Grace!" they all shout and wave at me as they disappear down the narrow hallway towards the front door.

"Bye, girls! See you on Thursday!"

I unplug my phone from the speakers and take a sip of cold

water. I gave two lessons today, one after the other, and despite not being too physically demanding, keeping so many girls in check for so long is as draining as it gets. Honestly, I don't think—

"Miss Grace?"

I almost jump at the sound of the little voice behind me. When I turn around, I see one of my students, Maddison Stevens, standing right outside the room with her little thumb on her mouth, chewing it nervously.

"Yes, sweetheart?" I kneel at her eye level. Her big brown eyes look worried, and I freak out. Why is she here? Where's her mother?

"Mommy isn't here yet." Mystery solved, I guess.

I soothe my voice before speaking. "Don't worry, dear. I'm sure she's stuck in traffic or something." I point to the small leather couch by the front desk. "Why don't you sit there for a bit while I call her? I promise I won't leave until she shows up."

Because I know how a kid's mind works, and the last thing I want is for Maddie to start crying because she thinks I'm going to abandon her in the studio and go home.

When she nods, I look through her file and dial her mother's number on my phone. No answer.

I ring her again. No answer.

Maybe she really is driving and can't pick up right now. I steal a quick look at Maddie, who's dangling her short legs on the edge of the couch, her eyes glued on me. "Did you call her yet, Miss Grace?"

I bite my bottom lip. "I'm on it, sweetheart."

As much as I need a shower, I wouldn't mind staying here with her until her mother shows up. It's not a big deal. But it only takes one look at the girl to know she's not enjoying this situation. She chews on her thumb nervously and can't sit still as she glances at the front door every few seconds.

Quickly, I scan her file again and... *Bingo*. There's a different number saved in here. Crossing my fingers so that the person picks up, I dial again.

Nothing. But I wait. And wait. Thirty seconds. Forty...

"Hello?"

*Finally.* A second later, however, I register that it's not a female voice greeting me on the other side of the line, but a very deep, masculine rumble.

A shiver runs down my spine, and this time it's not from uneasiness.

"Hey! Um, I'm calling you from The Dance Palace. Your... Your phone was listed in Maddison Stevens's contact information—"

"That's my sister," the man interrupts, a sudden edge to his voice. "Is she okay? Did something happen?"

"She's... She's fine, sir." I clear my throat. "It's just that her mother was supposed to pick her up a few minutes ago, but she hasn't shown up and I can't reach her on her phone."

"Shit." I hear a buzzing sound in the background, and the man covers the speaker for a second as he talks to somebody else. "Okay. I'm working right now, but I'll be there in twenty minutes. Maybe I could make it in fifteen."

And because the distress in his voice is so genuine, I say, "That's all right. Take your time. I can stay with her until you get here. This was our last lesson of the day, so I don't have anywhere else to be."

It sounds a bit sad when I say it out loud, but... Well, it's true. Other than a shower and eating with Em at the dining hall, I don't have any other plans tonight.

"You're a lifesaver." The man sighs into the phone, making my skin prickle. "I'll be there as soon as I can. Thank you so much."

"That's—" But before I can finish my sentence, he hangs up. Well then. I guess he truly is in a hurry.

"Did you talk with my mommy?" Maddie asks in a small voice.

"I talked to your brother." Her face lights up at my words. "He's coming to pick you up after work. He should be here shortly."

She beams at that. "Yay! Sammy!"

I smile, the tension gone from my body now that she looks happy again. "Hey, how about we dance some more until your brother gets here?"

\* \* \*

Exactly sixteen minutes after I take Maddie back to the classroom so I can show her how to do a pirouette (per her request), the doorbell rings. I locked the front door before coming back here, so I stop the music and Maddie and I stroll towards the front. She runs ahead, but because the lock is so high up, I don't worry about her reaching it and opening the door to a potential murderer.

"Sammy! Sammy!" I hear her excited squeals as I reach her.

And when I do, I freeze into place.

On the other side of the glass door is none other than the guy from the tattoo parlor.

*Callaghan.* Wait.

*That's* Sammy? *That's* Maddison's deep-voiced brother? He hasn't spotted me yet. His dark eyes are glued to his little sister, who jumps up and down while buzzing with excitement, and he wears the softest, most heart-melting smile I've ever seen on any man ever. It's kind of mesmerizing.

I unlock the door and Maddie instantly throws herself at Callaghan's long legs, the only part of his enormous body she can reach.

For real, the man is shaped like a brick wall.

"Hey, peanut." He bends down and picks her up. Then he

finally looks at me, and I can tell the exact moment realization hits him. "Grace?"

I give him a small smile. "That'd be me."

"I didn't know you worked here," he says, as Maddie clings to his neck. "Easy, baby. You'll tackle me to the ground."

She laughs, and the loving smile that touches his lips makes my stomach jump.

"Yeah, I'm a teacher here," I say awkwardly. Jeez, did I forget how to have a normal conversation with a guy? Well, not with a guy, really—Sammy right here screams *man* all over.

"Thank you for staying with her after closing," he says. "I owe you one."

I wave a nonchalant hand. "It's nothing. We had fun dancing some more, right Maddie?"

"Yes!" Her little finger traces the inked rose on Callaghan's neck. "I had so much fun with Miss Grace. She's the best teacher ever!"

And now I'm pretty sure I'm blushing. "I'm just fine."

Callaghan clicks his tongue. "Nah. I'll say you're way more than fine. More like pretty awesome. Right, Mads?"

God, is he flirting with me? An alarm goes off in my head, but I'm surprised to realize it's not the "you should flee right now" kind. It's more like "shoot, how should I respond to this?".

What the hell is happening to me?

"Right!" Maddie agrees.

"Well, thanks again for staying with her." Callaghan smiles, and something in my chest constricts at the sight of such a beautiful, genuine gesture. "Say goodbye to Miss Grace."

"Bye, bye, Miss Grace!"

"See you soon, Maddie." I smile, then nod at her brother. "I'll see you around."

Really? Will I be seeing him around? Why did I say that? *Oh, my god—*

He smirks. "You know where to find me if you ever change your mind about that tattoo."

And with that, they leave. Perhaps it's time to reconsider the tattoo, after all.

# chapter 5

## CAL

I don't take Maddie back to our mother's house after I pick her up from The Dance Palace. Instead, I buckle her up in the car seat I keep in the back of my car and drive to my apartment.

Meeting Grace at the studio was a pleasant surprise. Despite our scarce interactions and the fact that sometimes she looks a bit unsure about me, she seems like a cool girl. No, she's *definitely* a cool girl if she stayed behind with my sister while I finished Trey's back tattoo. I was lucky I wasn't with an actual client, or it would've taken me much longer to pack up.

But I can't even dwell on the fact that Grace is Maddie's ballet teacher—and that maybe I want to drop my sister off and pick her up from her lessons even more often than before—because my mother still hasn't answered the fucking phone.

As I hang up for the third time, I force myself to take a deep breath and keep the profanities to myself. Maddie doesn't need a reminder that our family life is fucked up.

When I tell her we're having a sleepover at my place, luckily, she doesn't object. She simply makes me promise we'll watch a princess movie on the couch before bed, and that's about it.

I don't know what I've done in another life to deserve such an angel as my little sister, but I thank past-life me for it every single day.

My apartment sits in the more residential part of town, although there are still some crowded bars and restaurants within walking distance. It's a quiet area where mostly families and old folks live, but I prefer it this way.

When I was apartment hunting years ago, I knew I couldn't live in the bustling Warlington downtown. I wanted to spend more time with my baby sister, and I wasn't going to be able to if some college kids started singing-shouting under my windows at two in the morning, drunk out of their minds.

"Wash your hands and we'll have dinner shortly, all right?" I tell Maddie as I open the front door and she rushes inside towards her bedroom.

"Yes!" she shouts before disappearing behind the kitchen.

My apartment isn't too big, but at least it gets a good amount of sunlight and it's quite modern. Right as you open the front door, there's a short hallway with a built-in closet, and straight on is the largest room of the place—the living room. It has a fireplace and everything, although it doesn't work.

On the right, there's an open concept kitchen and another narrow hallway that leads to Maddie's bedroom and bathroom. On the other side of the living room, there's the master bedroom with an ensuite.

The apartment is on the pricey side of Warlington, but I make good money at the parlor, and I don't mind paying extra to live comfortably. To get back here after a shitty day and be able to call this place my home.

"What are we having for dinner?" Maddie appears in the kitchen a few minutes after I've changed into a pair of sweatpants and an old t-shirt.

I help her sit on one of the stools at the kitchen island when she tries to climb it. "How about some mashed potatoes and sausages?" My fridge isn't exactly full right now, so I hope that's enough.

After an enthusiastic thumbs-up of approval, I get on with dinner after I put some cartoons on TV for her. The sausages are almost done when my phone rings in my pocket. I look at the caller ID and the heat of the stove has nothing on the raging fire blazing inside of me right now.

She doesn't bother with greetings. "Is she—"

"She's with me." I keep my tone low, so Maddie doesn't hear the venom in my voice. I can't exactly leave the kitchen while I'm cooking, and there's no wall separating it from the living room, so there's that. "Where the hell were *you*?"

At least my mother has the decency to sound apologetic when she speaks next, but I can't feel sympathy for her right now. "I'm sorry, Samuel. I really am. I got home after an exhausting shift at the grocery shop and I... I needed..."

"You needed to get blackout drunk until you forgot to pick up your own daughter from the studio?" I lower my voice to an impossible growl. "Who drove her to her lesson?"

"Taylor's mother did." I hear her gulp from the other side of the line. "She picks her up from school on Tuesdays because I have a longer shift, remember?"

I ignore her. "I had to leave the parlor to get her," I say between gritted teeth. "You know I would do anything for her, Mom, but being her parent isn't my responsibility. It's yours."

A charged pause. "I know."

*Then fucking act like it,* I want to say, but I don't.

"I'll get dressed and go pick her up," she says in a sluggish voice, the kind she uses when she's on her path to sobering up but not quite there yet.

"Don't bother. She's staying the night with me." I put some sausages on Maddie's pink plate, and the rest on a plain white one for me. "We'll drop by tomorrow morning to get her things before school starts. Any plans to get wasted this weekend, or will you be able to take proper care of your daughter?"

"Don't you dare talk to me like that, Samuel." For a second, she sounds like the authoritative, sensible mother I used to know.

A second later I remind myself that she doesn't exist anymore.

"Answer me."

A beat of silence passes between us. Then, "I won't drink this weekend."

I'm not sure I believe her. "Good. Then we'll see you tomorrow. Have a good night."

I don't give her enough time to answer, because if I hear any more of her half-drunken excuses right now, I might lose my fucking mind.

I finish the mash in silence and call Maddie to the table once dinner is ready. She loves my cooking, so it's no surprise that she devours her food in record time for a four-year-old.

After she helps me clean up, we snuggle together under a blanket on the couch and watch fifteen minutes of the movie before she passes out from exhaustion. I pick her up easily and carry her to her bedroom, which I let her chose the decorations of, so that's probably why it looks like a hurricane of all things girly.

Her 'big girl bed' has four posts and sheer white curtains, because *duh*—that's how princesses sleep. The white walls are decorated with stickers of flowers and stars, and I even got her one of those vanities for children I still don't understand the purpose of.

Trey teases me that I have too much great taste when it comes to designing princess bedrooms to be a coincidence, but I wanted to make her room at my apartment as cozy as possible, a place she wanted to spend time in.

So, yes, I pride myself on my amazing skills at room makeovers—*princess* rooms, specifically.

Maddie is so tired she doesn't wake up when I place her on the bed and tuck her in. "Sleep well, peanut," I whisper as my lips brush her forehead.

I close the door softly behind me and hope she has sweet

dreams.

I know I won't.

# GRACE

"Well, well, well. If this isn't Grace Allen going out for the second night in a month. Are you being possessed by a partying demon or something?"

I roll my eyes. "Gee, Amber. Thanks for the encouragement."

"You're welcome, sweetie."

I'm sliding into the booth at Danny's next to Céline when Em says, "She only agreed to come because it was my birthday on Wednesday, just so you know."

"Cut my girl some slack, will you?" Céline chimes in. "At least she's here, so stop being a pain in the ass."

I lean into her ear and whisper, "I love you the most."

"I heard that." Emily glares at me. I only stick my tongue out at her because she deserves it.

We chat about Em's birthday surprise from her parents, which consisted of the biggest bunch of flowers being delivered to her basketball practice when she was talking to "the hottest guy ever." Apparently, her parents have a thing for inconvenient public displays of affection that involve embarrassing their daughter at any given cost.

By the time our drinks—only water for me—and appetizers get here, Amber's eyes take on a mischievous gleam. She leans in conspiratorially. "So, babes, I was thinking... It's a Saturday night. We are at the hottest bar in Warlington right now, which happens to be full of sexy potential hookups. Who wants to go first?"

Céline arches a perfectly trimmed eyebrow. "I'm kind of seeing Stella now, remember?"

The blonde dismisses her with a hand gesture. "We know. And trust us—*about damn time*. You're not on the market, but myself and these two ladies totally are."

I shake my head as anxiety clings to my chest. I know Amber only has good intentions, but if she brings out her lawyer-to-be skillset tonight, I'm done for.

"Forget it," I tell her. "I'm not in the mood."

"Aw, come on," Emily whines before taking a sip of her beer. I can't even begin to understand how she drinks that *willingly*. Sure, I dislike alcohol in general and I almost never drink, but beer is on a whole different level. It tastes funny—a *bad* kind of funny.

She pouts. "Not even for my birthday?"

"You want me to hook up with some random guy as a birthday present?" I half-laugh. "I already got you those live-show tickets you've been pestering me about for months."

"But—"

"Sucks to suck."

"It doesn't have to be a hookup," Amber argues as she picks up a mozzarella stick between her long, red nails. "How about you go up to a guy and talk to him for a bit? Get his number? We'll be right here monitoring the whole thing, and I'll even let you choose your prey."

I roll my eyes. "Such a selfless soul you are. What's with you guys wanting me to talk to a boy all of a sudden?"

"We think you're ready for the next step." Emily shrugs. "Which is talking to someone. Only talking. In public. With us literally here."

I look at Amber and Céline, but I know I'm not going to find any allies at this table right now. They don't know about my assault, but they do know that I'm reticent about talking to men because of some past relationship gone wrong. It's not that I don't love and trust them. It's just that I refuse to see the inevitable pity in their eyes once they learn what happened to me.

Because trust me, the pity always comes. It chases me wherever I go.

When I told Emily about it, she started to treat me differently, more gently, for a whole two hours before I finally snapped and told her that I didn't need to be coddled.

I only want people to speak to me like they would any other person. I'm not the consequences of my assault. I refuse to let them define who I am.

I feel Céline's gentle touch on my arm. "If you're not ready, though—"

"She is," Amber interrupts with a decisive look in her eyes. "Come on, have a look around. Fancy any hottie?"

I can't believe I'm turning around. When I tell you Amber's a natural-born lawyer, I'm not kidding. And I find it super annoying right now.

Doing as she says, I scan the bar in a lazy search for... Who? I don't even know who I'm looking for. Perhaps if Dax were here, I would build enough courage to go up to him. We've been smiling at each other in class all week. Surely, he knows I exist now.

However, as the seconds pass and there's no sign of Dax anywhere, my confidence slowly melts away. Deep down it's not like I'm completely opposed to my friends' suggestion of finding a cute boy to talk to. If I were, I would've stood my ground, and they wouldn't force me anyway.

The truth is that something inside me shifted this summer. Sure, I refused to go to Paulson's party at first, but I ended up there, didn't I? And, despite what happened with that creepy guy after Aaron left, it didn't affect me as much as I thought it would. Maybe it's time to test the waters.

I talked to Callaghan a couple of times without having a panic attack and he's probably the most intimidating man I've ever come across, with his imposing height and biceps bigger than my head. I think it's a good sign.

"How about that guy over there?" Emily's voice drags me out of my thoughts. I follow her gaze towards a nearby booth, where a group of Warlington hockey players are laughing and drinking. "The blond one. He looks approachable, doesn't he?"

"And he's also in the middle of a conversation with his friends," I point out. "I'm absolutely not going up to their table. Are you insane?"

Em shrugs. "Fair enough."

I scan the bar again. It's packed, and we were lucky enough to find an available booth on a Saturday night. I'm sure Amber had something to do with it—there isn't a single person on campus she doesn't know, or any string she refuses to pull.

I'm about to tell my friends to drop it when I spot him. "What was the deal, again?" I ask absentmindedly.

Amber wastes no time reminding me. "Talk to him for a bit. Get his number if you're feeling bold."

Emily points an accusatory finger at me. "Don't you dare come back to this table empty-handed, young lady."

"Don't worry." I don't spare them another glance as my legs carry me across the bar on their own accord.

He has his wide back turned to me, but I would recognize those tattoos anywhere.

"Hey, Callaghan."

# chapter 6

## GRACE

Unlike at Paulson's party, this time I put a bit more effort into my appearance. And right now, I'm so glad I did. I'm only wearing a pair of black wide-legged pants and a red top, paired with the nude sandals I stole from Emily, but at least it's something. I can't deny that the heels give me a boost of self-confidence, even if I'm still shorter than average.

Callaghan turns his head at the sound of my voice, and when his eyes land on me they widen for half a second. A black man with a short beard and hipster glasses sits with him, beer in hand, but his smile looks kind enough, so I don't panic. Yet.

"Hey, sunshine." Callaghan throws me an easy grin and that nickname he gave me the first time we met. I kind of like it. "Did you change your mind about the tattoo?"

"Um, not really," I admit sheepishly. "I'm a bit scared that it will be too painful."

"Depends on where you want it," his friend chimes in with an equally friendly expression on his face. "And how high your pain tolerance is, I guess. You look tough enough."

"Thanks." Great, and now I'm pretty sure I'm blushing like a child in front of two grown men. So much for not embarrassing myself tonight.

Callaghan's friend nods at me. "I'm Trey, by the way. I work at the parlor with this one."

"Oh, you do? That's cool." And because that's not a socially acceptable answer, I add, "You two are friends?"

"Sadly," Callaghan mutters, but he's smiling.

Trey shakes his head with amusement. "Been friends since our teens. We grew up on the same street."

"And now I get to see his annoying ass at my shop five days a week," Callaghan jokes. "It's a privilege, really."

Their easy dynamic feels so genuine and refreshing that I don't find myself wanting to flee. Trey throws me another dashing smile before patting his friend on the shoulder. "Gonna talk to Oscar and Johnson for a bit. Nice to meet you, sweetheart."

And just like that, I'm alone with Callaghan and my heart starts to beat faster, although not from uneasiness.

"So, Grace. How was your week?"

His casual question surprises me, but I don't show it. "Piled up with too many assignments, unfortunately. How's your sister?"

His dark eyes light up at that. "She's doing great. Maddie really loves your ballet lessons, you know? She wants to become a professional princess-ballerina now."

I can't help but laugh at his sweet words. "A princess-ballerina? Well, sign me up for that too." Then, a thought crosses my mind. "Are you coming to our Christmas recital? We sent an email to the families last week, but maybe you didn't have time to read it."

He takes a tentative sip of his... Is that a soda? Why am I so surprised he's not drinking alcohol on a Saturday night? When he speaks again, his voice sounds slightly tighter. "I'll make sure to read it later, but count me in. I wouldn't miss it for the world."

That makes me smile. "I take it you're close with Maddie?"

"We spend a lot of time together," he says, but his tone doesn't sound quite right. Perhaps I'm only imagining things. I've only seen them interact once, but I'm sure anyone can see how devoted he is to his little sister and how much she loves him back. "You got any siblings?"

"Nope. I'm an only child." And because for some dumb, unknown reason I want him to know this, I blurt out, "I'm adopted. Gay parents."

He doesn't even bat an eyelid. "Neat. You get along with them all right?"

A rush of emotions builds up in my chest at the thought of them. "I love my dads. They're the best, but I don't see them as often as I'd like. They live in Canada."

He nods. "Canada must be amazing in the winter. I don't think I've ever visited, actually."

"Oh, you'd love it there." Before I know what I'm doing, I'm sliding into the empty stool next to him. "Winters are crazy, trust me. It's a pain in the ass to plan Christmas trips because there's always a blizzard or a snowstorm or something and flights get canceled left and right. Where did you grow up?"

I have no clue why I'm making conversation with this guy right now. Or why I don't feel like running away or throwing up, for that matter. There's something about Callaghan that puts me at ease, as if my brain somehow knows he's not a threat.

Which makes no sense because I don't *know* him. He's bigger, older, and I should probably be intimidated by his mere presence—but I'm not. Not anymore.

"Here in Warlington." He takes a quick sip of his drink. "It might be a fun city for you college kids, but it eventually gets boring."

"Oh, I doubt that," I tease him. I *actually* tease him. What the hell? "I love it here. I think I might stay after graduation."

"Really? Most students flee the city the moment they graduate. What could possibly keep you here?"

"My job, for one." I shake my head when the bartender asks me if I want anything. "I love working at The Dance Palace. And I don't know, there's something about this city that makes me feel at home. Maybe it's because Aaron lives here."

"He said the same thing after he graduated," he says with a smirk. "Couldn't see himself living anywhere but here."

"How about you? You never thought of moving away?" I ask, hoping he doesn't find my company annoying. God, what if he does but he's too polite to shoo me away?

"I lived in Boston for a while," he tells me and takes another sip. "A family friend took me under her wing and taught me the whole tattooing thing. Then I came back, worked for a bit, and eventually opened my own place."

"That's impressive," I say, truthfully. "I take it the business is going well, then?"

He smirks. "You ask your cousin about that. He could single-handedly keep it afloat."

I snort. Three years ago, Aaron got it into his chaotic head that tattoos were badass, and he wanted both of his sleeves done because "he'd absolutely rock that motherfucking ink." And sure, he does, but my cousin literally texts me a photo of a new tattoo every few weeks. His bank account must be bleeding right now. I know mine would be.

"Don't tell me about it. My aunt almost had a heart attack when she saw those flames you inked on his biceps."

Callaghan laughs. "Well, then she'd definitely pass out if she saw *me*."

At that, I can't help but marvel at the intricate artwork on his skin—both of his arms are covered in skulls, snakes, poker cards, flowers, and other jaw-dropping designs I would need a whole hour to analyze. The rose on the right side of his neck is impressive, with inked vines coming down his sleeves until they almost reach his long, thick fingers.

It's only now that I notice how stupidly ginormous his hands are, and I fight back a blush.

There's something wrong with me.

"Your tattoos are impressive," I say with honesty. I'm pretty sure I'm gaping at him because he chuckles in that deep rumble I've come to appreciate already. "Seriously. Did you do any of them yourself?"

"Only this one." He points to a minimalistic chain of mountains on his forearm. "I'm not a fan of tattooing myself. Too tiring."

"I can only imagine," I half-whisper as I narrow my eyes at the mountains to scan them more closely and hide the sudden urge to run my finger along the ink with a cough.

"Are you sure you don't want anything?" he asks me then. "It's on me."

"I'm all right. Thank you." A beat of silence passes between us, and suddenly I can't keep this a secret anymore. "Actually, there's something I want."

His eyes widen with interest. "Shoot."

I don't know why I feel so self-conscious about this now. I had no problem walking up to him, or actually *talking* to him. He seems like a naturally nice and laid-back guy, so why am I freaking out so badly over this?

What if he thinks I'm weird? He would never tell me to my face, not if he thinks I'll run to Aaron, and that makes me even more anxious.

"Okay, so," I start, catching my breath before I embarrass myself in front of the only man I've felt safe enough around for more than two seconds in four years. "My friends wanted me to come up to a guy tonight and get his number because they thought it would be good for me, but I don't feel comfortable talking to any random guys, let alone asking for their number, which—"

"Hey, hey. Easy." He smiles warmly at me, which means he doesn't find me weird, right? *Right?* "Let me see if I got it right. Your friends dared you to talk to a guy tonight?"

"It wasn't a dare. It was more like a trust exercise," I correct him.

"My bad." His eyes twinkle with amusement under the fluorescent lights of the bar. "And you came up to me because...?"

"Well, I already have your number from when I called you to pick up Maddie, and I need to show my friends proof, but it felt weird to flaunt it around without asking for your permission first. Plus, it was for a work thing so I'm sure using it for bragging is illegal, or something."

"Or something," he repeats with a smile. He smiles at me a lot, I notice. It's comforting, a contrast to his imposing body. "Tell you what, I give you permission to show my number to your friends as long as you know you can use it."

Holy shit.

Is he flirting with me?

"S-Sure." I give him a tight smile of my own because I don't know how to act anymore. My palms get all sweaty and disgusting, so I wipe them discreetly on my pants hoping he doesn't notice.

But he does, and quickly adds, "You know, in case you need some guidance about your tattoo."

I give him a curt nod. "Sounds good."

There's nothing wrong with a bit of harmless flirting. Callaghan looks harmless himself despite all his muscles and tattoos, and my friends are literally right behind me. I hate myself for closing off like this, damn it.

Is this what awaits me for the rest of my life? Not being able to have a proper conversation with a man without panicking?

Eventually, he finishes the rest of his drink in one big gulp and wipes his hands on his jeans in dismissal. "It was great seeing you again, Grace. Where are your friends?"

I turn my head in time to see the three dumbasses lowering their gazes. They totally weren't spying on us. Of course not. I point at their table with my thumb. "Just over there. It's a short walk."

He nods. "I'll see you around then. Take care."

And because I can't exactly keep him glued to his seat, I let him go as another loud alarm goes off in my head.

Why did I want him to stay in the first place?

# CAL

I fucked up, and I can pinpoint the exact moment I threw it all out of the window.

Most of the time, I have zero issues keeping my mouth shut. Hell, too many non-compulsory social interactions a day drain my energy as it is. I'm the textbook definition of an introvert when I'm around most people, or at least I thought I was—because I definitely don't know Grace well enough to suggest she calls or texts me.

And, seriously, *flirting*? When was the last time I flirted with a woman? A much younger one, at that.

I should've bitten my fucking tongue. It's obvious that Grace feels some kind of way about talking to strangers, and I shouldn't have pushed my luck. If she doesn't speak to me ever again, I can't say I didn't see it coming.

Trey joins me at the table, along with Oscar and Johnson who are regulars at the parlor and close friends of Trey. I let the conversation flow around me while I try not to turn my head to look at Grace, who's now standing at the bar with a bunch of girls I assume are her friends.

"You're sulking," Trey says and bumps his knee with mine.

"I'm not." I totally am, but I'm not about to admit it out loud. I take a mozzarella stick and pop it into my mouth. It's gone cold and it tastes rubbery, but at least I won't have to speak while I chew on it.

Trey looks over my shoulder in a not-so-discreet manner. "You tappin' that or something?"

I don't need to follow his gaze to know who he's talking

about. "No," I say, perhaps a bit more harshly than intended. "She's Aaron's cousin. Came by the tattoo parlor the other day but ended up backing out at the last minute."

"Yeah, I remember." He's still looking at her through his glasses, and for some reason it bothers me. "What's Aaron got to do with anything, though?"

I take another mozzarella stick and force myself to snap out of it. This is my best friend and Grace is practically a stranger, for fuck's sake. I shouldn't care if he looks at her or not. "He'll rip my dick off if I try anything with her. And why do you think I'm into her, anyway?"

Trey shrugs. "Just gave me that vibe." Before I can even begin to ask what the hell he means by vibe, he adds, "Yeah, no. You're definitely not tapping that. Or I hope you aren't, at least. She's talking to another guy right now."

My traitorous head turns at that and, sure enough, a kid I don't recognize has one elbow resting casually on the bar and is engaged in conversation with Grace. She doesn't look all that uncomfortable, but what do I know?

And most importantly, why do I even care?

Luckily, it becomes quite evident that I'm not interested in continuing our chat about my sulking, and Trey turns to our friends and starts talking about some upcoming video game release.

It's been weeks since I pulled an all-nighter to play with the guys, but now that plan is looking infinitely better than my current one—which involves sipping on a lukewarm drink, eating cold mozzarella sticks, and wondering why the hell I'm so worked up over Grace talking to a guy that isn't me.

If I hadn't noticed her sudden stiffness, I would've continued our chat until the bartender kicked us out. She's easy to talk to, and I would be lying if I said I didn't have a soft spot for the girl already. She stayed after hours with my sister so I could finish a tattoo, for fuck's sake. That's a solid ten in my book.

But, after tonight, I'm probably a solid four in hers. If that.

"Yo!" A strong, cold hand suddenly rests on my shoulder. I don't need to turn around to recognize Aaron's presence. "Man, if you wanted some good food you should've come to The Spoon." He picks a mozzarella stick between his fingers and shakes his head before tossing it back on the greasy basket. "Can't believe you're wasting money on this frozen shit."

"Johnson can't pick up chicks at your place. It's too fancy." I give my friend a knowing smile, and he shrugs as if to say, "Yup, that's exactly why I'm here."

Aaron boos and sits down in the booth next to Oscar. It's too tight for five grown men, but his eyes are scanning the bar so frantically I don't think he's even noticed that half of his ass is hanging out of the bench.

"Looking for anyone, Big A?" Trey teases.

"Yeah. She texted me earlier saying she was— Oh, for fuck's sake."

Aaron hides his face in his hands, shakes his head in desperation, and lets out the loudest sigh known to humanity. He's prone to dramatic outbursts, but I know him well enough to sense the genuine pissed-off "vibes" he's exuding right now, as Trey would put it.

"What is it?" Oscar asks.

I don't think I've ever seen Aaron look angry since I met him three years ago, but the icy rage on his gaze is unmistakable. "*That* is my problem."

His problem, as it turns out, is Grace and that kid chatting up at the bar. I give Trey a knowing look to tell him I wasn't kidding when I said Aaron would attempt to end my life if I tried anything with his cousin. Not that pursuing her is in my plans, anyway.

Aaron is usually a laid-back, go-with-the-flow kind of

guy—except when it comes to Grace. I knew he had a cousin at Warlington University and that he was protective of her, but we'd never been introduced. And now I'm starting to understand why.

"What's wrong with that?" Johnson asks before taking a sip of his beer.

Aaron runs a hand through his already messy brown hair. "Dax fucking Wilson is what's wrong with that."

There's an edge to his voice, cold and cruel, that I haven't heard from him before. A sudden burst of protectiveness claws at my chest, and I lean in. "He's bad news?"

He finally tears his gaze away and locks it with mine. "He's some college kid, but I've always thought he was shady as fuck."

"Explain." Oscar narrows his eyes. He shared a bunch of classes with Aaron back in the day, and he's the reason Grace's cousin got addicted to tattoos a few years ago.

"For one, he's a hockey player, which is a big ass red flag in itself." He keeps his voice low, and I know what he means. Playing college hockey in Warlington is one of those merits that inflates egos like none other. "And second of all, I overheard him the other day saying he wouldn't mind, and I quote, "fucking that girl Grace Allen's brains out any day." She's practically my sister. I shouldn't hear that shit." He fake-shivers, and I feel like going on a killing spree.

"You don't want him near her," Trey clarifies.

"Abso-*fucking*-lutely not. He's an ass," Aaron spits out. "Haven't you heard? This is only his second year at Warlington, and he's already hooked up with half of the cheerleading team, and then some. I don't want my cousin to get a fucking STD, thank you."

Trey snorts next to me, but I struggle to find any of this funny.

I lean in and lower my voice into an impossibly deep rumble. "Want me to go over there and tell him to fuck off?"

Aaron looks at me for a second too long. "That'll only freak her out."

"They were talking earlier, actually," Trey chimes in with a smirk, a traitorous finger pointing at me. "Weren't you, Cal? They're friends now."

When Aaron gives me a look I can't decipher, because I can't tell if he wants to murder me or if he's just surprised, I add, "She's my sister's ballet teacher and we talked for a bit."

"Ah." Grace's cousin diverts his gaze again. "Don't worry, man. I got it."

Next thing I know, Aaron is walking up to her and inserting himself between her and this Dax dude. The flash of disappointment in her eyes doesn't escape me, and it feels like a punch in the gut.

Who this girl does or doesn't hook up with is none of my business. My brain should know this shit by now.

Dax, clearly uncomfortable by Aaron's imposing presence, eventually nods goodbye and leaves. Good. But Grace doesn't come to our table with her cousin. Instead, she rolls her eyes at him, takes her phone out, and makes her way back to her friends. When Aaron sits back in front of me, the tension is visibly gone from his shoulders.

"Crisis averted," he says with a satisfactory grin. Then, he glances around the table and back at the bar. "What does a man have to do to get a drink in this place?"

# chapter 7

## GRACE

This is not a drill. Dax Wilson talked to me. I repeat: Dax Wilson talked to me.

I still don't know how it happened, but I'm also not going to question the universe's mysterious ways. The only thing I know is that one second, I'm chatting with Amber at the bar, and the next Dax is tapping on my shoulder and asking me if I had fun at Paulson's party all those days ago.

He remembered me.

And I'm not even mad about Aaron interrupting us out of the blue, because Dax Wilson *remembered* me.

By the time Emily and I reach our dorm and get ready for bed, I'm bouncing on my feet, unable to make my heart stop beating so frantically. She tells me how excited she is for me, and that I should sit next to him on Monday, but I don't want to rush it.

"What if he thinks I'm clingy?" I bite down on my bottom lip as I get under my cold bed sheets.

Emily is still folding her clothes and putting them away on the other side of the room we share. "He won't. He's clearly interested, G. Super popular guys like him don't go up to a girl if they don't want to hook up with them."

And that's exactly my problem, isn't it?

I might not have felt uncomfortable during our conversation at the bar, but that doesn't mean I'm ready to, I don't know, let him shove his tongue down my throat.

I haven't kissed anyone in four years, and I'm not a hundred percent convinced that I'm ready to start doing it now.

But it's Dax Wilson we're talking about. He's the first guy I've felt something for in a long time. This is a sign, right? A sign that it's time to move on.

I end up chickening out and not taking Em's advice to sit next to him on Monday, but I build up enough courage to come up to him after our Tuesday class.

"Hey." I approach him on my way out of the classroom. He's still putting his stuff away in his backpack, and I figured this would be the only opportunity I get to talk to him since he's not surrounded by his very loud, very nosey teammates.

"Oh. Hey, Grace." He throws me an easy smile when he notices me. "Tough reading this week, huh?"

"Don't even mention it." I let out an exasperated sigh. "Seriously, how does Mrs. Keaton expect us to read sixty pages by the next class? I don't think she knows we have a life outside this building."

Dax laughs. "Trust me, she knows. She just doesn't care." He finishes gathering his things and we walk out together. A few people turn their heads to look at us and do a double take when they see me by his side. Yep, *I'm* leaving the classroom with Warlington's hockey star Dax Wilson. This is even better than in my daydreams.

"Hey, speaking of having a life outside of Mrs. Keaton's classroom," he starts as we exit the building. The September air is colder than I anticipated, and I curse myself for deciding against wearing more layers this morning. "Are you doing anything this Friday night?"

I come to halt. Wait a damn second. Is he about to—?

"There's a frat party at Zeta House and maybe we could go together?" he asks, and he almost sounds shy about it. "I mean, if you want to."

There comes a time in everyone's lives where one must make a life-altering decision. To attend this party with Dax, or not to attend this party with Dax, that is the question. And the answer is:

"Sure, I'm not busy." I ignore the uneasy feeling settling in the pit of my stomach as I agree to...a date? Is this a date?

"Great. It's a date, then."

Well, there's my answer.

Dax pulls out his phone from the pocket of his jacket. "Let me get your number so I can text you the details later." Once he's saved my number—my freaking number!— he excuses himself because he has a study group in ten minutes, and then I'm all alone outside of the Humanities Hall.

It's not until five minutes later that it really dawns on me.

I have a date with Dax Wilson.

\* \* \*

Emily literally screams in my ear when I make her privy to my Friday plans, and I don't blame her. I went from not being able to talk to a guy without wanting to throw up to having a date with one of the hottest boys on campus. If that isn't a full-on glow up, I don't know what is.

"See? I knew pushing you to get some phone numbers at Danny's would be good for you," she tells me from the other side of the line as I make my way towards The Dance Palace for my evening class. "Are you nervous?"

"A bit," I admit. "I've never been to Zeta House before."

"It's like a fifteen-minute walk from our dorm. The place isn't enormous, so you should be fine," she reassures me, but I still feel mildly sick to my stomach. "You know you can cancel at any moment, right? You don't have to go if you don't want to."

"That's the thing." I bite down on my lip. "I want to go. This might be the only time Dax asks me out, and I don't want to blow it."

"I know, babe, but you shouldn't do something that makes you uncomfortable just because a hot guy asked you out. There are plenty more fish in the sea."

I happen to want this particular fish.

"I'll be fine." And because I know her and she's worried, I add, "I promise to cancel if I change my mind."

"Carly's birthday is on Friday too, but I can bail and go with you if you need support," she offers.

This woman, I swear. "Absolutely not, Em. You live your life. I'll be okay."

She lets out a loud sigh. "Fine, but text me when you get there and when you come back home. How about that other guy you talked to, though? What was his name?"

"Callaghan." My heart skips a beat at the reminder of our last conversation.

I thought he was flirting with me, and I freaked out a bit because I didn't know how to respond, but it's all good on my side. I wonder if he's dropping Maddie off today at the studio. The possibility of seeing him again makes my stomach jump with anticipation.

"He's a friend of Aaron's. He owns Inkjection, actually."

"Neat!" Em exclaims. "But he gave you his number, right? Why don't you use it?"

*I give you permission to show my number to your friends as long as you know you can use it.*

That's quite literally what he told me to do, didn't he? Still, thinking about texting him intimidates me. Plus, I have no idea what I could text him about in the first place. It's not like we're friends or anything. Outside Maddie's ballet lessons and me possibly getting that tattoo, we have no need to contact each other. He was probably being nice. If I texted him, I would just annoy him.

"Baby steps, Em." I round the corner and spot the dance studio in the distance. Its enormous pink sign is impossible to miss. "I've already got a date with Dax this Friday, which is way more than I could've asked for."

"Yeah," she says, "but, I don't know, Callaghan seemed cool. You looked at ease with him."

"He is, and I was." Something he told me a while back occurs to me then. "He's thirty, though. Maybe that's a bit old for me." That's eight years older than me, and I've never had friends that age.

"Nah. Remember when I dated Patrick Evans?" How could I forget? The man was so well-off he bought her five designer purses in the three months they were together. "He was ten years older than me, and it wasn't weird or anything. You'll be fine."

"Whatever. I don't want to date him, anyway." When I reach the studio, I spot Adelaide inside and wave at her. "I'm at TDP. We'll talk later, okay?"

"Sure, hon. Have fun."

And for the next hour, I do exactly that. Being with the girls always manages to lift my mood and wipe off all worries and remaining anxiety of the day.

We practice some more moves for the Christmas recital, and although I'm sure they will forget all about them by the end of the lesson, the fact that they exit the studio with wide smiles on their little faces is the best gift of all.

When I gather my things and head for the front desk, a pair of bulky tattooed arms catches my attention, and my heart does a stupid cartwheel.

"Callaghan, hey," I greet him in what I hope is a casual tone as he kneels to zip up Maddie's jacket.

"Hey, Grace." Today, a tight gray t-shirt with the logo of

his shop hugs his chest, and the thin piece of clothing is doing nothing to hide his ripped muscles. At least four mothers have checked him out on their way out in the past thirty seconds, and I can't blame them one bit.

"So, listen," I start, not really knowing why I'm bringing this up at all. "I've been thinking about the tattoo recently, and I'm still not fully ready to do it, but maybe we could talk about some sketches and budget or something?"

I've never felt more self-conscious in my life. I'm still wearing my ballet tights and slippers. My voice sounds too small and unsure, and he's right there in all his muscular, tattooed glory and I'm probably wasting his time and—

"Sure. I'm free tomorrow after six. We can talk about your options then. Sounds good?"

Oh. Maybe it's all in my head.

"I've got rehearsal at five thirty. Meet you at seven?"

"Works for me."

"Great." I give him a sincere smile. "See you tomorrow, then."

"Goodbye, Miss Grace!" Maddie waves at me as they leave the studio holding hands.

I wave back, smiling, until a voice behind me startles the shit out of me.

"Who was that?" Adelaide's looking at me with a knowing smirk, her brunette hair tied neatly at the nape of her slender neck, one thin eyebrow raised. She's in her late forties, but she doesn't look a day older than thirty and, frankly, she's one of the classiest women I've ever met. Because she's half-French, probably.

"*That* was Maddie Stevens's brother." I eye her carefully. After four years of being around her almost every day of the week, I know what she's about to say. "Don't get any crazy ideas. He's a friend of my cousin's."

"Uh-huh." She's not buying it. "That's why he was giving you those puppy dog eyes? Because he's a friend of your cousin's?"

I roll my eyes at her far-fetched assumption, even if my heart skips a beat nonetheless. Callaghan was absolutely not puppy-eying me. "You're seeing things," I assure her. "We don't even know each other that well."

"Mm..."

"I'm serious."

"Well, you look good together," she muses. "I'm digging the whole bad boy, good girl aesthetic you've got going on."

"Oh, my god."

*Aesthetic?* She's lost it. It's official—my ballet teacher and boss has lost her mind. Poof! Gone.

Adelaide has the nerve to laugh before winking at me and disappearing behind the desk to check something on the computer. Shaking my head, I take my phone out to add a reminder for tomorrow's appointment at Inkjection. This time, I'm not running away like a headless chicken.

It's time to put my big girl pants on.

# chapter 8

## GRACE

I forgot my big girl pants at home.

Well, no, that's a lie—this time, I actually make it to one of the stations. It's what happens afterwards that makes me want to run away and never come back.

"This is the tattoo needle." Callaghan holds up the devil-made weapon between his thick fingers and shows it to me up-close. "You'll feel a prickling sensation every time it pierces your skin, but it shouldn't be too bad. Because you want it on your ribs, though, it might sting a little more."

"How much more?" I ask, pale-faced.

Callaghan chuckles. "Don't worry. I'm sure you'll handle it like a boss. You wanted a short sentence, right? Shouldn't take me more than thirty minutes, max."

"Yeah, that's what I had in mind." I chew on my lower lip to prevent myself from asking any stupid questions. It's kind of embarrassing when I think about it. I had to come here and monopolize his free time because I can't grow up and take a few stings.

"Want me to sketch it for you now?" he asks as he puts the needle back in his workstation.

"Y-You don't have to do all this." I'm mortified by the thought that I might be nothing but a nuance, but that he doesn't tell me because he's scared of Aaron. "Especially when I still don't know if I'll go through with it."

"Oh, you will." He throws me a knowing smile that heats me up from the inside. "Come on. It'll only take me five minutes and I'll have to sketch it eventually anyway. What did you have in mind?"

Things will only get more embarrassing from this point on because my dumb ass hasn't told anyone, not a single soul, what I want tattooed. It's too personal, and telling people feels like peeling away a layer of myself and letting them judge my vulnerable interior. After all, this tattoo won't be in any visible place to others, and if I don't want people to know about it, they won't unless they see me naked and peek under my boob.

Which poses a whole different set of alarming issues. If I want my skin inked, I'll have to tell Callaghan exactly what design I want. *And* I'll have to let him touch the skin right next to my boob.

Oh, for fuck's sake.

"Grace?"

*Shit.* He asked me a question, didn't he?

"Sorry, what did you say?" I blink, hoping my face doesn't look as flushed as it feels.

Callaghan gives me an easy smile. "I asked what you had in mind for the tattoo. I'll work on a quick sketch so you can think on it at home."

"Um, sure." I pull out my phone, open an app and show him a font I like. "Something similar to this style, if you can."

"I can do that," he assures me in a soft, gentle tone. "Can I see the quote?"

"It's a bit silly, actually." I glue my eyes to the screen, although I don't need to. My dads' words have become a mantra for the past four years, and I know them by heart.

"I doubt that." He adjusts his stool, and in this new position one of his knees brushes mine. I don't pull away from the contact. It grounds me and, for some reason, that faint touch gives me the courage I normally lack to peel that first layer off.

"Something happened to me a few years ago. It was pretty bad, and, um..." I don't elaborate because I don't think I'm strong enough to do so right now. "Since then, my dads kept telling me this same thing and I guess it grew on me. They used to say, 'Wherever life plants you, bloom with grace.'" I give him a sad, pathetic smile. "Get it? Because I'm Grace."

I expect him to laugh at the cheesiness of it all. To make fun of the whole thing, maybe. Instead, he says, "It's beautiful. Great advice, too."

"It's an old French proverb, I think." I suddenly get the urge to explain it to him. "Or maybe they simply saw it online and went with it."

Callaghan chuckles and turns towards his sketching pad.

"Your dads sound pretty awesome."

I beam at that. "They're the best. When I told them about the tattoo, they offered to pay for it and everything. They're convinced I need to do something out of my comfort zone. Something I wouldn't normally do."

"Do they have any tattoos?" he asks without lifting his gaze from his design.

"Oh, no way." I stifle a laugh as I try to imagine either of my dads with a bunch of tattoos. "They're both these big, bad corporate lawyers. I'm not even sure they're *allowed* to get a tattoo even if they wanted to."

"I have a bunch of clients who are lawyers," he explains. "They should be fine as long as the ink isn't visible to others. Most of them go for their legs or their backs."

I eye him carefully as he works. Every inch of his arms is covered in ink, and so are his hands up to his knuckles.

My gaze lifts to the rose on his neck, and I ask, "Is your whole body tattooed? Or just the arms and the neck?"

"Pretty much only what you see." He erases something and

draws it again. "I've got a big one in my left calf and a few on my back, but that's about it."

"Oh."

He smirks. "You sound disappointed."

"I guess I imagined you all covered in ink, for some reason." Not like I'm imagining his naked chest right now. Or his muscled back. Of course not.

"I've always wanted both my arms done. Anything else, I will do if I feel like it. I have no idea what I want tattooed on the rest of my body, so it's bare for now."

Then, he finally shows me the sketch he's been working on for the past few minutes. And I let out a loud, totally embarrassing gasp.

He's not done only one design, but two.

The first one reads *'bloom with grace'* in lowercase and a cursive font even more stunning than the one I showed him for reference, followed by a comma. The second one is pretty much identical, except that the two 'o's in 'bloom' are in fact little suns, done in a delicate, minimalist stroke. Before I can even begin to form a single coherent thought, he starts, "I know half of the quote is missing, but since you're scared of the pain and the tattoo can't be too big anyway, I added the comma instead to symbolize that no matter what happens, you'll still bloom with grace."

I'm too stunned to speak, and that's probably why my voice sounds so rusty when I ask, "And the little suns?"

He gives me a small, sheepish smile I can't look away from. "All beautiful things in life need the sun to bloom and thrive. We might not know each other very well yet, but I have no doubt you're the brightest light of sunshine, Grace."

I remember, then. The nickname he gave me the first time I came here, and all the other times he's called me that. A fuzzy, warm feeling invades my chest.

"So, um," I'm surprised to see him so taken aback all of a

sudden, "take these home. Think it over, see which one you prefer, or if you'd like a new design that's fine too. No rush. Just hit me up when you've made up your mind."

I take the piece of paper between my fingers and fold it carefully. "Thank you. It... It means a lot that you've taken the time to do this for me."

"It's nothing. But if you want, you can consider it my way of thanking you for staying behind with Maddie the other day." He gives me one last smile before standing up from his stool. I do the same. "I'll walk you out."

My heart beats so fast as we walk to the front of the parlor that I don't notice the summer storm lashing outside until my hand is on the door handle. Above our heads, the already darkening sky is covered in heavy clouds.

My face falls. "Crap."

I feel the warmth of Callaghan's huge body right behind me, but his proximity doesn't startle me. "I hope you're not in a rush to get anywhere. Looks like it'll rage for a bit."

Glancing at the time on my phone, I notice that I've been in here for almost a whole hour. "I needed to finish a paper for tomorrow, and I wasn't looking forward to pulling an all-nighter, but..."

"Come," he suddenly says as he grabs a set of keys from the other side of the counter. "I'll drive you home."

"You don't have to do that," I quickly assure him.

"I'm done for the day, and Trey can close up the shop when he's done," he says, brushing my concerns off. "My car's at the back. You coming?"

"I could call an Uber."

"You could," he agrees. "Or you could accept my free ride."

I mean... When he puts it like that.

Without saying another word, I follow him towards the back of the shop. He opens a metallic door leading to a small carport where a black car is parked under the narrow roof. I get inside as quickly as I can, because the wind's picked up and I'm not wearing a jacket. I smile when I peep at what I assume is Maddie's black and pink booster seat in the back.

"Where to?" he asks me as he starts the car.

"Preston Hall."

"The dorm?"

"Yup."

"Got it."

Cocooned within a deep gray atmosphere, we ride in comfortable silence with only the sound of the rain hitting the windshield between us. Weirdly, I find myself at ease in his company as he drives through the flooded city. I've never liked heavy storms in the first place, so the fact that I'm not freaking out right now, while in a car with an older and stronger man, says a lot about where I'm at mentally.

My therapist would love to hear about this.

Despite the crazy rain pouring down on us, Callaghan sits behind the wheel as he would in front of the TV— relaxed, focused, also mildly bored. It's unfair how attractive he looks while driving, I think, as I ogle him shamelessly.

He's sporting one of those Inkjection t-shirts he uses as a work uniform, and his dark hair is pulled backwards except for that one rebellious strand that always falls on his forehead. His biceps flex as he grips the wheel to turn, and I force myself to peel my eyes away.

I must be coming down with a fever or something because there's simply no way I'm checking him out right now.

"That's your building, right?"

His deep voice drags me out of the very dangerous waters I was about to be drawn into.

"Yes, that's the one," I say, hoping my voice sounds steady even though I'm crumbling inside. "You can stop here."

He slows down the car, hesitating. The entrance to Preston Hall is still far away. Cars aren't allowed past the fence separating the dorms from the street, and I'll probably be soaked wet by the time I—

"Here. Take my jacket."

Callaghan reaches one long arm into the backseat and gives me a black denim jacket so large it would reach my knees if I put it on.

"It's not much, but if you throw it over your head at least you won't arrive in a complete puddle," he offers and unlocks the door.

"Thank you," I mutter, still unsure about the jacket. He's done way too much for me today, and I almost feel bad for hijacking his clothes now as well. But I also don't want to get my hair wet.

"No problem. Just text me when you get to your room safe." He nods towards the building and, sure enough, the rain falls so heavily I can't even see the huge front doors.

"Yeah, I'll do that." I give him one last smile as I put his jacket over my head. "Thank you for the ride, again. And for the jacket, and for the sketches. That was very thoughtful of you."

"It was nothing, Grace. Take care, yeah?"

And because I can't stand the intensity of his gaze for one more second, I simply nod and walk-run towards my dorm as fast as my feet can carry me without slipping in the torrential rain.

When I get to my room, Em isn't there, which is good because that means she can't see how closely I resemble a wet dog right now, or how flushed my cheeks are as I take out my phone and search for Callaghan's number. Before I text him, though, I place the miraculously dry sketch paper he gave me inside one of my writing journals.

**Home safe and looking like a wet**

> rat. *thumbs up*

Not even a minute later, my phone buzzes with his reply.

> I take it my jacket was useless
> after all?

> Not at all. I might resemble a wet
> rat right now, but at least my hair
> is dry

And then, because I might not have any self-control left when it comes to this guy after all, I double text:

> I'll drop your jacket off at the
> parlor tomorrow

> Ah, all worth it then. Can't have
> the complete rat look. And don't
> worry about the jacket, drop it off
> whenever.

> Do you like coffee? Because I
> totally owe you a coffee now

I bite my thumb as I wait for his response. I wouldn't be opposed to the idea of us grabbing a coffee together at some point, but if he refuses...

> You don't owe me anything,
> sunshine. I accept your offer,
> though. I'm physically incapable of
> saying no to an espresso.

I snort, imagining the tiny cup between his impossibly large fingers.

> Deal. I'm going to take a shower now unless I want to catch a cold. I'll see you around :)

Good call. See you around, Grace.

# chapter 9

## CAL

My car stays parked until Grace texts me that she's home safe. I don't know why I do it since Warlington's campus is one of the safest in the state, but for some reason the thought of anything happening to her on that five-minute journey to her room makes me want to punch a wall. And when she brings up dropping off my jacket at the shop, I resist the urge to tell her she can keep it. But I fucked up at the bar by being too forward, and I'm not stupid enough to do it again.

*Something happened to me a few years ago. It was pretty bad.* Her words have been drilling a dark hole into my head for days now. How vulnerable she sounded. How small she looked. Granted, she's petite as hell, but there's a sort of buzzing, cheery energy about her that certainly isn't.

A selfish part of me, the one that hated seeing the pain in her eyes, wonders what would happen if I brought it up to Aaron. It's obvious that he knows, and maybe that's why he behaves so protectively when it comes to her, but the most sensible part of me knows it's not his story to tell.

Still, it doesn't stop my head from spiraling for days, coming up with one terrible scenario after another. Each one makes my blood pressure spike higher than the last. I haven't seen her since Wednesday, so that's probably enhancing my shitty mood as well.

It's now Friday, and I should be paying attention to whatever Johnson is saying about this chick he hooked up with last weekend, because that's what a good friend does, but I can't.

Something's bothering me, and the fact that I can't pinpoint exactly what it is, is bothering me even more.

"Sorry, man. What was that?" I force myself out of it when I realize Johnson has asked me a question I didn't hear any single word of.

"Forget him. He's out of it today," Trey says as he comes up behind me at the front desk. "The fuck is up, bro?"

"Nothing's up," I lie. Well, not technically—something's up, I just don't know what.

"You need to get laid," Johnson deadpans. "How long has it been since your last playdate between the sheets? A year?"

"Fuck off," I mutter, which makes Trey laugh. "Definitely longer than that," he adds like the great best friend he is.

"Damn. For real?" Johnson frowns.

"Drop it."

"Nah. You know what you need? Exactly—a wild night out with the boys. Let's find you a hot date to take home."

"Absolutely not."

An hour later, I find myself in a booth at Danny's with the two fuckheads.

"See any woman you like?" Johnson smirks over the rim of his beer and nods at a tall redhead in a tight, blue dress by the bar. "That's a fine piece of ass right there."

Remind me again why I'm friends with this airhead?

Luckily, Trey senses my discomfort and jumps in.

"You know our man here doesn't do one-night stands," he tells our friend. I've done exactly two in my thirty years, and I regret both. "But he's right, Cal. Some tongue action might be good to bring down that stress."

I guess he's got a point, but I'm not going to shove my tongue down anyone's throat for two reasons. One, I don't fucking want to. And two, Grace is all I can think about lately.

It's not that I like her. Not like *that*, anyway. But her presence is a looming thought in my head, all day at all hours, and I can't shake the feeling that I should stop...and wait.

For what, I don't know. I don't want to know. The last thing I need is to get romantically involved with anyone right now.

It would only end in disaster.

As if my mind had summoned a distraction, my phone rings. When I take it out of my pocket and look at the caller ID, my brain stops working. Confused, I have to read the name on the screen again.

"Who's that?" Trey asks.

"I have to take this." I bolt from my seat and rush past the throng of drunk college kids until I'm finally outside. My heart is beating too fucking hard as I press the answer button. "Grace? Are you okay?"

Silence from the other line.

All I can hear are some muffled voices and distant electronic music. Panicking, I try again. "Grace. Where are you?"

Then, finally, *fucking finally*, I hear her broken voice. "I...I didn't know who to call. I'm s-sorry."

"Don't apologize." I'm already sprinting towards my car. "Are you hurt? Where are you?"

"I'm at Zeta House," she says in a weak voice. "I... Can you pick me up?"

"I'm already on my way," I assure her. "Don't hang up, all right? I'll be there in five."

She lets out a shaky sigh. "All right." A beat of silence passes between us. Then, "I think I'm about to have a panic attack."

I don't think I've ever gotten to my car faster in my life. "Breathe with me, okay, sweetheart? You're safe, and I'm five minutes away," I tell her in the softest voice I can manage while I'm feeling on fucking edge. "Come on. In." I do the breathing techniques with her. "And out. Again."

At this point, I care little to none if I get a speeding ticket as I race towards the frat house. Grace is still on the other line, breathing with me, but I know it's not enough. I know things will get worse with every passing second if I don't get there soon.

# GRACE

I don't regret going to the frat party with Dax right away. As I get ready in my room, I'm even excited for the night—following Em's advice, I opt for a casual black dress with a slit down my right leg paired with some heeled sandals. You know, because I'm feeling brave and all.

Well, that ends pretty quickly.

Within an hour of arriving at the party, Dax is halfway drunk and talking to a bunch of equally hammered frat boys I've never met before. Which, fine, I don't know many people as it is, and I wouldn't have minded making a friend or two...

If it wasn't for the tiny, insignificant fact that Dax forgets I'm there at all. As in, he turns around at some point, sees me, and asks what I'm doing here and if I'm enjoying the party.

I don't need to smell his breath to know he's drunk enough for two people.

So much for a date, huh?

But that's not why I end up crying and having an anxiety attack on the sidewalk in front of Zeta House.

Oh, no—I wish it was.

After Dax gets over the initial surprise of seeing me at the party, he asks me if I want to dance. He was been nothing but nice on our way to the frat house, through texts as well (I know that doesn't mean anything), so I say yes.

The moment he puts his hands on my hips, however, I freeze.

When his lips brush my cheek, panic grips at my chest. When he speaks in my ear in that slurred, rough way and asks me if I want to go somewhere quieter where he can make me feel good, I pull away like he's on fire and race for the front door.

I don't hear him shout my name behind me, telling me to stop, but I wouldn't have listened anyway. I don't even feel the cool late-September air on my bare arms as I exit the house and unlock my phone with shaky fingers.

My initial intention is to call Emily until I remember she's at someone's birthday party. Would she drop everything to come get me? Absolutely, but she also worries about me a lot and the most selfless and probably stupid part of my brain crosses her name off my list and moves on to the next option: Aaron.

Problem—he would know what happened within half a second, and I don't want him to be thrown in jail for beating Dax up. Not to mention Fridays are busy at The Spoon, and he likes helping around and talking to customers, even if, technically, he isn't part of the staff and only manages the business aspect of it.

And that sums up my list. I can't call my dads, obviously, since they live in a whole other country, and I don't want them to worry when they can't do anything about it anyway.

So, I call an Uber. And my ride gets canceled. Twice.

Friday nights are the worst.

I still don't know which part of my head convinced me to dial Callaghan's number. All I know is that, after three tones, he picks up and promises he's on his way.

He doesn't want me to hang up, so I stay on the line with him.

I want to tell him that it's not safe to talk on the phone while driving, but I can't.

I want to tell him that I feel pathetic, and like a piece of worthless meat—a complete stranger in my own body, but I don't.

I want to tell him that I can barely breathe, that my stomach is doing weird things and that my chest hurts, and this time I do.

"I think I'm about to have a panic attack."

I hate myself for putting him through this. For making me his problem. He was probably hanging out with his friends, or with Maddie, or alone and relaxed at home, perhaps with a woman. Now I've forced him to rescue me because I'm a pathetic piece of nothing who can't take care of herself—

"Breathe with me, okay sweetheart? You're safe and I'm five minutes away. Come on. In. And out. Again."

His voice grounds me. It's soft but firm, and I find myself following his instructions and breathing with him. For the next few minutes, Callaghan keeps soothing me with words, mixed with the unmistakable sound of traffic in the background, and it hits me that he's really coming for me. It's not that I didn't believe him when he said he was on his way, it's just that... He's really coming. For me. Right now.

I don't know how much time has passed when a black car pulls up on the other side of the road, and he gets out of the vehicle in a rush. I barely register my body movements as I hang up and put my phone back in my strappy bag. All I see is him, and all I feel is relief.

Before I know what I'm doing, I throw myself at him and wrap my arms around his torso, because that's the only part of his body I can reach, even in heels. Callaghan doesn't say a word as he wraps his own arms around me and pulls me closer against his chest. He smells like laundry detergent and that spicy cologne he always wears, and I don't ever want to let go.

"Grace," he calls my name so softly I'm surprised I can hear it between the loud voices in the back and the drumming of my own heart. "Talk to me. Are you hurt?"

I pull away to look him in the eye without breaking our embrace. I don't want to.

"I'm not hurt." A flash of relief crosses his face. "I... I want to leave."

He nods, still visibly tense. "I got you."

Callaghan keeps a comforting arm around my shoulders the whole way to his car. He opens the door for me. I get inside, he closes it, and I break down.

# chapter 10

## CAL

I've never taken a knife to the gut, but I suppose it feels a lot like seeing Grace cry.

Having a baby sister, I'm no stranger to tears. I don't feel awkward when someone breaks down in front of me, but the sight of her tears hurts all the same. I can only sit still and feel my chest tighten as Grace sobs quietly with her face turned to the car window, probably thinking I won't notice her breakdown that way.

"Grace," I call out gently. The last thing I want is to upset her any further, but I need her to calm down. "Look at me. You're okay."

She shakes her head. "No, I'm not. I'm broken."

The only thing that is about to be broken is my damn heart. "Why would you say that?"

"Because." She sniffles.

The distant sound of music from the party drifts over to the inside of the car. Something or someone inside that frat house upset her, so I figure the first step towards calming her nerves would be to put some distance. A quick glance at her tells me her seatbelt isn't on. "Come on, Gracie, I'll take you home. Buckle up," I say, hoping the nickname boosts her mood.

Without a word, she does as I say. It's evident how badly she wants to get out of here. However, not long after I start the car and take a few turns, Grace speaks again. "I don't want to go home."

I steal a quick glance at her. She isn't hiding her face anymore, and her eyes are swollen from all the tears. "Where do you want to go, then?"

Another sniffle. "I'm a bit hungry."

"Got you."

Mentally crossing my fingers so that the place I'm thinking of is still open, I turn the car down the next street. Grace sits in silence besides me, not quite crying anymore but still shaken up. My body aches to kill the engine right here in the middle of this dark street and pull her into a hug, but deep down I know that would be a mistake. I'm not sure she wants to be touched right now.

"Where are we?" she asks after a while, her voice strained.

I pull into the almost empty parking lot and point to the food truck a few feet away. "Over there. Fancy some vegan junk food?"

Grace narrows her eyes towards the vehicle and chuckles. The soft sound makes my heart do something funny. "Are you vegan?"

I mimic her smile. "No, but I appreciate all kinds of good food. Let's go."

Once she gets out of the car and we walk together to the food truck, I allow myself to look at the dry tears on her cheeks and the puffiness of her eyes. She's calmer now, and I can only hope she'll feel better after a full stomach.

"What do you want to get?" I ask her as she scans the menu, which is plastered on one of the truck's windows. "I've tried all the burgers and they're incredible. Tastes like meat."

"Mm-hmm. Okay. I'll trust you on this one." She turns to the woman inside the truck. "Can I get a double cheeseburger, please?"

"And two hot dogs. Do you want water?" I ask Grace. She

nods. "And two bottles of water, please."

I take my wallet out of my back pocket to pay for our food when I feel Grace's surprisingly firm grip on my wrist. "Nope. Put that away." She glares at me with such fierceness I can only stare at her in awe. "You've done enough for me tonight."

"Grace, I really don't mind."

"Well, I do," she states firmly. "Put that back in your pocket or I'm throwing it across the parking lot."

I chuckle at the mental image of sweet little Grace with her short arm tossing my wallet like a football. "Fine. No need to go through with your threats."

She gives me a proud smile as she takes her own purse and pays for the burger, hot dogs and two drinks. Luckily—because I hate eating in the damn car—there's an available picnic table right next to the truck.

Only then do I allow myself to take in what she's wearing. Just for a second, my eyes scan that tight black dress. It's not particularly low-cut, but the slit happening along one of her legs is enough to send my mind into overdrive.

*No. Get a fucking grip.*

I avert my gaze because I know it makes her uncomfortable, yet my head still pictures her beautiful, soft features. Anyone who says Grace isn't stunning would be lying out of their asses. Blonde hair; observant, big eyes; and plump lips. However, it's the way she lights up a room by simply walking in that makes my heart do fucking cartwheels inside my chest at the thought of her.

And I can't stomach, not for a single second, the fact that she's been crying her eyes out in my car. I don't want to bring it up, but I'm also not going home without an explanation.

"Hey," I start in the gentlest tone I can manage to get her attention. "What happened at the party? Did someone upset you?"

To my surprise, she doesn't dismiss the conversation. "You could say that," she whispers, biting down on her lower lip.

"Want to talk about it?"

"Not really." She sighs. "But I guess you deserve to know."

"You don't have to tell me—"

"The guy I went to the party with only invited me to hook up with me," she blurts out. The captive beast within me starts to roar, fighting to be set free from its cage. "I mean, I suspected he was interested in me, but...I don't know. He got really drunk and forgot I was there at all. Then he tried to take me upstairs and... Yeah. Not my best night."

The beast tears up the bars of the cage one by one, melting them into a pool of wrath. "Did he try to force himself on you?"

I don't know who this fucker is, and I've never been a violent man, but snapping someone's neck sounds way too appealing right about now.

"No," she says quickly. "I promise he didn't. I stormed out the second he suggested going upstairs."

"Good." My anger is nowhere near disappearing, though. Knowing some stupid fucker is the reason she left a party to cry her eyes out in my car is enough to make me see red.

Her small hand reaches out to touch mine. My eyes lock on those delicate, gentle fingers on my tattooed skin and my breathing calms down. "Cal," she starts, then promptly stops. "Wait. Can I call you Cal?"

I snort. "Why couldn't you?"

It's so dark outside that I can't quite see if she's blushing, but my bet would be yes.

"I don't know. I thought maybe only your friends called you that," she says with a hint of shyness.

I close my much thicker fingers around hers and squeeze before letting go of her hand completely. "Grace, we *are* friends."

She blinks. "We are?"

"Of course we are. Call me whatever you want."

The moment that mischievous gleam shines in her eyes, I

know I'm in trouble. "Even Sammy?" she teases.

Rolling my eyes, I watch as that beautiful mouth curves into a wide grin. "Maddie thinks it sounds funny, so it stuck, but nobody else calls me that. Don't push your luck, *Gracie*."

"'Gracie and Sammy' has a nice ring to it, don't you think?" she muses out loud, pursing her lips in the most adorable way I've ever seen. "It sounds like the name of a low-budget rom-com that got canceled after one season."

"Why a rom-com, though? Why not a show about two badass detectives or something?"

She glares at me with a serious look on her face. "Really, Cal? You think 'badass detectives' is the first thing that comes to mind when you hear *Gracie and Sammy*? Sounds more like a cartoon show to me."

"Okay, so maybe you have a point." My lips twitch. This girl. "We'll settle for a trashy rom-com about two badass detectives, then."

The sound of her laughter gets interrupted by the loud beeping of her phone's ringtone. She takes one quick look at the screen, and her face pales. "Shit."

"Who is it?" If it's the fucker that upset her at the party, I swear to fucking—

"It's Aaron." She swallows. "I told him I was going out tonight, and I totally forgot to text him."

"Well, pick it up." A pissed-off Aaron is the last thing either of us needs right now.

She's quick to slide her finger on the screen to accept the call. "Hey, sorry I didn't text you. I'm all right." A pause. "No, I left. I'm fine. Cal's here."

At the sound of my name, my spine turns rigid. It's not that I expect Aaron to beat me up for hanging out with his cousin, but I've got a little girl I worry about too—I know how he's probably feeling right now. Like nobody is good enough to share her breathing space. I get it.

So when she puts her phone on speaker with panicked eyes, I make sure to stay calm. This is my friend, for fuck's sake. And it's not like my tongue was down Grace's throat just a second ago.

Not that the mental picture is doing anything to help me out right now.

"Hey, man," I say casually. "We're at Monique's Vegan Cookout. The food truck. Wanna come?"

"Nah. I'm beat," he answers, but there's a weird edge to his voice that I shouldn't ignore. But I do because I'm a damn coward. "Everything all right over there?"

It's Grace who answers a bit too briskly. "Yeah. I got tired and Cal was around, so he picked me up."

"And you ended up at a vegan food truck," Aaron says with a hint of suspicion.

Grace looks at me and grimaces. I shrug, not really knowing how to handle this side of him that is so new to me. An overprotective Aaron isn't the kind of guy I'd like to deal with.

"I was hungry," she opts for. "Do you want me to die of starvation, A?"

He snorts. "Fucking dramatic." I can practically see him shake his head in my mind. "'Kay. I'll leave you to it. Text me when you get home, all right?"

"Okay, Dad."

"So funny, G. You're gonna be at the shop tomorrow, Cal?"

I swallow past the lump in my throat. "Yeah."

"Good." And he doesn't add anything else, which for some reason makes my skin prickle.

Thankfully, the woman at the truck calls my name at that exact moment to go pick up the food, and I bolt out of that bench as if it were on fire. I don't hear what Grace tells her cousin and, by the time I'm back with our dinner, her phone is back inside her small bag.

"Wow. This looks amazing." She beams at her burger as if she's never seen one before tonight. I can't hide my own smile at her excitement. "Want a bite?"

"Nah, I've had them before, but you must try the hot dogs. Here."

I grab one between my fingers and hold it over to her side of the table. When she takes a bite, I have to peel my eyes off her mouth to avoid doing something stupid, like keep thinking about her mouth.

"Oh my god." She moans. That's it. I've lost my fucking mind. "It's *so good*."

"I know, right?" I give her a smile that I hope doesn't come out too weird. "They make the best vegan food in town."

"I believe you now." She nods eagerly, talking with her mouth full. She's such a sight, eating a juicy hot dog in a tight black party dress with her immaculate skin and her slightly untamed blonde hair. I wish I could capture this moment forever, but I don't think we've crossed the taking-pictures-of-each-other line yet.

I'm a patient man, though. And I have the feeling that everything related to Grace Allen will be worth the wait.

# chapter 11

## GRACE

"You got any new books this week, dear?"

"Let me check at the back, Sloane."

I don't remember seeing any books on the box Olivia dropped off earlier, but it doesn't hurt to double check. The shop is quiet this morning anyway, with only Sloane and her ten-year-old granddaughter Pauline looking around. I push away the beaded curtain that separates the shop from the small storage room at the back and kneel beside the open box.

Clothes, clothes, a lamp, a jewelry bag, and... Yes!

"I've got one about... Oh, vampires." I send Sloane an apologetic look. It's not that I believe old ladies can't read about hot vampires, I just don't think it would be her style. She always gets the classics or historical romances.

Sloane sweeps her long gray hair over a shoulder and tilts her head towards Pauline. "Do you think it would be a suitable read for this one?"

I open the book at a random page and when my eyes land on the word 'cock', I snap it shut immediately. "Nope."

The woman chuckles at the more-than-obvious blush on my cheeks. "Aw, too bad. We'll take a look at the jewelry then, Pauline."

With a sigh, I put the book back in the box and make a mental note to label it correctly when we put it on display next week. I'll have to text Olivia about it so she doesn't forget. Once

I'm back at the front, I sit on the wooden stool we keep behind the front desk and look at the people walking outside the thrift store.

When I moved to Warlington almost four years ago, the first thing I did was look for a ballet studio. The second was to look for volunteer work at The Teal Rose Women's Shelter. I couldn't fathom the idea of other women going through the same thing I did—or worse—without me being there to help in any way that I could.

So even though I couldn't volunteer to assist actual survivors—which I totally understand—my people skills landed me a position at the shelter's thrift store in Melrose Creek.

My Saturday mornings here consist of putting out new stuff, keeping the shop clean and tidy, and helping customers with whatever they need. They are regulars who always, always leave with something. All profits go to help the women and children at the shelter, and knowing that may be the reason why I'm actually considering buying that vampire smut novel. Why not? I've never read erotica, but surely it can't hurt to try.

So, before I change my mind, I hop off the stool and grab the book from the box at the back. I leave the three dollars at the register and text Em.

> You won't believe what I got from the thrift store

Her reply comes only minutes later.

> Is it sexy lingerie?

> No, but it kinda has to do with it I guess??

> Now I'm intrigued. Spill, woman!!!!

A smutty book...about hot
vampires...

I'M DYING!!!! Pls let me borrow it
when you're finished

Ok but don't drool over the pages

I make no promises

I snort, which gets me an understanding smile from Sloane across the shop. I smile back as my phone buzzes again.

No, but really I'm happy for you.
Reading smut may not sound like
a big deal but I'm sure it'll help
you!!

That's what I thought too. We'll
talk later <3

Love you hon x

With a new purpose pulsing under my skin, and because Sloane and Pauline are regulars and I trust them, I open the book on page one and start reading. Sadly, I don't even get to page two (no dicks so far) when the old woman appears in my line of vision.

"We'll take this brooch, dear." Sloane sets the metallic bird on the counter and reaches for her purse.

"Of course. Didn't see anything that you liked, Pauline?" I ask her timid granddaughter, who only shakes her head. No matter how many times we've seen each other, the poor girl still hides behind Sloane when I talk to her. I never take it personally.

"We'll come back next Saturday to see if you've got any new

books," Sloane assures me with a warm smile as I take her cash. "Have a good week, sweetie."

"You both too." I wave them goodbye and open the book right where I left off.

So, apparently, this is a high fantasy novel about a witch who gets kicked out of her coven and has to make her way across the kingdom to join other fallen witches and start a revolution. Only that she gets kidnapped on the way there—by a muscled, dark-haired, hot-as-sin vampire of all people. Naturally they despise each other at first, but if their ever-growing sexual tension is any indication, they'll probably end up having hate sex sooner than later.

I'm not sure how I feel about that yet. I mean, am I ready to read explicit erotic scenes? With very specific descriptions of the male anatomy and everything? I have a vivid imagination, so I know for sure that I'll be able to see the whole thing in my head as if it were a movie.

Oh, my.

I'm so immersed in the story that I jump, heart racing fast, when my phone buzzes on the counter almost half an hour later. It's a...text from Cal?

> **You might want to book that tattoo appointment soon before I get sent to jail for beating up your cousin six ways to Sunday.**

What the hell?

# CAL

"Let me check if I got this right."

Not to be dramatic, but I might die today.

And that's saying something—with my bulky build, my

ability to knock someone unconscious without breaking a sweat, and how little fucks I give in general, the last thing I expected today was to be intimidated by a guy I've known for three years and who I consider one of my closest friends.

Well, I'm only *mildly* intimidated, but still.

Aaron continues without missing a beat. "My cousin was at this frat party last night and when she wanted to go home, you were *coincidentally* driving around the area and picked her up?" He crosses his arms in front of his chest, as if protecting himself from the truth he doesn't want to hear. "I struggle to believe that, Cal."

I take a deep breath and stare down at my friend with the cold glare I've mastered over the years. I don't care how good his intentions are or how much he cares about Grace. Not right now. He should know by now the kind of man that I am, and I'm sure as fuck not going to let anyone come into my shop and scold me like a damn child.

But I'm also not going to air Grace's business. She didn't want to tell Aaron what happened with that guy at the party, and although I don't get why, I refuse to break her trust like this, or at all.

"Look, man, if you're worried about me making a move on her, trust me that I'm not interested," I tell him head-on, perhaps a bit more harshly than I intended. Whatever. I don't deserve this reprimand in the first place. "I only took her to that vegan truck because she was hungry. She was the one to suggest we hang out, so tone it down a little, all right?"

Aaron scowls at me like I don't understand a thing. "You know why I'm telling you this, Cal. It's not because I don't think you're a good man—I know you are. This is about Grace and what is best for her."

A fucking classic. "And what do you think is best for her?"

"That she only surrounds herself with people who have her

best interests at heart, for one."

Ah, no. He's not going there. Over my dead fucking body.

I narrow my darkened gaze at him. "And you think I'm not one of those people?"

He has the decency to flinch. Just barely. "I don't know, Cal. You're one of my best friends and I trust you like a brother, but not with her. I don't trust anyone with her. It's not personal."

That, I can somewhat understand amid my growing rage. His words force a question in my head—who would I trust to keep Maddie's heart safe? Probably nobody but me, so I get it.

I let out a heavy breath and thank the universe that I've got an appointment in five minutes, so this conversation won't last much longer. "Look, A, I like your cousin. She's fun to be around, and I think she enjoys my company too. I've already told you there's no sketchy business from my end, so why the hell are you so defensive about her having a male friend?"

He seems to ponder his answer for a moment, as if he was choosing his next words carefully. I'm not dumb. I know Grace—and him—is keeping something big from me. Not that she has any obligation to tell me, but I know the secret is there. I have the nagging feeling that it's something that would rip my fucking heart apart.

So, when Aaron keeps being his vague self, I'm almost relieved by it. "Listen, men are shit and Grace knows it first-hand. She doesn't need friends with ulterior motives. She doesn't need to think they care about her, when all they've wanted from the start was to get into her pants. I'd rather she didn't take the risk."

Something lethal snaps inside of me. "Get the fuck out of my shop."

Aaron blinks. "Cal, man—"

"*Get. Out*," I grit out. I don't even recognize my own voice right now.

Thinking better than to fight back, Aaron gives me what my

furious eyes recognize as an apologetic look and rushes out the front door after muttering a "sorry" I don't give fuck about.

Before my foggy brain registers what I'm doing, I pick up my phone and text Grace. I don't even remember what the fuck I texted her as soon as I lock the screen. All I hear is a ringing in my ears, and all I feel is a deadly pressure in my chest that doesn't let me breathe.

*She doesn't need friends with ulterior motives. She doesn't need to think they care about her, when all they've wanted from the start was to get into her pants.*

He thinks I'm that kind of friend? Does he seriously think so little of me?

For fuck's sake.

Out of everyone in our friend group, I'm the one who would rather stay home than wild out at some random party. I'm the one who doesn't do drugs or get drunk. I'm the one who doesn't do one-night stands. I'm the one who doesn't pick up chicks at bars because that's not me. It's never been, and up until five minutes ago I thought one of my closest fucking friends knew that as well.

Wishful-fucking-thinking.

Fortunately for my sanity, my next appointment arrives only minutes later, and I focus on the beautiful traces of black ink on my client's skin for the next hour. Once I'm done, I realize I forgot about my text to Grace until I see the notification on my screen.

> **Not that I don't share the sentiment (he can be a little shit), but did something happen?**

For a second, I debate whether to tell her about Aaron's accusations and overprotective streak against me. Maybe it's not such a good idea to stir up drama between them. Aaron might be my friend, but he's her *family*.

And then I remember how he pretty much accused me of having ulterior motives to befriend her, and I decide to hell with it.

> **Wanna grab lunch? I'd rather tell you in person.**

An hour later, we are sitting at one of the cafés a couple of blocks away from the shop, waiting for our orders as Grace gapes at me like a koi fish. It's kind of cute.

"He said *what*?"

I don't know what I was expecting when I told her about my quarrel with her cousin, but seeing how she sides with me is surprising. And since it validates the hell out of my feelings, why lie?

We thank the waiter when she brings out our sandwiches, and I turn to her. "I suspected he was pissed when we talked on the phone last night, but I didn't see any of that coming."

"It's madness," she agrees before biting on a French fry. "I'll talk to him, don't worry."

"I'm not worried," I lie like a bastard. "I just don't appreciate him thinking that I have a hidden agenda when it comes to you. I thought he knew me better than that."

She shakes her head and takes a sip of her cold water. Anger and disappointment flicker in her hazel eyes. "He's not thinking straight. His overprotectiveness has gone too far, and I'm done."

I sit up straighter. "Grace, I really don't want you guys to fight because of this. Let me sort it out with him."

"You sort out whatever you need to with my cousin, and I'll deal with my own stuff," she says in a determined voice I've come to notice she uses a lot lately. I like it. "It concerns me as well, you know? He's going all caveman on me when I never asked him to, and I don't like it one bit."

"I get it." With a sigh, I dive into my sandwich, and I can't even appreciate it properly because this situation is too damn shocking. "Why does he always go caveman on you, though?"

She shrugs, but I don't miss the momentarily flash of panic in her eyes. "You have a little sister. I guess it's kind of the same thing. You get it."

I shrug back. "I can understand where he's coming from. Doesn't mean I will put up with it."

"Valid." She eats another fry before her eyes widen so much they almost come out of their sockets. "Oh! Oh! Guess what I bought today?"

The excitement in her voice clears the fog in my head. A change of topics is exactly what I need right now, or I'll go insane ruminating. "Let me guess—another plain white t-shirt?"

Grace fake gasps and puts a hand over her, indeed, plain white t-shirt. In all the time I've known her, she only seems to wear neutral tones and pastel colors; not that they don't suit her—she always looks beautiful. "You're one to talk, Mister I-Only-Wear-Black."

Well. She got me there.

"Don't distract me," I say. She chuckles, those pale cheeks turning the slightest shade of pink, and I nudge her feet with my own beneath the table. "Come on. What is it?"

"It's...kind of embarrassing," she admits with a lowered gaze as she wipes her hands on a napkin and reaches inside her tote bag. Then, she pulls out a book.

I blink. "Why would a book be embarrassing?"

But when she passes me the novel, I open it at a random page and the words 'hardened nipples' blind me like a freaking flashlight, I think I might know why.

My lips twitch. "Are you reading porn?"

Redder than ever before, she snatches the book from my hands, and I laugh. "Stop laughing at me."

"I'm not." I smile. "I'm laughing at how red you are right now. It's cute."

*You're cute.*

"Shut up," she mutters under her breath, and I laugh harder.

"So, what is it about?" I ask her once I've regained my breath. "Or is this a case of porn without plot?"

Her eyes have suspicion written all over them. "I'm not going to ask why you know about porn without plot in the first place." When I laugh, she rolls her eyes at me. Deserved. "It's a fantasy book about vampires and witches."

"Uh, spicy."

"Stop teasing me."

"Stop being so teasable."

"Is that even a word?"

"Don't know. Open that book and let's see if we can find it between hardened nipples and tentative touches."

"Ugh!" She groans. "I hate you. I shouldn't have said anything."

"Hey." My voice turns serious as I steal a fry from her plate. "I'm just playing with you. I think it's awesome books like that exist. Everyone deserves to explore their fantasies."

At my firm words, she looks down onto her lap and nods. "I've never done this before, and I guess I'm kind of embarrassed about it. I know other people read these books, but it's still a bit taboo. To admit that you read them, I mean."

I shrug. "Who the fuck cares? Anyone who shames other people for enjoying sex in any way, shape or form is an ignorant douchebag. Don't ever listen to those people because they have nothing intelligent to say."

Grace's lips curve into a small, sincere smile that I wish I could capture forever. I wish I could capture so many things about her forever.

"Thank you for saying that. And you're right. I have to get

used to it, I guess. It's a new thing for me."

I point at her with my index finger and give her my no-bullshit look. "You know what? You got me curious. Why don't you share some quotes from that book with me, and I'll decide if I want to pick it up myself?"

She chuckles. "Are you sure?" She challenges me with her eyes. "It might get...intimate."

I challenge her right back. "I can do intimate."

With an amused shake of head and a bright smile that lives up to her nickname, she says, "There's no backing out now, Sammy."

And damn it if my name on her lips doesn't make my head spin.

"Looking forward to those updates, Gracie."

# chapter 12

## GRACE

*"Fuck,"* Hunter grunts, the engorged head of his cock slamming against the very back of her core, earning a surprised whimper from Cordelia. *"You're so hot riding me like that. So damn good."*

*Her walls pulsate around him, choking him, and Hunter moans. Such a guttural, dirty sound she's never heard from him before. And suddenly she has the urge to hear it again, and again, and again. Knowing that she is making him come undone like this is enough to tip her over the edge.*

*Cordelia braces herself on his strong shoulders as she bounces faster and harder up and down on his hard cock. Her thighs ache and burn, but so does her desire for him. She doesn't ever want to stop. Her fingers curl in his long hair, pulling at it with abandon, exactly how he likes it. Rough, hot, primal. Hunter roars as her walls tighten around him. Her breathing hitches, and they—*

"Attention, class."

Professor Danner's voice drags me back into the present moment and I slam my book shut, earning a concerned glance from Sadie, one of my friends sitting a few rows in front of me. I grimace back.

Okay, so reading smut in class is a terrible idea. Who would've thought, huh?

"I know it's still quite early in the year, but as this class technically ends in April, I want to give you enough time to prepare."

Oh, god. Nothing good ever comes out of a speech that starts this way. I can already see myself buried deep in work for the next few months and I don't even know what he's going to say.

"As a final project for my class this year, I want you to try something a bit more...venturous."

And then he turns the projector on. And big, bad, scary bold letters stare right back at me. Mocking me.

## 10 STEPS TO START WRITING YOUR BOOK

My breath hitches. Deep down, I knew this day would come. I knew I would have to face my fears sooner or later if I wanted to pursue a career in writing.

I just never expected to have such a close deadline for it. Or to have my whole grade depending on it.

*Shit.*

"As I'm sure you've guessed by now, I want you to write or co-write a novella. A short book," Professor Danner explains with an easy smile. I can't even hate him for this damn assignment because he's such an amazing teacher. "It can fall in any genre that you like, but it would have to follow said genre's guidelines. I'll be uploading a worksheet and some PDFs on the course's page once we're done with the class."

He keeps going for twenty minutes, explaining how we have the choice to collaborate with another classmate and write it together. It would pose new and interesting challenges, he assures us—challenges I'm not interested in finding out about, thank you very much.

By the time the bell rings, the only thing I know for certain is that the only partner I'll be co-writing within the next few months is my impostor syndrome.

I've known I wanted to become an author ever since I was ten years old. I even wrote my first full-length, extremely cringy novel at thirteen and then another one, less cringy but still bad, the year before coming to Warlington. I haven't written anything for fun ever since. And nobody, no one, has ever read my books. Ever.

I hate the idea. I know, I know. If I want to become a published author someday, I'll have to snap out of it, grow a pair and allow my writing to exist out there in the wild for everyone to see and judge.

Although, to be fair, I'm not as scared of the criticism as I am of vulnerability.

Writing is such an intimate act for me, almost like stripping down naked but in a different way. In a mental way. And it freaks me out as much as the physical version would.

I need to get over it. I know I will. Maybe this project is exactly the kind of boost I need. As a firm believer that opportunities arise for a reason, I take a deep breath and force myself to not think about it until I'm sitting in front of the computer later. There's no point in fueling my anxiety right now.

And luckily, as I exit the Humanities building and my phone rings, I get the perfect excuse for a distraction.

"Hey, Daddy," I greet him with a genuine smile. Talking to my dads always manages to lift my mood. I don't know how they do it, honestly. Must be magic.

"How's my rockstar doing today? We haven't talked in forever, honey." There's no accusation in his voice. There never is, and I can only feel ashamed that I've gone this long without talking to them. I text them almost daily, but I'm not so good with calls.

"I'm okay. Just finished my last class of the day. The professor was telling us about the final project, and I want to pee my pants a little," I confess, chewing on my lower lip.

Daddy laughs. "Oh, baby. What is it? I'm sure it can't be that bad."

In theory, it's not. But he doesn't know of my internal

struggles when it comes to writing. No one does. "We have to write a book. The deadline is in April, and I have no idea what I want to write about."

"Well, you read a lot so that might inspire you," he muses. I hear the muffled sound of voices behind him. He must be at the firm. "What have you been enjoying lately?"

My mind immediately flashes with the image of Cornelia riding Hunter into oblivion. "Not much," I lie like a bad daughter. "I've pretty much read every genre, but nothing appeals to me right now."

"Give it a few days. No rush. You always figure it out and it's genius."

The pride in his voice makes my heart swoon. "Thanks, Daddy. I promise I won't stress out too much about it. How's Dad?"

Growing up with two fathers, one could think it would be confusing for me to distinguish them by name as there's no Mum/Dad distinction. Wrong.

Daniel Allen, a pale blond like me, is Dad. Marcus Allen, with short hair darker than coal and a dark and beautiful skin tone, is Daddy.

My two-year-old self assigned the nicknames at random, so don't ask.

"He's busy with a client right now, but he said he'll call before dinner. Are you coming home for the holidays?"

I sigh. "If the snowstorms allow it."

I love going home to my family, but last year's canceled trip made me paranoid about traveling on Christmas. Aaron and I spent the holidays alone at his apartment, eating ready-made lasagna. It isn't a bad memory by any means, but it forces out a more recent one.

I'm still angry with him. I haven't texted him back since yesterday, nor am I in the mood to confront him about it yet.

Definitely not now with the pressure of this unwritten book crushing down on me.

"I'm sure you'll be fine, sweetheart," he assures me before a woman's voice comes closer to tell him something. I know what he's going to say before he even says it. "I'm sorry, Gracie, but I've gotta go now. We'll talk again when Dad calls you tonight, yeah? We'll video chat."

"Of course, Daddy. Don't worry."

Both of my dads are top-notch lawyers, and it's never bothered me that they're so busy and always have so many things to take care of at work. They always make time for me, always make me their priority. I've never once felt like a rejected daughter. Not ever. And, for that, I couldn't be more grateful.

"I love you, honey. Take care."

"You too. I love you."

"I love you," he tells me again before he hangs up.

Feeling somewhat more at ease now, I make my way to the dorms and take the rest of the morning off until it's time to teach my ballet class in the afternoon. However, my plans to unwind and think about nothing but the whiteness of my walls shatter into pieces when I accidentally knock a notebook down and a small scrap of paper falls to my feet.

It's the tattoo sketch Cal made for me.

Sighing, I pick it up and stare at it blankly as if it held all the answers I'm looking for. I haven't thought much about the tattoo in the past few days, but it's something I still want to do.

Tingles dance down my spine when I remember that day at the parlor, how patient Cal was with me and how invested he seemed in sketching the perfect tattoo for me. Although maybe he goes out of his way for all his clients. It would make sense. He seems like a selfless man.

I swallow down the unexpected tang of disappointment and put the piece of paper back inside the journal. I have a book to outline—I shouldn't be focusing on my non- feelings for Cal.

And yet it's the only thing I do for the rest of the day.

# CAL

My little sister is upset.

I know it the second I walk into my mother's house, and she doesn't come running down the hall to greet me with a big hug like she always does.

My mother has her ass glued to the couch as the TV fills the house with superfluous chatter. To my surprise, Maddie's father—Pete—is right beside her.

"Where's Maddie?" I ask the room. Neither of them turn to look at me, as if I hadn't just walked right into their unlocked home. It could've been anybody, for fuck's sake. A child lives here.

"Bedroom," my mom answers, as always. Not like I ever expect Pete to give a damn about his daughter, or even know where she is.

"Why didn't she come to say hello?" Suspicion and worry lace my voice.

She shrugs, still not turning her head to look at me. "She was in a mood when I picked her up from school."

*In a mood.*

Taking a deep breath through my nose, I force myself to remember that flipping out right now wouldn't solve anything, and it's the last thing my sister needs. But I can't shake the horrible notion that my little girl is alone in her room, upset with the world, and her own parents don't give a fuck.

I storm out of there before I look at fucking Pete again and lose my cool for real. He's more like a sperm donor than a real father.

My mother tries. She's not going to win any awards for parent of the year, but when her head is clear, I can tell she truly tries to be a good role model for Maddie. It's when she's too tired, or too drunk, or around the stupid bastard that she retreats into herself and doesn't seem to find the strength to attend to her own baby daughter.

I'm trying to be understanding. Fuck, I'm trying hard not to be a judgmental dick. I know my mother has an untreated issue with alcohol, but I can't force her into rehab or a therapist's office. That's not how it works. You can't help someone who refuses to get help, and it fucking hurts.

When I reach my sister's room, the door's ajar but I knock anyway. It's important to me that she knows she has privacy, even from a very young age.

"Yes?" Her small voice sounds so dull my stomach turns.

"It's Sammy. Can I come in?"

"Sammy!" A second later, she throws the door open and hugs my legs with such force I almost stumble backwards. "I missed you."

"I missed you too, baby." I peel her arms away from my dark jeans and haul her up. She buries her face in my neck right away. "How are you doing today?"

It's not a question I was ever asked as a kid, and only when I had a sister did I start to realize how important it is to communicate with children like you would with any friend or adult.

"Mm-hmm..." she mumbles against my skin. I carry her to the bed and sit down on the soft mattress.

"Did something happen today?" I ask her softly. She's still not looking at me, clinging to my neck like a little monkey, but I don't peel her away. Maybe it's easier for her to talk when she's not looking at me. What can I say—it runs in the family.

"No," she answers a bit too quickly.

"Mads... You know you can tell me anything, right?" I prompt, rubbing her back. "I'm your big brother and I love you more than anything in this world. I want you to be okay, but I can't help you if you keep secrets."

I feel her nod. "I love you too, Sammy." She stays quiet for a few moments, and finally, "Someone made fun of me today."

My chest tightens, but I don't show her how upset that made me. "What did they say to you, baby girl?"

Before I can even blink, she untangles herself from my arms and reaches inside the small pink backpack she carries to school. When she takes out a wrinkled piece of paper, I frown. "What's that?"

Without saying a word, she hands me the note. The logo of her preschool sits on the right corner of the paper and big bold letters stand out:

## DONUTS WITH DADDY

It's some kind of father-daughter event taking place in a couple of weeks in which dads eat donuts while they watch their kid play.

I don't even get a chance to read through the whole thing before Maddie starts, "I asked Daddy to come with me, but he said he didn't want to." Her eyes glisten with unshed tears and my ears start ringing with silent, cold rage. "Everyone told Miss Laura that their daddies are going, but not me. And a girl laughed at me and said my daddy doesn't love me."

I don't hesitate before I kneel in front of her, clutching her hands tightly between mine, the note long forgotten. "Princess, look at me." I search her eyes that look like my own until she does as I say. A single tear rolls down her red cheek, and I gently wipe it away with the pad of my thumb. "Mommy and Daddy love you very much, more than anything in the world, and so do I."

She sniffles. "But Daddy doesn't want to come with me. He says he doesn't like donuts."

*Stay fucking calm*, I remind myself. *Lie through your goddamn teeth if necessary.*

"Daddy is very busy these days, baby, but I promise he still loves you," I reassure her. Pete might be very busy all right, just not with finding a fucking job. "You know what? I love donuts, and I'd love to come to this thing with you. Would you like me to?"

Another sniffle. "But you're not my daddy."

I might as well fucking be, seeing how I'm the only responsible adult here that cares about her. But I don't say that out loud.

I shrug like it's not a big deal, when in fact I don't think my heart has ever been so broken. "I'm sure the teacher won't mind. I'll talk to her if you want me to."

When she nods and throws her arms around my neck again, I let out a relieved sigh. "Thanks, Sammy. I love you a lot."

A small, sad smile breaks out on my lips. "I love you a lot too, peanut." Then, with a new resolve, I stand and pull her up with me. "Come on, we can have a sleepover at my apartment. Would you like that?"

Her eyes light up like a Christmas tree, her recent meltdown long forgotten just like that. "Can we have nuggets for dinner? With ketchup?"

And because I might be a strong man, but I collapse the second my sister cries—and it doesn't help that she has me wrapped around her little finger—I nod and she starts yelling with excitement.

There's not a single thing I wouldn't do to see her happy like this every single day.

While I wait for her to grab her favorite plushie for the night and after I get her school bag for tomorrow, my phone buzzes with a text from Grace.

> **I've had the shittiest day ever. Pls tell me you're free for dinner? :(**

My heart beats like a hammer inside my chest and before I know what I'm doing, I call to my sister, "Princess, would you mind if Miss Grace hangs out with us tonight?"

"Yay! Miss Grace is so cool!"

I smile. Well, then.

> **If you're in the mood to eat frozen nuggets and watch princess movies with a 4-year-old, I'm your man.**

# chapter 13

## GRACE

Three and counting. That's how many times my ovaries have exploded in the past five minutes alone.

The first explosion happens right as Cal opens the door with his sister clinging to his long leg like a baby koala.

*Same, Maddie, same. Wait, what?*

"Miss Grace!" The little girl greets me with the biggest smile. "Sammy is making nuggets. How many do you want?"

Cal chuckles and pushes the door open for me. "She isn't even inside yet, princess. Calm down."

Princess.

He calls her *princess*. Oh, god.

I know for sure I'm not going to survive this night as my ovaries explode again.

"I think I'll have a bunch," I tell Maddie. "I'm quite hungry."

And then he hauls her up with *one* freaking arm—a very muscular, very tattooed arm—and sets her on his hip like she weighs nothing as he lets me in.

Ovaries: shattered again.

I don't know what I expected of Cal's place, but his apartment may have just become my newest favorite place on Earth. It smells clean, the appliances and couches look modern. It's spacious with big windows, and the decoration fits him so well. He's got three skateboards mounted in one of the living room walls, a gaming setup in one corner, a big shelf full of figurines, and some comic books.

For some reason, getting a glimpse of his personality through his home makes my insides all warm.

"Miss Grace." Maddie tugs on the pink TDP sweatshirt I threw on before I took an Uber to come here. "Do you like ketchup on your nuggets? 'Cause we've got ketchup, but we don't have mustard 'cause Sammy doesn't like it."

I smile down at her. "Ketchup would be great, Maddie. And you don't have to call me Miss Grace when we aren't in class. Grace or Gracie is more than okay."

She blushes. "Okay."

I follow her to the open-concept kitchen overlooking the living room and find Cal already heating up the air fryer. "So, you hate mustard, huh?" I tease him.

He makes a face. "It's disgusting. Sorry I have taste."

"I'm your friend after all, so you *do* have some taste. Just not when it comes to food, apparently."

He pinches my side, making me squeal. Maddie tugs on Cal's t-shirt like she did with me earlier. "Can I put the nuggets in the fryer? Pretty please?"

"All right, but do it gently."

He hauls her up and she starts picking up and tossing the frozen nuggets into the fryer with her small fingers. Watching them interact in such a domestic way feels overwhelmingly intimate. Cal's whole face relaxes when he looks at his sister, his voice softens, and his eyes hold a kind of love that I've only seen before when my dads and Aaron look at me.

I clear my throat and grab my phone, suddenly needing a distraction from the lump forming in my throat.

"All set," Cal announces as he places Maddie back on the ground. "Go change into your PJs, peanut. Dinner will be ready soon, yeah?"

"Yeah!" She holds her little hand out to high five him, and

then she turns around so she can do the same with me. I chuckle as our palms connect.

"She's such a bubbly kid," I say once Maddie leaves for what I assume is her bedroom. Wait. "Does she have a bedroom here?"

Cal busies himself with taking a few plates and glasses out, not meeting my eyes. "Yeah. She... She stays here sometimes."

There's an edge, *something*, to his voice as he says it, but I brush it off. It's probably nothing.

"She has school tomorrow though, right?"

He nods. "I'll drop her off. I brought her backpack with us."

When he doesn't add anything else, I can't help but think it's a bit odd, but I'm not one to push. We might be friends, but we aren't *that* close. The tightness in his voice he's trying so hard to mask tells me there's more to why his sister has a whole bedroom at his place. But I haven't exactly opened up to him about my personal issues, so I refuse to get upset about this. It wouldn't be fair.

As I sit on one of the kitchen stools after Cal leaves to change, my mind drifts off to the not-so-unlikely-anymore scenario in which I tell him what happened to me all those years ago. And it's a shocking realization, really, since some of my family members aren't even aware of what went down, and Em is my only friend who knows.

So why do I feel this nagging ache to open up to him?

And why am I not panicking over it?

My derailed train of thought is interrupted by Maddie entering the kitchen with a monkey plushie on her grip. Her yellow pajama bottoms and long-sleeved white shirt with a huge sunflower right in the middle are both oversized, and she looks like the most adorable doll.

The moment she spots me, her little face lights up, and she tries to climb up the stool next to mine.

"Here, let me help you." I lift her up so she's sitting safely.

She's so tiny she barely reaches the island. "Who's your little friend over here?"

She sets her monkey on the countertop. "This is Monkey."

I blink. "Your monkey is called Monkey?"

She nods eagerly. "Yep. She's a girl."

My lips twitch. "Is she your favorite toy?"

Before she can answer, Cal's voice echoes from somewhere behind us. "It tends to vary. Last week her favorite toy was that mermaid doll, Nessa."

Maddie never takes her eyes off me. "Yes, but I like Monkey the most now."

Cal comes up behind her and ruffles her hair, making her squeal. Soon the nuggets are done, and I help him set up the small table in the living room while Maddie washes her hands and puts Monkey on the couch, under a thick pink blanket.

"She's watching the movie with us later," she explains to me because duh, I'm new here so I wouldn't know.

It feels nice being part of their routine, even if it's only for tonight. I already knew Cal was a laid-back guy, but seeing him with Maddie solidifies my suspicions. He's soft spoken but firm when he talks to her, gives her a lot of hair ruffles and light kisses, and his eyes fill with undying love every time he looks at her. It's clear that she loves him, too.

And when she accidentally knocks her plastic cup full of water during dinner, Cal doesn't make a fuss and instead hands her some paper towels so she can clean up after herself. Maddie never once complains.

When we finish dinner, I offer to do the dishes while Cal puts on the movie. He refuses at first, *of course*, but eventually I push him out of the kitchen and win the fight. "What are we watching?" I ask as I plop down next to Maddie on the couch a few moments later. Cal is on her other side, tucking her in with her pink blanket. Monkey sits on her lap.

He gives me a side look full of agony. "A princess movie. Again."

I chuckle. "You watch those a lot?"

"Every time she sleeps over." He shakes his head as he says it, but even the darkness of the room can't hide the smile tugging at his lips. It's kind of cute.

Not that I think Cal is cute.

Wait, are friends allowed to think each other are cute?

I'd have to Google that later.

"Movie! Movie!" Maddie squeals as Cal presses play. She's sandwiched between us although the couch is quite big, but she seems so immersed in the opening scene that I don't think she's even noticed.

Not even a minute into the movie, my phone screen lights up with a text from Cal.

So...

I side-eye him and grin, my heart beating faster for some dumb reason.

So...

**Sorry for dragging you into movie night, you've probably seen this a million times.**

**What?! I wanted to come. And this is one of my favorite movies too**

**Don't tell Maddie or she'll pester you forever.**

I think I can deal with both of you

Oh so I pester you?

All the time

How?

Let's see. You pester me about the tattoo, for one

Shut up. You want to get that tattoo.

But you still pester me about it

He sends me a look over Maddie's head, and I stifle a laugh.

Did anyone ever tell you that you're a little shit?

Don't get all cocky on me now, Sammy. I still have your jacket, remember?

You can keep it.

I frown at him, and he only shrugs.

But it's yours

And now it's yours, congratulations.

**It's too big for me**

**That's what she said.**

I snort out loud. For some reason, his text catches me off-guard.

**Ok Michael Scott**

**Is that supposed to be an insult?**

**Never**

**I don't believe you, give me my jacket back.**

**No, now it's mine**

**Brat.**

I'm about to write a snarky reply when I feel a heavy weight on my left arm. Cal looks over and whispers, "She fell asleep."

Sure enough, Maddie is already snoring softly against me, Monkey gripped tight in her little hand. Cal stands up quietly and picks her up with such care I'm pretty sure my ovaries are going to explode again. I've lost count at this point.

"I'm putting her to bed," he whispers, and I nod.

I pause the movie and when he comes back only a few moments later, I feel out of place all of a sudden. Now that Maddie's gone to sleep and neither of us wanted to watch the movie anyway, doesn't it make sense that I go home? It's not too late, but—

"Wanna watch *The Office* for a bit?"

My stomach jumps. "In the mood for some *'that's what she*

*said'* jokes, huh?"

He smirks at me, and I melt like a foolish piece of chocolate on a hot summer day. "It's your fault if you think about it. You called me Michael Scott."

I roll my eyes playfully. "Mm-hmm, sure it is. Can we start on season four, though? It's my favorite."

"Your wish is my command."

As he looks for the show on the TV, I throw one of Cal's fluffy blankets over my legs and settle against the cushions, not bothering to move. He doesn't move either, so there's only a child-sized gap separating us when the first episode starts. I can feel his body heat through the fabric of my sweatshirt, through the blanket, through my skin, and for some reason it makes me shiver.

"Are you cold?" He notices right away. How the hell does he pick up on everything?

"Um, no. Just a random shiver." It sounds stupid when I say it out loud, but luckily his attention goes back to the screen. Mine doesn't.

It doesn't take a genius to see that Cal is more of an introvert, even if he doesn't go all hermit mode when he's with me. I know he likes his space and to be alone. So why did he offer me to stay? Does this mean he's comfortable around me?

*Of course it does. You're friends.*

Two episodes later, my overanalyzing brain still doesn't get it. Why would he want to spend time with me, of all people? I've seen him with friends, so I know he has them. As much as he likes his me-time, he's not an antisocial man. I'm pretty sure the only reason he isn't kicking me out right now is because he doesn't know how to do it without looking like a jerk. He doesn't want to be rude or make me feel bad. So he would rather sit through however many *The Office* episodes I want to watch until I take the hint and go home.

Okay, hint taken.

"I, um…" I start, my palms getting sweaty. I wipe them on the soft blanket. "It's getting late. I better get going."

He pauses the TV. "You sure? You can stay here for a bit longer if you want."

*Lies, lies, lies. He's being polite.*

I shake my head in a useless attempt to make the self-destructive thoughts go away. "No, I… I don't want to bother you."

His eyebrows shoot up in surprise. "You're not bothering me, Grace. I invited you here. I wasn't expecting you to leave as soon as you swallowed the last nugget."

I stand up despite his words, folding the blanket neatly and placing it where it previously was as I look away. "You're probably tired, and Maddie has school tomorrow, and—"

"Sunshine."

It's the nickname that makes our eyes meet again. "Come here."

Still unsure if he's just being polite, I do as he says and sit back down, closer to him this time. When I feel the weight of his muscled, tattooed arm around my shoulders, my breath hitches.

"Is this okay?"

Taken aback by the question, I nod. It's more than okay, I want to say, but I can't.

"I know what's going on in that chaotic head of yours right now, Grace, and I need you to understand that you're not bothering me in any way. Yeah?"

I glance down at my lap. "Yeah."

"And," he squeezes my arm with his ridiculously big hand, "you're my friend, and I want you to stay if that's what you want as well."

Okay, so maybe he's not lying. Maybe it was all in my head after all.

"All right," I say, releasing the breath I'd been holding for the past few minutes. "I'll stay a bit longer."

He grabs the remote and presses play again. "You have any classes tomorrow?"

"Not until noon."

"Good."

Steadying my breathing, I settle back into the comfort of the couch, and I notice that Cal's arm is still around my shoulder at the same time he does. He starts to remove it, but then my mouth opens, and I can't control the words that escape me.

"Leave it," I say. His arm freezes on the spot. "It's... You're comfy."

His chuckle relaxes me just barely, but he doesn't fight back and puts his arm right back where I want it to be. I wasn't kidding when I said he was comfortable. His body is so ridiculously large I could completely hide from view if he stood right in front of me. Despite his *very obvious* muscles, he's surprisingly squishy and his body warmth feels nice against my side.

At some point during our fifth episode, his fingers start moving up and down my arm, leaving a trace of goosebumps in their wake. My brain must check out for the day because I snuggle closer to him and place my head against his chest. His breathing is even, relaxed, and it coaxes me like a spell.

The last thing I feel before my eyes close are his lips grazing the top of my head.

# chapter 14

## GRACE

When I wake up, it's still dark outside and the first thing my mind registers is that my body is inside a huge, very warm cocoon. There's a heavy weight on my stomach, right against my skin, as if whatever it is had crawled beneath the fabric of my sweater and settled there. My eyes flutter open, and I take in the shadows in the living room. Cal's living room. Shit. I never went home last night, did I?

So that means that my warm cocoon...

My heart starts racing as if it were running a freaking marathon inside my chest. This wasn't supposed to happen. Friends don't fall asleep together, cuddling on the couch, and wake up with tangled bodies. We shouldn't be doing this.

*Shit, shit, shit.*

I attempt to sit up, but Cal's hand on my stomach pulls me back against his chest and a soft grunt escapes his throat. The sound is almost erotic, and it crawls beneath my skin.

*Well, fuck me.*

*But not literally.*

*God, no, I didn't mean it like that.*

*Shit.*

Desperate to get away so my heart can get a damn grip, I sit up abruptly which ends up waking him up. Before he can even open his eyes, though, I'm already on my feet.

"Grace?" The deep and raspy sound of his morning voice

makes my thighs clench, and I hate myself a little more. "What time is it?"

I quickly grab my phone from the coffee table. I must've left it there at some point last night after our texting session. "Six-thirty."

He rubs the sleep away from his eyes with those massive fingers and sits up on the couch. When he takes me in, he frowns. "You look like you've just seen a ghost."

I gulp. "We fell asleep."

His arched eyebrow is nothing short of sarcastic. "That's what happens at the end of a tiring day."

I scowl at him. "I know. That's not what I meant."

"So, what did you mean?" I have a feeling he already knows, but I also suspect he will force me to say it anyway.

When he stretches his arms above his head, those muscles flexing and contracting, I look away.

"I meant that we...you know."

"I really don't." I'm not looking at him, but it doesn't matter because I can practically hear the smirk in his voice.

"Don't make me say it."

"Why? Are you embarrassed?"

I glare at him. "Yes."

He lets out a low chuckle that makes my insides tingle.

"Aw, come on. Did you not sleep well?"

"I slept well, but that's not the point." I don't think I've had such a great night's sleep in a long time, but I don't tell him that.

"The point is that we fell asleep all cuddled up and warm, I get it." He winks at me as he stands up and I think I stop breathing for a few seconds.

When he stops right next to me, his arm brushing mine, his voice drops with concern. Or maybe it's my imagination. "I didn't make you uncomfortable, did I?"

I lift my chin to look him in the eye, so he can see the truth in every word. "No. You never make me uncomfortable, Cal."

He gives me a small nod, his darkened eyes never leaving mine. I suppress the urge to lick my lips, because I know that's where his eyes would settle, and I don't think I could take the sight of his stare on my mouth without doing something dumb.

*Something dumb, like what?*

"Don't overthink this," he tells me, voice still roughened from sleep. "We're still friends, right?"

"Of course." There are no doubts in my mind about that. And just to lighten the mood because I know he needs it, I add, "I didn't know you were such a big cuddly bear."

His features relax at my teasing tone. "I do love my hugs, not gonna lie."

I tuck away the information for later. "Hey, can I, um, use the bathroom?" I ask awkwardly. I don't think my bladder can take it anymore.

"Sure thing. Um, come with me."

I follow him into the sole room on the opposite side of the kitchen. "This is my bedroom. It has an attached bathroom. There's another one, but it's right next to Maddie's room and I don't want her to wake up yet," he tells me as he opens the door, and suddenly my cheeks heat up.

I'm in his space. *That's* his bed, with his white sheets and gray comforter. It's too dark to make out a lot of details, but I spot a couple of picture frames on his bedside table and some artwork on the walls. Too stunned to pay attention to anything else but the fact that I'm in *Cal's room*, I don't even hear him open another door until he flips the light switch.

"This is my bathroom. You can take a shower if you want, and... Wait." As he looks for something in one of the cabinets, I glance around the space like the nosey person I am. It's clean and tidy, with black and white modern touches. "Found it."

My eyebrows shoot up in surprise when I notice the brand-new yellow toothbrush, still in its package. "Thank you." I don't overthink why he might have one of these lying around because I really could use some dental hygiene right now.

"I'll leave you to it. What time did you have to be at your dorm, again?"

It takes my mind a moment to remember what day it actually is. "Not until noon."

"Good. I'll drop you off after leaving Maddie at school, 'kay?"

"You don't have to do that," I tell him quickly. He's already done too much for me. "I can take an Uber."

"No."

"No?"

"No."

My lips twitch. "Fine."

He only winks at me before closing the bathroom door behind him, leaving me all alone with a confused heart.

\* \* \*

When I come out of the bathroom a few minutes later, I find Cal already dressed in jeans and a clean t-shirt. I don't know when he applied that cologne, but jeez. He smells amazing, like wooden spice.

"And now I feel like a stray dog," I blurt out, because of course I do.

He raises an amused eyebrow. "You don't look half bad."

"And what happened to the other half?" When he only laughs, I mutter, "Asshole."

"I'm joking." He nudges my arm playfully. "I'm waking Maddie up in a bit. I must warn you that she tends to get a bit cranky in the mornings, though."

"That's fine. What do you usually have for breakfast?"

He crosses his arms, and I try *so hard* not to look at the way his biceps flex. I fail. "You don't have to make anything. I'll cook."

But I shake my head. "You cooked last night. Plus, it'll give me something to do while you're with Maddie. Come on, grumpy man, tell me what you want to eat."

His eyes darken with something similar to confusion for a moment. When he blinks, it's gone. "Buttered toast is fine."

I frown. "Absolutely not. That's boring, Cal. No wonder your sister wakes up in a bad mood."

He rolls his eyes playfully. "What do you suggest, then?"

"How about some pancakes?"

"Mm-hmm." When he reaches up to open the cabinet above the sink his t-shirt rides up his stomach, giving me a first-row view of his defined abs. I look away, cheeks warm. "We're out of pancake mix."

"Do you have flour?" He nods. "Sugar?" Another nod. "Milk and eggs?" When he nods again, I can't help but chuckle. "Then you don't need pancake mix, dumbass. I can make them from scratch."

"Okay, chef." He pulls my hair playfully. "I'll get the ingredients for you."

Once everything is neatly laid out on the counter, I grab a bowl and start on my pancakes—they're my specialty. He asks me if I've got everything I need, and only when I reassure him for the third time does he disappear into what I assume is Maddie's half of the apartment. It's kind of cute that she has her own space, bedroom *and* bathroom, in her brother's home. Despite their age difference, they couldn't be closer.

And because I'm not getting any less nosey, I purposely sharpen my ear when I hear a door opening. "Good morning, princess. It's time for school." A small, tired grunt answers him. I smile.

"Grace is making pancakes, but you have to be quick, or we'll eat them all."

"Grace is here?" Her voice sounds so quiet I can barely hear it.

"Yes, peanut. And she's making you the yummiest breakfast. Come on, let's get up."

I go back to mixing the ingredients in my bowl, pretending that I wasn't eavesdropping just a second ago. Soon Cal enters the kitchen with a very sleepy Maddie in his arms. She looks so ridiculously tiny against his wide chest and big arms that my ovaries do a flip. Again.

"Good morning, Maddie." I smile warmly at her. "I'm making pancakes, see?"

"With butter?" she asks with her cheek pressed against Cal's shoulder.

"Yes. They'll be ready very soon."

"Let's get dressed while Grace finishes breakfast." Cal sends me a soft smile as he disappears down the hall again, and my insides melt.

Forty minutes and a few pancakes later, we are ushering a still grumpy Maddie out of the door and into the backseat of Cal's car. In her own words:

"I don't wanna go to school. I wanna sleep."

I can't say I don't share the sentiment. This only confirms that I would be a terrible big sister, because unlike my lazy ass— who would be more than down to stay home and take a nap—Cal is having none of it.

"Tough luck, peanut." And there's that.

She's so quiet during the ride that I keep glancing back at her, fearing she'll fall asleep. Cal assures me she's just being dramatic, hoping her antics will work and he takes her back home.

"She does this every time." He smiles fondly at his sister through the rear mirror. "And then she forgets about me the second she sees her friends."

I chuckle. "I was the same. I liked the idea of staying at home, but then I had so much fun with my friends that I forgot all about my bed."

Maddie's preschool isn't far from his apartment, in one of the fanciest areas of Warlington. I wish her a good day when Cal opens the door for her, and I watch with a small smile as they leave hand-in-hand. I can't help but notice the drastic, almost hilarious contrast between his huge intimidating build and the rest of the parents', all clad in suits and office clothes. That could never be me at eight in the morning.

Once Maddie's given her brother a kiss on his cheek, I see firsthand how Cal's words become true. Another little girl runs up to her and tugs at her sleeve, urging her to go inside with her. Maddie waves at Cal one last time and disappears inside the brick building.

As he makes his way back to the car, I can't help but think he's truly a sight to behold. At what I would guess is around six foot three or four, he towers over most people in the street, the black ink in his arms shining under the early morning sun. If I didn't know him, I would pin him for a broody asshole. I know, I know. I'm a superficial ass, yes. It's just that I've never had a friend with so many tattoos, or a friend so huge, or so imposing, or so—

"Take a picture; it'll last longer," is the first thing he says when he slides into the driver's seat, and I kind of want to die because of it.

The only solution? A death stare. "In your dreams, Sammy."

The corner of his lips twitches in what I've learnt to recognize is the beginning of a teasing smirk. "You take a lot of pictures of me in my dreams, Gracie?"

My cheeks heat up at the question, so I force my eyes down to my phone screen with zero notifications on it. "I'm not going to answer that."

"Aw, come on." He nudges my shoulder playfully. "Hey. Now that I think about it, you never updated me on your vampire book."

I give him the side-eye. "I thought you were joking about that."

"I'm absolutely not joking."

"Uh."

"So, how's it going? Have they sixty-nined yet?"

I groan, and he laughs. "No, they haven't." God, we really are having this conversation. "I haven't had much time to read, so for now they've only hooked up a little."

"What does it mean to hook up *a little*?" he asks with a smile he can't hide anymore.

"Um." How do I tell him that I have no idea? "I... You tell me."

Something similar to a choking sound comes out of his throat. "Why would I tell you?"

I shrug, wondering if it will shock him too much if I open the door right now and jump. "I figured you have, I don't know, more experience? Do you have a girlfriend? Boyfriend?" I blurt out, because self-control is something I haven't quite mastered yet when I'm around this man.

He doesn't look too fazed by my question. "No boyfriends for me; I'm into women, but I don't have a girlfriend currently. My last relationship ended around the time Maddie was born."

I want to ask him if he's had more girlfriends and why the relationship ended, but I bite my tongue. "See, that counts as experience."

He hums and stays quiet for a couple more minutes.

Then, "I'm guessing you don't have a boyfriend?"

I shake my head until I realize he's paying attention to the road and can't see me. "No."

"Girlfriend, then?"

"Nope."

"Have you ever been in a relationship, then?"

I don't feel ashamed when I say, "No. I mean, I've kissed a

couple of boys, but I've never dated any of them."

"Interesting," he muses. "Why not? If you don't mind me asking."

My head starts spiraling before I can get a hold of it. *Why not?* The question echoes inside my brain as I fight to stay afloat in this imaginary ocean of anxiety and unwanted memories.

Because I was a shy kid.

Because I feared being hurt, only to end up shattered anyway.

Because after the worst day of my life, a piece of me broke and sometimes I don't think it will ever heal.

Because although I keep telling myself that I'm moving on, that one day I'll crave intimacy like I deeply want to, that impossible future feels like a dark tunnel with no light at the end.

"Hey."

The feel of fingers on my chin, lifting my head, brings me back to reality. When my eyes collide with Cal's, I notice they're full of worry.

"Where did you go?" His voice is soft, his fingers gentle on my skin. The monsters retreat.

"S-Sorry, I zoned out." Lame excuse, I know. And I also know he's not buying it.

"Are you okay? What happened?"

"I don't want to talk about it," I confess, voice hoarser than I would've liked. I force myself to break the spell between our eyes and I notice he's already parked in front of my dorms. "Thanks for the ride."

My hand is on the door handle when his deep voice stops me. "Sunshine."

I look back at him, and the moment I see his hands twitching in his lap I know he wanted to stop me by grabbing my arm, but he didn't. "Yes?"

He swallows, and I don't think I've ever seen him look so stoic. "I want you to know that you can tell me anything if you ever feel ready to, all right? I'm your friend, I care about you, and I'm here to support you."

A lump forms in my throat, and I'm moments away from ugly crying. His honesty, the safety of him hits me right in the middle of the chest and knocks all the air out of me. "I know," I half-whisper. "I-I'll think about it."

"Okay." His voice softens along with his eyes. "Don't forget to text me your reading updates, though. Now I'm invested."

I can't help but chuckle. And just like that, the heaviness in the air goes away. "I don't know if I should be amused or scared."

"Both," he says. When I laugh again, he winks at me. "Have a good day today, Grace."

"You, too. I'll text you later."

"I fed you nuggets last night, so you'd better."

With one last laugh, I exit the car and wave him goodbye. When I reach the front door of my dorm and look behind me, his car is still there.

# chapter 15

## CAL

"Yo, dude."

Grace stayed the night at my place. Grace fell asleep in my arms.

She made breakfast in *my* kitchen with *my* ingredients.

My sister absolutely adores her, in and out the ballet studio.

Fuck this, fuck life, and fuck *me*.

"Earth to Cal."

She told me she's never dated anyone, that she's never done anything with any guy or girl besides kissing. And why the hell am I focusing on this right now?

Something about that conversation made her upset, and although I *know* there's something serious underneath that thick layer of reticence, I would never push her to talk about it. But in return, being in the dark is killing me.

"Yo!"

I feel it before I hear it. Trey comes up behind me and smacks me between my shoulder blades. Hard. "What the fuck, man?"

"Exactly." He grins at me. "You zoned out. Been calling your name for a good two minutes."

I roll my eyes at my best friend and co-worker. "Wow. Two minutes, you must be exhausted from all the waiting. Go take a seat."

"Fuck you." He laughs. "For real, though. What's up with you today? You've been out of it since this morning."

We might be close, but I'm not about to tell him my mind's been on Grace since the moment I left the parking lot of her dorm. Knowing Trey, he'll make a mountain out of a molehill and start planning our wedding or some shit. He's been pestering me about getting with someone since I broke things off with my ex, and the man is annoyingly persistent.

But because he's also annoyingly smart and he's known me my whole life, lying to him and hoping he won't notice is a luxury I don't have. So, I tell him a different truth that's also been on my mind all day.

"Maddie had to spend the night again."

He curses under his breath, knowing exactly what it means. "Shit, man. You talked to your mom?"

I nod. "She picked her up from school today. I called her to confirm." I even made her put Maddie on the phone so I could be sure. That's how fucked up this whole situation has become.

Trey shakes his head in disbelief and plops down on the leather couch by the front desk. His last client left five minutes ago, and we're about to call it a day. "I'm sorry, dude. It sucks ass, but at least Maddie's happy with you, no?"

I shrug. "I guess."

I know for a fact that my sister loves me and is happy to stay with me, but she's a goddamn child—she needs a stable home and a healthy family life, and she sure as hell has neither right now.

I try my best for her, I really do, but it's not enough. And I'm terrified that she'll grow up into a resentful woman one day—maybe even with severe addiction problems like our mother—as a result of a childhood full of parental neglect.

A wave of nausea threatens to climb up my throat and I have to push the thought away.

"Ever considered therapy for her?" Trey asks, and not for the first time. He started seeing a therapist himself a few years ago, and he insists it was the best decision he's ever made. Maybe I should consider it for myself, although god knows I'm messed up beyond repair.

I shrug again, as if having this conversation wasn't killing me inside. "I don't want her to think there's something wrong with her. You know how kids are. Therapy may be a good thing, but a lot of parents still think you only need it when you're borderline crazy, and they pass those beliefs onto their children. I don't want her getting picked on at school. We don't need to add bullying to the mix."

"I get it, man, but if it's the best thing for her then fuck everyone else."

He might be right. I can't think about this right now, though, or I swear I'll throw up. I'm so damn tired of this mess.

Trey gets up and claps me on the back. "I'm beat. You good to close up?"

"Sure. Have a good night."

"I'll see you tomorrow." Before he disappears out the front door he gives me an overly enthusiastic thumbs-up. "You got this, Best Brother of the Decade."

"Fuck off," I tell him, but I'm smiling. This dude, I swear. It doesn't take me longer than ten minutes to make sure everything is tidy and clean, every light is switched off, and the alarm system is armed. On my way to the car, my phone buzzes in the back pocket of my jeans. Thinking it must be Grace, I pick it up without a second thought.

The last time we texted she told me she was stressed out about some project for class, and that she couldn't wait for her ballet lessons in the afternoon. It clears her mind in the way the gym clears mine.

But it's not Grace texting me. Close enough, though. It's Aaron.

**Hey, man. Meet me at The Spoon**

**when the shop closes? I want to
talk to you**

I haven't heard from him in a few days, which isn't unusual
for us. He's a good friend, sure, but our schedules rarely align,
and we don't frequent the same places. While he goes out to bars
and parties, I prefer quieter outings.

I'm assuming he talked to Grace, and she scolded him good,
so he wants to make amends with me now. Smiling at the mental
picture of little, tiny Grace putting her older, much bigger cousin
in his place, I text him back.

**Sure. I'm on my way.**

* * *

The Spoon is one of Warlington's hottest restaurants among
locals and students alike. With its sleek touches and the friendly
ambiance created by the cheery staff, along with the quality food,
it's easy to see why.

Since Aaron opened it nearly three years ago, I don't think
I've seen or heard of a night when it wasn't full to the brim.
Tonight is no exception.

I tower over most patrons as I walk in. People eat and laugh
around crowded tables, and some others are standing on the bar
and other high tables. Because of my build or tattoos, though—
maybe both—the crowd parts for me and I spot Aaron behind the
bar in seconds, talking to one of the waitresses.

The second his eyes lock with mine, he tells her something
that makes her leave, and he sends a tight smile my way.

"Cal, hey. Thanks for coming."

"No problem."

"Let's go somewhere quieter."

I follow him towards the back, where he keeps a small office. He's not at the restaurant every day since he only manages the business aspect of it, but he once told me that he hates working from home, hence the office.

It only consists of a big desk, two chairs and a couple of filing cabinets. He takes one of the chairs and I sit on the other one.

He leans back, so obviously uncomfortable it's almost awkward, and starts, "So, um, I asked you to come because I want to apologize." I'll give him credit, at least he doesn't break eye contact.

"Apology accepted." I'm not one to hold grudges, anyway. They're a waste of time and energy, and I've got more important things to worry about. Unfortunately.

He blinks. "Just like that? I had a whole speech prepared and everything."

I smirk, and he visibly relaxes. Leaning into the backrest, I gesture for him to continue. "By all means, enlighten me. I wouldn't want a perfectly good speech to go to waste."

He smirks back, but a second later his features sober up. "Listen, what I said was out of line and I hate that I hurt you. We're friends, dude, and friends don't pull that shit on each other."

I don't say I agree; I only nod.

"It's been hard for me." He shakes his head, and I see the heavy storm raging behind his eyes before he blinks it away. "I sound like a fucking asshole, don't I? Grace's got it much worse and here I am, whining about my protective tendencies."

I must be staring blankly at him, or maybe with a shocked expression on my face, because he frowns. "She didn't tell you?"

"Tell me what?" My heart starts hammering inside my chest. I have a feeling I know what he's referring to, but I promised I wouldn't push her or him and I intend to keep my word.

I'm not surprised by his loyalty. "Forget I said anything." He clears his throat. "I don't want you to think it's an excuse, but the only reason I said that shit to you is because I love her, and I feel this primal need to watch out for her. I promise it wasn't personal, but I'm ashamed nonetheless for what I said to you."

*She doesn't need friends with ulterior motives. She doesn't need to think they care about her, when all they've wanted from the start was to get into her pants.*

His words still sting, all right, but I'm one hell of an understanding bastard. I might not know what happened to Grace, but I bet my life it's the kind of evil that would make me want to rip a fuckhead or two apart once I find out.

Who knows how I would act if this was Maddie we were talking about. Perhaps worse than Aaron did, so I get it.

"All's good, man. No bad blood between us," I assure him. "What you said pissed me off, but it's water under the bridge."

"Thank you." There's a hint of relief in his voice. "And by the way, not that I'd have a say in this, but I'm fine with you and Grace being friends and all. You're a good man, and she's the greatest fucking thing that's ever happened to me."

I swallow, unsure how to respond. Aaron loves his cousin, that much is clear, and it sounds a lot like what I feel for my sister. There are many things about their relationship I don't know about, I realize then. Two people don't become so close just because, even if they're family. Something bonds them along the way, good or bad.

And I suspect this is the bad kind.

Before I get the chance to say anything, though, he keeps going, "I still don't know what the hell I could tell her to make her forgive me, because I know she's pissed. She hasn't replied to my texts in days, man. I've been worried sick."

"She's fine." I almost reveal that she spent the night at my place and I dropped her off at her dorm earlier, and that we've been texting back and forth all day, but it's probably the worst thing I could add to this conversation right now. Just because he approves of our friendship doesn't mean he'll be okay with anything else.

Not that there's anything else between us.

Only a friendship.

"I still gotta talk to her." He leans back and sighs. "I know she doesn't like it when I get overly protective, but I can't help it."

"Listen to her. Make an effort. Compromise. She won't stay mad at you forever, don't worry."

"Yeah..."

"I'm serious."

"I know, I know." Another sigh. "Okay, enough about my cousin. We're good, right?"

I give him a firm nod. "We're good, Big A."

The nickname does it. He leans forward and pats my arm in a brotherly way. "Thanks, dude. Appreciate it. Come on, you can grab a burger and some fries to take home."

"No, it's okay—"

He winks. "It's on the house."

Oh. Well, then. I'm not dumb enough to say no to free food.

# chapter 16

## GRACE

It's been almost a week since Professor Danner dropped the bomb on us, and I still don't have a clue what I could possibly write about. What genre, what plot, which characters... Nothing.

Mind: blank.

Anxiety levels: spiraling out of control.

That's how I know I need a ballet class more than my next breath.

Adelaide isn't teaching my group when I get to The Dance Palace, but she lets me tag along anyway. She knows my head is troubled for real when I drop in here unannounced, agreeing to dance in whichever class she's choreographing at the moment. This one is less advanced than my usual group, and they're rehearsing for the Christmas recital, but I follow the flow of the lesson as if it were my own.

Forty minutes later, the class ends and my boss, teacher, and friend comes up to me with her signature bright smile. "What a lovely surprise, Grace."

I don't even pretend to have it together. I shake my head and let out a dramatic sigh. "I have a lot on my mind today."

She gives me a motherly frown and puts a comforting hand on my arm. "Do you want to talk about it?"

Do I? The project isn't the only thing I'm worried about, and that's the worst thing about all of this. Because it's not just *one* thing.

To start off, I still haven't talked to Aaron. He sent me a text yesterday asking me if I was alive, and because I love him too much and don't want to be a jerk, I replied a concise "yes" and left it at that. I'm aware that we need to have an honest conversation. But I don't feel ready enough to confront everything that lies dormant in my heart.

And then there's Cal. Stupid, caring, cuddly Cal.

Ever since he assured me I could confide in him whenever I was ready, the dangerous idea of taking the lid off my past and setting it free advanced to the forefront of my mind.

The sole reason I'm not more open about my assault is because I refuse to be pitied and treated differently for it. What I went through shouldn't have happened in the first place, and it changed the way my mind and heart worked, but I'm not going to be defined by it.

I refuse to. I'm more than a victim. I'm a survivor.

I'm a whole woman. I'm not broken even if smaller parts of me might be.

I'm a fighter, and I *will* rebuild myself no matter how long it takes or how uncomfortable it makes me feel.

When a vase shatters and you try to put the broken pieces back together, they never fit again. Not perfectly. Not in the way they used to. There may be cracks in the new vase, but it's thanks to those fissures that sunlight filters through. Life thrives under its glow, grows through the cracks, and blooms anew.

I guess that makes me a broken vase, but I couldn't be prouder of it.

"Just stressed about school." I shrug. And for good measure, I add, "I also got into an argument with my cousin Aaron and I need to talk to him, but I keep putting it off."

She gives me a sympathetic smile. "I know how close you two are, dear, and I'm sure whatever it is that happened you'll figure it out because that's what people who love each other do."

"Thank you." I mimic her warm smile. Adelaide radiates so much calm and confidence I can't help but agree with everything she says.

"As for school, what is it that you're stressed about?"

Another dramatic sigh escapes my lips. "I have to write a book for class, and I have no idea what I want to do. Literally nothing. Not even the genre."

"When's the deadline?"

I tell her.

"Oh, you've got plenty of time! Don't worry one bit, Grace. Inspiration always comes when you least expect it."

Waiting for inspiration has always worked for me, but each time I'm afraid my philosophy of just sitting and thinking about the story until creativity strikes will fail me. It might take me a bit longer to figure things out, but once inspiration comes knocking at my door, I'm unstoppable. I can't force myself to do anything, ever—not choreographies, not going out, and certainly not writing, if I'm not in the right mood for it. It has to *feel right*. It's a damn curse.

"Crossing my fingers." I give her a small, almost weak smile, as I indeed cross my fingers.

She shakes her head, amused. "You're such a gem, Grace. You'll be fine. How's the rehearsal going with the little ones, by the way?"

We keep chatting for a bit until her next class starts ten minutes later, and by the time I'm out on the street again, the fog in my brain has cleared. Not completely, but enough to text Aaron.

\* \* \*

My cousin lives in a one-bedroom apartment a couple of blocks away from The Spoon. Since he's always roomed with his friends, I asked him shortly after he moved in if he missed coming home to a house full of people. He snorted and told me he would rather eat dog shit.

Apparently, he's too old and sophisticated now for the Warlington-student lifestyle even though he still attends every official and unofficial party in town. Figure that one out.

I ring his doorbell a little over an hour after leaving TDP, and it doesn't take him long to answer the door.

"Hey, G. Come in."

When he greets me at the door with that wide smile of his, no one would guess we aren't exactly on speaking terms right now.

Gah. I love him too much to stay mad at him for long. Still, there are a couple of things I need to make very clear, and I won't leave without his understanding and a promise to do better.

"Can I get you anything?" he asks me as I sit down on one of the tall kitchen stools. "I've got some of that iced tea you like so much."

I can't help the smile. "Sure, I'll have one."

He passes me a bottle and opens a can of strawberry flavored soda for himself. "I know why you're here," he starts after taking a sip and making a face. As much as he loves strawberry-flavored anything, he can't stand sparkly drinks. "And I just wanted to tell you that I'm sorry. So fucking sorry, Grace. I shouldn't have acted like an ass, and I'm ashamed of the things I said to Cal. I already apologized to him and all's good, but I can't stand the thought of you being angry at me. I can't."

I already knew he'd talked to Cal and even bought him dinner, or so he'd texted me a couple of days ago. But despite everything, Cal isn't the reason I'm here.

"Okay, let's start from the beginning." I take a moment to collect my thoughts, making sure I remember everything I wanted to tell him. His eyes never leave mine. "You're the closest thing I have to a brother, Aaron, and I love you as one. I know you didn't mean any harm and for that I forgive you."

His chest shakes with a deep, relieved sigh. I raise a hand. "But."

"There's always a but." He smiles weakly and takes another sip of his evil drink.

"I know you love me and always try to do what's best for me, but this whole..." I gesture towards him. "This whole overprotective act needs to stop. Now."

"Grace—"

I hold up that same hand again. "No, I'm not done." When he purses his lips, I continue. "I really appreciate you looking out for me, but that's all. This time you've crossed a line coming for one of my friends, Aaron, and I don't want you to do it ever again.

"Trust me that I know better than anyone that what happened to me was awful, and it changed us. Both of us. I know that, but I refuse to be coddled. I refuse to be treated like I'm made of glass, and anyone could break me any second. I'm tough, Aaron, believe it or not, and I'm not naïve. I can tell when someone wants to be my friend and when they only want to get into my pants. Cal is the former."

His lips are pressed on a thin, hard line and it's painfully obvious that he's having a hard time processing everything I've just said. But I'm on a roll and I can't stop now, or I'll never get this weight off my chest.

"I know my fathers trust you to keep me safe, but I can do that on my own. I'll always appreciate that you have my back like I've got yours, but that's it." I choose my next words carefully. In the end, it all comes down to this. "It's...insulting that you think I'm not strong enough to take care of myself. That because of what happened to me, I'm this broken person with equally broken judgment. It makes me feel like a child."

The horror on his face almost makes me wince. "Grace, no, I... Fuck." He pinches the bridge of his nose and takes a deep breath. "I didn't know you felt like that. *Fuck.* I'm such a fucking asshole."

"No, hey." I get up, round the counter, and grip both of his arms firmly. "You're not an asshole, okay? You're just an overprotective, caring cousin who made a mistake. But I need you to do better from now on. Can you do that?"

Slowly, he nods. "It will take time. I'm used to...to this behavior, I guess."

"I know." I give his arms a squeeze. "All I wanted was to hear you say you'll try."

"Of course I'll try, Grace. Whatever you need of me, I'm here. I'll always be here." There's a new resolve in his voice, and when he pulls me into a hug, his grip feels stronger than ever before. "I'm sorry I made you feel like a child, and I'm sorry I snapped at Cal too. It was a dick move."

I would agree, but I don't want to rub salt in his wound, so I stay quiet and squeeze him tighter. "I love you," I murmur against his chest.

"I love you too, G." He kisses the top of my head. "I'm sorry again."

"Stop apologizing."

"But—"

"I'll literally kick your ass, A."

His deep laughter shakes me right before he pulls away. "Damn, you've gotten aggressive."

I narrow my eyes at him. "Always have been."

"Not sure about that." He takes another sip of his soda and somehow, I know what he's going to say before the words come out of this mouth. "So... You're friends with Cal, huh?"

My narrowed eyes stay narrowed. "What about it?"

He shrugs like he's not all that interested in my answer. I know damn well he is. "Just surprising. I don't remember your last guy friend."

Smooth. That's because I've never had any. Sure, I was friendly with a couple of guys in high school, but we never made plans together outside of class. My friend groups growing up consisted exclusively of girls and still do.

Except now there's Cal.

"He's cool to hang out with. Laid-back. Funny." I stop myself right there because despite his promise to not be an overprotective mother hen, I suspect Aaron is going to read too much into my words anyway.

Sure enough, he looks at me like he already did. "He doesn't know about the assault."

"I haven't told him yet."

He raises an eyebrow. "Yet?"

"I've been toying with the idea of talking to him about it for a while now," I admit with a shrug. "It's always the same thing, though. I don't want the pity stares or my friends to treat me differently, so I don't know what I'm going to do."

He sighs. "I kinda hate to say this because I'm still adjusting to the whole 'not being a protective shit' shebang, but I know Cal and yes, he's going to get mad and he'll want to murder that fucker with his bare hands, but he won't treat you differently. Tell him what you told me, and you'll be fine."

"I'll sleep on it." I nod, unable to think about this any longer. I've had the longest day, and I can't deal with another heavy thought right now.

Fortunately, Aaron always comes to the rescue. "A couple of friends asked me to come to the bar for a bit. Wanna tag along?"

I think about it. On the one hand I know I need a distraction as Emily is busy tonight, but on the other hand, I don't think I'll be comfortable around his friends.

So maybe because I'm a little shit, I ask, "Can I ask Cal if he wants to come?"

Aaron glares at me. I flash him the most innocent of my

smiles.

"Fine." He rolls his eyes. "But don't get too cozy while I'm nearby."

"*Aaron.*"

"I'm joking. Just joking."

"You totally are not."

He gives me a guilty look, and I shake my head.

"Love you, G." I smack his arm as I reach for my untouched iced tea.

"You're lucky I love you too, dumbass."

# chapter 17

## GRACE

"Please tell me you're not reading vampire porn at the bar."

Gasping, I look up from the book hidden on my lap under the table in time to see Cal sliding into our empty booth.

Aaron is somewhere with his friends, talking to a couple of guys they stumbled upon. I wasn't in the mood to meet new people, so I offered to guard our booth. Like a coward and all that.

My hand flies to my chest, making sure my breathing still works. "Holy hell, Cal."

The little shit laughs and leans in until our arms are touching, not-so-subtly glancing down at the book I'm so desperately trying to hide. Thanks to my texts, he already knows Hunter and Cordelia have...done some stuff. Knowing him, though, he'd want to read the whole thing with his own eyes and then I'll die.

"Why are you reading at the bar?" he asks.

"What about it?"

"The lighting sucks. You're gonna hurt your eyesight."

I arch an eyebrow. "Really? *That's* the reason I shouldn't read at a bar?"

He shrugs. "You do you. How many times have those two fucked?"

*Oh my god.* The word "fuck" shouldn't leave Cal's lips like, ever. No, no, no.

Heat climbs up my cheeks. "Don't say that."

"Say what?"

"Fuck."

"Why not?"

*Yes, Grace, why the hell not? It's not like you haven't heard him curse before.* Or have I?

I shake my head. "Forget it." As I put the book away, his quick hand snatches it from my grip. "Hey! Don't you dare—"

He dares.

Cal opens it on the page I was on and starts reading. Out loud. *"The sight of Cordelia's plump lips wrapped around the thick head of his cock sent a bolt of electricity through him. Gripping the back of her hair—"*

"No. Nope. We're not doing this." I snatch the book back and the traitor breaks out in such a deep laughter I'm scared he'll run out of air. "Dumbass."

He continues laughing as he wraps an arm around my shoulders, pulling me into his side. "Damn, Grace, you really were reading erotica *right here* with a straight face. Wow."

I roll my eyes and ignore the way my belly heats up by being so close to his warm, safe body. "Judge me all you want. I was getting bored, so I did what I had to do."

He chuckles again. "Not judging. You've got balls for that, and I fucking love it."

"Mm-hmm."

*Don't freak out. Don't freak out. Don't freak out.*

Too late, I'm freaking out.

Because he loves...what? That I'm antisocial enough to read smut in the middle of a crowded bar instead of hanging out with my cousin and his friends? I'm getting lightheaded.

"Where's Aaron?" he asks, and I'm grateful for the change of topics.

I point to a couple of tables away. "Over there with some guys."

He frowns. "How come you're sitting here all alone, then?"

"I'd rather be here." It's the truth. I dislike big crowds in general, and although it's not too bad anymore, the idea of being introduced to three more men tonight holds zero appeal to me. I've had enough with my cousin's two friends, who definitely checked me out for longer than necessary when Aaron wasn't looking. And I'm not even wearing anything exciting, jeez. My black jeans, go-to white sneakers, and pink jumper are nothing worth breaking necks for.

Luckily, Cal doesn't ask any more questions. "I'm going to get a drink. Want anything?"

I shake my head, and he leaves. I've still got some iced tea left in front of me, although it's probably warm now.

When he comes back after exchanging a couple of words with Aaron and ordering a soft drink, he slides into the booth next to me again. I can't help but frown at his drink of choice, recalling how he'd been having the same thing back when I pretended to get his number to amuse my friends. "You don't drink alcohol?"

He shakes his head, a brief shadow of somberness passing his eyes. "No. Never have."

"Are you serious?" I wasn't expecting that. Even I have had alcohol before, and I'm not a huge fan.

"You sound outraged." He smirks.

I blink. "No, no. Not that. I... I don't know, I wasn't expecting it. Almost every guy your age drinks. Or has tried an alcoholic drink at some point."

He attempts a casual shrug, but his shoulders are tense.

"Never seen the appeal in hangovers, I guess."

Nodding, I press my lips together. I don't want to pry, but it's starting to feel painful how little I know about Cal.

Sure, I'm aware of the basics—where he lives, that he has a sister he's completely devoted to, and that he owns a tattoo shop he's proud of. But that's it. Granted, I haven't exactly been an open book when it comes to my past, but I was hoping we would get there eventually. Maybe he doesn't trust me as much as I thought he did. Maybe—

"My mother has issues with alcohol."

I freeze. He's looking right ahead, avoiding my gaze, and gripping his bottle so tightly I'm afraid it may shatter. "They started before I was of legal age to drink, so when I turned twenty-one, I'd already seen what alcohol could do to a person and I didn't want that for myself. I'm her son, and I was scared it was in my genes or something, so I never risked it."

My throat clogs up, and I only get the words out by sheer determination. "How's she doing now?"

He shrugs like none of this is a big deal. "It varies. I thought she was finally sobering up for good this year, but it's not..." He clears his voice. "I'm not too hopeful."

I don't even think before I take his big paw of a hand and press it between my much smaller ones, warming it up. I notice that he's freezing. Huh. He's usually a human heater.

"Has she ever asked for help?" I wonder out loud, my voice soft.

Cal shakes his head. "She doesn't think she has that big of a problem, so no. She thinks rehab is for real alcoholics, and that she's not one. Says going there would embarrass her."

"I'm sorry," I whisper, hoping he can hear me over the loud music. When he laces his fingers through mine, I know he has.

I want to ask him how he's doing because of it. I want to ask him how it might be affecting Maddie, but I don't want to be insensitive. It's obvious he's shared more than he probably feels comfortable with, and while I may be curious, I'm a good friend above all.

But then a thought crosses my mind, and my body freezes all over again.

Could it be... Could his mother's problems have to do with

the fact that Maddie has her own room in his apartment? Because her episodes get so bad he has to take his sister away?

*God.* If I don't stop this train of thought now, I'll end up bawling my eyes out right here. An urgent change of topics is due.

So still holding his hand tightly between mine, I tell him, "You know the thing I've been stressing over this week?" He nods, his shoulders visibly relaxing. "Well, it's a final project for one of my classes and I have to write a *freaking book.* And yes, my mind is completely empty in case you were wondering."

"Wait, that's neat. You haven't come up with anything yet?"

Over the next fifteen minutes, I tell him about my frustrated dream of becoming an author and how difficult it is to make it in the publishing industry. I tell him about the books I've written in the past and how much they sucked, hence why I'm so scared of screwing up this project too. He listens attentively, asking me a few questions and reassuring me time and again that I don't suck even though he's never read anything I've written.

It's kind of cute.

"This is how I see it," he starts as he puts his drink down. I breathe a little easier at how at ease he looks now, the conversation about his mom long forgotten. "I'm warning you it's probably going to sound cheesy as hell."

"Enlighten me." I smirk at the thought of a cheesy Cal. His hand squeezes mine, and my next breath dies in my lungs.

"You're still going to keep teaching at TDP after you graduate, yeah?" I nod. It's a job I love and pays well. Adelaide already offered to give me more responsibilities once I can commit to a fuller schedule. She's thinking of opening a second studio across town and everything. "Well, since you say making it as an author takes time, it's good that you already have a stable source of income to support yourself while you get there. You can write in your spare time and sleep well at night knowing you're working towards your dream while keeping a safety net beneath you."

It makes a lot of sense. "I guess I'm scared that I'll never make it at all, you know? Trust me, many people want to become authors and most of them never get to publish anything. What if I'm one of them? And yes, fine, I write for myself because it helps me clear my head and gives me a purpose, but I can't lie and say I don't want people to read my work."

He hums. "No, it makes sense. If you pour your heart and soul into something you're proud of, you'd want to share it with the world."

"Exactly."

"This is how I see it, and here comes the cheesy part. You only get one life, and while I'm sure it's gonna be a long one, I don't want you to wake up one day in forty years regretting that you never were brave enough to write a damn book and try to publish it."

Unconsciously, I tighten my grip on his hand as he keeps talking. "It's true that you might never make it. It happens, but what if you *do* make it? What then?" He shakes his head. "You know how you're one hundred percent never gonna make it? If you don't write a book and pitch it. Your unfinished drafts won't ever see the light if you don't choke that impostor syndrome to death and finish that story. And if you try your best and still fail, at least one day you'll die with no regrets."

His words are something I've told myself time and again over the years, yet hearing them from him makes my chest feel lighter. A sudden rush of confidence in my future and inspiration to work on my dream explodes inside my body, and I find myself a little choked up when I try to speak. "Thank you, Cal. You are..." *Everything.* "You're a great friend."

He gives me a smile. "You're a great friend too, sunshine. I'm sure you'll figure this out with time, and you know I'm always here if you need to talk. I'm a good listener."

"Thank you. I know. I'll let you know if inspiration strikes."

"*When*," he corrects me.

"When," I repeat, a shy smile playing on my lips.

"Good." He starts toying with my fingers, bending them into weird angles. "You think your professor will pass out if you turn in a smutty book?"

I'm the one about to pass out now. "What? I... No, I could never write that."

"Why not? You read them."

"It's not the same thing as writing them." My cheeks heat up. "I don't think I'd be good at it." Not to mention that I don't have any experiences to draw from, but that's a conversation for another day. Maybe.

"You're good at everything," he says with such confidence I almost believe it.

I'm about to tell him that he couldn't be more wrong as three tall figures appear in my line of vision. When I lift my head to look at Aaron, his eyes are already locked on Cal's hand holding mine. To his credit, Cal doesn't let go.

My little speech from earlier might have worked, because instead of threatening to cut off Cal's arms if he doesn't stop touching me right this second, my cousin takes a deep breath and focuses on me. "We were gonna hit the pool table. Wanna come?"

"Sure."

We spend the next hour playing pool with my cousin and his two friends. I thought one of them was quite nice and funny at first until he touched the small of my back as he walked behind me when he absolutely didn't have to. I jolted, shaken up by the unwanted touch, and Cal was by my side a second later like a rabid beast waiting to strike. From the other side of the table Aaron glared at his friend.

Jeez.

They don't say anything or make a scene, so technically I can't get mad at them. Whatever.

Because it's a weeknight, we decide to leave early and Aaron offers me a ride home. He doesn't say it, but of course the only reason he's so eager to jump into driving me is because he knows I'll ride with Cal otherwise. He only had one beer over an hour ago, so he's fine to get behind the wheel and we take off.

Later that night after my usual catch-up session with Em, my phone lights up with a text from Cal.

> **Confession time. I'm more intrigued by that book of yours than I should be.**

I grin at my screen like a total fool, glad that Emily's focus is on her tablet and not me or she'll be asking too many questions I don't have answers for. Before I get the chance to unlock my phone and type a reply, a second text comes through.

> **I had a lot of fun tonight. You're easy to talk to. I'm picking up Maddie from TDP, so I'll see you tomorrow. Sleep well, sunshine.**

> **I had fun too. I'm 100% turning to you for motivational pep talks from now on, btw. It's a threat :)**

> **I'll see you tomorrow. Sleep well, Sammy <3**

> **I didn't know people still sent hearts like that.**

> **<3**

# chapter 18

## GRACE

Almost five weeks and two major mental breakdowns later, the blank Word document belonging to my stupid unwritten book still haunts me. And it continues to do so after Professor Danner dismisses us, and I lean back in my seat with a groan.

"Same." A nearby masculine laugh reaches my ears. Turning around, I lock eyes with Luke Elms. "How's your project going?"

With his tall, slim build, bright blond hair and big blue eyes, I've always thought Luke was the spitting image of a cherub. I've known him since my first year at Warlington, although we couldn't have exchanged more than a handful of words in total.

He's also Olivia's son and sometimes helps her carry the heavier boxes into the charity shop I volunteer at. It's a small world after all, huh?

From what I've gathered, he's a quiet lacrosse player who gives me more surfer vibes than anything else. Maybe it's his chill attitude.

I sigh, unable to hide my frustration. "I don't have much planned yet." Nothing at all, in fact. "What about you?"

He gives me an easy smile as he puts his laptop away in his shoulder bag. "I think I'm gonna give a shot to crime fiction. I've watched way too many crime shows, it has to pay off somehow."

"Oh, wow." That sounds way too complicated and far more interesting than anything I could ever come up with.

"I'm just outlining it, though."

"That... It sounds amazing, Luke." I give him a genuine, encouraging smile because I don't want to project my own insecurities onto this poor guy. "I'm sure Danner will be impressed."

He chuckles and rubs the back of his neck nervously. Is he... blushing?

"Well, that's if I actually dare to start it." He laughs again. "Anyway, thanks for the encouragement. I...I gotta get to practice now but I'll see you around, Grace. Maybe I'll stop by the shop this Saturday. And good luck with the project."

"Thanks, Luke. You, too." I wave at him like a loser as he descends the stairs and exits the classroom.

Once he's gone, I close my eyes and wonder if I'll ever be able to talk to a man ever again without feeling like a fool or having my stomach turn. So far, the only man I can be myself with is Cal and while I'm not complaining, I would like to test my social skills with someone else.

Maybe cherub-looking Luke is the perfect candidate for that. He hasn't given me the creeps so far, and he's Olivia's son. I like Olivia.

"He's totally into you."

I turn my head in time to catch Sadie's knowing smirk.

I blink. "Who? Luke?"

"Totally."

Sadie, with their pastel pink hair and their nose piercing, is one of those people I tend to gravitate towards even if we're not really friends. I've known them for a couple of years, but we've never talked outside the classroom. I sat next to them in one of our classes last year because they gave me good vibes, and we've even worked on a group project together. When they learned I was adopted by gay parents, they declared themselves my number one fan and we've sat near each other since then. However, they hang out with an off-campus crowd and I'm not comfortable enough to make new friends, so this is all we get.

"I don't think he's interested like that. He was just being friendly," I tell them as I grab my things. "I work with his mom."

They shrug like they don't believe me. "Trust me, he's into you. I've got an eye for these things. I haven't seen a guy blush over a girl in a very long time."

I laugh and shake my head. "Thanks for the heads-up, but I'm not interested in a relationship right now." It's not exactly a lie.

"You can hook up with him, no strings attached," they offer as any good ol' matchmaker would. I know they mean well and it's not like they know about my past, so I don't take offense at their insistence.

"I'm not into hooking up, either."

"Oh, that's cool. I'll mind my business then," they say with a smirk.

I smirk back. "It's fine. I'm used to my friends pestering me to get out there."

"But still. If I made you uncomfortable, I apologize."

I shake my head. "I appreciate it, but it's not necessary. I mean it."

A smile breaks out on their lips. "Okay. I'll see you around then, Grace."

After waving them goodbye, I hook my tote bag up on my shoulder and exit the almost empty classroom. I feel more tired than usual, and the constant messy thoughts in my head don't help me relax.

In the past month, I've gone to one party with my girlfriends, and, to my surprise, it went fairly well. Which for me means that I didn't want to run away, and no slimy weirdos approached me at all. It was one of the best nights I've had with Em, Amber, and Céline, and I promised them we'll go out together again soon.

Part of my newly found confidence stems from—listen to

this—reading smutty books. That's right.

I've gone through three of them already, one high fantasy novel and two contemporary romances, and I must say that living vicariously through those characters has helped me immensely.

Did you know there's something called safe words? Before having sex both partners can agree on a word to say when they need to stop. I didn't know it was a thing, and it eased some of my internal worries. When he touched me four years ago, not even the word 'stop' would make him—

*Beep.* It's Cal.

**Vegan food truck tonight?**

Smiling down at my phone, I fight to shake the feeling of my assault away. Two weeks ago, I became *this* close to finally telling Cal about it, but it didn't feel right at the time. I don't even know what that means or why it matters, and yet...

**Yup**

**I'll meet you at the shop at closing time?**

**\*thumbs up\***

Seeing and texting him always manages to lift my mood, so even though I still feel somewhat crappy, the storm in my head clears away as I make my way to my dorm. Emily told me the other day I totally have a crush on Cal, but that's...not true.

I can't have a crush on him. Sure, he might be charming, and patient, and funny, and wickedly hot with those bulky tattooed arms. And he's so patient with his sister, and—

No.

Absolutely not. I'm not going down this rabbit hole. Not right now, and not ever. Nope.

Cal and I share something special—my first real friendship with a man I feel safe with—and I'm not going to even attempt to think about my tiny little crush on him and jeopardize it.

Not that I have a crush. Because I don't.

I find him attractive both physically and mentally, so what? Sue me. It doesn't mean anything.

Anything at all.

\* \* \*

As I let myself into the tattoo parlor hours later, I'm relieved to find out my stupid hormones carry all the blame about my earlier breakdown over Cal. Because right when I got home from my last class of the day, I got my monthly visit from Aunt Flo. Which means I'm dying inside right now, and I barely feel my legs, but hey—at least I can blame my not-crush on a period-induced lapse in judgment. All is good and under control. Mostly.

"Hey." Cal's right by the front desk when I enter. He gives me a quick once-over before glancing down at his laptop again. "You look pale. Paler than usual, I mean."

Am I surprised he notices my shitty state of mind and body right away? Not really.

"I don't feel so good." Carefully, I lower myself onto the leather couch and hiss when another cramp attacks my abdomen.

In a heartbeat, he's kneeling beside me, whatever he was doing behind the counter long forgotten. Worry bathes his features. "What's wrong? Are you hurt?"

I shut my eyes and adjust my posture on the couch, but nothing I do helps at all. "I'm dying." Then, because I can't see it but I can imagine the look of horror in his face, I add, "Period cramps."

His relieved sigh hits me a second later. "Did you take any

painkillers?" Nodding, I tell him that they usually take too long to take effect. "Stay here. I'll be back in a second." The only non-humiliating thing about all this is that at least the shop is closed, so I can be miserable in peace. I don't think walking in for an appointment and seeing a random woman all sprawled out on the couch groaning like she's two seconds away from death would make a great impression.

True to his word, Cal comes back a few moments later with some kind of red package between his hands. "Heat pack."

"Why do you have that in here?" I manage to ask in the middle of the pain.

"You'd be surprised by the random shit we keep in the breakroom. I'm gonna put this on your abdomen now, yeah?"

I can only nod and watch as he kneels in front of me again and presses the heat pack over the thin material of my leggings. He does it so gently my stomach jumps, and this time it has nothing to do with cramps.

"We'll leave this here for fifteen minutes." When he shoots me that same pity look he gives Maddie when she wants to go to the park but it's raining, I almost want to cry because I know what he's going to say next and I don't want to hear it. "I don't think we should go to the food truck tonight."

I groan in pain as I try to sit down straighter. "No, it's okay. I'm fine. I want to go."

"We can if you really want to, but I don't think we should if you're in pain." He runs his fingers through my hair in a comforting gesture.

"Can we still hang out?" I swallow because I can't believe I'm feeling so stupidly emotional right now. Fuck hormones and fuck periods. "I'm not sure I want to be alone right now."

His eyes soften, and I lean into his touch.

"Okay. If that's what you want, we'll hang out here."

"Really?" I beam.

"Really. I don't know how to say no to you."

*Oh, man.*

"Are you hungry? I can order some food if you want," he suggests, as if he hadn't just left my heart in complete shambles.

"To the shop?" He nods. All right then. "I'm craving mozzarella sticks."

"Whatever you need. Let me grab my phone and I'll get us some dinner."

By the time our food arrives, I'm already feeling way better. The painkillers have—mostly—kicked in and stuffing my grumpy stomach with some homemade delicacies from The Spoon helps a whole lot.

Once dinner's done and we clean up, Cal grabs the laptop from the counter and puts one of those reality shows we've become so addicted to. This one is about hot single people not being allowed to have sex while on a dream island vacation, and it's a great distraction from the remains of my cramps.

He sits on the couch next to me. When he wraps an arm around my shoulders and I lean into the comforting warmth of his body, I realize two things.

One—the tattoo shop is eerily cozy at night.

And two—I trust Cal with my mind, my body, my heart, and my secrets. And it scares the hell out of me.

# chapter 19

## CAL

"Samuel, can I speak to you for a second?"

I'm finishing up some yard work in my childhood home when my mother's voice breaks through the mental barriers I put up every time I come back here.

Trey was fine with me taking Saturday morning off, and although Maddie is on a playdate with a friend from school and Pete is who-the-fuck-knows-where, I still wanted to come and see my mother.

If her stiff tone is any indication, however, I may regret having dropped by after all.

I follow her into the kitchen, and it only takes me a second to notice the picture of Maddie and me on the Donuts with Daddy party at her school a couple of weeks ago. In it, I'm kneeling next to my sister with an arm around her as we show our donuts to the camera with huge smiles on our faces. An exact copy of that photo hangs proudly on my fridge.

But as my mother picks it up, I notice the troubled expression on her wrinkled face and I know something's wrong.

"I found it at the bottom of Maddie's backpack." She looks at it with sad eyes before redirecting her gaze towards me. "What is this?"

I blink, confused. "What do you mean?"

"When did you go to Maddie's school, and why are the two of you eating donuts?"

I look at her like she's just asked me about the meaning of life and expects an accurate answer. "What? Mom, this is Donuts with Daddy. Maddie came home with a note from her teacher weeks ago, didn't you read it?"

Why do I even bother? By the guilty face she's making, it's obvious that she didn't. I rub the mental exhaustion off my face as she asks me, "If this is a father-daughter thing, why did you go with her?"

"Because her sorry excuse of a sperm donor refused to go since he doesn't like donuts and, apparently, that's more important than spending time with his daughter. That's why."

I count to three in my head in a failed attempt to calm down. This is what bothers me the most about my mother—her inability to see the harmful shit right under her nose.

Her relationship with Maddie's father has never been healthy, but she's so scared of being alone after my father left us that she won't dump his sorry ass even if he deserves it. Which he does.

Pete's not abusive to her or my sister, or else he'd be ten feet under the ground already, but he's a lazy fuck. He doesn't help my mother at home or with their own daughter, and he loses his job every few months for who knows what reason.

My mother's shifts at the grocery store aren't enough to pay all the bills, the car, Maddie's school, and her ballet classes, so that's why I've been helping her financially since my sister was born. I don't mind doing it at all; not when that means a happier and easier life for both of them. I can afford it with how good my business is going, so it's not a struggle.

But *shit*. It's her father who should be doing all of this. It's my mother who should be demanding at least the bare minimum from him. But it's been nearly five years and it's still the same fucking nonsense. And maybe that's why I'm tired of holding my tongue any longer.

"Samuel," she warns. "Don't talk about Pete like that. You know I don't appreciate it."

"And I don't appreciate him not spending time with Maddie and not raising her like a good father should." I've never yelled at my mother, not since I was a moody teenager who needed to be put in his place, and I sure as hell won't start now. I'm not losing my temper over rat-ass Pete.

Setting the picture down on the kitchen counter, she pinches the bridge of her nose and shakes her head. "Did the teachers say anything?"

Really. That's what she's worried about. That's what she's deciding to take from this conversation. Not that the literal father of her child forgets he has a daughter at all, but what other people might say about his absence. I can't say I'm surprised that she keeps ignoring the truth, but it sure hurts like hell.

"No. I told them Pete couldn't make it and that's why I went instead."

She nods. "Good."

"No, Mom, it's not good." I step closer so she can look at me. She doesn't. "Maddie was crying, for fuck's sake. She told me her father didn't love her, and I had to stand there with a broken heart and fucking lie to her and tell her he did."

That's when her eyes, the exact same dark shade as mine, snap up to me. "Don't you dare accuse Pete of not loving his own daughter, Samuel. You don't know a thing."

"*I* don't know a thing?" I can feel my temper rising with every breath I take, and I know I'll have to get out of here soon if I don't want to explode. "How can you be so confident that he loves her when he never pays attention to her, never plays with her or takes her anywhere? Never buys her presents or candy, and lets her down when it counts the most? If he loves her like you're so confident he does, he sure as hell doesn't show it. I act like a father to her, Mom, not him. Open your damn eyes once and for all."

She slams her palm on the counter, the rage in her eyes mirroring mine. "Enough! You're not here all the time. *I'm* the one who sees Pete with Maddie and I can assure you he tries his best. He's under a lot of stress right now with his job search, you know this."

I roll my eyes. "His job search from the couch while he watches TV, you mean? Then yes, I'm aware of it." Shaking my head, I pin my mother down with a hardened stare. "He's a disgrace, Mom, and you're not going to change my mind about him. He's not a good father to Maddie and I'm scared to fucking death that one day she'll notice how distant he is and grows up with some kind of trauma. Why can't you see how serious this is?"

"That's not going to happen. Don't be dramatic." She rubs her temples. "Samuel, I...I can't do this right now. I need a moment."

"Of course. I have places to be, anyway." It's a total lie, but I don't want to be here anymore. I lean in to kiss her forehead. "I'll come over to see Maddie tomorrow."

She only nods, and I leave. I don't look back for fear of seeing her reach into the liquor cabinet because I don't need another piece of my heart shattering right now.

Once I'm sitting behind the wheel in my car, I take a deep breath and try to calm down. The first thing I learned when Trey's dad taught us to drive at sixteen was to not get on the road while you're upset, and the last thing I need is to get into a damn accident. Pulling out my phone, I don't even hesitate as I open our chat.

> **Where are you? I could use some Gracie and Sammy time right now.**

By the time she texts back minutes later, my boiling anger has significantly subsided.

**What's wrong?**

**I'm at The Teal Rose in Melrose Creek**

**Wait, I'll send you the address**

**You can come now if you want**

I smile at how she always double and triple texts me and is completely unapologetic about it. I love it.

When she sends me the location of some place I've never heard of, I finally pull out of my mother's driveway with a lighter feeling in my chest. The mere prospect of spending some time with Grace manages to push all my worries and anger away, and I don't know what to make of that.

\* \* \*

I've always been a laid-back dude, which means I don't do the whole possessive and jealous act. I've never felt that way towards a woman, no girlfriend of mine at all, and I have no plans to start now.

Too bad my plans go out the fucking window the second I walk into The Teal Rose.

Grace is standing behind the front desk, wearing a bright blue wool jumper that makes her look like an angel on Earth along with that breathtaking smile I always crave. I'm so distracted by her beckoning aura that I almost don't notice the blond guy talking to her.

Almost.

Try-Hard Dude has this whole surfer vibe to him, even though the nearest beach is miles away from Warlington. Backwards cap, loose hoodie and jeans, a surfboard necklace hanging from his neck. You know what I mean. And yes, you guessed it—he looks ridiculous as hell.

On top of that, the way he talks to Grace makes it painfully obvious that he's into her, and I want to rip his head off and feed it to wild dogs just because. He leans into the counter with a gesture that seems oh-so-casual but instead looks oh-so-practiced-in-front-of-the-mirror. I want to wipe that damn smile off his face and stick it up his—

"Cal, hey!" When Grac e notices me, her smile widens, and my shoulders relax at the way her eyes shine. What the hell is happening to me? "I'll be done in a second. You don't mind waiting, do you?"

And because I'm a petty bastard and I want this fucker to know she's mine, I smile easily and say, "Of course not, babe. Finish up, don't worry about me."

Her cheeks redden and she looks away, visibly affected by the nickname.

Cal, 1. Try-Hard Asshole, 0.

Wait.

What the fuck am I doing?

Barely a month ago, she gave her cousin hell for behaving like a territorial caveman and here I am now, doing the same thing when I don't even know why I'm feeling this way in the first place.

I don't have a claim on Grace. I know this. The only thing going on between us is a beautiful, genuine friendship I've just jeopardized again by opening my stupid mouth.

Seeing her with another guy, though, has triggered something ugly and deeply buried inside of me. There wasn't anything I could've done to fight it, not when every sensible part of me went numb at the sight of her laughing with another man. Boy. That kid's got nothing on me. He's all lean limbs with no real muscle. And sure, he might be tall, but I still tower over him a few good inches.

All right, and now I'm comparing myself to this random guy. Am I a damn high schooler or some shit? When have I ever done such a foolish thing? I'm thirty years old, for fuck's sake.

"Hey." Try-Hard Dude holds out his hand to me as Grace disappears into the back of the shop. His eyes are too blue, and his smile is too white. "I'm Luke. I share some classes with Grace."

If I shake his hand, it's only because my mother raised me right. "Callaghan."

I can't tell if he doesn't care about my stiffness or if he's oblivious, but he keeps talking to me like I give a fuck. "You work at that tattoo parlor, right? Inkjection? I think I've seen you around."

"I own the place." Because it's extremely important that he knows this.

"Oh, that's dope! I've been thinking about getting a tattoo, but I can never make up my mind on a design, or a spot."

And only because I've just told this asshole where I work and that the shop is mine and we can't afford whispers of the owner being a douche, I put on my fakest smile and tell him, "You can come by any time. I'm sure we can work something out."

"Nice, man. I'll take you up on your offer." He nods eagerly as Grace comes back to the front. Try-Hard knocks on the wooden desk twice with his knuckles. "Right, gotta take off, but I'll see you on Monday?"

She smiles, and I want to glue his eyes closed so he can't see her beautiful face ever again. "Sure, Luke. Have a nice weekend and tell your mom I said hi."

His mom? Grace knows *his mom*?

"Will do." After he winks at her, I don't even bother to answer when he turns to me and says, "Bye, Callaghan. I'll stop by the shop soon."

The door closes behind us, and I still don't move an inch or even glance at her, too scared of what I'll find in those expressive hazel pools. I can feel her looking at me from the corner of my eye, but no. I'm not doing this right now. "Babe, huh?" Her voice sounds teasing and not angry, so there's that.

Even so, I don't look at her. Instead, I focus on the shop around me. I've never been to this part of town or The Teal Rose before, and I wonder why Grace is working behind the counter on a Saturday morning. Does she have a second job? She told me once that her position as a ballet teacher pays well. On top of that, her dads help her cover most of her expenses until she graduates and finds a full-time job so she can focus on her studies. So maybe it's not about money.

When my eyes land on the big teal sign behind her, though, I understand.

I understand everything.

The Teal Rose is a charity shop.

And all profits go to a local women's shelter.

Just like that, everything comes crashing down on me like a deadly avalanche.

*My friends wanted me to come up to a random guy tonight and get his number because they thought it would be good for me. Something happened to me a few years ago. It was pretty bad.*

*Listen, men are shit and Grace knows it first-hand.*

The reason she freaks out when she's around men.

Why Aaron behaves so protectively and doesn't trust any guy near her.

"Cal?"

I can't breathe.

I can't feel my pulse, my arms, my legs.

I can only feel my fucking heart shattering inside my chest.

"Cal?"

This can't be true. She couldn't have been...

"Cal."

I blink. "Sorry."

When I finally look down at her, her hand is on my arm and her whole face screams worry and confusion. "Are you okay? You look pale. Let me get you some water."

"You don't have to." I manage to let out somehow past my burning throat. Speaking more than one word right now seems like an impossible task. But it's too late, because she's disappeared behind the beaded curtain again, leaving me all alone with this fucked-up realization.

The last thing I need is to jump to alarming conclusions, but it's too difficult not to when every little hint points to my suspicions being right. Her volunteering at a women's shelter of all places isn't a coincidence. I know it deep in my soul.

When she comes back with a plastic cup full of cold water, I can only stare at her like a complete fool.

I need to hear it. I need her to tell me it isn't true.

"Cal, you're scaring me."

Taking the cup from her small hand, I take a sip and collect my thoughts to avoid stepping over the same line I've almost crossed far too many times now. She doesn't owe me a thing. I have no right to demand an explanation. "Sorry." I leave the empty cup on the counter and debate whether to pull her in for a hug, because I need to feel that she's safe and whole right now, against my chest.

I decide against it. "I didn't know you worked here."

"Yeah." She looks around the place shyly, avoiding my gaze. "I volunteer to run the shop on Saturdays. Luke is my supervisor's son, and we happen to share some classes too. Small world, huh?"

I can't even find it in me to be bothered by Try-Hard Luke's mere existence at this moment. Not when something so painful is brewing inside of me. Clearing my throat, I say, "It's nice of you to volunteer for such a great cause. I'm sure your help is much appreciated."

She gives me that gentle smile of hers that usually makes my heart beat faster and my stomach jump. Today, though, I only feel hurt. "Yeah, it's a... It's a cause that means a lot to me."

I can only nod. Every single word I thought of saying dies on my lips, choked to death by the heavy lump forming in my throat. And when she looks at me and her eyes are glassy in such a raw, naked way I've never seen before, every hope of all this only being a bad dream dissipates into thin air.

"I volunteer at the women's shelter because I...I know what it feels like to be in their shoes." Her hands start to shake, and so does her voice, and suddenly neither of us are breathing. "I... I was... I was raped four years ago."

Every single living thing inside my body shuts down. My brain, my heart, my soul.

Six words.

That's all it takes to break me.

# chapter 20

## CAL

No. This isn't true.

My ears start ringing, my pulse accelerates.

This is only a cruel nightmare, and I'm going to wake up any moment now. I'm sure of it.

A beat passes. Then another, and the bitter realization hits.

This isn't some kind of sick joke, as much as I wish it would be.

I can't even manage to repeat the words in my head. My beautiful sunshine...

"I..." She opens and closes her mouth several times, unable to get the words out. I know that feeling all too well right now. "Not a lot of people know. Only my best friend Emily, Aaron, and my fathers."

I can't even begin to unpack what it means for us that she trusts me enough to tell me. That she trusts me enough to spend time with me, *alone* with me, in my apartment, letting me wrap my arms around her. What it really means for her to get that tattoo.

"It happened at a party the summer before I came here. He was a guy in my class. We weren't friends, but I knew him. I thought he was cute, and..." She lets out a quivery breath. "He made a move on me that night. We kissed, and then he touched me under my skirt although I said no. He kept going further, his fingers..." She pauses, takes a deep breath, and continues. "He was very strong, but I managed to push him away and ran for my life."

My hands start shaking, and before I know it, she's wrapped her small fingers around mine, holding me steady as if I were the one in need of comfort and not her, who has just relived the worst day of her life only to share it with me.

"Cal." Her soft voice is beckoning. Looking down at her and seeing unshed tears in those beautiful eyes ends me. "I'm okay now, I promise."

My hand twitches in hers, begging me to wipe those tears away and pull her closer, a gesture that felt natural until a few minutes ago. Now, I only feel nauseous at myself for having the urge to touch her when she's just confessed the most horrible thing that has happened to her.

But because she's Grace and those assertive eyes always manage to strip my soul bare, she places one of my hands on her cheek and leaves it there. "I'm okay," she whispers with such fierceness it startles me. "What happened to me doesn't define me, and the last thing I want is to be coddled because of it."

The contrast between my tattooed knuckles and her pristine pale skin sends my mind into overdrive. Her words make sense, and yet...

I pull my hand away and hurt flashes in her eyes. "I don't want to make you uncomfortable," I whisper, my voice coming out rough, throaty and wrong.

"You don't," she reassures me, but I still can't process any of it. When seconds pass and I'm still unable to speak, her gaze hardens. I feel her slipping away between the invisible fingers holding her close in the way my real ones are aching to. "You're treating me differently."

It's the cold disappointment in her voice that snaps me out of this trance. Sobering up, I fight against all my instincts to give her space and cup her cheeks, keeping her close like her eyes are asking me to.

When the tears start to fall, I wipe them away as gently as I can with the pad of my thumbs. "Sunshine." Swallowing, I try to remind my brain that this is the same Grace we've held in our arms before, the same Grace who teases us and feels safe around us.

She shuts her eyes in an effort to keep the tears from falling. It doesn't work. "If I didn't tell you before, it's because I didn't want you to see me like a helpless victim. I didn't want you to pity me," she says, and my heart shatters a little more. "That's why I don't tell many people. I can't stand... I've never blamed myself for what happened to me. I'm not made of glass. I'm not going to break any moment if I'm not handled carefully. I'm a survivor, yes, but I'm also much more than that."

I find myself nodding at her words, my hands shaking while they hold her face. "You're strong, sunshine. You've got fire in you. I knew it the second I met you," I tell her, because I need her to know how I see her. And I should've told her before. She deserves to know how fucking amazing she is every single day, and I vow right here right now to always make sure she remembers it for as long as I keep breathing.

She opens her puffy red eyes again, and the mere sight is enough to make me want to cry with her. "Promise me nothing will change between us." She swallows thickly. "Promise me you won't treat me differently."

I lean my forehead against hers and shut my eyes. "I won't treat you differently, Grace. I promise." She releases a relieved breath at my words, but I'm not finished. "It breaks my fucking heart. I'm torn between crying with you and killing the fucker who did that to you with my bare hands. I can't stand the thought of you being hurt. Your tears are killing me, and all I want is to make you feel like the amazing, strong woman that you are."

"You already make me feel like that," she whispers, her breath caressing my lips. "Being with you feels right, Cal. Being your friend feels right. I don't want our connection to change."

Her words shake me again, but this time a whole different feeling settles in.

*Being with you feels right.* Yes, it fucking does.

There's nothing in this world I wouldn't do to see Grace's happiness shine through.

I ache to get on my knees for her and promise her she'll be forever safe with me, as friends or as...

No. I shouldn't even be thinking about this during such a vulnerable moment. Whatever might be starting to bloom inside my heart will have to remain hidden until I can root it out for good.

"I promise you, Grace. I'll always be your friend." Above anything else. Of that, I'm sure. "No matter what, I'm here."

"And I'm here for you, Cal."

"I know." My thumbs wipe the remaining of her tears, and her lips curve into a soft smile that steals my breath and my sanity. "There you go. There's my Gracie."

Her smile only widens, and I can't help but mimic it. "And there's my Sammy," she whispers.

That's right.

Forever and always, whatever life throws at us, we are here. Together.

# part two: growth

# chapter 21

## GRACE

The awaited Christmas recital is only a few weeks away, and the custom-made outfits Adelaide ordered for the girls have finally arrived at TDP.

Their tutus are bright red, paired with a matching bodysuit and a black belt. On their hair, they're supposed to wear one of those big dramatic clips with a huge Christmas present attached to it (if they manage to keep them in place, that is).

Everything looks super adorable, and I can't wait for the girls to try them on. Their parents are going to die of cuteness—I know I will.

Grabbing one of the outfits, I double check it's Maddie's size before putting it away in my locker. Cal texted me earlier that she was feeling a bit under the weather, so I promised to take it to his apartment before dinnertime later today.

It's been a couple of weeks since I told him about the assault, and while things haven't really changed between us, they also have. Kind of.

Don't get me wrong—he's never once coddled me so far, although I've caught him looking at me with pity a couple of times. But it's all right. Can I really blame him?

Learning that one of your closest friends was raped years ago and still deals with the consequences can't be an easy truth to stomach. When I told Em about our conversation at The Teal Rose, she reassured me that Cal was taking it way better than she did back in the day.

She also insisted that I totally have a crush on him. Bah. On another note, I've finally come up with an idea for my final project—a historical romance between a noble woman and a stableboy. You don't have to tell me it's mediocre at best. I know that.

The twist is that the male protagonist isn't really a stableboy, but a nobleman in disguise who's plotting the demise of the female protagonist's father by making his daughter fall in love with him.

I know, groundbreaking.

I still haven't made up my mind about whether I want to add smut or not. Since Professor Danner will be reading it *and* grading it, probably not. On top of that, I still haven't figured out if I'm comfortable with writing spicy scenes in the first place. Sure, I have no problem reading them and I enjoy most of them, but writing them takes some form of talent that I lack. Experience, probably.

Somewhere between me telling Cal about my past and devouring erotica, the sheer determination to "put myself back on the market"—as Amber would so eloquently say— spiraled out of control. Well, maybe that sounds overdramatic, but the sentiment remains the same.

As crazy as it might sound, romance books are teaching me that healthy, safe sexual relationships can be created with trust and the right person. That it's okay to refuse or demand things from your partner.

Everything changed for me when I unwarily picked up a book about a sexual assault survivor at the local library almost a week ago. I returned it the next day after staying up until four in the morning to finish it. I *couldn't* put it down.

In the book, the protagonist is a young woman whose main issue is to overcome the toxic notion that survivors shouldn't have any kind of physical relationships after their assault because they're too traumatized. And while I've never personally struggled with such a mindset, it solidified some truths for me— that trauma doesn't define a person, that everyone is different and each survivor has a different timing, and that we'll know when we are ready to move on if ever.

And I am. I *feel* it.

The question, however, is who am I ready to take this next step with?

Am I truly ready to flirt with a guy and see where it goes?

The image of Luke crosses my mind briefly. In the past few weeks, we've talked more often after class, and he stops by the thrift store every Saturday morning. He hasn't given me any reason to believe his niceness is only an act—like, come on, he even tags me in memes sometimes.

Maybe I could ask him on a date or something? Grabbing a coffee together at campus seems innocent enough, perfect to test the waters. Sure, I might not be super attracted to him, and he might not make my heart beat and my soul fill with undying love, but we could get there. Right? Rome wasn't built in a day.

Before I chicken out, I grab my phone as I prepare to leave TDP for the day and message him on Instagram since we haven't exchanged phone numbers yet.

> **Hi, Luke. I'm wondering if you wanted to grab a coffee after class tomorrow? You can totally say no!**

I'm already in my Uber to Cal's apartment when my phone buzzes with a reply from Luke.

> **As if. Looking forward to it :)**

Good. Great. Yes, this is good. Putting myself out there is what I'm ready to do. Perfect.

Before my head starts spinning in all possible directions—like, *'What if he ends up being like Dax?'*—my ride arrives at Cal's fancy neighborhood, and my focus switches to Maddie's excited little face when she sees the costume. Hopefully she isn't feeling too poorly anymore.

When the elevator stops on Cal's floor, his front door is slightly ajar, so I let myself in. "Hey, it's me." I peek my head inside and, sure enough, he's cooking something on the stove. By the smell of it, I would guess it's an omelet.

"Hey." He smiles at me over his shoulder. "Maddie's in bed. She's feeling better, though, so if you could make her come here for dinner, that would be great."

"Sure." But first, I walk up to him and give him a side hug. It's something we do a lot—hugging. Turns out both of us love physical touch, and he's the best hugger ever. So, win-win. "How was your day?"

"Fully booked, so I can't complain."

"But..."

"But I'm exhausted." The corner of his lips twitches, giving me that side smile I like so much. It shouldn't make my heart beat faster, but it does, and I'm not going to sit here and unpack why. Nope.

I rub his back in a comforting gesture. "The day's over, so forget about it." That's what my dads always used to tell me when I came back from school all stressed out. "I'm going to get Maddie."

Before I get the chance to step away, though, a strong pair of arms wraps around my middle and pulls me against a hard chest. Cal holds me tightly and rests his chin on top of my head. "Gotta give you a proper hug."

I chuckle and rest my hands on his bulky, tattooed forearms.

"Your omelet will get burned."

"Then let it burn." He pulls me even closer to the point where I'm struggling to breathe, but I would be lying if I said I didn't love his monster hugs. They make me feel cocooned. Sooner than I would like, though, he releases me. "Maddie's way too excited about the costume. Did you bring it?"

I smirk and show him the bag I'm holding. "It's in here. Let's see what she thinks."

When I go into her room, she's sitting in bed watching something on Cal's tablet. The second she spots me at the door and notices what I'm carrying, she jumps off the mattress and sprints towards me. "I wanna see it! I wanna see it!" she chants with a kind of excitement that is difficult to match. I guess she's feeling better after all.

I laugh and pull out the costume from my bag, watching as her eyes fill with light and joy. "What do you think? Do you want to try it on and show your brother?"

"Yes!" Quicker than lighting, she grabs the tutu and I help her change like we do at the studio. She doesn't have her tights or shoes here, but she doesn't seem to mind. Once she's ready, I put her hair up on a tight bun and place the Christmas present pin securely on her hair.

She's got one of those huge wall mirrors in her room, and she spends a good couple of minutes staring lovingly at her reflection. Smiling to myself, I can't help but marvel at the princess explosion that is this bedroom. The soft pink and white tones, the big canopy bed and vanity, the fluffy blankets and rugs, all the toys... Cal wasn't joking when he said he'd splurged to make her comfortable here. And for some reason, the thought of him putting this princess bedroom together makes my breathing a little more difficult.

No.

I shouldn't... It shouldn't tingle like this. It's nothing. I'm

PMSing, that's why my mind is wandering to such dangerous territories.

"Let's show Sammy," Maddie resolves once she's done admiring her cute outfit. Taking my hand, we walk together to the kitchen where Cal's just finished making three cheesy omelets. "Sammy! Look!"

She twirls around like a ballerina so he can see the full effect. I steal a quick glance and him and—

*Oh, hell.*

His face softens, eyes lighting up with such raw love that I almost have to look away. He looks at her like she holds his entire world in her hands and trusts her to keep it safe forever.

"You look beautiful, princess." He takes her hand in his much larger one and twirls her around, making her laugh. "Are you feeling better? I made dinner."

"Yes!" When she stops dancing around, she turns to look at me with a serious expression on her face. "I can't get the tutu dirty. Can you help me change?"

I smile at her thoughtfulness. "Of course, sweetheart."

Maddie disappears down the hall a second later, jumping and babbling with pure excitement, and before I follow her, I make the mistake of glancing back at Cal.

He looks at me like I hold his world in my hands, too.

\* \* \*

"That baby is his."

"You're sure?"

"Positive."

"But they haven't hooked up since... What? Last season?"

I shrug. "Don't care. The baby is Jonah's. Wait and see."

After we finished *The Office*, Cal and I decided to start a new show that neither of us had seen before. This one is about a high-profile law firm where every character is messier than the last. Cue the drama stemming from an unplanned pregnancy in which the identity of the father is unclear, and I'm hooked. As much as Cal tries to deny it, he is too.

My feet rest on his lap while we both lie on the couch like the true lazy pair we are at heart. In this moment with the lights off, the TV playing softly with a good show, and Cal's comforting presence by my side, I don't think I've ever felt more at ease in a long time. I could fall asleep right here, but I know I shouldn't.

Ever since that first time I came to his place and accidentally fell asleep, I haven't spent the night here. Why would I? It's not like I don't have my own place. Plus, it would be weird to do sleepovers at our age. Sure, I'm only twenty-two and he's thirty, but it would be strange anyway. I'm not his girlfriend. I shouldn't stay over.

And why am I imagining now what it would be like to be Cal's girlfriend?

Before I can convince myself that going down this road is the worst idea I've had in years, I'm already there.

If we were dating, I have no doubts in my mind he'd treat me like a true princess. I mean, you just have to see how he's with his sister—Cal is the kind of man who does anything for the people he loves. I know for sure he'd take care of me, shower me with affection but also give me space if I asked for it. He'd take me out on the most thoughtful dates and make me feel special every day no matter what we were doing, because that's who he is.

And intimately... My forehead starts sweating just thinking about how gentle and attentive he'd be in bed, but I also feel like he has a rough, dominant side to him he doesn't show often. Exactly like the men in my books.

If I close my eyes, I can feel his big hands on my waist, guiding all my movements as I straddle his lap, positioning his cock right at my damp entrance and—I start coughing.

"Don't die on me." He grabs my ankle and gives it a squeeze.

*What the hell was that?*

"You look flustered," he comments, eyes narrowed in my direction.

"What? I'm not flustered." Very convincing.

"You are." Of course, he's not letting this go. "What's going on? Are you nervous about something?"

Then he goes and makes it worse by glancing down at my ankle and removing his hand, and I blurt out the last thing I wanted to tell him. "It's not you, Cal. Your hand is fine, leave it. I... I kind of have a date tomorrow, and I'm a bit anxious about it."

His hand stills mid-air on its way back to my ankle. "A date?"

I sit up straight on the couch. "Yeah. Remember Luke, from the thrift store? Blond hair, blue eyes..."

"I remember him."

His stiff tone catches me off-guard. "All right... Well, I asked him to grab a coffee after class tomorrow and he said yes."

"Cool." He runs a hand through his dark hair, and as I follow the movement, I catch myself staring a bit too long at his huge bicep as it flexes. I swear it's bigger than my head. I'm serious. "If you like him and he's a good guy, go for it."

"Thank you." And I mean it. "I appreciate your support more than you think. As much as he tries, Aaron would be freaking out right now."

He chuckles at that, but it doesn't sound right. "Well, you let me know if he's an asshole and I'll go beat him up."

"Cal!" I slap his oh-so-muscled arm, and when he laughs this time, it sounds a little bit more real. "Don't say stuff like that. He's nice."

He shoots me a side glance like he isn't buying a word. "Sometimes nice isn't enough."

I roll my eyes. "Trust me, I'm aware. I'll watch out for the signs. It's just coffee at campus, so I should be fine."

"I trust your judgment," he reassures me. "But my offer still stands."

"Thanks, Sammy." I pat his arm again in a friendly gesture, totally not because I want to touch him again, as I get up and stretch my arms over my head. "It's getting late. I'm gonna call an Uber."

"All right." He pauses the TV and gets up with me. "Text me when you get home, yeah?"

I roll my eyes again, but I'm smiling. "As if I ever forget." With a small grin, he ruffles my hair like the annoying ass he is. As I leave his apartment fifteen minutes later, though, I can't help but think something's off with him—I just can't put my finger on it. He said he was exhausted, didn't he? It's probably that.

Only that, when I get to my empty bedroom—Em is spending the night at a friend's—there's a nagging feeling inside of me that tells me it's something else.

# chapter 22

## GRACE

"I've heard some rumors about him around campus," Emily tells me over the phone the following morning. I'm literally walking to our date, so these rumors couldn't have come at a worse time.

"Of the bad kind?" I ask, although I'm not sure I really want to find out.

"Mm-hmm. Not necessarily. I heard Luke is... You know, *experienced*."

"So what? He sleeps around?"

"He's had a handful of hookups here and there." There's some shuffling in the background and I think I hear a distant masculine voice.

"Where are you?" I frown. It's not typical of her to not tell me where she's at, especially when she's with a guy. Her fear of being sold to traffickers is too real, and I don't blame her.

"With a friend, don't worry about it," she answers a bit too quickly.

"Spending the night at a friend's, huh?" I tease.

I can practically feel her rolling her eyes from the other side of the line. "Let's focus on the topic at hand, yeah? Don't distract me."

I chuckle. "Sure, whatever. Okay, so he's slept with a handful of people. I can handle that."

"Are you sure?" She sounds genuinely concerned, and I

know what she's thinking.

"I promise it's fine. At our age, most men I'd want to be in a relationship with are bound to have way more experience than I do."

"True, but I still thought I should give you a heads-up."

"Thanks. I promise I'm fine, though. Nothing to worry about."

Turns out, however, that I had a few things to worry about.

I meet Luke at Warlington University's most popular— and most crowded—coffee shop. It may not be an ideal place for a first date, given how I can barely hear him through the commotion of students and the obnoxious sound of the coffee machine, but here's where I feel safest.

Here, if anything happens, there would be many witnesses and people to help. It eases some of my nerves.

As the date goes on, I start growing more comfortable and realize that Luke is in fact a very decent guy. His family is originally from California, where he spends every summer facing the waves, but he also appreciates the colder weather of the East Coast. He tells me about this new job he started only a couple of weeks ago, how annoying his two brothers are, and a party he attended last weekend. The whole conversation feels friendly and safe enough.

At some point, I tug at the dress my friends swore looked so flattering when I sent a picture to the group chat this morning. Sexy, even, and with the right amount of autumnal vibes. Now, however, I wonder if Luke would think it's too short. Sure, I'm wearing a thick pair of black tights underneath because it's cold as hell outside, but the fabric still clings too much to my curves and it barely covers my ass.

I wonder why I thought this was a good idea. I'll blame it on choosing an outfit at nine in the morning when my brain is still very much asleep.

With each tug at my dress the front goes lower, so I stop. The V neckline is too pronounced to keep doing this unless I want my boobs to come out and say hello. And trust me, that's the very last thing on my long list of wishes right now. I don't want Luke to get the wrong idea or give him the impression that I'm interested in him like that. He might be cute enough and not creepy so far, but I don't exactly want to shove my tongue down his throat yet.

Once our food and drinks are gone, we exit the coffee shop and I walk him to his car. Suddenly, I feel a bit awkward for the first time since our date started. What am I supposed to do now? Kiss him goodbye?

"I had a really good time today," Luke says, leaning onto the vehicle. I think I'm supposed to find his casual pose hot.

Shaking the thought away, I give him a tiny smile. "Me too."

Luke is staring at me in an odd way. Before I can process what's unfolding right here right now, he moves his head closer to mine. Frozen, I stand still from both fear and anticipation.

In a moment, he presses his lips against my cold cheek.

He does it so softly I think I might have imagined it.

Alarms go off in my head, but then his hand travels to my forearm and gives it a small squeeze. "See you around, Grace."

I can only nod goodbye.

What the hell has just happened?

* * *

"And then he kissed my cheek."

Amber's mouth drops. "He did *not.*"

Céline nudges her arm. "Shut up, you knew this already." She does. I sent five voice notes to the group chat the second he drove away.

"There's not much more to tell." I shrug, locking eyes with my drink. It's been hours, and I still have no idea how I'm feeling.

Did it feel invasive? Not really. I didn't ask for it, but I guess most kisses just…happen. Nobody asks for permission, right?

"Are you going on a second date?" Emily asks. "We haven't talked about it, but I suppose?"

When I broke the news over our group chat earlier, they demanded an emergency meeting at Danny's, hence why we're now in one of the booths with drinks in our hands. We all have work and classes tomorrow, so we won't be staying long.

Amber scans my face with her all-seeing eyes like she's looking for something specific and when she finds it, she points at me with one of her long, red nails. "Something's bothering you. What is it?"

She's probably my most assertive friend besides Cal, so I'm not surprised that she picks up on my weird mood right away.

"Honestly? I'm not even sure. He wasn't creepy or anything, but there also wasn't a spark between us."

"You read too many romances," Céline points out, always the voice of reason. "They can set unrealistic standards for relationships, you know?"

"I do, but it's not like I was expecting this grand show of fireworks either." I shrug, not really knowing how to put my feelings into words. So much for an aspiring author. "My body didn't *tingle* all over, if you know what I mean."

"You weren't horny, you mean," Amber deadpans.

"Oh my god." I cover my face with my hands and chuckle at her bluntness. "No, I wasn't horny either, but that's not what I meant."

"What she means is that she didn't feel an instant connection with him," Emily chimes in as if she could read my thoughts. She turns to me. "Do you feel super excited to have another date with him?"

I mull it over. "It's not like I'll die if I don't see him again."

"So that's a no." Amber turns to Emily. "Next question."

"Did your stomach jump when he kissed you?"

"No," I answer right away. "But in his defense, I didn't expect it so I couldn't prepare."

Em looks at me like she wants to ask me if I'm all right after that, so I give her a faint nod and she relaxes.

"That's not an excuse. When Stella kissed me this summer, I wasn't expecting it either and I still felt all the fireworks," Céline adds with a longing smile.

I shrug. "Maybe it's me. Maybe I can't feel fireworks with anyone."

The moment the words leave my lips, though, I know it's a lie. I did feel fireworks the first time Cal held me, while we were watching TV at his apartment. I did feel fireworks when he showed me the thoughtful sketch of my tattoo. I do feel fireworks when he plays with his sister, or when he sends me a cute text, or when he teases me about my smutty books.

But I don't think those count.

"Absolutely not." Emily's sharp tone brings me back to reality. "It's not you, Grace. It's okay not to feel a spark on the first date. It can happen, but it's not an omen for anything."

Amber nods. "You can go on another date with him and see where that goes. It's possible that your special connection needs some time."

I nod back, but something at the back of my head is telling me that I don't really have any kind of special connection with Luke. He's a great guy and not creepy in the slightest, but that doesn't mean I have to be attracted to him. Being a decent human being isn't enough to make me fall in love with a person.

"He's experienced, too, which I guess is intimidating," I add as I play with my pink straw. It reminds me of Maddie and her all-pink and all-princess obsession.

"If you have any questions, babe, here I am," Amber says with twinkly eyes and a knowing smile. "But Google has the answer for everything these days. People write blogs about anything. Wait!

One of my hometown friends talks about sex and relationships on her page. She's a certified sexologist. I'm texting you the link."

I blink. "She's a *what*, now?"

Amber chuckles as she types something on her phone. A second later, my own screen lights up with her text. "A sexologist. They study human sexuality, anatomy... That sort of thing."

"She's basically a sex expert," Céline quips.

"And a great one at that," Amber reassures me. "I'm serious, look at her blog tonight. She covers all kinds of topics, things you've probably never even asked yourself before."

Later that night, I come across a post about having healthy sexual relationships after sexual abuse in her friend's blog. I read it three times.

It says that one key aspect to keep in mind if I want to learn about positive sexual relationships is to experience them with someone I trust and feel one-hundred-percent safe with. Is Luke that person?

No.

But I know who is, and I know who to ask for help.

# chapter 23

## GRACE

In the past few months, Cal has become an anchor of sorts; a constant—someone I can rely on to always make time for me and have my best interests at heart.

When I told him I was thinking of getting a car after graduation since I already have my license, he gave me advice on insurance and maintenance. When Em's desk was wobbly and we didn't have the tools to fix it, he dropped by our dorm on his lunch break and sorted it out in under five minutes. It was a bit embarrassing how quickly he fixed it, to be honest, but we still appreciated it a lot.

So, yes, it's safe to assume that Cal will do anything for me. He wouldn't hesitate to help me if I asked, which is why I've decided he's the only one I can go to about my current problem.

When I drop by Inkjection a couple of days after having read that blog post and having chickened out twice or a hundred times, I find him clearing his workstation. It's closing time soon and Trey usually leaves first, hence why I chose this time to come.

I need us to be alone for this, or I'll die from embarrassment. Even more than I already will, I mean.

Sure enough, Trey is walking out the door right as I walk in. He gives me a wide welcoming smile and points down the hall. "Cal's just finished up. See you around, lil' Grace."

I snicker at his nickname. He started using it after I told him I was five-two, and I'm sure he'll never get rid of it at this rate.

"Have a good night, Trey."

The door shuts behind him, and I take a deep breath before I approach him. This might be the best or the worst idea I've ever had to date. I'm leaning towards the latter.

Knocking on a metal cabinet since there's no door, he glances at me only for a second before he says, "Grace, hey. I didn't know you were coming."

Too bad I'm too stunned to speak. He's sitting in his usual stool, but he's wearing a black sleeveless shirt I've never seen on him before, and *holy mother of everything.* It shows off his toned arms and muscles that look out of this world.

Before he glances up and catches me ogling him blatantly, though, I clear my throat in an attempt to find my voice again.

"Yeah, it's um, kind of a last-minute thing," I opt to say, while trying not to think too hard about how the hell I'm going to breach this subject once he's done.

The universe must hate my guts because barely thirty seconds later he's all done and staring right back at me. "Came to finally get that tattoo?"

I glare at him. "No. And stop pestering me about it."

He laughs and pats the tattooing chair with one big, gloved hand. My eyes land directly on the veins in his arms. "Come here. It'll only take me thirty minutes max." Seriously, I need to stop fixating on how huge his hands are. It's not doing my poor sanity any favors. But now that I know how they feel around me, on my skin...

No.

I gulp. "Maybe another time. I'm here for... Um, something else."

He eyes me with caution as he takes off his latex gloves. "What's up?"

I've been thinking about this for days, and now that it's about to happen all I want to do is run away. How mature of me.

I can always tell him that I want to go to that vegan food truck, or that I'm stressed with my final project and want to hang out with him. Yeah, none of those things would raise any alarms. This, though... This probably will.

Before I can say anything, he asks, "What's wrong, Grace?" The genuine concern in his voice makes me feel like a terrible human being.

"Nothing's wrong," I say quickly. "I just have a problem, and I was wondering if you could help."

He doesn't miss a beat. "Of course."

Damn him and his willingness to help me out no matter what. I smooth down the blouse I'm wearing, suddenly noticing my palms are sweaty.

"So, um. Remember Luke?"

"I do."

"You know we went on a date the other day and, um... He kissed me." When I see his whole body tense I quickly add, "On the cheek."

There's a storm brewing inside Cal's eyes when he asks in such a low voice I barely hear him, "Did he make you uncomfortable? Did he cross any lines?"

"No, I promise he didn't. I mean, I wasn't expecting the kiss, but it didn't feel invasive."

His shoulders relax at that. "Okay. You said you have a problem. What is it?"

I chew on my lower lip. This is it, isn't it? Oh hell. "I've heard that he's, you know, experienced." I can sense the gears turning in his head. "And I'm not."

He blinks. "You've never had..."

"No. Not before the assault, and after that I didn't... I couldn't be with anyone like that."

"I understand," he says tightly. His expression remains open. "But you've been kissed before, right?"

"Yes, years ago, but that's not the kind of experience I'm talking about." I can feel my cheeks flushing as Cal looks down at his discarded gloves.

I'm not ashamed to admit that I'm a virgin. Because what does that *mean* in the first place?

When I was a teenager, being a virgin felt like a big deal. "Virgin" would be used as an insult by the same people who would then shame you if you weren't one. Because, apparently, women can never win.

Back then I felt pressured to find a boy I liked and "lose it" before it was too late and people started making fun of me. As an adult, I've realized it's all bullshit.

My assault didn't make me "lose" anything. I'm whole in many ways, including sexually. And when I finally consent to having sex with a man for the first time, I will choose to give that person a vulnerable part of myself. *On my terms.* And then I'll continue being a whole person, but with a new experience under my belt.

Sure, I'm a virgin—whatever that means for different people—but it isn't something to be ashamed of. Who cares what you do with your life and when you decide to take that step.

My friends know this, and I guess Cal now does too. I enjoy living vicariously through my friends' experiences and romance novels, so it's not like I yearn for sex or anything like that. But telling a man, telling *him*...

It doesn't feel as unsettling as I expected. Not because I feel embarrassed, but because I can't believe I'm having this conversation with *a man*.

And, on top of that, I'm admitting that I'm nervous about having sex for the first time. Because, sure, "losing" your virginity isn't that big of a deal in the grand scheme of things. But the perfectionist control freak inside of me wants to know exactly what she can expect so she's prepared.

"It's just..." I start again when he still doesn't say anything. His gaze remains locked somewhere on the ground. "I feel like I'm ready to take that step and learn the basics, so I'll know what I'm doing."

I'm sure he gets it by now, but since he refuses to establish eye contact and if I don't get the words out now, I never will, I blurt out, "Will you teach me about sex?"

A few seconds go by, and Cal still says nothing.

At this point I'm not even breathing anymore. I gather the little dignity I have left and look away. "It's fine, never mind." I swallow. This was a shit idea anyway. "I can always look it up online. God, how have I not thought of that before? Silly me. I'm sure a lot of people—"

"Sit down."

The firm command in his voice makes me do as he says. Walking to the tattooing chair, I keep my eyes down and sit awkwardly on the edge. I'm not scared of him by any means, but I've never heard him sound so authoritarian, and I don't know what to make of it.

Embarrassment clouds my sight. How did I get to this point?

"Is that really the reason you're here?" he asks me a lot more softly.

I shrug. "I'm freaking out a bit over this whole thing. I know it's not that big of a deal. It's just nerves. I don't know what to expect when it comes to dating, and I don't want Luke to think I'm pathetic. Or any other man for that matter."

"No one worthy of you should make you feel like you're pathetic for something as inconsequential as being a virgin, Grace."

"I know, but still. I want to know what I'm doing. Not particularly because I want to date Luke, which I'm not even too sure about in the first place, but for myself. I'm ready for this. It's time."

"That's amazing. I'm happy you're feeling this way."

I give him a small smile and finally look at him. "Thank you."

"If you don't mind me asking, why haven't you gone to your friends? You're close with them, right?"

"Yes, and I already talked to them about this. But I also want a man's perspective to understand what they like and what to expect." I swallow back my nerves. "I want someone I trust to teach me."

He looks away, lips pressed tightly into a thin line. When he still says nothing, I continue, unable to stop myself.

"You're the person I trust the most, Cal."

For a fleeting moment I'm tempted to ask him how many women he's kissed, how many he's slept with, but I suddenly realize I don't want to know the answer. The mere thought of Cal holding, kissing, or sleeping with another person makes me nauseous. Figure that one out.

Finally, he sighs before giving in. "All right. Tell me what you want to know."

His voice might sound more relaxed, but his shoulders and jaw remain tense. Mentally, I shake my head and sit up straighter. Some small part of me can't believe he's agreed to it. As much of a great friend he is, talking about sex with me can't be his ideal Thursday night plan. This might mean that my request wasn't that weird after all, and it gives me a tiny boost of confidence.

There were so many things I wanted to ask Cal, but since I never envisioned myself actually asking or him agreeing, my mind is now blank. So naturally, I blurt out the first thing I come up with. "What does it feel like to have sex?"

Cal looks like he's about to run away. *He's doing this for me, so I don't find myself unprepared*, I remind my brain. I can be patient. This is probably as awkward for him as it is for me, no matter how much we trust each other or how close we are.

"Well," he starts, but his voice betrays him, and he has to clear his throat. "I'm afraid I can't tell you how it feels for women, if that's what you're asking."

It makes sense, I'm just dumb. "I'm worried it may hurt too much," I confess. I don't think I've ever said this out loud, not even to Em.

His expression is serious. "It depends. Some women barely feel pain the first time, while others can't take how much it hurts."

Knowing my luck and despite having done ballet for most of my life, my first time will probably hurt like hell. "Do guys think it's disgusting when... When women bleed during their first time? I've heard that can happen."

"Boys might." Cal looks at me so intently his gaze burns. "Men won't."

Right.

Cal is no boy. That is painfully obvious. He's the tallest man I know. Broad. Big. There's no other way to describe him—Cal is simply *huge*.

"There's one thing I want you to learn above all others." He sounds so serious I stiffen. I don't think I've ever heard him like this, almost furious with the world. And Cal never, *ever*, gets angry. "And that is to say no. Don't feel bad or embarrassed if you're not ready to do something, Grace. You say no and that's it. No. There is no room for arguments, no convincing to do. And if he still tries to persuade you, get out of there, call me and I'll break his goddamn legs."

His sudden possessiveness makes me clamp my legs together, and the desire to feel any kind of friction down there grows until it becomes almost painful.

*No, no, no.*

I shouldn't be thinking about Cal like this. Not when Luke is a great guy who shows genuine interest in me, and Cal is no more than a friend. A best friend with whom I've developed a connection that is more special than anything I've ever felt. And I'm not going to risk it. Not when he would never see me in such a light, anyway.

"Noted," I say, hoping he doesn't notice how flustered I feel.

"Any other questions?"

Many. I've got many, and none of them are appropriate.

"How would I know when to take that step?"

"You'll feel it."

I arch a skeptical eyebrow at him. "I'm afraid that doesn't help much."

Without saying another word, he gets up from his stool and stands between my legs. I feel the urge to look away so he can't see my reddened cheeks, but he holds my chin gently to make our gazes meet. He looks at me with dark eyes and something else I don't understand. He brushes the pad of his thumb over my flushed cheek, just like he does when he wipes away my tears, and as he leans down, I lose the privilege of breathing. He stops only a couple of inches away from my face and asks, "Do you feel it?"

*Oh, my god. This can't be happening.*

"Yes," I let out a raspy whisper that doesn't sound like my voice at all. "I get what you mean."

He stays there, still and silent, watching me with intent. His face has never been this unreadable before. "Good girl." He pulls away without warning. My skin instantly misses the warmth of his touch, and my body longs for the proximity of his. "The right moment will feel like something similar. You'll know."

I shift in my seat, the ache between my legs now unbearable. Forget the words and technical explanations. Something in me wants Cal to show me. I want him to show me how it feels to break down my walls.

"And then what?" I ask almost shyly.

"Intimacy is more instinctive than you think." His voice is low as he speaks. "Let it flow, learn what you like, say no when you feel uncomfortable, and always make sure he's using protection. If he refuses to or says his dick is too big, you get up and leave because he's lying out of his ass."

I chuckle at that, normalcy slowly settling over us again like a comforting blanket. Until my mind decides to wonder how big Cal is, and the ache between my legs comes back. I hate myself.

"Thank you." I force myself to have decent thoughts again. "And I'm sorry if this was a bit weird."

Cal's eyes shine with understanding. "It wasn't weird, Grace. Don't worry about it. I'm glad you asked me. You know I'd do anything for you."

*But would you show me how it feels?*

*No. Stop it.*

I shouldn't be entertaining this careless idea. If it went to hell and I lost Cal over it, how would I move on? He's become such an important person in my life that the mere idea of losing him makes me nauseous.

But another, much tinier part of me wonders what would happen if our relationship didn't go to hell. If something else bloomed from the change.

I choke that thought to death.

# chapter 24

## CAL

*Fuck, fuck, and fuck.*

Oh, did I say *fuck*?

When Grace told me a few hours ago that Try-Hard Dude had kissed her cheek on their date, I lost my goddamn mind. And when she asked me if I could teach her about sex so she wouldn't feel embarrassed when she did it—with *him*—I wanted to find out where he lived and burn his house down.

This isn't supposed to be happening. I'm not supposed to get angry at the world because Grace is interested in someone else. For fuck's sake, I don't even want her to be interested in *me*.

I can't commit to a serious relationship when my sister and her stability should be my number one priority. If I let someone in, Maddie will get attached and when they leave—because trust me, they always do—it will make her more upset than I can afford to handle.

Not to mention that I don't *want* to be in a relationship right now. My last one ended nearly four years ago after I found out she'd been cheating on me for three months out of the seven we were together. After she denied everything and I showed her proof—the other guy also thought she was single until he saw us together, recognized me from the shop, and told me—she threw both a fit and my computer screen across the room and into the nearest wall.

So yeah, not traumatizing at all.

Even if I wanted a girlfriend, deep down I know it shouldn't be Grace.

I've never had such a close, special relationship with a woman before. I can't pinpoint exactly in what way, but ours is so different from every other friendship I've ever had—even the one with Trey that goes back so many years.

It's like fate clicked into place when we met. Like having her walk into my tattoo shop was meant to happen.

This primal need to see her, to text her, to talk to her, to make her laugh and wipe away her tears... It's tearing me apart to think everything could be destroyed if we took that next step and it didn't work.

But I'm not scared. I simply don't want to date Grace, that's all.

Why am I tossing and turning at one in the morning while thinking about her, then?

Fuck my life, honestly.

I close my eyes in an attempt to shut my brain down and listen to the silence in my apartment. Since Maddie isn't here tonight, I could turn on the TV and watch something until I fall asleep or play whatever video game will make me fall asleep the fastest, but I know neither of those things will make me unwind. Not when my mind is such a fucked-up mess.

Lying on my back on top of my covers, it becomes clear after a while that sleep won't overcome me as if by magic. My brain starts spinning—not like it ever stops—and imagining scenarios I should ignore. Especially because they involve my mouth between her legs and such a pretty sight won't help my current state in the slightest.

How her breath hitched when I stood so close to her, her flustered cheeks and her parted lips...

*No. Get a fucking grip.*

I shift my weight to the other side of the bed, hoping the cold sensation of the untouched covers does something to calm me down. It doesn't.

I take my shirt off, thinking it's the next best thing I can do. Perhaps it's the heat of the room that doesn't let me sleep.

It doesn't register what I'm doing until my hand is inside my boxers, stroking my length ever so slightly.

Well, then. If this is the only thing that will get me to fall asleep, so be it.

My hand roams the base of my cock, debating whether I'll go to hell for this. As I reach the conclusion that I most likely will, I wrap my long fingers around the shaft and start pumping it up and down, slowly at first. I squeeze at the base every time my hand comes down to mimic the delicious clenching of the body I wish I was sinking into. But she's not here, and my twisted imagination is all I have. I can feel guilty tomorrow—and I will. But tonight, I want to close my eyes and imagine that it's Grace pleasuring me as I teach her about sex like she so badly wants me to.

Throwing my head back, my movements become faster and deeper as my head conjures the wicked image of my sweet little Grace wrapping those plump lips around my cock, sucking and choking on it. Fuck. She'd be a natural, I'm sure, milking me so good until I come down her throat.

I'm sick, so fucking sick for this, but I don't care. I can't stop.

My other hand grips the covers, and I suppress a loud groan as I picture myself fucking her mouth, pulling her blond hair in my fist and shoving my fat cock down her eager throat. God, she'd be so tight everywhere.

*Fuck, fuck, fuck.*

My dick twitches in my hand, and I start pumping it faster as the first drops of precum soak my fingers. The thought of Grace is all-consuming. I bet she'd scream as I pound into her, give me the sweetest moans I've ever heard. Desperate, needy, so ready for me as I fuck her from behind like an animal.

The mental picture of her pussy swallowing my cock is all it takes to make me come down from this fucked-up high. With a throaty groan, I come harder than ever all over my hand.

*Fuck.*

*Holy fucking shit.*

What the hell was that? I am a sick asshole.

Allowing myself a moment to lie there and catch my breath before I take a shower and clean up, I decide this can't happen again. It's wrong in so many ways I'm getting a headache just thinking about it.

Grace deserves better than a friend who jerks off to her when all she wants is an innocent friendship. She deserves better than me, and the realization fucking hurts. I don't want to lose her, and if I don't cut this kind of shit off I will. So I erase the last five minutes of my life from my memory, and hope they don't come back to haunt me later.

\* \* \*

They come back. Oh, yes, they do.

As I wait outside The Teal Rose for Grace to finish her shift, I can't help but steal a few quick glances in her direction. A pair of tight jeans hug every sinful curve of her legs and ass, and she's wearing a black turtleneck that has no business making her look so damn good. Her hair falls like a soft cascade around her shoulders, the golden rings on her fingers glinting under the chandelier on the ceiling.

She's breathtakingly stunning, inside and out.

And I should get a grip before the evidence of my thoughts starts straining my jeans. She doesn't see me that way, and I shouldn't see her like that either.

The last thing I want is to ruin things between us when I don't even want a relationship in the first place. I don't think she's looking for one, either. Hell, she'll probably flip out and never talk to me again if she found out I touched myself at the thought of her a couple of nights ago. She might be starting to be interested in sex, but I'm still sick in the head for even imagining her in such a sexual scenario without her consent.

"All done." She gives me the brightest smile when she comes outside to lock the front door, and it makes me feel even worse. She trusts me and she's healing, and I had to go and do that. "Ready to go?"

She texted me this morning asking me if I could drive her to a couple of the bigger bookstores around Warlington so she can soak up some inspiration for her assignment. I had nothing better to do, and how was I supposed to say no anyway? She's got me wrapped around her little finger.

We drive in silence for the most part with only my rock music filling the car, although it's never awkward with her. And luckily, things between us haven't changed much since she asked me about sex earlier this week. In fact, it's as if our conversation had never happened.

I can't decide whether it makes me feel better or worse. "What are we looking for?" I ask her as we make our way through the crowded shelves of our first stop.

She comes to a halt right at the historical romance section and bites her lower lip, thinking. My eyes linger on that innocent gesture, and I hate myself a bit more. "Would you kill me if I told you I'm not sure?"

I chuckle. "I thought you had the book outlined already."

"And I do, but it's not quite clicking, you know?"

"Is it too cliché? Maybe that's why you're unsure. Because it's been done many times before."

But she shakes her head. "Clichés aren't that bad. Each author can make them unique if they're original enough, and most readers enjoy them anyway."

I can't help myself. "What's one cliché you enjoy?"

"Only one?" She snorts. "Okay, let's see. When they have to stay the night somewhere and... Gasp! There's only one bed." Her whole face lights up as she speaks, and I swear she's never looked more beautiful than right now. "When they hate each other at first, but then inevitably fall in love and it's all very messy. Oh, and when the guy is the girl's bodyguard, but they can't be together. That always gets me for some reason."

"Those are quite specific." I smirk.

She shrugs and sends me a mischievous glance. "I know what I want."

*Me too.*

No. Nope. I don't.

We spend the next twenty minutes browsing the historical romance section until she gives up and drags me to the smutty bookshelves. She browses through each paperback, taking her time scanning the blurbs and telling me all about the ones she's heard about.

I fucking love it. I love how she enjoys these kinds of books unapologetically, and how she includes me in her passion.

After nearly half an hour, she ends up choosing seven novels. "I can't buy them all, so I think I'll narrow it to two or three."

"Why can't you buy all of them?" I frown. Also, why doesn't she own an electronic reader if she reads so much? It would save her a lot of money for sure.

She looks at me like I don't get it. "Cal, these are around fifteen bucks each. That's a lot of money."

On a whim, I grab all seven books and gesture to the register. "Let's go. We have another bookstore to raid."

She blinks once, twice. "Cal, I'm not buying all those books."

"I know. *I'm* buying them."

"What? Absolutely not! That's more than a hundred bucks. I can't let you do that."

I shrug. "These aren't for you. I happen to have developed a recent obsession with porn without plot, and I want these."

"Oh, is that right?" She arches a playful eyebrow, but rushes to snatch the books from my grip. "Seriously, I'd feel terrible if you bought them for me. It's too expensive."

And because I know she's not giving up, I stare down at her with the most stoic expression I can muster. "Grace, I make more than a hundred bucks every day before lunch time. Let me get these for you, please."

She swallows, and I can practically see the gears turning in her head. "Why do you want to do it?" she asks in a small voice.

"Because I love how your eyes fill with light when you read your sneaky smutty books," I reply honestly before I can stop myself. "And when you're happy, I'm happy."

"Simple as that, huh?" The slight blush on her pale cheeks makes me want to cradle her face and do something very stupid right now. "Okay, fine. But I want to check out the children's section and get something for Maddie. You always read her the same bedtime story, and that won't get you any new brotherly points."

"In my defense, she loves that book." I tell her as I follow her across the store.

"Uh-huh, sure."

I'm not thinking clearly—or at all—as Grace browses the different colorful books. It's obvious by their interactions that my sister and her get along, but the fact that she wants to buy something for my princess...

I stop my thoughts before it's too late.

"I think she'll like this one." She proudly shows me one of those pop-up books about some mermaid princesses. "Is it brother-approved?"

"It is." I give her a warm smile. "Thank you. You don't have to get her anything."

"I was going to grab a book for her anyway. I loved reading

when I was her age, and it's so cute that she does too."

She opens the book one more time, and an enormous pop-up marine castle jumps out of the page. "Yeah, Maddie's going to lose her mind over this." Grace smiles. "I mean, it's no Gracie and Sammy adventure book, but it'll do."

"Well, that one would be a bit difficult to find." Then, something in my mind takes shape and I blurt out, "Unless you write it."

Grace looks at me with a blank expression, and for a moment I wonder if I've said the wrong thing. "You're serious?"

"Well, yeah." I shrug. "Why? Is it such a shit idea?"

"No, no," she mutters. Her gaze seems lost, locked somewhere behind me. "I never thought of it, I guess."

"Can you write a children's book for your final project?"

"Let me check." She pulls out her phone and starts typing furiously, then skims through what I assume are the project's guidelines. "It says I can write books for any age group and genre, but I have to reach a minimum word count."

"Good, so there you go."

She blinks up at me. "I assumed I was going to write something for adults, but this makes sense. I like this idea a lot, Cal."

I give her a smile. "I've never been more excited to read a children's book in my life."

She blinks. "You'd want to read it?"

"Of course."

She blushes, and the sight makes my heart sing. "I'll have to think about what kind of mystery I want Gracie and Sammy to solve. They're supposed to be these badass detectives, remember?"

"I never forgot." My damn face hurts from all the smiling I always do around her. This is the kind of pain I'll take every single day if I could. Then, something else comes to mind. "Hey, are illustrations allowed in your project?"

She browses her phone again. "It doesn't say here, but I could ask my professor. Why?"

"Because I'd love to draw a few to go with your story, if you want."

Grace looks at me like she's never seen me before. "Put the books down."

Without question I do, and not even a second later she throws herself in my arms. I hug her back at once, inhaling her intoxicating perfume. "You're the best, Cal," she murmurs against my chest. "Thank you for everything you do for me."

I hide my foolish smile by pressing my face on top of her hair. "You deserve this and much more, sunshine."

She squeezes me tight, and I let out a wheeze. Damn, she's stronger than she looks. "If you illustrate my book, I'm paying for it." I open my mouth to protest, but she beats me to it. "No, I don't wanna hear it. It's non- negotiable."

"But you won't be making money with that book since it's for class. It wouldn't be fair," I point out.

"Don't care." She shrugs, still in my arms. "I value your time, and I want to pay you as anyone else would."

Already knowing there's no way I'm winning this argument, I give in. "Fine, but you're getting a discount."

"Deal." She pulls away and I instantly miss the warmth of her small body against mine. Then she holds out her hand so I can shake it. "You can't back out now, Sammy. A handshake is right up there with a pinky promise, and you know how sacred those are."

"Of course. I wouldn't dare to break this super licit contract." I smirk.

She smirks back. "Dumbass."

"Ditto."

She opens that pink mouth to say something else, but she doesn't get the chance to when her phone buzzes in her hand. A frown breaks out in her face as she reads it, and I swear I can see the panic in her eyes slowly settling in as the seconds pass.

"Hey, everything all right?" I put a hand on her shoulder and shake her slightly.

"Huh? Yeah, it's nothing."

"Grace."

"Um?"

"You look pale. Who is that?"

She shrugs, and for a moment I fear she's not going to tell me. But then she does, and I see red.

"It's Luke. He wants to take me out for dinner tonight."

# chapter 25

## GRACE

"Are you going to say yes?"

For the past ten seconds, I don't think I've blinked once. "I don't know. Should I?"

"That's up to you." It is, isn't it? Ugh.

Shaking my head, I start walking up to the register.

"What if he tries to kiss me?"

Cal's steps falter beside me. "Would that be a bad thing?"

When Luke kissed me on the cheek after our first kind-of-date over coffee, I didn't find it weird or awkward, just... unexciting. My friends are right—chemistry between two people can take a while to manifest, and I shouldn't expect fireworks right away. And yet...

"I don't think I'd run away if he tried to kiss me," I say truthfully. "But I'm not sure that's what I want, either."

He sets his books down on the counter and the woman behind the register starts ogling him so blatantly I almost cringe. Is professionalism out of style?

I mean, it's not like I can blame her for staring—most of his tattoos might be covered by the long sleeves of his dark gray Henley, but his impressive muscles are all the more noticeable. When he pulls out his credit card and hands it to her, she gawks at his tattooed knuckles and actually blushes. The audacity.

A sudden wave of possessiveness rushes through me, so strong that I can't choke it to death this time. The moment Cal notices her staring and grins at her, though, I lose it.

"I'm going to say yes to Luke," I announce louder than necessary like it's some kind of grand decision. Before I can change my mind and think too hard about why I'm suddenly so eager to agree to our date, I grab my phone to text him.

Cal sends me an unreadable look over his shoulder. "If you're sure."

"I am."

"All right."

The stupid cashier flashes him another smile while asking him if he needs a bag. I can't help but snort out loud, which earns me another unreadable look from him. Whatever.

Of course he wants a bag, what kind of question is that? Is he supposed to carry all seven books around in his arms all day? Please.

*Okay, slow down, girl. Why the hell are you being so petty?*

Great question. Too bad I refuse to ponder it right now. Sure enough, the woman barely makes eye contact with me when it's my turn to pay. Instead, she sticks to the professional attitude and dull voice she probably uses with all customers. Those who aren't hot, at least.

Because who am I kidding? Cal is hot as sin.

"The cashier was totally flirting with you, by the way," I tell him once we're back in the car.

"Mm-hmm..." He puts on his sunglasses despite it not being sunny and starts the engine. "Well, too bad I'm not available then."

My heart jumps to my throat. "What do you mean?"

He said he didn't have girlfriend, but maybe he started seeing someone in the past few weeks? Although, frankly, it doesn't make sense that he's in a relationship when he spends most of his time working, with his sister, or with me. Perhaps it's a long-distance thing. Or maybe—

"I'm not looking for a relationship. Or a hookup."

"Oh." And now my brain is picturing him hooking up with some random, unidentified woman, and I hate it so much I want to cry. "Why not?"

He shrugs as we stop at a red light. "It's not where I am at this stage in my life."

"Yeah, I get it." I do, but it doesn't mean I don't feel a tang of disappointment as his words settle in.

I don't know what I am expecting, anyway. That he fall heads-over-heels in love with me, and we live our own fairytale? Yeah, right.

We're already friends, the *best* of friends, and neither of us would want to jeopardize that. Especially since we don't like each other *like that* in the first place. Because we don't. I might find him attractive and caring, but that's all. A lot of people I know share those same traits and it doesn't mean anything.

I decide to skip on the bookstore raid, and he takes me home instead so I can get ready for my date with Luke. I'm not dying to go, but it'll be a welcome distraction.

I need to get Cal out of my mind at any cost.

# CAL

Working out does nothing to ease my shit mood. And trust me, I've tried.

The gym is within walking distance from my apartment, and once I arrive back home, I check that there are no missed texts or calls from my mom or Grace before plopping down on my gaming chair and starting the first game I see on the screen. Whatever will help me get through the next few hours, I don't care.

No matter how hard I try, however, no amount of pretty graphics or intricate storylines are enough to keep me from glancing at the clock every ten minutes.

Grace's date started nearly an hour ago, and I assume it's going well since I haven't heard from her. I urged her to text me if she needed me for anything at all, and she assured me that she would. She even sent the location of the restaurant just in case, so I'm not worried about her safety. I know she can take care of herself.

I'm worried about what this raging jealousy is doing to me.

Yes, whatever, I'm jealous. There, I said it.

Does it make sense? Not at all, but this train has already gone off the rails, and I can't do shit about it now.

The fact that she seemed annoyed at that flirty cashier earlier isn't helping my case, either. Only a fool would believe she has feelings for me, and that's the last thing my confused heart needs right now.

I still don't want a relationship, not only due to the nightmare that was my previous one, but also because Maddie deserves stability. I can't afford to have women walking in and out of my life. There's this nagging feeling in my chest telling me it's all going to hell sooner than later.

And what then? What happens when the inevitable goes down and I have to move Maddie in with me for good? She is and will always be my priority, and not every woman would be willing to share that spotlight. Not to mention that if the relationship goes well, we'd eventually move in together and my sister would have to move in with us too.

I'm only thinking ahead, analyzing every possible scenario.

None of them look promising.

As much as it pains me, Maddie and I are in for a difficult ride these upcoming years—I feel it deep in my bones—and dragging a girlfriend into it would be unfair to everyone involved.

So yes, no romantic relationships for me anytime soon. Especially not with Grace. I should get a damn grip once and for all.

For the next hour, I pretend to care about whatever is going on in this game. All I've been doing for the past twenty minutes is chopping down wood to get character points, so can you blame me?

At around eight, Aaron logs into the same server so we can talk.

"Hey, man." There's some shifting in the background as he adjusts his chair. "How's it going? I haven't seen you in a while."

He came by the shop a couple of weeks ago to bring Trey and I some new tapas his chef is trying out for The Spoon in exchange for our honest opinion, but other than that I haven't seen much of him.

"Adult life is a pain in the ass. We're always way too busy." I sigh. "How come you're not going out? It's a Saturday night."

"I'm getting old, Cal." He sounds dramatic for a whole second before he bursts out laughing. "Shit, I sound depressing."

I chuckle. "Weren't you eager to settle down?" Aaron might be all over the place most of the time, but he's told me before that if a good woman came along and made him happy, he wouldn't mind planting roots.

"Um, yeah." He coughs. "When the time comes."

"Right."

"You don't?"

My mind goes back to Grace and the feelings I refuse to take flight. They're better off hidden under piles and piles of fear.

"I guess." I clear my throat, hoping he doesn't pick up on my sudden awkwardness. "Not anytime soon, though."

"How come?" I shouldn't be surprised that someone as nosey as Aaron won't drop the subject, and yet...

Choosing to be honest is the best thing I can do. "My sister."

"Shit. Is she living with you or something?"

"Not yet, but I have no doubt it will happen eventually." And it fucking terrifies me. I'm expecting this bubble to burst any moment, yet I know I won't be ready when it finally goes down.

"Have some faith, man. She'll get better." He's talking about my mother, and I don't understand how he could have so much blind trust in her after the shit she's been pulling all these years. It's obvious he doesn't know her like I do.

To the outside world, my mom is nothing but a poor victim of her circumstances. She is, in a way, but the real victim here is her four-year-old daughter. There's no point pretending otherwise. She's a damn adult, for crying out loud. If you fuck up, you own it and change for the better—so far, she's not even acknowledging her mistakes. Done with this heartache of a conversation, I change topics to something related to the game I don't care about that much, but Aaron buys it and goes on to tell me all about the new updates. About an hour later, I fake a few yawns and tell him I'm tired and that I'll stop by the tapas bar next week to grab some dinner.

After checking my phone and finding no texts from Grace, I take a quick shower to clear my mind. I already showered at the gym, but if I don't do something right now, I might go insane.

Why hasn't she texted me with any updates? I hope it's a sign that she's enjoying herself, at least. No matter how much it stings to imagine her laughing with him, kissing him, going home with him—

My phone rings with a call as I'm exiting the shower, and because I'm a worrier at heart and I took it to the bathroom with me, I see right away that it's Grace on the other line.

"Hey. Are you okay?" My heart stops, impatient and worried, as I wait for a response.

"Cal, I'm..." She sighs, and I immediately know something isn't right. "I'm downstairs. Can you buzz me in?"

"What? Wait, yes, give me a second."

It's dark outside and although this is a safe neighborhood, I don't want her to be alone in the street for longer than necessary.

I wrap a clean towel around my waist and rush to let her in. When her small form appears down the hall, I hold my breath. She looks breathtaking with her skin-tight jeans, heeled boots and blazer. However, one glance at her face is all I need to go back into concerned mode.

"Hey." She gives me a shy smile as she enters my apartment. "Sorry, I should've let you know I was coming sooner—" Her next words die in her lips when she looks me up and down and notices I'm practically naked. "Um, am I interrupting something?"

I give her an incredulous look. "I wasn't having sex a minute ago, if that's what you're worried about."

She rolls her eyes but is unable to hide the intense blush on her pale cheeks. "Whatever. I'm sorry anyway for dropping by unannounced."

"Don't apologize. Is everything okay?"

"Kind of," she says, hesitating. "Luke, um, wanted me to go back to his place. I said no."

Relief crashes through me, and I immediately curse myself for it. "Did he make you uncomfortable?" Because I'm ready to break some arms and legs if the situation calls for it.

"No. Well, not on purpose," she says, and when she takes off her blazer revealing a tight black top underneath, I lose my mind a little. "He didn't hide that he wanted us to hook up, and I thought I was ready to take that next step, but..."

She stops herself, and the panic in her eyes makes me react. "Okay, here's what we're going to do," I start, placing a hand on the small of her back and guiding her to the couch. "You stay here while I put on some clothes, and then I'm going to give you some milk and cookies while we talk about this. Sounds good?"

"Milk and cookies?" She arches an amused eyebrow. "You're such a big brother."

"Not to you," I blurt out before I can think the words through. Whatever. I need her to understand there's nothing brotherly about the way I feel about her, no matter how hard I fight it. "I'll be right back."

It takes me a couple of minutes to put on a clean pair of boxers, sweatpants, and a t-shirt, and then I'm off to the promised milk and cookies. Grace is sitting on the couch with a blanket draped over her shoulders when I set everything on the coffee table. "Thanks, Cal."

"It's nothing." I tuck a loose strand of blond hair behind her ear, and she shivers under my touch. "Tell me what went wrong tonight."

She sighs and takes a bite off the first cookie. "Nothing, really. It's me. I'm the problem."

"I know for a fact you're not."

But she shakes her head. "The date itself went great. I had fun. But then he tried to kiss me and asked me to go back to his place, and I couldn't do it."

"He *tried* to kiss you?"

There's a cookie crumb on the corner of her lips, and she looks so damn adorable I should turn away from her. Because I love torturing myself, though, I don't.

"He went for my lips, but I moved my head a little at the last second and he kissed me here instead." She points right at the breadcrumb, and when she touches it, she chuckles and eats it before frowning again. "I wasn't feeling it, and it's got nothing to do with him, honestly. He was the perfect gentleman, and I'm sure many girls would die for a date as great as the one we had, but..."

"Grace, it's okay if you weren't into him. Not every guy you meet will be the guy for you, and that's normal," I assure her, convinced I'm a sick bastard for feeling so comforted that she's here now and not with him.

Her throat bobs as she swallows thickly. "I thought... Never mind."

"No, tell me."

She brushes it off. "It's nothing."

I poke her arm. "It's something, and I want to know what."

After a couple of minutes of silence, she finally lets out a defeated sigh and says, "I'm broken, Cal."

"You're not broken," I tell her without hesitation. "Look at me." She does. "Just because you're ready to take the next step doesn't mean you have to do it with the first guy that buys you dinner."

"I know that." She sends a pointed look my way, but her face falls again a second later. "The thing is, I was ready to do it. Maybe not sleep with him, but kissing, fooling around... I was mentally prepared to cross those lines."

Taking a deep breath, I remind myself that she did none of those things. There's no reason to freak the fuck out right now. "That doesn't mean you're broken, only that it didn't feel like the right moment."

Her gaze is lost somewhere across the living room. "It didn't feel like that time you showed me at the tattoo shop," she whispers.

I recall how I stood between her legs, my hand on her chin, our breaths intertwining, my soul leaving my body. I remember thinking it had never felt like that with anyone else for me, either. And I doubt it will again.

"Grace." I don't mean for my voice to lower, but between the darkness and the soft aura that surrounds her, I can't help myself. "I'm not sure anything else will ever feel like that again."

Her beautiful hazel eyes meet mine, and something unspoken passes between us. A feeling, a jolt of electricity, a truth neither of us want to admit.

"I think I could feel like that again," she murmurs.

My voice drops down an octave. "Yeah?"

Her full lips part, her eyes curious and afraid, her breathing uneven. I need her to say it. I won't move a fucking muscle if she doesn't—

"Cal," she whispers my name like it pains her to do so. My leg brushes hers, and the scent of her sweet perfume blinds all my senses.

"Yes, sunshine," I breathe.

She's so close to me, every fiber and nerve in my body roars back to life. *Stop. What the fuck are you doing? She's your friend. Don't cross any fucking lines.*

Despite the blaring warnings, time stops around us all the same. The air thickens with electricity and it's like my brain knows this is a shit idea, but the damn organ in my chest refuses to listen.

Mine.

She's *mine.*

And I'll be dead before I'm anyone else's.

Leaning in slowly, she holds my heart and my soul in her delicate hands as she whispers, "Show me I'm not broken."

And when I feel the soft pressure of Grace's lips on mine, one of my walls collapses.

# chapter 26

## GRACE

My lips brush his in a shy kiss, testing the waters. For a moment Cal's whole body stiffens, and panic rushes through me like a deadly wave.

I shouldn't have done this. I should've asked him if he wanted to kiss me. I know what it's like to—

"Come here," he whispers roughly against my mouth, pulling away only for a second before kissing me again.

*Oh, my fucking god.*

One of his big hands grabs the back of my neck, pulling me closer until I'm straddling his lap. My hands come to rest on his shoulders, not really knowing what to do with them. It's been years since I kissed someone like this, and it wasn't even like *this* when I did. I'm scared I'll do something he doesn't like, like biting his lip or something. "Relax." He pulls away again, reading my mind. "Just follow my lead."

I shut my brain down and do as he says.

Cal kisses me like he wants to memorize the taste of my lips. Holds me like he wants to remember my skin under his touch forever. The world stops as he parts my mouth with his tongue, deepening the kiss. Every single one of my senses comes alive with each caress of his tongue, soft and gentle against mine, and a small whimper escapes my throat.

My heart jumps with embarrassment. I debate whether to pull away and run off, but then Cal's grip on the back of my neck tightens and he brings me closer. He...likes it?

Something pulls at my heart, screaming at me to lose myself in him. For once, I listen.

When his other hand comes to rest on my waist, sending a jolt of electricity through my spine, my hips rub against his on their own accord. Another throaty sound leaves me at the hardness now pressing against my center, and he gives me a grunt in response but doesn't pull away.

*Oh, god. This is really happening.*

His mouth takes mine in a hungry kiss as I keep rubbing my jean-clad core against the obvious hardness of his length. The hand at my nape lands on my waist, prompting me to keep going.

I pull away, gasping for air, and he rests his forehead against mine. His eyes follow my every movement on top of him, as if he didn't want to miss a second of this.

"That's it. This is where you belong. Here *with me*," he growls. The praise and possessiveness in his tone make my head all dizzy. "You're gonna use me to get yourself off, sunshine? Is that it?"

The pool of wetness between my legs grows at his dirty talk. *Holy shit.*

His big hands—*god, those hands*—give my waist a squeeze, and he stops. "Talk to me, Grace. Tell me what you need from me."

I hold his face between my hands. This sweet, sweet man never fails to make my heart melt. "I only need you to let go," I whisper, my movements slow but not halted. "I'm not fragile. I won't break."

A grunt leaves the back of his throat. "I don't trust myself right now. I don't want to be too rough with you."

There's nothing that would drive me more insane than seeing Cal's rough side in bed, but maybe he's right. Maybe that wouldn't be wise tonight.

"Then simply follow my lead," I repeat his own words.

The doubt in his eyes only lasts for a moment. Our lips find each other's again, and my pace quickens. I'm panting, whimpering at the hardness between my legs that feels so imposing it both terrifies and thrills me.

I throw my head back as my impending orgasm grows and grows inside of me. In an instant, his mouth finds the exposed skin on my neck. Cal kisses, nibbles, sucks on it, and I lose my mind.

"*Fuck,*" he mutters under his breath. "You look like a fucking goddess on top of me. So sweet, so perfect."

His praise is my undoing. I bury my face in his neck, tired and spent, as I struggle to chase my release. He immediately takes over, guiding my hips with his strong hands.

"Come for me, sweetheart," he rasps in my ear. "Rub yourself on my cock and *come.*"

I can't hold it in any longer. With a strained, loud moan, my walls clench and I finally, *finally* come undone.

Holy shit. Did I just dry hump him?

I've pleasured myself before with my fingers, but nothing can compare to orgasming with another person. And he hasn't even touched me.

I hug him around the neck as I slowly regain my breath. He sits still under me except his hand rests on my lower back now, drawing small circles on my covered skin.

When I sit back, his darkened stare meets mine. Raw dominance radiates off him, and I wonder if he's about to unleash the beast I know he keeps hidden. If he's about to make me come again.

I wouldn't be opposed to that, even though I'm so exhausted I could fall asleep in minutes.

Instead, he opens and closes his mouth twice until he finally manages a whisper. "Sorry."

My heartbeat picks up until I'm sure he can hear it through my chest. "Cal, you don't have to apologize. I initiated it." And I don't even want to ask myself why.

His hands are still on my body, as if he wants to let go but can't. "Grace," he starts, and I know I'm going to hate whatever comes out of his mouth next. "We shouldn't have... This isn't..."

"Yeah." I gulp. I would rather break my heart in two before he does. Although it may be too late for that now. "I'm sorry if I crossed a line. I should've asked you for permission first."

"It's all right," he reassures me. "You didn't do anything I didn't like or wanted."

I blink, unsure if I understand what he's saying. He wanted to kiss me? Dry hump me, even? He's thought about it before?

"What if I want to do it again?" I ask, biting on my lower lip. Not as an act of seduction trying to prompt a round two, but because I feel so self-conscious I could scream.

He rubs his eyes, that tattooed hand catching my eye again. "I don't think we should."

My face falls. "Oh."

"Do you still think you're broken?" His question surprises me, but more so does my answer.

"No. I don't think I ever was."

Like a shattered vase that has been glued back together, I'm not broken—I'm simply new.

And the man in front of me is as responsible for this realization as my own healing soul is, even if he's hurting my heart right now.

Instead of pulling away, he brings me closer against his chest and hugs me tightly. Silent confessions pass between us, only to die in each other's hearts. "You're one of the best things that's ever happened to me, Grace," he murmurs. "I want to keep being your friend, but I understand if you can't do that right now."

I feel confused and a little scared, but if there's something clear in my mind it's this. "Of course I still want to be your friend, Cal. Always. That's never going to change."

With a sigh, he lets me go and scoots back on the couch.

"I shouldn't have let it happen."

"I initiated it," I repeat. If only he could get it through his thick skull. "I told you to follow my lead, and you did."

"Yes, but you are..." He doesn't finish his sentence.

"I am what, Cal?" I snap against my better judgment. "Broken? Is that what you think?"

"No," he says firmly. "No, you aren't. Not at all."

"What is it, then?" When I make a move to get off his lap, he lets me go. Standing between his legs, I cross my arms and glare down at him. "You made me feel good, so what if I want to return the favor?"

"You made me feel good, too."

"You know what I'm talking about."

He sighs and drops his gaze to his lap. This isn't how it should've gone. The last person I need to treat me like a fragile doll who can break at any moment is doing exactly that.

And when the seconds tick by and he says nothing, I tell him, "I shouldn't have come here tonight." The lie tastes sour in my lips, and I force myself to move. "I... I'm going home."

He swallows and follows me to the door. "I'm sorry," he tells me again, as if those words could make the pain go away. "I... I can't offer you anything more than my friendship right now. I hope it's enough."

Right. He doesn't do relationships and, to be fair, I don't think I'm ready for one either. Not if I can't have something like this. I nod. "I understand. I don't want anything else. Of course your friendship is enough."

He nods back, and I give him a tight smile and a promise to text him when I get to my dorm before disappearing down the hall and into the cold night. It helps that I can barely feel a thing right now, my face and hands included, or else I'd be freezing to death.

Is this what heartbreak does to you?

* * *

I'm not ignoring Cal.

It's just that I haven't seen or talked to him in three days, but it's purely a coincidence.

He texted me earlier today asking if I was all right, I said yes, and that was it. He didn't stop by The Dance Palace to pick up his sister, either, which I guess is good news. It means his mother is taking care of her daughter, as she should be doing.

Still, it doesn't mean I don't miss him. It doesn't mean this feels right.

I'm as dumb as they come. I could drop by Inkjection right now if I wanted to, and he would be there. He wouldn't refuse to see me. We could talk. I could apologize again for being distant these past few days, and we would go back to our regular scheduled programming.

The only issue with that plan is that I can't face him right now, not without dying of embarrassment and heartache.

Because on top of being dumb, I'm also irrational. The whole package, I know.

He doesn't want a relationship. I know that, and to be fair I'm not sure I want one either. My curiosity about sex and pleasure is just that—a sign that I'm on the path to healing. It doesn't have to come with a marriage contract.

I'm just confused.

Confused, and a whole lot of heartbroken.

Hiding my head in my hands, I let out the most dramatic sigh known to humanity, and it earns me a snort from somewhere behind me.

"I take it the book's not going well?" Em asks.

I grunt and stare one last time at my blank Word document before shutting my laptop for the night. "I can't do this. Maybe I'm not meant to be an author."

The covers shuffle around as my best friend gets out of bed. "Bullshit. You're not inspired right now, that's all it is." She sounds so convinced I almost believe her. Keyword: almost.

"It's late, Em. Why aren't you asleep?" I ask, changing the subject. She's usually knocked out cold by this time during the week.

She holds up her phone with one hand. "Carly hooked up with Laila last night, and she wants to tell me all the juicy details in person. I'm waiting until she texts me to go to her room. You don't mind, do you?"

"Of course not." I'm glad Em is going to her room instead of her coming here, or else I would be looking at a three-hour gossiping session.

As Em yawns and stretches her legs, I realize something. "You didn't grab dinner at the hall tonight. Amber was asking for you."

I can't tell if her shoulders freeze with tension or if I'm seeing things. "I was out with a friend," she says casually enough, but there's something off about her voice. I just can't pinpoint what. "We went to The Spoon, actually."

"Oh, cool. Did you see my cousin?"

She plays with the fluffy hem of her pink blanket.

"Yeah, he was around."

"I don't get why he insists on being there almost every night," I muse out loud. "It's not like he helps around much when it's crowded."

"He does help the staff most of the time," Emily blurts out. "Bringing out food and drinks, and things like that."

"How do you know that?"

"No reason." She shrugs. "He told me once, when I asked."

It makes sense. Emily is too nosey—*curious*, as she'd put it—for her own good, and the fact that she's never afraid to ask questions or start a conversation is something I admire a lot. I'm always worried whether I'm being an inconvenience, so I'd rather keep quiet.

I'm about to say something else when someone knocks at the door. "Must be Carly." Em reluctantly gets out of bed to answer it.

As I turn back to my desk, debating whether to open my laptop again and face the disappointment and insecurity, my best friend's voice fills the room again. "Um, Grace? It's not Carly at the door."

"Huh?"

When I turn around, Cal is standing on the other side of the threshold, in all his tattooed glory.

*Holy shit.*

"Cal?" I hurry out of my chair and practically shove Em out of the way. I look nervously around the deserted hallway before grabbing his hand and yanking him inside. "You can't be here this late at night! How did you even get in?"

He looks around Em and I's shared dorm room, and it hits me that he's been here once before—to fix Em's wobbly furniture. Our dorm might be spacious enough for two decent-sized beds, two wardrobes and two desks, but his enormous size makes it look like a tiny shoe box. He would dwarf my bed for sure if he lied on it, and great— now I'm imagining Cal on my bed and my cheeks are already tomato red.

"Trey's brother is the security guard at your building," he explains. I guess it's really that simple. When he finally looks down at me, my breath hitches. "I, um, came here to talk to you. But I can leave."

Em clears her throat behind us, one hand already on the doorknob. "I'm going to Carly's room. Text me."

I nod, and she leaves. Cal is still waiting for an answer, I realize, so I sit down on my bed and pat the spot next to me. "We can talk."

I was right about him dwarfing my furniture. The mattress squeaks under his weight, and why the hell am I finding our size difference so hot right now? I open my mouth before my mind can drag me to the exact place it's been stuck in for the past three days—our kiss. And our dry humping. *God.*

"What did you want to talk about?"

Cal doesn't beat around the bush. "Are you mad at me?"

"A little," I tell him honestly. "I needed...time to think, I guess."

"About what?" He turns his head to look at me, and before I can help myself my fingers tuck away the unruly strand of dark hair that always falls on his forehead.

I put my hand back on my lap, where it's safe. "Our kiss confused me," I admit, hoping he doesn't take it the wrong way. "Not because I want you to be my boyfriend or anything. It... It left me with this weird feeling inside. And then we did...that other thing, and I wanted to do more, but you refused. I get why, and I'm sorry for pressuring you."

A beat of silence passes between us. "I was afraid I'd ruined everything between us."

"Cal, no." I take his warm hands between my cold ones. "You know why I've been distant? I was embarrassed."

"Why?"

"Your rejection threw me off. I was scared you'd see me again and want nothing to do with me."

He shakes his head and squeezes my hands in a comforting gesture. "Never, Grace. Listen to me, we're adults, all right? I don't do petty drama or miscommunication shit, and I know you don't either. So, let's talk about stuff like this like adults from now on."

"I like that idea." I smile. "Are we good, then?"

"We've always been. I want to keep being your friend—if

you'll still have me."

My lips twitch. "Don't be dumb. Of course we're friends."

He pulls me towards him, and I fall onto his lap. My arms wrap around his neck on their own accord, and my heart is about to bungee jump out of my chest. Cal doesn't seem to mind this new position one bit, though. "That isn't the only reason I came here tonight."

Yes, my heart is definitely not doing well right now. Keeping an arm around me, his other hand goes to the pocket of his jacket, and he pulls out a bunch of papers.

"For you."

Unfolding them, I blink once, twice, not sure if the darkness of the room is making me see things. "Is this...?" I look at the first drawing, then the second, and the third. A lump forms in my throat.

"Gracie and Sammy." He rests his chin on my shoulder, and I feel his heart beating as fast as mine when he presses his chest to my back.

I'm at a loss for words. Between my shaking fingers are three stunning sketches of the main characters of my non-existent novel, and the only thing I want to do right now is to kiss him again. And then cry.

The drawings aren't colored, but they're detailed to a tee. Gracie wears her short hair on two low pigtails and holds a big magnifying glass in one of her hands. Next to her, Sammy has a big pair of chunky glasses on, ready to take notes with his pen and notebook. They both sport the whole detective gear—cool hats and even cooler raincoats with belts and everything.

The first drawing is of them doing some heroic pose that I can already see on the cover of the book; in the second, Gracie is bending down, looking at something with her magnifying glass while Sammy takes notes; and in the third, they're taking pictures while hiding behind a bush.

I can't even begin to form a comprehensible thought. "Do you like them?" he asks in a soft voice, as if he were scared that I would actually hate them.

Still holding the three sketches in my hand, I turn around and throw myself at him. He hugs me back, laughing as he falls backwards. "Should I take it as a yes?"

"Take it as a hell yes!" I press a loud kiss on his cheek. "This is the best thing I've ever seen, Cal. Holy shit. When did you make these? They're so different from the tattoos you draw for your clients."

He chuckles. "I can pretty much draw any style. And I finished them today. They're not much."

Realizing I'm still on top of him, I sit back on the bed and marvel at the little detectives again. "These are amazing, Cal. I don't even know what to say."

He smiles. "You don't have to say anything."

I don't want to cry, but it's getting harder to keep the tears at bay. Everything he does for me while asking for nothing in return is almost overwhelming—in the best way. My heart screams at me, demanding to stop this confusion. I wish I could.

"I... I haven't talked to my professor yet," I admit in a quiet voice, and now I feel terrible. What if he's worked on these beautiful sketches for nothing?

"Don't worry about it." I feel his hand on my back, tracing soothing patterns with his fingers. "If you can't put them in your book, you can use them for inspiration. I'll make as many as you want. And I'm thinking they could have a badass pet helping them with their mystery-solving."

I'm not breathing anymore. I swear I'm not. "That's a great idea," I manage to let out. "What pet would you want?"

"How about a dog?" he suggests, his fingers still soothing my growing nerves. "He can catch the bad guys and smell for clues while looking cute."

I don't think this man is real. "I'd like that. A lot."

"I'll start working on it tomorrow, then."

"I don't deserve you," I mumble against his chest as I hug him again, unable to stay away. If I could hold onto him forever like a clingy koala, I would.

"I'm the one who doesn't deserve you, sunshine," he whispers back, and his voice sounds almost pained.

That isn't true, but right now I don't trust myself to carry on with this conversation without bursting into tears, so I change topics. "Do you want to stay and watch a movie?"

He tucks a strand of hair behind my ear. "I want to, but Trey's brother warned me it would be best if I got out of here as soon as possible. I could get you into trouble."

"Right. It makes sense."

"And I guess your roommate would want to come back to bed," he says, smirking.

"Oh, don't worry about her. She left to gossip with a friend, so she's all right."

"Still, I should get back." He gives me an apologetic look. "Vegan food truck tomorrow, though?"

We agree to meet after the shop closes, and he gives me a faint forehead kiss before leaving. The heat of his touch lingers on my skin as I text Emily, and when she comes back an hour later it's still there. I don't think it'll ever leave, and the thought is nothing short of comforting.

Emily takes one look at me as she gets into bed and deadpans. "He's totally in love with you."

I don't answer. I wouldn't know what to say.

# chapter 27

## GRACE

I can't do this. Not to myself, and not to him.

Luke has been nothing but a gentleman. He deserves better than to be led on by a girl who can't stop thinking about how right it feels...with somebody else.

My feelings for Cal have been changing for the past weeks and although I don't know what to make of that yet, there's still some decency left in me. Enough to talk to Luke, at least.

However, I can't bring myself to tell him over the phone. Come on, that's just cruel.

So even though guilt eats me alive as I ask him to meet for coffee outside of campus, deep down I know this is the right thing to do. Because even if Cal and I will never be more than friends, I still have to call things off with Luke before the situation escalates and he gets his hopes up. He'll never make me feel what Cal does.

It's not like I'm cheating on anybody, but it kind of feels like it. Luke took me on two dates, and he was nothing short of fun and charming, but this whole thing is...wrong. It's a recipe for disaster, because I'll never be able to fully commit to him, focus on loving him and developing a real relationship with him when Cal is the sole owner of my thoughts.

Where does this leave me? Surely, Luke can't be the only person I'll ever want to date, so what happens when I meet someone else, and this exact scenario repeats itself? Will I never get over Cal?

My head starts spiraling out of control. Luke must be only a few minutes away. There's no easy way out of this. He's probably excited about our third date, hopeful even about moving things forward, but I'm here to break things off instead.

Luke gets to the café just in time, and I feel like the worst person on the planet when he plants a small kiss on my cheek as hello. "How was your week?" He gives me a sweet smile as we make our way to the counter to place our orders. He looks so oblivious I want to rip my heart out just to stop feeling so damn guilty.

"Uneventful," I lie. It has been eventful, all right. But he doesn't need to know about Cal kissing me and making me come with our clothes on, does he?

Luke keeps the conversation going for the most part, talking about his classes and some funny stories about the lacrosse team. The moment he starts rambling about this new Greek restaurant we need to try out, though, I know it's time.

Enough of dragging out his hopes. It's cruel, it's unnecessary and, to be fair, telling him won't be the end of the world. I'm not the love of his life and clearly, he isn't mine either.

We'll both be fine by this time next week. I think. I hope.

"Luke," I start slowly, a soft smile on my lips. I remind myself to be gentle about this. We may be in a public place, and he might seem sane enough, but I know first-hand that a man who feels rejected is a dangerous man. "There's something I wanted to talk to you about."

He tenses at that. "What is it?"

Breathing in and out, I keep convincing myself that this is the right thing even if my little pep talk doesn't make things any easier.

"I love spending time with you," I say, because it's true.

He's a great guy, just...not for me.

"Okay." He nods, probably sensing where this conversation

is going.

This is it. I can do it. He won't yell at me or hit me. He's not like that.

"But I don't think we could...you know, work out as a couple in the long run."

The background noise around us gets a lot louder once the words leave my mouth. My throat goes dry, my palms become sweaty, and I don't think I've ever felt worse.

Luke seems to genuinely like me, and I'm breaking things up before they even start because of what? Because of Cal? My best friend who won't ever become anything more, no matter how badly I want it?

There, I said it.

*Fine.*

I want more between Cal and I. Whatever there is between us, it feels...wrong not to explore it.

But us together as a couple will never happen. There'll be no wedding, no babies, no happily ever after, nothing. It's not in the cards.

"I understand," Luke says after a small eternity. His voice is calm, but his face has visibly dropped. "Can I ask why?"

"I'm not ready for something more between us," I opt for, which isn't exactly a lie. I can't bring myself to tell him about Cal, not when we'll never be together anyway. "But you're a great guy, and I really enjoy our time together. I'd love to keep being your friend. If you want to."

"Of course." His excitement has clearly worn off, but I appreciate that he's taking it so well. "I'd love to be your friend, Grace. I hope you still want to beta read my crime novel."

"Are you kidding? I'd love to! How is the writing process going?"

We stay at the café a little longer, catching up as if nothing had happened. Maybe I've imagined the whole thing, and he wasn't that interested in dating me in the first place. That thought brings me the slightest amount of relief, so I selfishly cling to it.

When we part ways, he gives me a hug and promises that there are no hard feelings on his end and that he'll keep coming to the thrift store on Saturdays to see me. Maybe it's because I expected a disaster and ended up with a friend, but instead of going home, I knock on Professor Danner's office twenty minutes later. Even though I didn't schedule an appointment, I know these are his office hours and sure enough, luck is on my side today.

"Grace! Good to see you, please take a seat," he greets me with his usual wide grin. "Are you here to talk about your final project?"

I take a seat in front of his desk. "I am, if you have a minute to spare."

"I've got at least ten, so ask away."

Immediately at ease by Danner's easygoing attitude, I start. "After spending some time going over a couple of ideas, I've finally decided to write a children's book."

"That's wonderful!" He reclines on his chair, interested. "Did you take a look at the minimum word count? What's your age group target?"

"Yes, I'm keeping the word count in mind, and my target would be readers from ages seven to ten."

He nods. "Sounds good to me."

That manages to ease some of my nerves. "The reason I'm here is because I have an idea for the book, but the guide you provided doesn't cover it, so I wanted to check with you first. Would illustrations be allowed as part of the project?"

Danner hums and pinches his lips, considering. "Would they serve a real purpose to your story?"

I don't miss a beat. "All children's books include illustrations nowadays. If I sent my manuscript to a traditional publishing house, I wouldn't need to include a cover or any illustrations, but those are some key aspects to take into account when self-publishing. My intention for this project is to make it as realistic as possible."

He stares at me with a frown, and my hands start sweating when I can't read his expression. "Well, I made it clear that you have free rein to turn in your manuscript in whichever way you prefer. Covers are optional and won't get you a higher grade, as mentioned in the guide, so I guess illustrations would fall into the same category. Are you drawing them yourself?"

"No. A friend volunteered for the job." I give him a weak smile and try to control my blushing. Just thinking about Cal coming to my dorm to show me his sketches, sitting on my bed and pulling me into his lap... I clear my throat. "I'll of course credit them in the copyright page as I would in a real book."

"Sounds like you've got it all covered, then," he resolves. "Feel free to include any illustrations you want in a way that makes sense to you, but know that your grade won't be influenced by the aesthetics, as you kids put it nowadays. I'm here to critique your writing, and that's it."

"Thank you. I understand." My shoulders relax, and I breathe a little easier knowing I'll be able to put together the story that I want, however I want. Hence why Danner is one of my favorite professors, and I'll miss his guidance after I graduate. He understands that writing is a feeling, and when it comes to your own book you must follow your heart.

And my heart is telling me that Gracie and Sammy deserve some cute illustrations to go along their adventures.

"Glad I could help, Grace. Take care." He smiles before going back to his laptop.

I'm so excited about the news that I don't want to tell Cal over text. Instead, I take advantage of this rush of motivation and walk to Inkjection to tell him in person. He might be busy with a client, but I can wait.

As I make my way to the parlor, I send a quick text to Em. She fell in love with the sketches right away and threatened to egg Danner's car if he didn't allow me to put them in the book. I guess my professor not only saved my sanity today, but his vehicle too.

When I spot the shop's sign at the end of the block, I start walking a little faster. It's dumb to feel this excited about telling him, I know, but I can't help the smile that takes over my whole face as I imagine how happy he's going to be for me too.

But the second I stop in front of the shop and look inside, my smile falls. And so does my heart.

Laughing, Cal leans into a tall woman with a dark bob and pulls her into a hug. The woman wraps her arms around his back, smiling at something he says. I'm frozen in place, unable to look away but also dying to unsee this.

Why do I feel like throwing up right now? Why is my chest being ripped apart?

Cal shakes his head with laughter one last time before lifting his gaze, eyes colliding with mine.

I don't smile. I don't wave at him.

I only turn around, my heart clogging up my throat, and I leave.

# chapter 28

## CAL

"Shit, Sophia. I haven't seen you in what, a year?"

She pushes her rolling case to one of the tattooing stations at the front of the shop and plants her hands on her hips, smiling so widely I can see all her bright white teeth. "Insane, I know. But in my defense, it's been super busy at the shop for the past few months."

"That's always good to hear. How are Kevin and Lance?" Sophia has been a family friend since I was a teenager. She used to work with my mother at a sketchy road diner outside Warlington before moving to Boston, where she's been tattooing now for the past few years—and doing a damn good job at it. Seriously, her technique is insane.

She was the one who convinced me to move to Boston all those years ago to learn the ropes with her. I must have been no older than fifteen when she saw my sketches for the first time and thought I had potential. In a strange way, I owe her my whole career.

Now she's thirty-eight and married to her long-time boyfriend Kevin, who she has a little boy with. Despite not having seen her for so long, she looks exactly like I remembered—black hair that barely reaches her chin, equally black eyes and tanned skin.

"Lance is going through the terrible twos right now, so not great." She winces. "Is it bad that I feel relieved to be away from home for a few days? Because I totally do."

I chuckle. "I'm sure Kev will manage."

She shakes her head. "Those two are dangerous together, Cal. Trust me, you're lucky Maddie is such a sweet angel. Boys are unhinged. If you ever want kids, ask the universe for a little girl."

My head goes straight to my sister, and how I'm raising her in all the ways that count. Would having my own children be similar?

I've never thought about it much. Growing up in a fucked-up family, the idea of creating one of my own someday rarely crossed my mind.

For one, I've never had a father figure to look up to. Her boyfriend at the time got my mother pregnant when they were sixteen, and he fled before I was born. I've never known him, and thirty years later I still don't want to. He could be dead for all I know. Who the fuck cares?

And when I was a teenager, my mother became a shadow of the strong woman she once was. My uncle's death took a toll on her that she never fully recovered from, and I have to live with that. We all do.

Then my sister came along, a surprise pregnancy my mom never saw coming. She didn't think she could have another child at forty, but she wanted Maddie from the moment she found out she was growing inside of her.

When her dependency became alarmingly worse and Pete did nothing for his own family, I stepped into the main caretaker role without thinking much of it—all I knew was that I loved Maddie and I'd sacrifice anything for her to grow up happily and safely.

I know all about potty training, schooling, play dates, kiddie foods, doctor appointments, princesses, and mermaids, so I guess having my own child wouldn't be much different from what I'm already going through with my sister. Especially if I end up having a girl.

And now I can't stop thinking about it.

Against my will, my traitorous brain shows me a nitid image of Maddie holding a pink bundle in her arms. She'd be so excited to be an aunt, especially to little girl. Maddie would hold her carefully in her small arms, in awe at how small the baby was, how beautiful.

And I'd fall in love all over again—with my sister, with my wife, with my daughter. She'd have her mother's blond hair and delicate skin, a spitting image of Gra—

*No.*

*No. No. No.*

*What the fuck am I doing?*

"Cal?" Sophie's voice pulls me out of my head. "Where did you go, hon?"

My heart is hammering inside my chest and my palms are sweating. Wiping them on the rough fabric of my jeans, I shake my head. "Nowhere, sorry. What were you saying?"

She smirks knowingly. "My first client is coming at two, right?"

"Yes. Right."

Pushing Grace and a future I have no right to imagine out of my head, I force myself to focus on the woman in front of me. Sophia is here for a few days as a guest tattoo artist at Inkjection, and I want to catch up with her after all these months apart. I should be looking forward to that, not...not marriage and babies with my best friend.

Seriously, what the fuck?

After Sophia gets settled at her booth, we come to the front so I can show her how to work the laptop. It's still early in the morning and she's got a few hours to spare. She tells me she's going to stop by her hotel to take a shower, and after the shop closes, I invite her over to grab dinner at The Spoon with our friends. She hasn't seen Trey in a while either, so I'm sure they'll want to catch up.

"How's your mother?"

The question shouldn't catch me off-guard, considering they were close friends once and she always asks me about her, yet it startles me anyway. Sophia crosses her arms in front of her chest, visibly uncomfortable with the conversation but wanting to find out all the same. I don't think my mother's reached out to her since she left Warlington, but Sophia's always kept in touch with me.

"She's still the same." I scratch the back of my head. "But I guess that's good. Things could've taken an ugly turn."

She frowns, pursing her lips. "I really thought having Maddie would change things. I'm sorry it didn't, honey. I have no doubts that she loves you both. I hope one day she learns to love herself, too."

And that is the problem, isn't it? Granted, my mother doesn't bring up her personal issues with me, but one could spot her lack of self-confidence and self-love from a mile away. Having a man abandon you and your unborn child tends to do that to a person. Not to mention rat-ass Pete, who may not be abusive towards her, but it's painfully evident he doesn't love her or my sister. Not like a boyfriend and a father should.

"How are you handling things with your sister?" she asks me, concern written all over her features.

I sigh. "We're doing okay, considering how fucked-up this whole situation is. I take care of most of her expenses, visit her every day, and she still stays at my place at least once a week. She's a happy kid. For now, anyway."

"You're doing a great job at providing her with a stable and loving home, Cal. And I'm proud of you for that." She strokes my arm affectionately and squeezes my wrist. I'd forgotten how touchy she's always been, and one of her crushing hugs right now would be more than welcomed.

"I'm scared of fucking up," I confess. She's a mother, so I know she understands. "Maybe not now, but when she's older. I don't want her growing up hating her dad, our mother, or me."

"I assure you she won't." She holds my hands tightly between her own and gives them another squeeze. "She'll grow up to be a bright, beautiful lady and she'll only love you more when she finds out everything you're doing for her. Your mother will get better one day, too. I'm sure of it."

I want to believe her. I really do, with all my heart, but it gets more difficult every day.

"You're a good man, and you're doing so well for yourself. Look around." She gestures to the shop. "I'm sure the ladies are lining up to snatch you away."

That manages to get a sincere snort out of me. "I'm out of the market, I fear."

"Oh? Met anyone special?" She wiggles her eyebrows.

I shake my head, smiling. "It's complicated. I'll tell you about it later."

"Promise, or I'll team up with Trey to tattoo a penis right in the middle of that forehead."

I burst out laughing. "Ah, I missed you, Sophia." Smiling, I pull her into a hug.

"I missed your secretive ass, too."

Shaking my head with laughter, I say, "I promise I'll tell you later. Believe it or not, a penis on my forehead doesn't sound too appealing right now."

She chuckles, and an invisible pull forces me to turn my head. Right there on the other side of the door, is Grace.

I'm about to let go of Sophia and wave at her, tell her to come in, anything. But she sucks in a breath, face falling, and leaves.

"Hey, you okay?" Sophia asks, noticing how tense my whole body has turned. My eyes are glued to the outside of the shop, wondering if I've imagined it all. "Cal?"

"Sorry. I... I saw a friend."

Sophia turns her head towards the street. "Like...a special friend? Because you look pale as shit right now, honey."

"Something like that." I swallow. "Hey, do you mind if I send a text real quick?"

She gives me a knowing smile. "Don't worry about me. I need to leave for the hotel anyway. Go talk to this friend." With a wave goodbye and a "See you in a few hours" she exits the shop. I pull my phone out of my back pocket before she even closes the door behind her. There's a nagging feeling in my chest that barely lets me breathe.

> **Were you at the front of the parlor just now?**

She doesn't answer right away. Not like I expected her to. If you asked me to capture her face the moment our eyes met, I'd know exactly what emotions to translate to the paper—confusion, sadness, anger. But I don't understand why she would feel any of them.

Is it possible that she thinks...? Surely not. She can't possibly believe I'm involved with Soph... Right?

I try to picture how it would've looked from the outside. A man and a woman laughing and hugging shouldn't raise any alarms, yet I'm sure that's what it did in Grace's mind.

Is she mad at me because she thinks I have a girlfriend and I didn't tell her? Or is it something else?

My head is about to fucking explode when she finally texts back twenty minutes later.

> **Yeah. I wanted to talk to you but you were busy.**

And now I'm overthinking the tone of her message. It's only a text, for fuck's sake. There's no way I can tell her mood through it.

> I have an appointment in 5, but we can grab lunch together?

> I have plans. Maybe another time.

Yeah, she's pissed. That much is fucking obvious, and not only because she's now adding periods at the end of her texts.

If she were any other woman, I would tell her to piss off and move on with my life. I don't do drama. Yet I can't bring myself to throw in the towel when it comes to Grace. If she's hurt, I want to take her pain away and reassure her that everything is fine. I'm not lying to her nor am I seeing anyone behind her back.

Not when she's the only one in my mind.

And if it takes begging and chasing for her to understand, then I fucking will.

# chapter 29

# GRACE

"I will literally drag you down the street, Grace Allen. Don't try me." Em rarely uses my full name, so when she does, I know I'm in trouble. She reminds me of Dad sometimes, which usually makes me snicker. Not tonight.

"I'd pay to watch that," Amber chimes in.

"And I'd pay for some chicken tenders right about now, so hurry the hell up," Céline urges with no short amount of moodiness. She gets cranky when she's hungry.

The only reason I keep walking instead of running back to the dorm is because I consider myself a good friend, and frankly Céline scares the crap out of me when she's hangry. So yes, I walk, but I also drag my feet all the way to Aaron's restaurant because I'm pissed off and I need everyone to know. The soles of my boots would give me the middle finger right now if they could.

I didn't want to go out, all right? Granted, they promised me we were only going for a nice dinner, no wild parties afterwards or anything too crazy, but my heart isn't in it. Staying under my covers while listening to sad playlists and crying over how miserable my life is sounds way more appealing if you ask me. Sue me.

Not so deep down, I know I'm acting like a petulant child. It's just that I can't bring myself to care anymore.

So, what if I saw Cal hugging and laughing with another woman, a beautiful woman at that, and it made me want to throw up? Am I not allowed to feel like shit?

As I reluctantly follow my friends to The Spoon, I realize three excruciating things.

One—that woman, with her arm tattoos and pierced nose, looks exactly like his type. I don't even know if he has a type, but if he does then it's her. Undoubtedly.

Two—I like Cal. As in...I *like* him. As in, "I'd climb him like a tree and cuddle him all day afterwards" kind of like.

And three—I'm fucked, and not in the way I'm hoping for.

Falling for a friend is bad enough, but falling for a friend who has made it crystal clear that he isn't interested in a relationship? Yeah, that's bad.

And all right, we kissed once and it was everything I imagined it would be and more, but I guess it meant nothing. Our relationship isn't going to change.

"Come on, babe." Em links her arm through mine, urging me to walk faster. "Dinner with the girls is exactly what you need right now. You'll have enough time to sulk tomorrow."

"I'm pathetic, aren't I?"

"Not at all." She surprises me by stopping in the middle of the sidewalk. Her eyes are hard on me as she says, "Are you overreacting a bit? Totally, but you're not pathetic. He told you he wasn't in a relationship, and I don't think he's lying. That woman is probably just a friend, you'll see. Cool off tonight and talk to him tomorrow."

"I'm so embarrassed." I let out a heavy breath. Might as well confess it. "What do I even tell him? That I was jealous because I thought he was seeing someone else?"

She shrugs. "Sounds honest to me."

I give her an unimpressed look. "And then what? I tell him I felt jealous because I'm the one he should be seeing?"

"That's a solid plan right there, babe."

"You're kidding, right?" She has to be. That, or she's gone

insane in the past two minutes.

"Listen, Grace, I'll say this once and you'd better get it through your thick skull, okay? That man isn't seeing anyone because he *likes* you. And frankly, it's painful to watch him give you those puppy eyes when you're not looking because he's so damn obvious!" She throws her arms up in exasperation.

But I'm not buying it. "Don't you think I would've noticed his crush on me if he had one? We see each other pretty much every day. He can't pretend for that long."

"Oh, sweetie, he's not pretending. You're just blind as hell."

I think Emily is being too optimistic. There's no way I haven't noticed Cal's crush on me (if he even has one, which I highly doubt). Jeez, I'm not *that* naïve. I know when someone is interested in me, let alone when that someone is such a close friend. The signs should be right there under my nose, and they aren't, hence there's no crush. Simple as that, easy math.

Sure, he kissed me back, so he might be somewhat attracted to me. It doesn't mean he feels anything deeper. He's made himself very clear.

I'm still ruminating over it as I step into the warmth of the restaurant behind my friends. Shrugging my coat off, I notice right away that it's packed—no surprise there. But then I do a quick scan of the room, and my whole body freezes when my eyes collide with a pair of black orbs, as deep as the night. Eyes I've gazed into more times than I can count.

"You have to be kidding me," I mutter under my breath, but loud enough for Em to hear.

"What is it?" She follows my gaze, and I know the second she spots him because she says, "Oh."

Yeah. *Oh.*

Sitting at one of the tables with a bunch of friends is none other than Cal. Around him, I recognize Trey and my own cousin, who apparently chose not to help the staff tonight in favor of hanging out. And sure enough, right on Cal's left sits the woman he hugged at the shop.

I would be lying if I said it doesn't feel like a knife to the gut.

"Come on, let's sit down." I'm so numb all over I barely feel Emily tugging at my hand and dragging me to the other side of the restaurant.

My back is turned to Cal, a small miracle. I tell my friends I don't care what they order—I know the menu by heart, and I like everything—and eventually the food arrives, but it's not enough to distract me and neither is whatever conversation around me.

The back of my head tingles, as if someone was drilling their eyes directly into it. I know he saw me when I walked in, so I have a fair idea whose eyes they could be. I don't turn around.

"G!" I feel his hand on my shoulder before I see him. Aaron gives me the brightest of smiles as he moves his hand up and squeezes the spot between my neck and my shoulder. "I didn't know you were coming tonight. How are you ladies enjoying the food?"

"It was a last-minute thing," I mutter, doubting he can ever hear me over the loud chatter around us.

It's Em who says, "It sucks, as usual."

I choke on my water, but Aaron doesn't hesitate. "I've got something else you can suck on later if you want."

"Aaron! What the fuck?!" I slap his arm harder than I probably should in front of his employees, but his only response is a deep belly laugh. When I look at my best friend, she's fighting to suppress a smile.

"It's all good." Em waves it off.

"Well, this is interesting," Amber says, propping her chin on her palm. She points between my cousin and our friend. "I didn't know you two were close."

Yeah, I didn't either. I know they exchange hellos when they see each other in passing and they've talked a couple of times at parties, but this level of...of familiar comfort is throwing me off. I'm not sure I want to find out what it is about, either.

"We aren't." Em pops a bite of Spanish omelet into her mouth.

"Cal is here, by the way." Aaron changes topics drastically, although it doesn't faze me. He does this all the time. It makes sense, seeing how he hates small talk.

"Oh, okay," is the only reply I offer him.

Of course, it earns me a curious look, and I lower my gaze to Céline's chicken tenders. I would lose my arm of I even *attempted* to touch one. "Are you fighting or something?" Aaron asks me in a low voice, close to my ear.

"No," I mutter. We're really not. I'm an idiot. A very jealous one.

"Huh. Cal is acting all grumpy too, so I thought... Never mind. It was good to see you girls, I'm going back to my food before it gets cold." He smiles and gives my shoulder one last squeeze.

"Don't choke," Emily offers without lifting her gaze from her plate.

Again, my cousin doesn't miss a beat. "That's your thing, sweetheart. I wouldn't wanna steal it."

"Okay, enough," I snap. Aaron is already on his way to his friends, laughing. I turn to Em. "What was all that about?"

She shrugs. "Don't know what you're talking about."

I pin her down with what I think is my best death stare, but she only bats her eyelids at me like the not-so-innocent friend she is and goes back to her food. Okay then.

Almost half an hour goes by with chatter around me, coming from my friends and the various crowds scattered all over the restaurant. I barely speak ten words in total. I'm thinking about how great of a job Aaron is doing at creating such a dynamic and cozy space at The Spoon when Amber's words freeze me over for the second time tonight. "Phew, are those the guys from Inkjection over there? They're hot as hell."

I'm not even hungry anymore, but I stuff my mouth with a mozzarella stick so I have an excuse to stay quiet. Luckily, Em saves me from having to add to the conversation. "Why, Amber? Interested?"

My blond friend smirks. "I wouldn't mind enjoying their company for a night or two. I mean... Look at them, jeez. Do you think I should shoot my shot?"

I clear my throat—it's either that or choking on my food. I have no issues with Amber hooking up with Trey. I think they'd look quite cute together, actually. Cal, on the other hand...

Over my dead body.

He's mine.

"I'm going to the bathroom," I decide, keeping my gaze down as I leave the table so they can't see the lie in my eyes. So mature of me to pretend to need the restroom to escape an awkward conversation, I know.

What can I say? I'm resourceful like that.

In all honesty, I don't hold it against Amber to find Cal hot (who doesn't?), but today isn't the day to hear about it. Seeing him at The Spoon, sitting a few tables away from me, is painful enough. Another reminder that he's out of reach is the last thing I need right now.

My heart is a goddamn mess as I descend the stairs to the basement area of the restaurant, where the bathrooms and a single storage room are located.

Cal is my friend, one of the best I've ever had, and I'll have to talk to him eventually. I want to, that's the thing. Pure embarrassment clouds my judgment, but the longer I ignore it the worse it will get. What if he decides I'm not worthy of his time and moves on? It would be entirely my fault and—

As I'm closing the bathroom door behind me, a strong hand

comes up above my head and holds it open. I see his reflection in the mirror in front of me, and goosebumps break out all over my skin.

"What are you doing?" My voice comes out hoarse as Cal steps in the small but clean bathroom and closes the door. *Locks it.* "Cal?"

"We need to talk," he says, staring down at me with a mix of stiffness and softness that does nothing but confuse me even more.

I arch an amused eyebrow despite the tension in the air. "In a restroom?"

"I'd talk to you in the middle of a dumpster if it came to it." The resolve in his voice makes me shiver.

I swallow. "Okay. So talk."

He takes a step forward, his chest almost brushing mine, but I don't move. His dark eyes see right through my soul as he half-whispers, "Tell me why you're mad at me. Again."

"I'm not mad at you," I say, but we both know it's a big fat lie.

"Don't give me that crap," he growls, getting closer until he hovers over me. "Tell me what the hell we're doing, sunshine, because my patience is running thin."

Now is definitely not the time to notice how hot he looks when he's angry.

For a second I think of making another joke about this whole talking-in-a-bathroom situation before I take in the sternness of his face. This isn't the right time—this is the time to put my big girl pants on and face the music, whatever the outcome might be.

*Wherever you're planted, bloom with grace.*

Well, I hope I can bloom somewhat graciously in The Spoon's unisex bathroom.

"I was jealous," I admit, my eyes never leaving his. All or nothing, right? "I didn't know you were seeing someone."

A shadow crosses his gaze. "I'm not," he drops his voice.

"Sophia is a family friend and a mentor, the one who introduced me to tattooing. I've never been with her in that way nor am I planning to."

"Why should I believe you?" I challenge him. Wrong move.

His hand comes around my neck, holding me tightly but not tight enough to hurt. He lowers his forehead to mine, his heavy breaths meeting my skin. "Because I haven't stopped thinking about those little moans you made while rubbing yourself on my cock, that's why."

My breath hitches, his possessiveness making me rub my legs together in search of that friction nothing and nobody but him can replicate.

"You didn't want us to do it again," I point out in a hoarse whisper.

His fingers squeeze my neck a little tighter. "You're poking the beast, sweetheart," he warns, but all I want is to make him lose control. "Tell me why you were jealous," he demands.

If there's one thing my romance novels have taught me, besides all about sex, is that keeping important things from people you care about always ends up in a big (avoidable) disaster. And I'm not ashamed to admit that books are the reason I say, "Because I want you all for myself, Cal. That's why."

A lifetime passes by between my last breath and the next.

My own words echo in my head, through the walls, between our bodies mere inches apart. An olive branch of sorts I'm not sure he's going to take.

Cal's eyes are on me, stripping my soul bare and ripping it to shreds with every moment that goes by in such deafening silence.

And then he speaks again, taking the remains of my poor heart with him.

"I'm going to kiss you right now."

I nod.

And just like that, his lips are on mine.

My arms move on their own account, fingers tangling on the back of his head and pulling him closer while his mouth devours mine. There's nothing tender about this kiss, a far cry from our first one—not as his rough hands leave my neck and settle firmly on my hips to press me against him.

His tongue melts against mine in a way that makes my knees buckle. I whimper, he groans, and suddenly his hands are on the back of my thighs, silently begging me to wrap my legs around his torso. He's so strong I don't even need to jump before I'm in his arms, and he's pushing me against the door.

Cal's muscled body is pressed even closer against mine when I feel something hard between my legs. Far from freaking out, though, it only fuels the unrestrained desire pooling low on my belly.

"Is this okay?" he asks me, panting, when he pulls away. I can barely manage a nod before my lips find his again. Wrapping my legs around his hips even tighter, a small whimper escapes the back of my throat when the hardest part of him rolls against my center. With a grunt, Cal moves his hands under my shirt and caresses the naked skin on my back, leaving a long trail of goosebumps in his wake.

"*Fuck.*" He pulls away only to kiss me again. And again, and again, like he can't get enough. "Tell me this isn't a mistake. Tell me this feels as right to you as it does to me."

My poor heart leaps in my chest, and I whisper, "Nothing has ever felt so right, Cal. Kiss me. *Please.*"

He doesn't hesitate, not for one second, before capturing my lips between his own again. I sigh into his mouth, melting under his touch, and in that moment, I understand it's always been him.

It's always been Cal who I was meant to find, who I was meant to share this with.

When he pulls away and lowers me to the ground again, hands never leaving my hips, I stare into his deep orbs and see a blurry future unfold before me.

"My sunshine." He gives me a butterfly kiss I'm afraid I'll never recover from.

It's hard to believe this man is real. He can't be.

"Go back to your friends and we'll talk later," he says. "We'll figure this out together, yeah?"

"Yeah," I whisper.

"Good." He doesn't kiss me again. "Later."

# chapter 30

## CAL

The moment I kissed Grace again, every worry and insecurity plaguing my mind faded away. There was nothing else in my head but the way her body fit perfectly against mine, the softness of her lips and the little sounds she made as I devoured her.

God, those fucking sounds will be the death of me.

When I came back to our table, Sophia eyed me knowingly and so did Trey, who had seen me run after Grace. Thank fuck Aaron was too busy to notice both his cousin's absence and mine, between a conversation with Oscar and making sure everything ran smoothly at the restaurant. Just because he's toning it down a little and is now used to the idea of Grace and I being friends doesn't mean he'll be okay with me hooking up with her at his restaurant.

He'd skin me alive, probably.

Grace and her friends leave before we do, and as discreetly as possible I send her text telling her I'll pick her up from her dorm once we're done. Which is where I'm standing now despite the cold November wind, leaning against the hood of my car as I wait for her to come out.

And when I finally spot her blond hair coming towards me, my stomach does a fucking cartwheel. I remind myself that I don't want a relationship, that Maddie is and should always be my priority and that a distraction isn't welcomed right now.

But then she smiles at me.

That sweet smile, bright enough to blind the fucking sun, and I forget my own resolve.

Because my head might think a girlfriend would be a distraction, but my poor heart can't keep up.

"Hey." The wind carries her soft voice. She stops mere inches away from me, taking me aback with her delicate beauty. Those sincere eyes, those lush lips, that sweet mouth...

"Hi," I say, voice hoarse. "Do you want to talk at my place?"

Her features soften. "Sure."

The ride to my apartment is quiet but not uncomfortable, all while I fight back the urge to reach out and hold her hand. But I don't, because we need to talk, and I *must* get my shit together within the next ten minutes it takes us to get to my place.

We park, ride the elevator, and reach my apartment, and I still haven't made up my mind. I have to think about my sister and the stability she deserves, but... What if my mother never goes off the rails? What if the moment I fear the most, me having to take my sister away, never comes?

Am I really going to sabotage what my heart desires for an uncertain future?

"What did you want to talk about?" Grace asks. She looks so adorable in leggings and a puffy red coat. I want to hug her tightly against my chest and keep her there forever.

"Let's sit down. Do you want anything to drink or eat?" I offer.

She shakes her head as she takes off her jacket and takes a seat on the couch, in the exact same spot where we once fell asleep together. "No, thanks. I'm fine."

"Okay." I sit down next to her, wiping the nervous sweat off of my palms on the fabric of my jeans. She's staring at me with such an honest, open expression that it only fuels my need to get this over with. I still don't know where I'm going with this, because my head is a fucking mess. Putting all my blind trust in my heart, I tell her, "I don't know what to do with you, sunshine."

Grace gives me a sympathetic grin. "Not a single clue?"

"Not one."

"All right. You once said we were adults and needed to talk as such, so let's do that." Her expression sobers up and my heartbeat goes insane at how insanely attractive confidence makes her look. "I tell you one truth about my feelings for you, and you tell me another. Deal?"

Little by little, step by step. I can do that. "Deal."

She takes a deep breath, and sighs. "I really like it when you kiss me."

Well, there goes my sanity. "You do?"

"Yes. I can't stop thinking about your hands on me, either." Bye sanity, hello boner. "Your turn."

Imitating her, I gather all my remaining courage and say, "I love being your friend and I don't want that to change, but I also think about kissing you way more often than I should. I think about your smile, your jokes, your smutty books, and it fills my heart with joy. I look forward to seeing you every day and sometimes texting you isn't enough. I don't know when my feelings for you changed into something more, but the mere thought of you in my arms keeps me up at night, and I hate myself for wanting you this way when I can't have you."

Her mouth is slightly parted, her eyes wide with shock, and for a second, I consider leaning over and capturing her lips in mine. "Why do you think you can't have me?" she half-whispers.

It all comes down to this, doesn't it? My desires versus my duties. Years ago, I would've made an excuse to avoid having this uncomfortable conversation in the first place. But since I'm not an immature ass anymore, and I care about Grace way more than I ever imagined I could, I decide to lay the truth bare.

"You know about my mother's issues with alcohol, and I'm afraid it'll only get worse from now on. She forgets about picking up my sister, sometimes about feeding her or taking her places. She's barely home as it is since she works a lot, and I know Maddie feels neglected. I don't want to disrupt her home life, but if things escalate and I do nothing about it, social services will take her away."

Grace's face visibly drops. "I didn't know all that, Cal. I'm so sorry."

"Don't be. It is what it is. What I mean by this is that Maddie comes from a very unstable home, and I don't want her to grow up in a dysfunctional family. I... I can't afford to be in a relationship right now because it wouldn't be fair, not to Maddie and not to you. She'd always be my priority and she already likes you so much—if you walked away it would disrupt her routine again. I don't want that for her. I *can't* allow it."

Her throat bobs, and she nods. "I understand, Cal, but I would never do anything to hurt either of you. Never. Maddie is your priority, I know it, and I would never want that to change. You're such a good brother, and I admire that a lot about you. I don't... If this is what you think is best for the both of you, I understand."

Maybe I expected her to fight me, to try to convince me that we should be together despite my reasoning, and that's why her compliance makes me feel like I'm dying inside. I swallow. "You... You understand?"

"I promise I do." Her bottom lip trembles, and I fight the urge to cradle her face between my hands. "You're my best friend, Cal, but it also feels right to kiss you and... when you hold me, it feels right too. I don't know why I feel this way, but I'll get over it. Maddie is the sweetest angel, and she deserves to grow up in a stable home with you. I would never walk away from you or hurt either of you, but I understand if you can't trust my words. I promise I get it, Cal."

"Grace..."

"The last thing I want is to make you feel bad about this." She shakes her head and when she gets up from the couch, some part of my heart cracks. "You made it very clear that you didn't want a relationship. Several times. I'm being unfair."

"Don't say that." I stand up too and take her hands in mine. "It's more complicated than that. It's not that I don't want to be in a relationship with you, it's that..."

"It's not what you should do. It's all right." She gives me a small smile and squeezes my hands. "I'm glad we had this conversation. The only thing I want is to keep being your friend."

"That will never change," I promise, but I don't tell her that I can't imagine my life without her anymore. "Grace, I..."

She shakes her head. "It's okay, you don't have to say anything. I'll get over it."

I don't fucking want her to get over it, because I don't want us to part ways like this in the first place. My head is screaming one thing, and my heart is yelling another, and I don't know what to do.

"You're the best older brother Maddie could ask for," she tells me in that sweet, soft voice that I wish I could capture in a bottle and listen to on an eternal loop. "I'm still going to be your friend, you know? You won't get rid of me that easily."

But I don't want to be just her friend. I want to be able to kiss her, hold her, make love to her every night and every morning until she comes around me in pure ecstasy. Yet there's this invisible hand pulling me away, preventing me from reaching out and...going for it.

I fight against it every time I see her, every time she laughs or makes a joke or looks all proud and happy. But it isn't enough, and now she's walking away from me while I'm unable to do anything about it.

Could we be friends with benefits? Not in this fucking lifetime. That will only make my complicated feelings for her grow, and I won't be able to stop them. I can't do the whole only-physical thing with her. I can't. She means so much more to me.

"I would never want to get rid of you." I bare my truth to her, my throat clogging up with emotion. "I'm sorry. You deserve something better than this."

Her sad smile crushes my soul and sweeps away the remains. "You too, Cal."

I can't move while she zips up her jacket and gathers her things. I can't breathe when she stands on her tiptoes and gives me a lingering kiss on my cheek. I can't feel my own body as she tells me goodbye and walks out of the door.

I can't.

I can't do this anymore.

# chapter 31

## CAL

The day before she goes back home to her husband and son, Sophia eyes me carefully from her spot behind the counter and says, "You look like shit, hon."

Don't I know that.

All my focus is on the tablet resting on top of my thighs. The worn leather couch at the front of the shop isn't the most comfortable place to sit, and this position isn't optimal to draw, but I tell myself I deserve the discomfort. Apparently, I like kicking myself down when I'm already at my lowest.

"I'm fine."

My friend doesn't buy my half-assed response, though. I know it when a moment later I hear a tired sigh and quiet footsteps coming towards me. The couch shifts as she sits, and I don't need to turn my head to know her burning eyes are on me.

"Tell me what's up, Cal."

Instead of acting like the grown-up, thirty-year-old adult that I am, I choose to ignore her and keep drawing in silence. It does nothing to calm the raging storm in my heart. Not while I trace the delicate lines of Gracie's blond pigtails, nor when I fill in Sammy's trench coat with a light brown brush. And not when I add a little detective hat to the children's black Labrador and my soul aches a little more.

It's been days since I've last seen Grace. We've texted back and forth in that time, but things aren't fine.

I know for certain I didn't imagine the hurt flashing in her eyes, the sheer disappointment, while she told me she understood why we couldn't be together. And it burns like a motherfucker, this persistent sensation inside of me that screams, howls, and roars that none of this is right.

I wonder, and not for the first time since she left my place, if I've made a terrible mistake. One I can't come back from.

"All right," Sophia's voice softens and, with an equal amount of gentleness, she takes my tablet from my hands and puts it away. "You're family, Cal, and you know I love you as such. So please tell me what's up because you're scaring me. You don't look good, so don't even bother trying to convince me it's nothing."

With a sigh, I turn to her and the concern in her eyes stares right back at me. She's right—there's no point in lying. Not to her, not to the woman who's been reading me like an open book since I was fifteen. So that's why I finally confess, "It's about a woman."

"I figured," she says. "Is it the one you followed to the bathroom at the restaurant the other day?"

A nod and another sigh later, I finally let the whole story out. "She's my best friend, but we're so right together, Soph, it's insane. We've kissed twice and... She's everything I've ever wanted in a partner and in a friend, but..."

"But what? She isn't ready to take the next step?"

I let out a humorless laugh. "*I'm* the one who's not ready, and I told her just that. She said she understands, but... Fuck, Soph, it feels so fucking wrong and I don't get why. This is what I fucking wanted, isn't it?"

Her hand finds my back and rubs it in small, comforting circles. "Seems to me like that's not what you truly want, hon."

"It's what I *have* to want."

Her voice is still firm but gentle when she says, "Tell me why you're not ready for a relationship. Is it because of your ex?"

Sophia knows all about my last relationship and the

dramatic, off-the-rails way it ended, so she doesn't need to elaborate. "No. I don't give a fuck about that cheater anymore. It's more complicated than that." I blow out a breath and rub my eyes with the heels of my hands. "It's about Maddie."

A beat of silence passes, and then, "Ah, I get it now."

She shifts on the couch, her hand leaving my back only to grip my forearm tightly. "You don't want a relationship because this friend would become a big part of not only your life, but your sister's, and you're worried about the consequences if she leaves one day. You're worried about how it could affect Maddie. Correct me if I'm wrong."

Damn her and her innate ability to read a person in three seconds flat. "You're not."

"Good. Now that we've got that out of the way, let me tell you why you're making a huge mistake," her tone hardens, and I instantly recognize the reprimanding voice she used on my mother every time she came by and found her drunk, sprawled out on the couch like the cockroaches under our fridge.

"I understand you want stability for your sister, and I have no doubts you will provide her with that. I also know she'll be happy, so happy with you. The problem comes when you sacrifice your happiness in favor of a future that could simply not happen."

I knew this, but hearing it from her mouth brings me a new sense of awareness. She asks, "How serious are you about her?"

"I've never thought about getting married or having babies until I met her, Soph. That's how serious I am." Because I want both of those things, with Grace and with her only, and now I feel like that future I imagined for us is being ripped away. And it's only my fault.

"So, let's say Maddie ends up living with you and you're dating this woman... What's her name, again?" I tell her. "Okay, imagine you're now living with both Grace and Maddie. Everything works out until it doesn't, and you guys split up. How do you think it would affect your sister?"

"Grace is her ballet teacher, and she already admires her so much. They get along well, so if we all lived together... My sister would eventually fall in love with her and get attached." Like I'm doing right now. "She'd feel devastated if Grace left our lives one day."

"All right. Now imagine this other scenario. Your mother gets her shit together and Maddie never moves in with you. You both get to have a normal, healthy family life. Would you date Grace then?"

"Yes." Hell, I would've asked her out ages ago if that was my reality. Only a fool would let such an incredible, kind-spirited, fun, strong woman walk away without a fight.

I guess that makes me a fucking idiot, then.

"Congratulations, you're dating the woman of your dreams in this hypothetical fairytale we've made up." She pins me down with one of her stern glares, and that's how I know I'm in trouble. "But, oh wait, I'm sorry. No, you can't date her, my bad. Wanna know why?"

I gulp. "Why?"

"Because, Cal, what if you guys have a baby and get a divorce one day? The poor little thing would suffer so much."

My heartbeat picks up. "What?"

"Yeah, hon, think about it." Sarcasm rolls off her tongue. "You can't ever date Grace, or anyone else for that matter, because you'll want to start a family one day and so will she. But relationships are so unpredictable that your love story might end someday, and then what? What happens to your child?"

I swallow past the lump in my throat, the mere possibility of being the father of Grace's babies constricting my chest. "Well, um... I... Divorced parents are a thing, and not every kid ends up with irreversible trauma. Trey's parents are divorced, and he and his brother are fine. Their parents don't get along, but it hasn't affected them in a dramatic way. Aaron's parents are divorced, too, I think."

She arches an unimpressed eyebrow at my little speech. "Sounds to me like the possibility of breaking up when there are children involved isn't reason enough to justify not being ready for a girlfriend."

My eyes land on my tablet's still lit-up screen, Gracie, Sammy, and their dog staring right back at me. They're chanting *"Idiot! Idiot! Idiot!"* in my head, and that's when it dawns on me.

It clicks like a light switch turning on, filling the darkness with long-awaited answers.

I've been such a short-sighted, stubborn bastard.

Grace and I don't have to break up. There's a fifty-fifty chance we won't, in fact, and fuck me for even considering not giving us a chance purely out of fear. That's not me. I've never been a coward, so why am I acting like one now that something I treasure with all my damn heart is on the line?

It wouldn't be the end of the world if we split up. Sophia is right, because parents get divorced all the time and it doesn't have to turn into a nightmare for the kids. Maddie doesn't have to suffer the consequences if we play our cards right.

Would it hurt to say goodbye to Grace if it came to it one day? It would shatter my fucking soul, I know that.

But it would hurt even more to push her away now when we haven't even had the chance to become.

My friend must see the realization in my eyes because her features soften. "You understand why this is a mistake now, Cal?" I nod. "Maddie likes Grace, you say? Well then, I don't think she'll have any issues with you dating her. She'll be delighted with the news, I'm sure."

"Fuck," I mutter, rubbing my face again. My last headache is still lingering when I get a fresh one. "I haven't even thought about that. Maddie is my everything, and I don't want her to feel like... Like I'm replacing her."

"That's something you'll have to speak with her about, but don't worry too much. Kids are more understanding than we give them credit for, trust me," she reassures me.

"What if it's too late now?" My chest burns just thinking about it, our picture-perfect future fading away if Grace doesn't want us anymore. It would be entirely my fault, and I'll blame myself for the rest of my days for letting her walk away when she's mine.

Mine to cherish. Mine to take care of. Mine to love.

Sophia rubs my forearm in the comforting way only a good friend can. "There's only one way to find out."

\* \* \*

"Sammy! Look at me, Sammy!"

I squint my eyes against the bright sun, which isn't hiding behind the dark clouds anymore. "You're doing amazing, peanut!"

Maddie gives me the widest of smiles and a thumbs up before going down the slide, only a few feet away from where I'm sitting. The cold afternoon breeze makes the park an almost deserted land, but I prefer it this way.

There are enough children for Maddie to play with and none of those ogling mothers who always flirt with me when they coincidentally happen to sit in the same bench I do. Sometimes with their husbands right there. Savage.

My last appointment of the day ended a little over an hour ago, and I drove to my mother's house straight away and brought Maddie here. I guessed she didn't have any exciting plans for the rest of the day, and I was right.

As I look at her now, though, speed-talking to a little boy and going up the slide again after him, none of that matters anymore. Not my mother, not Pete, not my not-so- dormant fears.

Because my sister smiles, and I breathe a little easier.

"Hey."

Despite the thick jacket I'm wearing, I shiver at the sound of her voice. I haven't seen her in almost a week, and I thought I was ready to take her in after all this time, but I'm not. Grace sits next to me on the empty bench. Her hair is up in a high ponytail, and she's wearing a cream-colored long coat and dark jeans. It's nothing I haven't seen her wear before, yet she still takes my breath away.

I'm starting to learn she always does.

"Hey." I take my eyes off her and bring them back to my sister before I do something impulsive like kiss her again. "How have you been?"

"We've been texting non-stop," she teases. It's not the first time we haven't seen each other in days, yet it feels different this time. For me, at least, it does.

"Still. I want to hear it from you."

She puts her small hands on her pockets. "Good. I got your email with the digital sketches last night."

"Do you need me to change anything? Or add something else?" I ask, keeping my gaze trained ahead for my own good.

"No, they're... They're perfect, Cal. I have more than enough for the book, thank you," she says with a hint of shyness. Keeping my eyes away from her has never felt so damn hard. She always looks so adorable when she shies away. "Don't think I've forgotten about paying you, though. I'm not letting you do this for free."

I can't help the small smirk. "Stubborn."

"Like you're one to talk." She nudges my knee with hers. "What did you want to talk about?"

Right. That's why I texted her earlier. I clear my throat. "I wanted to see you." Which isn't a lie, but it's a far cry from the real reason I asked her to come to the park in the first place.

"Oh. Well, you've seen me now. So, bye," she jokes, and actually tries to leave. My hand shoots up and when I grab her arm to sit her ass back down, she laughs. "Cut me some slack, Sammy. Can I at least go say hello to Maddie?"

I grunt and she laughs again, leaving my side to go up to my sister and her new friend. The moment she spots Grace, Maddie squeals with happiness and throws herself at her open arms, proceeding to tell her all about the game she's playing. Grace crouches next to her and listens attentively, asking both kids questions and nodding along with whatever they answer back.

My heart can't stand it.

For a moment, I forget everything I've been worried about for the past few weeks and focus on the only truth that matters—I want Grace in my life, for however long she'll have me, as my best friend but also as everything else.

As my confidant, as my partner in crime, as my lover.

As the sunshine to my stormy heart.

So that's why, when she comes back to the bench with a smile on her beautiful face and pinkish cheeks from the biting cold, I reach out and grab her by the waist, pressing her against me. I'm still sitting down, and my chest collides with her stomach. Looking up at her, I say, "You sure you want to pay me for those illustrations?" I know she does, and I couldn't care less if she didn't, but it would make her feel better if I gave in. So that's why I do.

She nods, out of breath. "Yeah."

My grip on her body tightens. "Go on a date with me, then."

She blinks down at me. The warmth spreading on her cheeks now has nothing to do with the cold. "A...date?"

"You'll be paying, of course." I smirk. "A date in exchange for the illustrations. What do you say?"

"You don't want cash instead?"

"I'd rather be with you." In every way that counts. "So, is it a yes?"

She pretends to think about it. "What kind of date?"

"Whatever you want, since you're paying," I say with a grin. When she smiles back at me, my insides melt. "Sounds great. If you're sure."

I squeeze her waist through her thick coat. "I'm sure," I tell her with a serious expression.

If there's something about us, it is that a simple look into each other's eyes is enough to understand what our vulnerabilities won't allow us to say out loud. I know she can read between the lines when she says, "Don't make any plans for Sunday, Sammy. You're all mine then."

# chapter 32

## GRACE

A date. A freaking date with Cal. What am I supposed to do with my life now?

It's not that I don't want to go, but I'm confused. Only a few days ago he was telling me how he didn't want a relationship while looking at me with the kind of love I've only read about in books.

Whatever we're doing is stupid as hell, I know that. We're friends, but we're also something else neither of us are brave enough to put a label on. He's not my boyfriend, all right, but he's also not just my friend. Luke is just my friend. Em is just my friend.

I don't go around kissing my friends, hooking up with them in random bathrooms and wishing they could show me what it feels like to be worshiped.

I trust Cal with my body, my heart, and my soul.

And I'm tired of hiding it.

However, that's not what I'm thinking about when I spot his car waiting for me in front of my building, or when I get into the passenger seat and greet him with the kind of smile only he pulls from me. No—instead, I turn around and high-five the little girl in the backseat, forgetting about the worries and the what-ifs.

"Ready, Maddie?" I ask her with a knowing grin.

"Ready!" she exclaims. "Sammy, let's go! We'll be late!"

"We won't, princess," he assures her in a calm voice as he starts the car. "We still have twenty minutes until it opens. Plenty of time." God, he looks too hot when he's so under control.

I could've picked any location for our date, and I almost went for the usual Italian restaurant until I realized we didn't have to be boring. Not when Maddie, the least boring person I know, could tag along.

So after a quick search on the internet, I came across a kid-friendly farm not far from Warlington where we could go apple picking and visit the petting zoo. After getting Cal's brotherly seal of approval, I booked three tickets and now here we are.

Clovester Farm sits on a bright green countryside, surrounded by breathtaking landscapes, and engulfed in chilly air. As soon as she gets out of the car, Maddie makes a beeline for the farm until Cal picks her up easily and sits her on top of the trunk of the car, which makes her giggle. My chest constricts with an inexplicable amount of warmth as he zips up her little jacket and gives her a pink wool hat she puts over her head.

"Grace, look! Princess hat," she calls out to me with a level of excitement difficult to match.

"You look like a real princess, Maddie," I beam at her and take my own hat from my bag. "Mine's white, though. Do you think it's still a princess hat?"

"Yes, because you look like a princess. Right, Sammy?"

Cal finishes up her zipper and gently sets her down on the ground again. "You both look like princesses."

I send him a smile as Maddie grabs my hand.

"Come on! We'll be late!"

She's quick to grab Cal's hand too, and just like that we're rushing to the main entrance. He mouths a "sorry" while his sister swings herself between us, jumping and urging us to walk faster. I shake my head, smiling, because the truth is that Maddie's happiness is both contagious and what we need right now after a week of confusion and tumultuous feelings.

My poor heart still hasn't decided whether this date means

Cal has changed his mind about relationships, or if this is nothing but a friendly outing with his sister. Either way, I'm set on having fun. Nothing will ruin today for me, not even myself.

After grabbing a map of Clovester Farm and a basket for apple picking, Maddie lets go of our hands to run through the endless field. Families with children and couples stroll around us, and for a moment I wonder what it would feel like to lace our fingers together.

Is he holding back because of Maddie? Maybe he doesn't want to make things awkward for her, or for me, or—

"Thank you for organizing this today," he says after waving to his sister, who's picked her first apple of the afternoon. He clears his throat before continuing, "It was very thoughtful to think of her."

"Of course. I thought you'd want to spend time with her since it's the weekend and all." I lower my gaze to the green grass, hoping he won't notice the blush on my cheeks. Even I know blaming it on the cold won't work this time. "And I really like spending time with her. She's a fun kid."

He stops. "That... That means a lot to me, sunshine."

I stop too, finally gathering the courage to look him in the eye. "Cal..."

"Sammy! Grace! Look!" Maddie's excited voice breaks the moment and we both sober up at once. "There's a worm in this apple!"

We both laugh before resuming our walk, and I take comfort in the fact that, for a second, Cal's eyes twinkled while looking at me. He might not want to take this thing between us further, and I'm ready to accept it, but dammit if it doesn't hurt. Because for the next hour or so, we walk through the fields together as if we've done this a million times before.

Maddie holds my hand and fills the comfortable silence with lively chatter about apples and animals and whatever pops into her little brain. Cal takes a dozen pictures of her and then carries her on his shoulders on the way back because she's too tired. And I can't help but think that all of this feels so right.

I know Cal worries that I would feel left out if we were together because Maddie is and will always be his priority, that's not the case at all. Jeez, I would be worried if he didn't put the best thing that's ever happened to him (in his own words) first. Maddie and I could both be important to him, only in different ways—but he doesn't see it, and I'm not going to force him to change his mind.

I'd rather have Cal as my best friend—have him be with somebody else, even—than losing him completely. My heart wouldn't be able to take it.

After we buy the apples we've picked, Maddie insists on visiting the petting zoo. However, once we're there, she hides behind her brother's legs when a goat tries to get close to her. Cal chuckles. "The animals want to be your friends, see?" He kneels to pet the goat, who doesn't so much as flinch at his touch.

"Look, Maddie, I'm doing it too." I mimic Cal and pet another goat called Greer, according to its name tag. "They're very friendly."

One of the workers spots her hesitation and comes towards us with a huge smile on her face. "Hello, sweetheart. What's your name?"

"Maddie," she tells her, still hiding behind Cal. "Will the goats bite my fingers?"

The woman chuckles. "No, Maddie, don't worry. They're really well-behaved." She demonstrates by petting another goat called Maggie. "You can pet a little goat too. See, your parents are doing it."

It takes me a fraction of a second to realize that by "your parents" she means us. As in, Cal and me.

Oh, boy.

He stares at me, and I look at him, and the air between us thickens with something I'm too scared to identify. Before either of us can correct the unaware woman, though, Maddie starts giggling.

"Sammy is not my daddy!" she tells her. "He's my brother. And Grace is his girlfriend."

I'm his *what*?

"Oh." The poor woman's cheeks match the shade of the apples we've just picked. "I'm so sorry. I shouldn't have assumed."

"It's all right," Cal says with an easy smile. "We two do look alike, huh?" He winks at Maddie, who isn't hiding behind him anymore.

"You do," the woman agrees, visibly more relaxed that we didn't take her assumption the wrong way. "Which goat do you want to pet, Maddie? I promise they're all very friendly."

"Come on, Mads, be brave like a princess," I encourage her. That seems to do the trick, because a second later she's carefully approaching Greer and tangling her little hand in its soft fur.

"Well done, peanut." Cal kisses the side of her head and I melt.

Once she grows tired of the petting zoo, we decide to head to the farm's restaurant and have a couple of their homemade pizzas for dinner since it's already late for Maddie. I'm walking ahead of them, texting Aaron back, when I hear Cal tell his sister, "And Grace isn't my girlfriend, baby."

"Oh." I can't see her face, but her voice sounds disappointed. "Why not?"

It takes him a little longer to answer, a few seconds in which my heart goes insane behind my ribcage.

"Why? Do you want her to be?"

Suddenly my locked phone screen is the most interesting thing in the world. Or that's what I want Cal to think because I'm totally eavesdropping.

"Yes, I want her to be my big sister!" she exclaims in that excited voice of hers, and breathing comes a little more difficult. I knew Maddie liked me, but not to this extent.

Cal coughs. "Well, Maddie—"

"If you have a wedding and a baby, can it be a girl? Please? Boys are so boring."

"Mads—"

"Will your baby be my sister?"

"No, peanut. She'll be your niece, and you'll be her auntie."

"Yay! I want to be an auntie, Sammy. Pretty please!"

"Maybe one day."

"One day when? Next week?"

I suppress a laugh and Cal sighs. "That's not how it works, Maddie. Come on, let's get our pizzas."

Since it's a Sunday and the children visiting the farm have school tomorrow, the restaurant is nearly deserted when we walk in except for some couples and a family of five. Maddie is quick to grab a table next to the big windows overlooking the apple fields. She's too short to reach the top, so Cal slides a booster seat under her.

"Did you have fun today?" I ask her as we dive into our pizzas. She's already making a mess of her slice, and all the tomato sauce around her mouth makes her look even more adorable than usual.

"Best day ever." She nods eagerly. "Sammy, can I skip school tomorrow?"

"Absolutely not, but good try."

She directs her puppy dog eyes at me. "Grace... Can I?"

I exchange a quick glance with Cal, amusement glinting in his eyes. "Sorry, Maddie. Whatever your brother says, goes."

"Oh, man." She pouts.

I grab another slice of roasted garlic chicken pizza. "But we can come here another day. I'm sure they'll do something special for Christmas."

Her little face lights up at that. "I love Christmas! Can we go ice skating some day?"

"Sure we can." I smile while pointedly ignoring Cal's focus on me. I'm not ready to find out what he's thinking, and I'll know with one look at his face. His dark eyes are like bottomless windows, allowing me to see everything he consciously hides.

"You're super fun," Maddie tells me with her mouth full. "Do you think you can have a wedding with my brother so you can hang out with me all day?"

Cal chokes on his drink and I struggle not to stagger as I speak. "We can hang out whenever you want, Maddie," I assure her. Thinking of marrying my best friend is the last thing my sanity needs right now. Nope.

Seemingly satisfied with my answer, she nods and goes back to her pizza. Not even two minutes later, though, she tells me, "I'm nervous for the Christmas recital."

Cal smooths her auburn hair away from her forehead. "You have no reason to be nervous, kiddo. You're a princess and a ballerina after all."

"That's right. You know all the steps, and you're a great dancer," I add with what I can only hope is a reassuring smile.

She turns to her brother. "Are you coming to see me?"

"Of course I am, Mads. I wouldn't miss it for the world."

"Are Mommy and Daddy coming too?"

I see it clear as day, the way Cal's wide shoulders stiffen and his whole expression morphs into something akin to pain. He's never talked to me about Maddie's father, but I can only assume their relationship is almost non-existent. Growing up with two attentive and overly cuddly fathers, I wouldn't know how it feels to be neglected by your own family, but it doesn't take a genius to see it can be traumatic.

I know Cal is trying to give his sister as normal of a

childhood as he can. The fact that he does it so well makes me fall even harder for him.

"I don't know, peanut. Maybe they'll have to work that day. We can ask them later," is the answer he opts for, although the underlying hurt is still there. Under the table, I poke at his leg with my foot, silently telling him he's doing his best. The smile he gives me in return lets me know he got the message.

The rest of our dinner goes smoothly, with Maddie talking non-stop and us prompting her to speak even more. Cal's eyes light up whenever he looks at his sister, and it's a sight so beautiful I wish I could engrave it in my mind forever.

When we leave the restaurant, Maddie clings to her brother's legs and begs to be carried to the car since she's too tired. Cal is only so happy to oblige and by the time I open the backseat door for them, she's already fast asleep. To my surprise she doesn't wake up as he starts the car, nor when he starts speaking to me in a low voice, "Did you have fun today?"

"A lot," I whisper. "Did you?"

"Yeah." He holds my hand in his much bigger one and places it over his thigh. My heart isn't beating anymore. "We barely got to talk, though."

Hypnotized, I watch how the pad of his thumb caresses my skin. "Maddie might have school tomorrow, but we don't."

"Are you inviting yourself over to my place, sunshine?" He smirks.

"Yep."

He chuckles, a low manly sound that goes straight to my core. "It's a plan, then."

A little over twenty minutes later, we arrive at an area of Warlington I'm not familiar with. We pass by a park and a few local shops, but the rest is all rows and rows of one-story houses and bungalows. Eventually Cal stops the car in front of a small home. "This is where I grew up," he tells me. "Maddie lives here with our mom and her dad."

I don't know what to say, so I simply nod. I've seen their mother a couple of times when she picked Maddie up from The Dance Palace, but the mental picture I have of her is fuzzy. I remember tan skin and long, dark hair but that's all.

Shame creeps up on me when I allow myself to admit that I'm not a huge fan of the woman. I'm trying not to be judgmental, I really am, especially since I know she has issues with alcohol and sometimes people are victims of their own circumstances. But then I remember how she's treating Maddie and the stress she's putting Cal through, and my blood boils.

"She's still asleep. I'm gonna drop her off real quick. You can stay in the car," he tells me, and I nod again.

Maddie barely stirs as Cal picks her up and disappears through the front door, allowing me to take a moment to breathe.

When he comes back, we're going to his apartment, and we are going to talk...or maybe not.

I want to kiss him so badly it's not even funny at this point, but I can't tell if we're on the same page. Maybe all he wants is to tell me how we're better off as friends, so I shouldn't get my hopes up. But I do anyway.

Because a moment later he comes out of the house as the night descends over our heads. I watch as he strolls towards the car, all big and tall and tattooed and masculine, and my body tingles. He's all I've ever wanted—a friend, a lover, a partner for life. He's right in front of me, and I can't have him.

"My place, then?" he asks as he sits behind the wheel and closes the door behind him.

I can't tear my gaze off him. His dark, soft hair. His strong tattooed neck and that sharp jaw. Those kind eyes and plush lips that are begging to be kissed. He's so damn perfect in every single way it physically pains me not being able to be with him the way I want to.

"Grace?"

"Huh?"

His chuckle is the hottest sound I've ever heard. "Are you listening to me?"

I shake my head. "Not really."

That sound again. "Why not?"

My gaze moves to his lips on its own accord, and he notices. Breath hitching, I look back up to his eyes but it's too late.

"You want to kiss me?" he teases in that low voice that drives me insane. And I nod because I might be a bit of a coward but I'm no liar. "Come here."

His hand cups the entire side of my face as our lips touch, gentle as a feather, before he pulls away again. I almost whimper at the loss of his touch.

I don't know what this means.

Did he change his mind? Is he ready for more?

His nose brushes against mine as he whispers, "Let's go home and I'll take care of you."

# chapter 33

## CAL

My mouth is on hers the instant I close the door behind us. Concealed by the shadows of my apartment, I'm unable to see the blush on her cheeks but by the way her hands grip my jacket, shaking slightly, I know it's there.

Before we get carried away towards the inevitable, I force myself to pull away. As I cradle her gorgeous face between my tattooed hands I whisper, "We can't do this as friends, sunshine. Do you understand me?"

Grace licks her lips, a pained expression mirroring mine. "No, I don't. Tell me exactly what you mean, Cal, or just let me go."

Still with her head between my hands, I lean down again to kiss her lips gently. "I'm scared as fuck, Grace, but I would rather give us a chance than wonder for the rest of my life how it would feel to make you mine."

Her breath hitches, mouth agape in shock. "Are you sure?"

"Yes, I'm sure." I brush my nose against hers and breathe in her familiar scent. "I'm tired of being a coward and ignoring this connection between us just because there might be a chance it doesn't end well."

"Cal, listen to me." Now it's her small hand cupping my cheek. The pad of her thumb caresses the skin under my eye, lighting it up on fire. "I would never, *ever*, hurt Maddie or you. You said it yourself—we are adults, and we'll navigate this relationship as such. I care about you more than I've ever cared about anyone. I care about Maddie too as if she were my own sister, and I would never want you to put me above her. Do *you* understand *me*?"

There's a lump in my throat that won't let me utter a single word, so I only nod.

I can't for the life of me remember the last time I cried, but fuck it if I don't want to burst into tears right now.

How is she real? What good have I done to deserve her?

The words I know I've felt for a while are on the tip of my tongue, but I don't dare say them out loud. Not yet.

"Do you want to be with me?" she whispers into the darkness, her hand falling from my cheek to rest over my heart, which beats only for her.

"Yes." There's no hesitation in my voice. "A million times yes, Grace. I want you in my life as my friend, my girlfriend, my everything. If you'll have me."

She smiles. "I can't believe you have to ask."

A throaty groan escapes me as she kisses me again, my hands settling on her waist. Grace throws her arms around my neck, fingers tangling in the back of my hair and pulling at it with the right amount of pressure, exactly how I like it. I press my body closer to hers in response, and suck in a breath when my boner brushes against her stomach.

Slowly, so slowly, my lips part and my tongue slides across her bottom lip. "Cal..." she breathes.

The warmth of her body and the comfort of her touch are enough to make my head spin. "Let me take care of you, sunshine."

She sighs and nods, but there's something in her eyes akin to fear that I can't and won't ignore. So that's why, when we walk into my bedroom, I sit down on the mattress and pull her onto my lap.

"We don't have to do anything tonight. Or until you're ready," I assure her. "And if you're never ready, that's all right too.

I want to spend the night with you, but we can do plenty of things before going to bed. We can play a videogame if you're into that."

Hesitation is written all over her face, and it takes her moment to swallow and ask, "Can we watch a movie?"

I place a soft kiss on the side of her head. "Of course we can. You pick."

As she changes into the clothes I gave her—one of my old sweatpants and a t-shirt—I get a bag of chips and a couple of sodas from the kitchen. When I come back to my room she's already settled under the covers.

I don't think she's ever looked more beautiful than right now. In my clothes, in my bed.

All mine.

"What's that face for?" She arches an amused eyebrow.

Clearly, my poker face game is on the floor.

"Just thinking about how beautiful my girlfriend is." It feels surreal calling her that, but it's also...right. In every single way.

"I was thinking about how amazing my boyfriend is, actually. What a coincidence." She smirks.

After climbing into bed, I wrap my arms around her and pepper her face with kisses, which makes her squeal. She looks so small in my arms yet so strong and unbreakable inside, it makes my breathing a little harder.

The movie starts—some romantic comedy she's seen a million times already—and Grace settles between my arms. With her head resting against my chest, calmness washes over me like a tidal wave.

Being with her feels so right, I can't even remember how I managed to live without my sunshine. And I hope I never find out again.

A little over an hour into the movie, Grace starts shifting. First, she drapes a leg over mine. Then, she presses her body closer to my side while I pointedly ignore the growing bulge in my sweatpants as she accidentally rubs herself on my hip bone.

*Breathe, Cal. Fucking breathe. In and out.*

But it proves to be an impossible task when the woman you are falling for is so close yet so far.

"Cal," she whispers, so low I think it comes from the TV at first.

"Yes, baby."

She shifts again, this time *very clearly* rubbing herself on me. I'm going to lose my fucking mind.

"You said you were going to take care of me."

My heart stops and my throat goes dry like a damn desert. "I'm taking care of you right now, aren't I?"

She hums. "That's not what I mean."

"What do you mean, then?"

"Are you going to make me say it?"

"Yep."

She props herself up on one arm and glares at me.

"You're evil."

I smirk. "I can't read your mind."

In a flash, she sits up on the bed and dangles one leg over my lap until she's straddling me. I lose the privilege of breathing as all my blood descends to my hardening cock. "Grace?"

"Can you read body language? Or do I need to spell it out for you?" she challenges, and fuck if her sassy tone doesn't turn me on beyond reason.

I place my hands on her hips and squeeze her there. I cover the span of her hips with both of my hands, and it turns me on beyond reason. "I need to hear you say it." My voice comes out strained.

"I want you to make me feel good," she says, and there's not an ounce of hesitation in her. "I'm ready."

"Okay." My hands are fucking trembling on her skin with anticipation. I want to make this right for her more than

I've ever wanted anything in this world, and the weight of that responsibility crushes down on me with an unstoppable force.

"Do you know what a safe word is?" she asks me, and I nod. "Can we have one?"

"Sure. But if you tell me to stop, I will right away." Carefully, I place a loose strand of wavy blond hair behind her ear.

Her eyes glisten under the moonlight filtering through the windows. "You would stop?"

It breaks my heart that she doubts that, not because of an ego thing but because someone has broken that trust for her. "Of course I would, Grace. You tell me to stop, and I will. Always. Right away."

Her hair falls over her shoulders as she nods. "So, 'stop' is our safe word?"

"Yeah." Taking advantage of the fact that my hands are steadier now, I hold her face between my wide palms and let my thumb brush the corner of those luscious lips I love kissing so much. "Is there anything you don't want me to do? Any triggers?"

She chews on her lower lip, a nervous habit of hers I've started to pick up on. "No... I don't know. I've never done this before."

"We'll figure it out together. Always at your own pace, yeah?" I sit up straight on the mattress, my back pressed against the bed rest. She places her head on my shoulder.

"Grace?"

"Yeah?"

"Look at me." When she does, it takes all my willpower not to kiss her right now. But what I need to tell her is far more important than my impulsive needs. "You want to stop, you tell me. It doesn't matter what we're doing. I want you to be selfish about this, okay? Don't worry about me at all. Tell me you understand."

She gives me a small nod. "I understand."

A relieved sigh escapes my chest, and I tangle my fingers on her soft hair. "This is what's going to happen now. I'm going to grab a condom from the bathroom in case we need it, but don't feel pressured into doing anything. I'm getting it just in case, yeah?"

"Okay." She looks more at ease now, and I keep going. "Then we're going to take things slow, at your pace, and we're going to explore this together. Anything you need, even if it is to turn on the lights or keep your shirt on, you tell me. The only thing I want is to pleasure you and make you feel safe."

Emotion swells in her eyes, and I can't take the sight of her like this. "What's wrong, sweetheart?"

Grace shakes her head quickly, blond hair flying everywhere. "You are... You are the best thing that's ever happened to me."

My soul leaves my fucking body at her admission, and before I lean in to kiss her, I whisper, "And you're the best thing that's ever happened to me, sunshine. I hope you know that."

There's nothing in this world I wouldn't do for her, I realize then. It doesn't matter if it would hurt me in the process—Maddie and Grace are my light, my girls, my princesses. Having them in my life is the best thing that's ever happened to a lost soul like mine.

Grace closes the slim space between our lips and kisses me slowly, so slowly I melt under her touch. The feel of her hands roaming under my t-shirt, skin on skin, lights me up on fire from the inside. And when she runs her fingernails down my stomach, I can't help the involuntary jerk of my hips against her warm core. A small, almost timid whimper escapes her throat at the contact, which makes me even harder under my revealing sweatpants.

It takes all my willpower and then some to keep my hands firmly on her hips, right above her—my—clothes because I don't want to freak her out. But we keep kissing, and she keeps exploring, and eventually she grabs my wrists and slides my hands up her sides until my palms are cupping her boobs.

And *fucking hell*, she's not wearing a bra.

She sighs against my lips as I caress her breasts over the thin fabric of the t-shirt, playing with her nipples until they harden under my touch. She's so fucking responsive it's driving me wild with need.

"Can I take off my shirt?" I ask her, and she nods. The moment my chest is bare, she trails her fingers up and down my muscles, and the tattoos on my shoulders and neck. I watch her as she watches me, in awe of her curiosity, and it hits me that she's never touched a man like this before.

I'm going to be her first. Maybe not tonight, maybe not all the way, but I am. When she asked me to teach her about sex all those weeks ago, I didn't think we would end up here—with me teaching her about pleasure, hands-on—but I can't say I'm sorry it led to this. There's nobody else for me. Nobody I would want to do this for, or with.

I take a deep breath when she sits up on my lap and takes her t-shirt off. I take another deep breath when I finally see her full breasts, so round and ripe for the taking.

So fucking perfect. My hands find her narrow hips, my thumbs caressing the soft skin on her stomach.

"You take my breath away, sunshine," I say in a rough whisper, entranced by the utter perfection of her naked skin. "You're beautiful."

Her lips curve into a shy smile, and I see her cheeks flushing despite the darkness surrounding us. "Will you touch me, Cal?"

*Fuck. Me.*

"I didn't get the condom," I blurt out, because I know for a fact I won't be able to think clearly later, and I need to do it now.

But Grace has other plans. She leans over until her breasts are pressed against my chest, hot skin against hot skin, hearts racing, and she whispers against my mouth, "Later. Now I want you to take care of me like you promised you would."

I'm a fucking dead man.

I hoist her up with one arm around her waist and place her back down on the mattress, positioning myself above her. Her lips are agape with surprise, and she runs her hands down my biceps as I finally lower my mouth to her delicious breasts.

The second I suck on her pebbled nipple, she moans, and the sound goes directly to my impossibly erect cock.

"You all right?" I pant.

"Yeah... I... I didn't know it could feel like this." She tangles her hands on my hair and pushes my head down. "Keep going. *Please.*"

I chuckle. "So needy, my girl."

Goosebumps break out all over her skin, revealing exactly what I wanted to know.

She likes it when I call her *my girl*. She likes it when I claim her as mine.

My tongue keeps swirling around her nipple, sucking and biting until she's wriggling beneath me, consumed by the pleasure I'm drawing from her. As I'm placing open-mouthed kisses on the skin between her breasts, her hands lower and drag down the hem of the sweatpants she's wearing.

I detach my mouth from her and cover her hand with mine. "Want me to take these off?"

She nods, biting her lower lip. "It hurts."

"What hurts, baby?"

"Between my legs." She arches her back as my other hand engulfs the side of her waist. "Cal... Make it stop."

I close my eyes and count to three in a failed attempt to calm my cock down. It's the most pointless thing I've ever done.

"How do you want me to make it stop?" I whisper roughly as she starts lowering the sweatpants with my hand still covering hers.

My breath hitches at the sight of her lace underwear.

"With your mouth. Please."

*Fuuuuuck.*

Gently, I help her take the last of her clothes off until she's lying under me only on her black panties, so ready for me I could cry from anticipation. I lower my body on the bed and press a soft kiss against her stomach. "Relax." Another kiss. "I'm gonna make you feel good, yeah?"

Her hands slip back into my hair, desperate to grip at it.

"Remember what we said earlier. You tell me to stop, and I will." Another kiss, lower on her abdomen this time. The hem of the lace tickles my chin, and it takes everything in me to breathe normally and calm the fuck down.

"I know." She swallows. "I'm ready."

The confident gleam in her eyes tells me she's never been this sure about anything. So that's why the next time I press my lips on her skin, it's against her covered sex. It earns me a loud whimper in response and a tug on my hair. But because she isn't telling me to stop, I kiss her there again.

The intoxicating scent of her arousal blinds all my senses until all I can think about is tasting the sweetness between her legs. I press my tongue flat against her, giving her a preview of what's to come, and she half-screams, "Oh my god!"

As I grab the hem of her panties to drag them down her smooth legs, my heartbeat picks up. I've never been this nervous when in bed with a woman, but that isn't surprising.

None of them were her. None of them were my sunshine.

The lace comes off and she's completely naked in front of me. I take a moment to appreciate such a mesmerizing, privileged sight and take comfort in knowing that nobody else will ever see her like this. Because she's mine, and I'm hers, and we're it for each other. Of that, I'm sure.

"Cal..." The hesitation in her voice makes me stop right on

my tracks. "I'm nervous."

I smooth my palm up her thigh in a comforting gesture.

"That's normal. I promise you'll like it."

"Will it hurt?"

"No, I promise. You'll only feel pleasure."

She looks at me like she trusts me with her heart and body, and it makes me feel like the luckiest man on fucking Earth. When she nods, giving me permission to claim her with my mouth, that's exactly what I do.

I will always remember my first taste of Grace like the closest thing to fucking paradise I've ever experienced.

When my tongue parts her sealed folds, I'm instantly met with a pool of warm desire I wish I could get drunk on. She would be the most delicious of hangovers.

She's sweet on my mouth, so damn wet I can only imagine how she would feel on my cock later. And as I devour her, she squirms beneath me, moans and screams in pleasure while urging me to keep going with her words and her grip on my hair.

I lick her slowly, savoring every taste as if her pussy were my last meal. The tip of my tongue pierces her small entrance, and she cries out at the intrusion. I repeat the action again and again, picking up my pace until she's riding my face, begging for release. I know for a fact I will be too big for her, but fuck it if the mental picture of Grace being filled to the brim with my fat cock doesn't drive me insane with need.

"Cal..." Her walls clench around my tongue and I know she's close. My hips buck against the bed, my rock-hard cock screaming for release. "I'm so close, Cal. Oh my god. I'm going to..."

I grunt against her pussy, and pull away long enough to say, "Come on my mouth, sunshine. Ride my face and let me lick you clean."

My hands keep her in place by the waist as she comes down her high with the most erotic scream I've ever fucking heard. Her arousal coats my tongue, my chin, her thighs, and it physically hurts to pull myself away from her pussy.

I need to take her more than I need the air I breathe.

One taste. That's all it took. Now I'm addicted.

"I'm... Wow." Her lips twitch with the beginning of a smile and my poor heart swoons at her satisfaction. "Was it good for you?" she asks, out of breath.

Instead of answering, I climb back on top of her and press the swell of my rock-hard, covered cock against her stomach. "What do you think?"

When she smirks up at me, that confidence gleaming in her beautiful face, I know I'm in trouble. "I want to feel you inside of me, Cal."

# chapter 34

## GRACE

If I wasn't already on my back, the sight of Cal's head between my open legs would have brought me to my knees. The way his powerful shoulders contracted with each of his movements, how his strong hands held me in place while I squirmed under him, how his expert tongue broke me and glued me back together...

Yeah, I've been missing out.

I've touched myself in the past, but it's nothing compared to the numbing orgasm he's just given me. I've been thrown over a metaphorical cliff, free falling to then land in the safety of his arms.

His tattoos seem to shine under the moonlight filtering through the blinds in his room. "I want to feel you inside of me, Cal," I tell him without hesitation, because right now there's nothing else I need more.

He kisses me, and I taste myself on his lips. "Condom," he whispers roughly before pushing himself off the bed and disappearing into his bathroom.

When he comes back, not even the night can hide the long, thick curve of his shaft pressing against his sweatpants. My mouth waters, aching to know what it would feel like to take care of him with my mouth. He must be wondering the same thing as he stops at the foot of his bed, dark eyes boring into mine with such raw intensity it makes my legs all wobbly.

Without another word, Cal slides his sweatpants down his

legs and stands almost fully naked in front of me. I've never seen his bare legs before, long, powerful, and covered in dark hair. I remember him telling me he's got a tattoo on the back of his calf, but I forget all about asking him to show it to me when his fingers grab the hem of his black boxers. He stops.

"If you feel uncomfortable at all..." he starts.

But I shake my head, and he stops talking. "I won't. And if I do, I promise to tell you."

His features relax at that, and my heart swells at how thoughtful he always is with me, especially tonight. Some people might think asking for permission before every little move kills the mood, but I find it hot as hell. If anything, it's turning me on even more that he wants to make sure I'm okay. It shows he takes my trauma seriously, while also accepting that I'm ready to move on. With him.

Asking for permission is sexy, and so is the sight of Cal finally, *finally* taking his boxers off.

My mouth waters and my thighs clench at the sight of him.

He's...enormous. There's no other way to describe it.

His dick is long and thick, making me wonder how the hell he's going to fit inside of me. Veins run along his shaft, and I fight the urge to lick them and suck on the reddish head that's already leaking precum. I swallow, intimidated by his size, as he tears the foil open and rolls the condom over his cock in one easy movement.

It hits me then that he's experienced. How much I don't know, but it's obvious he's done this before and most likely enjoyed it too. Cal doesn't sleep around, yet that hasn't stopped him from getting women into his bed and pleasuring them like he's about to do with me.

And what if I can't meet his expectations?

What if I can't pleasure him like he pleasured me?

"I can hear you thinking." He fists his long shaft and gives it a few slow, captivating pumps.

"I... I don't know how to do this," I confess. "What if it's not good for you?"

He's right in front of me in one long stride, his hand cupping my cheek like he always does when he wants me to listen carefully.

"Sunshine, you could lie there and do nothing at all, and you'll still throw me over the edge. You know why?" I shake my head. "Because I want you, and only you. I love everything you do, and you could never disappoint me in any way. I told you to be selfish tonight and not worry about me, and I meant every word."

"But..."

"Shh... Listen to me, sweetheart." He presses his forehead against mine and my stomach jumps at the term of endearment. "I'm going to make love to you and it's going to drive us both insane, okay? Focus on your own pleasure, and trust that I'm gonna enjoy every second of your sweet pussy wrapped around my cock."

I suck in a breath, head spiraling out of control at his dirty talk. This side of Cal... I love it.

He sits down on the mattress, his wide back against the headboard, and drags me by the waist until I'm straddling him. I arch a confused eyebrow. "I thought you'd want to be on top."

"No. You're in control tonight." He hauls me up by the waist so easily I blush at his show of strength. Then he settles me further up, the tip of his cock pressing right at my entrance. He hisses. "Fuck."

I whimper at how good it feels, even better than his tongue if that's even possible, and rub my folds along his thick shaft, coating it with my arousal. The ache between my legs is now unbearable. "Cal..."

"Tell me what you need, baby, and I'll give it to you."

One of my hands finds his shoulders, using his strong

body to hoist myself up, as the other reaches between us until my fingers are wrapped around his shaft. I can barely curl them around it, and the realization that his thickness might rip me in half makes me even wetter.

"I want it inside of me," I whisper.

Cal's eyes don't leave my pussy as I bury his length past my lips, first the tip and slowly taking the rest. I whimper as he fills me up, stretching my tight walls like I knew he would. His grip on my waist becomes so strong he'll leave a mark, but I don't care about that right now. Throwing his head back in pleasure, Cal lets out a borderline animalistic groan that travels straight to my core.

"*Shit*," he mutters under his breath. "You're so fucking tight. You're a fucking wet dream."

It stings a little at first, but soon the pain transforms into raw pleasure and I start moving. It feels weird to have something inside of me, let alone something this big, but it feels so damn good too.

Using his strong shoulders for balance I start moving up and down his cock, slowly at first until the pleasure runs away from me and I start to chase it. Breathing heavily, Cal watches my breasts bounce with each of my movements. "That's it. Fuck yourself on my cock. Good girl."

I throw my head back and moan so loudly I'm sure his whole building can hear us right now, but I couldn't care less. My fingers reach between us until I'm touching the base of his cock, sliding in and out of me, fully covered in my arousal.

"Feel how I'm pumping into your pretty cunt," Cal grunts as he looks at my exploring fingers. "You take my cock so fucking well."

His praise elicits another moan out of me, and I start bouncing faster. Cal grips my ass and starts ramming into me with abandon, until all we can hear are the sounds of our moans and the slap of our bodies coming together. My fingers move to my clit, and I touch myself as he fucks me relentlessly.

"I'm gonna..." I start, but I'm interrupted by his lips on my neck. "Cal..."

"I know. I'm right there with you," he sounds gentle now, a contrast with the force of his thrusts. "Tell me when you're about to come, and I'll come with you."

He keeps trailing open mouthed kisses along my neck, and it doesn't take me long to reach the point of no return. "Cal... Shit, I'm gonna *come*."

"*Fuck*." His thrust become faster, sloppier, and I find myself crying for release. "Come on my cock, sweetheart. Come for me."

I scream as my walls clench around him, and he roars with the force of a thousand storms as he comes inside of me. The condom is the only barrier between our bodies, and for a moment I wonder what it would feel like to feel his release inside of me, filling me up to the brim until it leaks down my thighs and on the bed. But I'm not on the pill, and the orgasm-induced fantasy leaves as quickly as it came.

Cal is panting beneath me, his strong arms wrapped around my body in a comforting hug. Moments later, when we're both a little less flustered, he kisses the top of my head. "How are you feeling?"

"Amazing," I blurt out. "That was amazing."

He chuckles, his chest vibrating against mine. "Took the words right out of my mouth, sunshine."

I tilt my head back to look at him. "Do you mean that?"

"Of course I do." He tucks a strand of my now messy hair behind my ear. "You'd better believe it was the best sex I've ever had in my life."

And I do. I truly do believe him. "It wasn't too bad of a first time, either." I smirk.

He chuckles again before kissing the tip of my nose. "And

that's nothing compared to what I plan to do to you from now on."

My breath hitches and my cheeks boil. Even though it's dark in here and he can't see my blush, I know he feels it all the same. "But for now," he kisses my nose again, "how about we take a shower and go to bed? It's getting late."

"A shower...together?" I stutter, suddenly nervous about the idea. I'm not sure I'm ready to let him see my naked body in the bright light of the bathroom, and somehow, he picks up on my hesitation. He always does.

"There are two bathrooms, so you can shower in mine while I take Maddie's." He gives me a reassuring smile. "Sounds good?"

I nod, and when he pulls out of me and helps me out of bed, I realize two things.

One—I will never get enough of the filthy, dominant, dirty-mouthed side of Cal. He's like all my book and real-life fantasies come to life.

And two—at this rate, if he keeps taking such good care of me, it's going to be impossible to avoid the fall.

Because I am, dramatically and helplessly, falling in love with my best friend.

# chapter 35

## GRACE

Four days later, I stand in front of the building where everything started.

With full confidence in my stride, I push the door open and step inside the empty tattoo parlor. It's way past closing hours, but Cal insisted on doing this alone. Just the two of us.

I press a soft kiss on his lips before sliding into the tattooing chair, more at ease than I ever thought I would feel.

It's thanks to the man adjusting his black rubber gloves in front of me, and thanks to the fact that I'm growing into who I was always meant to be. Before everything happened, and despite my circumstances.

I can feel it inside my bones and in a few moments, I'll have it inked in my skin forever.

"Ready, sunshine?" He smiles, pure adoration and silent encouragement radiating from those beautiful dark orbs.

"Ink me up."

As the sharp needle pierces through my skin on the side of my ribcage, I feel the weight of my past sliding off me. There will always be a remaining layer of pain within me, a scrape of reminisce that will always walk along beside me, holding my hand even if all I want is to run free.

I've come to terms with it in the past four years, and my resolve to water this seed that is me so I can grow and bloom has only intensified in the past few months.

This journey of uncomfortable healing won't end with this tattoo—I never expected it to, anyway. From now on and for the rest of my days, I will walk beside the pain, the grief, and the fear, and I will learn to let go of their hand so I can be free. I'm already starting to.

When Cal finishes his art on my skin, he silently hands me a mirror. My eyes swell with unshed tears the moment I spot those two little suns and the beautiful calligraphy staring back at me.

A reminder by the two men I love the most in the world, sealed into my body by the man I'm slowly starting to realize is the love of my life in all the ways that matter— my best friend, my confidant, my partner, my forever.

"I love it," I mutter through the tears as the pad of his gentle thumb wipes them all away. "I love it, Cal."

*I love you.*

His smile is nothing short of devastating, but so are his next words.

"Bloom with grace, my sunshine. Whatever happens, like you were always meant to."

# part three: bloom

# chapter 36

## GRACE

I know better than most people that healing isn't linear, and that happiness doesn't last forever. The fact that I allowed myself to hope differently is purely my fault. Four weeks before everything goes to hell, I'm sitting on the worn leather couch at the front of Inkjection as I finish the last details of the outline for my final creative writing project.

I tend to be humble, but *Gracie and Sammy: Undercover Detectives* is looking very promising if I do say so myself. Luke offered to give it a read once it's done, and I plan on reading it to Maddie too.

So yes, for once, I'm excited about this project now that I finally see the light at the end of the tunnel.

Cal's last client of the day, an ex-military man with an impressive tattoo on his buzzed head, comes out to the front of the shop with my boyfriend right at his heels.

God, *my boyfriend*. How can saying something feel so right and so surreal at the same time?

He winks at me before turning to his laptop to type something in, and I melt against the leather. As he talks to his client, my unapologetic eyes drift over to his hands and stay there for longer than it's probably acceptable. All I can think about as I stare at those strong but gentle palms, those thick and talented fingers and his tattooed knuckles is how good it felt last night when he grabbed my ass as he pounded into me, my legs tangled around his narrow waist to take him even deeper.

*Holy shit*, when did it get so hot in here?

For the past few days, I've slept at his apartment every single night. Emily isn't complaining about my absence—if anything, she's encouraging me to stay with him even more often. As if that was possible.

"Move in with him," she suggested one day, so casually it threw me off and I almost choked on my morning coffee.

"What?! Em, are you insane?"

She only shrugged and said, "He's it for you. I can feel it. Why are you wasting your time?"

Her words have been echoing back in my head ever since. Not like I'd act on them any time soon. Cal and I are only recently learning to navigate this new connection; we don't need any added pressure.

And talking about added pressure... We haven't told Aaron yet and hiding our relationship from him is killing me. Not because I'm scared he'd lash out at Cal if he found out before we tell him ourselves, but because it would hurt him that I'm keeping this from him. It just...never came up. The moment never felt right enough.

I know they are bullshit excuses, but I'll tell him soon.

Eventually.

My attention drifts back to Cal's hands, so rough and beautiful at the same time. Capable of pleasuring me, holding me, taking my pain away. More than once I've caught myself daydreaming about what it would be like to feel his fingers inside of me, but every time I'm about to suggest it in bed an invisible leash holds me back.

We have all the time in the world, and I promised myself I wouldn't rush any stage of my healing journey. Cal understands this and never pressures me to do anything I'm not sure about, which helps. Yet every time those fingers touch my body, I wonder...

"Sunshine."

I blink, waking up from my daydreams at the sound of his voice, in time for him to bend over and capture my lips in a sweet, short kiss. When he pulls away, a warm smile adorns his handsome face. "How's the outline going? Are you finished?"

I mirror his sheepish smile and notice for the first time his client is gone and we're alone at the shop. "It's all done. I'll start writing it tomorrow, actually. I'm so excited."

His lips descend over mine again, pecking them so gently my heart combusts. "I'm so proud of you."

The words are on the tip of my tongue, just like they've been for a while now. But it's still too soon to set them free, especially when we aren't on the same page yet. He's barely admitted to himself that being in a relationship won't ruin his sister's life. I can be patient. For him, I'll always be.

His hand engulfs the side of my ribs, below the now healed tattoo. I get tingles just thinking about his ink on my skin, his beautiful art on my body forever. "Are we still going to the vegan truck?" I ask him, voice breathy. I'm not fully used to this touchy, more intimate side of him yet, but I'm also not complaining.

"Yeah, I'm starving," he says, and the double entendre isn't lost on me. Goosebumps appear all over my arms as he takes a step back and holds out his hand, helping me up. "Ready? My car's out back."

Once he closes the shop, we step outside the freezing December air, and I press my jacket closer to my limbs. It's so darn cold, I curse myself for having forgotten my hat at the dorm.

I tell him about the outline of my book as he drives across town, and for the first time since Professor Danner told us about the project, I'm thrilled to start writing my book. This gut feeling I've been harboring for the past few weeks is screaming at me that I'll be all right, and this time I'm going to listen.

"What do you wanna try tonight?" Cal wraps an arm around my shoulders as we scan the menu at the vegan truck.

"Mm-hmm... How about the tacos? Are they any good?"

"Oh, yeah. I think I'm in the mood for one of the sandwiches. We can share if you want."

"Deal."

After getting our food, we go back to the car as it is unbelievably cold outside. He only complains once—he hates eating in the car, but I don't want to freeze my butt off. Cal moves Maddie's car seat to the front, and we take the back.

"I was thinking," Cal starts as he wipes his fingers on a napkin. I follow the movement with my eyes like a starved animal. "Trey's birthday is coming up, and he wants to grab some drinks at Danny's to celebrate. He told me to ask you if you wanted to tag along."

My eyebrows shoot up in surprise. "He did?" I mean, I like Trey and we joke around sometimes, but I didn't think he liked me enough to invite me to his birthday party. Or it could be because I'm now Cal's girlfriend and he feels obliged to...

*No. Stop it right there.*

*He invited you because he wants you there. End of the story.*

"Yup."

"When's this thing?"

"Tomorrow after we close. You in, sunshine?"

A few months ago, it would've taken me *hours* to think this through. But now, as wary of crowds as I still am, I say without hesitation, "Sure. It sounds fun."

Because Cal will be there to shield me from everything, but even if he isn't, I can hold my own ground now.

If the past few weeks have taught me anything, it is that the soil I've been planted in is fertile enough to make me bloom under any circumstances. Slowly, at my own pace, but I'm getting there and that's all that counts.

"Good." Cal sets our empty takeout boxes aside. "Now come here. I miss those lips."

# CAL

There are endless little things about Grace that drive me insane.

The way her whole face lights up when she talks about books. How she unconsciously reaches for me when we sleep together. Her dancing around my living room with Maddie while I make dinner.

Seeing her in a tight, short dress is one of those things.

When I pick her up from her dorm, I physically have to stop myself from throwing her over the hood of my car and making love to her right there. She's addictive in the way happiness is addictive, and I want to feel her in my veins every fucking day.

Tonight, though, I can't.

Because something else that is currently driving me insane—in the worst way possible—is the fact that I'll have to keep my hands off her all night.

Aaron is here, and he doesn't know about us. The only people who do are Trey and Grace's group of girlfriends, who have been sworn to secrecy until we tell Aaron ourselves. I'm not sure what Grace is waiting for, but I vowed to follow her lead and I won't break my promise now.

Hopefully, my cock gets the memo too.

And trust me, it's not easy to make him understand. Not when Grace's warm body, clad in such a sinful dress, is pressed against my side as the crowd moves around us. We've been at Danny's for an hour and so far, my hands haven't reached past her elbow. Anything lower than that and I know for a fact I'll have Aaron breathing down my neck in a second, demanding I explain why I have a semi.

Because this is Grace, so naturally any type of contact between us sets my whole body on fire.

At one point she stands on her tiptoes to say something in my ear, but she's so short compared to me that I still have to bend over a little. "Bathroom," she says simply, and with a firm nod I let her know I'll keep an eye on her as she leaves.

She's just disappeared into the women's bathroom when the strong grip of a hand lands on my shoulder. "Cal, man. Long time no see," says Anderson, one of the regulars at the shop.

I keep an eye on the bathroom door as I talk to Anderson, who's more Trey's friend than mine, but he's a solid guy and I don't want to be a grumpy asshole to him. My shoulders relax when I spot Grace coming out to the bar, and then they tense again as some jock stops right on her path, a smug smirk on his dumb face.

I'm this fucking close to throwing him out into the streets when I remember Grace's conversation with Aaron. She was annoyed at him for being so overprotective, as if he didn't believe she could take care of herself. So while Anderson keeps talking to me even though I'm not hearing a damn word, I keep my eyes on her.

One panicked look my way and I'm breaking his legs.

But the guy doesn't cross any lines, and Grace seems calm enough. She nods at something he says, then she laughs and shakes her head. He's obviously into her, probably offering to buy her a drink, but she only turns her head to look at me and winks.

My smirk is a promise of what's to come when we're alone later.

Their conversation lasts less than a minute, and I breathe a little easier when Grace is back at my side. Not being able to help it—and not caring, either—I wrap my arm around her waist and pull her closer. Once Anderson spots somebody else in the crowd and leaves, I turn to her. "Are you okay?"

"Yeah." She gives me that small, adorable smile that does wicked things to my heart. "He was just flirting."

"Flirting, huh?" I tug her closer and drop my mouth to the shell of her ear. "So what you're saying is that some fucker was hitting on my girl."

Her breath hitches, and the fact that my possessiveness turns her on is not lost on me. "Maybe."

My hand moves down to rest a little lower, the sudden urge to claim her in front of all these people—Aaron be damned—crawling up my spine at a dangerous speed. "Can't have that now, can we?"

She tips her head slightly, so my lips are brushing her nose. This is dangerous territory, but neither of us are thinking too clearly right now. "Come with me," she whispers before tugging at my hand and leading me across the bar and down a dark hallway.

We pass the crowded bathroom line and step inside what seems to be a coat closet. A tiny one.

"Grace?" My heart pounds like crazy when I understand what it means that she's dragged me here.

The closet isn't completely dark as there's a ventilation grid above the door which lets in the faintest hint of light. Somehow, Grace finds a lock on the door and turns it. When her eyes find mine, lust is pouring out of her.

Her hands land on the button of my jeans and my cock stirs. "I need you in my mouth," she whispers so roughly I almost come right there.

"Fuck, babe." Almost as a second instinct, I grip the back of her hair tight enough not to hurt her.

Determination gleaming in her eyes, Grace carefully slides the zipper down and then my jeans until she comes face to face with the prominent bulge on my boxers. I can't hold back the groan that pours out of me when she strokes my cock through the thin fabric. She's given me oral before, but never like this. She's never looked so starved, so eager to put me in her mouth. So confident.

*Fuck*, her confidence is so fucking sexy.

After a few strokes, she finally pulls down my boxers and wraps her hand around me. And *shit*. The mere sight of my dick between her small fingers is enough to make me desperate with need. She licks her lips, and I tighten my grip on her hair.

"You're gonna suck my cock like a good girl?" I grunt, marveling at the woman on her knees before me.

She looks up at me with big, innocent eyes, and I fight the urge to shove my cock down her throat as punishment because the last thing she's right now is innocent, and she knows it. "Is that what you want me to do?"

I angle my hips forward, the tip parting her rosy lips. "Let me fuck your mouth," I breathe. My girl whimpers at my possessive demand, and fuck if it doesn't make me even harder.

She keeps her eyes on me as she spits on the swollen head of my cock, getting it all wet and ready for her. She plants an open-mouthed kiss on my sensitive skin before swirling her tongue and sucking hard on my length.

"Fucking hell," I groan, already losing control. My hand on her hair tightens, holding her in place. I don't dare take my eyes off her in case I miss a second of her pretty mouth around my shaft.

Grace strokes the base of my cock with her hand, adding a small twist as she works me since she can't fit all of me in her mouth. It turns me on beyond reason that I'm too big and thick for her. Throwing my head back in ecstasy, I remember how my cock stretches her so wide when I fuck her.

*Shit, shit, shit.*

Like a man possessed, I start thrusting into her mouth until the head of my cock hits the back of her throat, making her choke on it. But she doesn't stop even as her eyes water, and the lust I feel only keeps growing.

"You look so fucking beautiful like this," I groan as I keep thrusting my hips. "You like how I fuck your mouth, don't you? That's right, I want every inch of my fat cock buried deep in your throat."

She moans at the rough command, and the sound makes my balls tighten. I push even deeper, careful to not hurt her but still aching to see her choke on me. The sight of her on her knees, with my cock in her mouth, gagging on it, moaning around it...

I'm so fucking close.

Tears roll down her cheeks as I fuck her mouth with abandon. "I'm gonna come in your mouth," I warn her, but she only moans around my shaft and doesn't pull away. "And you're gonna swallow every drop of my cum like a good girl, understood?"

She loves it when I manhandle her like this, when the rough side of me comes out in bed. I can only imagine how fucking wet she is between her legs, how exquisite she would taste right now. "Your throat is so fucking tight, babe. I bet your pretty little pussy is gonna choke my dick when I fuck it later."

She whimpers with need, desperate to be filled in other places too. I thrust into her like an animal for another few seconds until I can barely hold myself together any longer. "If you want me to pull out, say it now."

Grace only manages to shake her head. Looking right into her eyes, I pump into her one last time before spilling down her warm throat while she moans around it. Her throat moves up and down as she swallows my cum, and it's the most erotic thing I've ever had the fucking privilege to witness.

My dick eventually softens inside her mouth, my grip on her hair eases, and we're both breathing heavily by the time I pull out. Still on her knees, Grace's eyes follow my movements as I crouch down and kiss her hungrily, not minding the taste of myself in her lips at all.

"You okay, sweetheart?" I wipe her tears away with the pads of my thumbs. "Was I too rough?"

"You were perfect," she reassures me with that bright smile. "I never thought I would give you a blowjob in a coat closet, but here we are."

I throw my head back with a laugh and pull her up with me, hugging her to my chest. "I don't think we should risk our luck by doing part two here." I lower my mouth to her ear and whisper, "I'd rather fuck you good and slow in my bed."

Her breath hitches. "Looks like we'll have a busy night, then."

# chapter 37

## CAL

The day before Maddie's Christmas recital, I'm not surprised to find out my mother has decided not to go but it still pisses me off enough to dampen my mood.

"I'm too tired from work, Samuel," she told me over the phone when I asked her for the very last time. Like a fool, I was being too hopeful. "But you can film her on your phone, will you? I still want to see her."

*Then drag your ass from the fucking couch and come with me* is what I want to tell her. Instead I say, "Sure." And there's that. Nothing too surprising here.

Last week I mentioned it to Pete as well on the off chance that he suddenly decided to act like a proper father and support his daughter. Our conversation went like this:

*"You want to come to Maddie's ballet recital next Friday?"*

*He didn't even look away from the TV. "How long will that thing last?"*

*"Around two hours. Probably less."*

*"I'll pass."*

*I'll pass.*

If I didn't slam his head against the fucking screen it was only because I wasn't in the mood to deal with the consequences.

By the time the big day comes, though, I've shoved all the hurt away for Maddie's sake. And my own.

She asked about her parents coming to cheer her on,

319

naturally, and although she didn't make a fuss about them not showing up it still broke my fucking heart to tell her it was just going to be me in the audience.

I'll never forgive either of them for this.

"How are you feeling, peanut?" I crouch in front of my sister, unzipping her puffy jacket before I drop her off at the back entrance of the local theater so she can get ready for her performance. When I spot Grace at the door, ushering little girls and boys inside, I wink at her and her cheeks flush.

"I'm a little nervous." Maddie bites down on her lower lip. "Sammy, do you think I can do it?"

"I *know* it, Maddie." I cradle her whole face in the palm of my hand, and she leans into the touch. "And I'm not saying it because you're my little sister, but because you're an amazing princess-ballerina. Just remember to have fun. That's all that matters."

Without warning, she throws her arms around my neck.

"I love you, Sammy. You're the best big brother ever."

A lump forms in my throat, and I swallow past it. "I love you too, Mads. More than I love anyone else."

She gasps. "More than Grace?"

I chuckle as I tuck her brown hair behind her ears. "I love you both in different ways," I explain. Saying that I love Grace out loud doesn't feel the least bit weird at all. "But yes, baby, I love you even more than I love Grace. More than anyone. You're my number one person in the world. Don't ever forget it."

She gives me a big smile followed by a loud kiss on my cheek. I drop her off with the promise of something yummy for dinner when she comes back home with me tonight. With us.

Maddie runs straight to Grace, who kneels to whisper something in her ear that makes her laugh. Both turn their heads in my direction and giggle, a secret passing between them that I'm not privy to.

My heart swells until it fucking hurts to keep breathing, and

I don't think I've ever loved anyone so much in my life.

My sister and my girlfriend, the air I breathe and the sunshine that feeds my soul. It hits me then—there's simply no way I could live without them. They give me a reason to wake up every morning, to be a better man.

If anything happened to them...

I stop my thoughts before they trespass forbidden territory. I refuse to go there, not when everything is so damn perfect right now it's a struggle to believe it's real.

After Grace ushers Maddie inside, I hop back into my car and drive to the shop for my last appointment of the day. The recital doesn't start for another few hours, so I have more than enough time to finish work.

Last night, Grace told me they require the girls to get there early so each group can rehearse on the actual stage at least a couple of times to get familiar with the layout. Also, because they're so little it takes all the patience in the world to help them with their outfits and hair. Maddie was super excited for Grace to do her bun.

Three hours later, I'm finally sitting in the very crowded theater. I don't think I can spot a single empty seat from here. I knew TDP was popular in Warlington—when I looked for a ballet studio, I made sure it was the best—but holy shit. Apparently, it's not only parents and friends that come to this thing, but talent scouts as well.

So yes, The Dance Palace is *the shit*.

The fact that my sunshine is talented enough to work here only makes me even prouder of her.

The first group starts at four sharp, and because Maddie belongs to the younger groups, hers is the second performance of the afternoon. Excitement and pride fill my chest, and I completely forget about taking out my phone and filming the whole thing. My eyes are glued on my little sister, shining like a star as she follows the routine.

It's too fucking adorable.

She waves her hands and points her feet, a perpetual smile on her face, and I'm relieved she doesn't feel scared at all. Maddie's not a shy kid, but there are a shit ton of people here and it would be understandable if she got nervous. But no—she follows the choreography with ease, and when she bumps into one of her friends her only reaction is to giggle and move on.

Seeing how happy and in her element she looks out there, dancing with her friends like it's a fun game... I could cry right now.

*This* is what I want for her. Unconditional love. Total happiness. A normal life.

I know it's unrealistic to expect her to always be joyful—I'm not that delusional. But there's a difference between being a happy person who has bad days, and harboring a sad heart and being distracted by temporary happiness.

If Maddie moving in with me is what it will take to give her that kind of normalcy, so be it.

Once the performance ends, I clap and cheer for her as loudly as I can, not caring about the side looks from all the stuck-up parents around me. I want my princess to know she killed it.

The only downside to my sister dancing so soon into the event is that I still have another hour of this to get through without any real excitement. Don't get me wrong, I appreciate the art of ballet and I find it beautiful—more so now that both of my girls are into it. Some of the songs are catchy, even. Who would've thought classical music had some solid bangers?

A while later the owner of TPD, who's also been introducing each group before they come up on stage, announces the last performance of the night.

And when the dancers get on stage, I lose my breath.

Grace is right in the middle of the stage, clad in a beautiful white and gold ballerina outfit that makes her look all the more angelic.

The music starts, and I'm completely and utterly mesmerized by her elegant moves. I've never seen her dance beyond those times she dances with Maddie at home, but she wasn't like *this*. Majestic like a swan, gentle like the touch of a feather, and so bloody talented it makes me wonder why she's not a professional ballet dancer instead.

My heart fills with the promise of undying love as I watch her. So confident, so breathtaking, so *graceful*. Her own name has never fit her this well. I'm so dumbfounded by her that I can't even bring myself to cheer along with everyone else when their performance ends. I only have eyes for her, her beautiful smile and the twinkle in her eyes as she waves to the crowd and bows.

After everyone fills the stage again to say goodbye and I cheer for Maddie again, I follow the crowd of eager parents outside to wait for the girls.

The second Maddie spots me, she sprints in my direction, and I catch her in my arms. "You did so well, princess. I'm so proud of you."

I pepper her warm cheek with loud kisses, and she laughs. "You're proud?"

"Of course, I am. You're my little girl. I'll always be proud of you."

She beams at me and I lower her to the ground, grabbing her hand. "Let's wait for Grace, and then all three of us are going home and eating some hot dogs. Sounds good?"

As she jumps happily, I don't think my life has ever felt so full.

\* \* \*

It's not until we have dinner and Maddie dances around the living room for a bit to wear off her excitement that I can finally put her to bed and have Grace all to myself.

I keep the door to my room ajar, just like every time Maddie sleeps over so she can come for me if something happens, but my burning hands find Grace's waist and pull her against the wall all the same. "You didn't tell me you were dancing tonight," I whisper, our foreheads pressed together.

She runs her hands along my arms, a trail of goosebumps spreading on their way. "I'm sorry I kept it from you, but I never tell anybody. I hate all the attention."

"It's all right." I kiss her nose. "You killed it anyway."

"Thank you." She smiles sheepishly.

"I wasn't prepared for the angelic sight of you in that stage," I whisper roughly in her ear. "So, be a good girl and give me a warning next time, yeah?"

"Yeah." I can practically hear the arousal in her throaty voice.

"Good." Knowing my sister is sleeping on the other side of the apartment and we can't do anything tonight, I give her a quick peck on the lips and pull away before our tension escalates. "Want to watch a movie?"

"Sure."

Once we've changed into more comfortable clothes and Grace's had a shower, we climb under the covers. When I hold her in my arms, I forget all about the movie. "I'm gonna miss you," I whisper, burying my nose in the familiar strawberry scent of her hair. I bought this shampoo specifically for her since I know she loves it so much.

She chuckles softly against my chest. "I'll be gone for less than a week. You'll hardly have time to miss me."

"I beg to differ," I say, hugging her closer. She's flying out to her hometown in Canada for the holidays to see her dads, and I'm a selfish prick who wants to keep her all for himself. "Want to do something special for New Year's?"

"Sure. What did you have in mind?"

My lips graze her forehead. "I could book a table in some fancy restaurant..."

"Yeah?" she prompts, amused. "We could watch the fireworks..."

"Uh-huh."

I shift on the bed so I'm on top of her, caging her small body under mine. She laughs as I bury my face in her neck, tickling her with my stubbled cheek. "Or we could stay at home so you can spread your legs like a good girl and let me have my first meal of the year."

She throws her head back in laughter, and I can't help but chuckle as well. "Oh, Sammy, you're naughty."

"Is that a yes, then?"

"It's a hell yes, babe."

I kiss her again and force myself to pull away once more. We still have tomorrow to fool around before she leaves, and I'm not risking my sister walking in on us. I can't imagine a more mortifying experience.

Grace sighs placidly when I wrap her in my arms again and press play on the movie, which paired with the wear of today's high emotions lulls us to sleep in minutes.

It isn't until much, much later that a faint whimper pulls me out of the darkness.

At first I think it's only a product of my dreams, until a powerful instinct makes all the alarms go off inside my brain.

When I peel my eyes open, I see a small shadow standing near the foot of my bed. I blink once, twice, and the shadow transforms into my little sister.

I jerk up and reach for her, sleep long vanished from my system. "What are you doing here, princess? Is everything okay?"

That whimper again. She comes closer, and I notice she's holding Monkey firmly on her grip. "Nightmare," she mutters.

"Come here, baby."

I haul her up since the bed is too high for her to climb on and hug her tightly against my chest, rocking her back and forth. "It's okay, Maddie. It was just a bad dream, nothing was real."

The little hand that isn't holding Monkey grips my t-shirt. "You... You left."

My chest constricts with emotion. "I would never, ever, leave you. Never. You're my little girl, remember?" I whisper and press a soft kiss on the crown of her head. "Try to fall back asleep, yeah?"

"Can I stay here?" she asks so quietly I almost miss it. "Of course you can, peanut. Let's get some sleep now."

The bed shifts and a confused groan comes from my right side. "Cal? What's going on?"

Before I can say a word, though, Maddie leaves my arms and settles between Grace and me. Facing her, she whispers, "I had a nightmare. Can I sleep with you?"

Grace's eyes are barely open as she smooths a hand down Maddie's hair, and my stomach flips. "'Course you can, sweetheart. Want me to tell you a story?"

And so I watch, dumbfounded, as my girlfriend starts narrating in a lulling, calming voice, the story of Gracie and Sammy to my sister. Within minutes, Maddie is already snoring against her, and Grace's words slowly fade into silence as she falls asleep too.

Fuck me if I don't know now.

Fuck me if I don't know, without a single shade of a doubt, that Grace is so much more than the love of my damn life.

She's my fucking soulmate.

# chapter 38

## GRACE

"No, no, no. This can't be happening."

I pace my empty dorm room back and forth, silently and then not so silently cursing the fuckery I've read fifteen times already on my phone to make sure it's real. Because I can't believe this.

And still in disbelief and with my heart pounding so fast I fear it might explode, I send a screenshot to the group chat I share with my fathers. Not even a minute later, my phone rings with a video call.

"I'm freaking out," I say as a way of greeting.

Dad is holding the phone, a stern grimace on his face while Daddy puts on his glasses before coming to stand behind him. "Okay, sweetheart. Breathe in, breathe out," Daddy instructs. I do as he says. "Now we can talk."

"Did you guys see what I sent you?" I try to wipe the anxiety off my face with my sweaty palm, but it doesn't work.

"We saw," Dad confirms. "It was to be expected, Grace. Snowstorms are not uncommon at this time of the year, and right now the weather is awful."

"My flight is *canceled*, Dad, with no rescheduling. What am I supposed to do now?" Because the thought of not seeing my family for the holidays is leaving me freaking breathless, and not in a good way.

Aaron left for Toronto the morning of my ballet recital,

already expecting that the weather would only get worse as the days passed, but I couldn't fly out with him for obvious reasons. And now I'm stuck in Warlington, alone for the second Christmas in a row, with not even my cousin to make it better.

"I wouldn't want you to fly in this weather anyway, Grace," Dad says in his usual serious tone that I've officially branded as his "lawyer" voice. "Snowstorms aren't a joke, and it looks like this one will last until Christmas Day."

My hopes skyrocket. "I can fly out that day, then. It wouldn't be ideal, but..."

"Listen to us, sweetie." Daddy takes the phone from Dad and sits on the couch. "Christmas Eve is tomorrow, and I don't think this storm is going anywhere. We thought of driving down there and spending the holidays together even if it's in some hotel room, but the roads aren't safe enough either. Aaron is here already, but are you sure none of your friends are staying at Warlington too? I'm sure they'll have no issue accommodating you for the holidays. We can still see each other at New Year's, eh?"

I nod, but the sadness doesn't fade away. "My friends went home days ago, and..."

I freeze. How have I not thought of him before?

Dad frowns. "And...?"

But I can't ask him for this. Sure, we are together, but... Isn't it too soon to spend Christmas together? With his family, no less? Because with Maddie in the picture, he's spending the holidays with them even if the tension is bound to kill him.

"Grace."

I blink. "Sorry. I was thinking... There's a friend staying here for Christmas, I think."

"That's good." Daddy's face relaxes at that. "Do we know her?"

I bite my lip. "Um, no. You don't know...him."

Silence falls over the three of us like a thick blanket. My

dads have never been the overprotective, overbearing type, but they also know I haven't had a male friend in... Well, ever. The shock is understandable.

Daddy speaks first. "If this isn't a surprise," he mutters, but he doesn't sound angry. "Well, please, do tell us about this young man. Is he in your class?"

"Um, no. He's thirty, and... Yeah, we're friends." I'm not about to break the news that I have a boyfriend over a video call. "His name is Cal, and he's from Warlington. I met him when I went to the tattoo place all those months ago. He owns the shop, actually, and he's also Aaron's friend."

"Interesting," Daddy muses, narrowing his wise eyes like he can see right through the truth I'm veiling. "And he's a good friend to you?"

"The best," I blurt out, making Dad's eyebrows shoot up in surprise. Clearing my throat, I add, "I told him about the assault. He's... He's a great person."

"You saying Aaron knows this Cal guy?" Dad asks. I nod. "They're friends."

"Good. Well, if you're such great friends I'm sure you can spend Christmas Day with him," Daddy says, but there isn't a hint of bitterness in his tone, only surprise. "As I said, you can still fly out for New Year's and stay here a few days. We really want to see you, sweetie."

My features soften. "I really want to see you both too. So much."

I go on to tell them about my book, and they beam with happiness at my progress. The topic of Cal isn't brought up again, but it's obvious they would conduct a full-on interrogation about him if they could. While I don't blame them for their curiosity, I can't help but feel relieved that they don't ask me about him again.

I'm not ashamed of our relationship, nor do I intend to keep it a secret from my family. It's just that I've never had a boyfriend before, and this is a huge step for me and my healing. Telling my parents and Aaron will happen, hopefully soon, but now I have other more pressing matters to worry about.

Namely, asking Cal to spend the holidays with him and his family.

\* \* \*

Cal says yes immediately and encourages me to "move in" to his apartment for the holidays so I'm not alone at the dorms. I say yes immediately, too. Duh.

As we get ready to leave for his mother's house on Christmas Eve, though, he warns me. "It's probably gonna get really awkward."

"I don't care," I reassure him. Walking up to him, I peel his fingers from the small buttons of his white shirt so I can do them for him. He looks hot as sin dressed in such formal clothes that I struggle to breathe normally. "I only care about Maddie and you."

His shoulders still don't relax. "Pete is an asshole."

"I don't care."

But because apparently Cal enjoys self-flagellation a little too much, he adds, "*I* might behave like an asshole."

I finish up the last button of his shirt, which barely fits his wide shoulders and large biceps, and I adjust the collar to keep my hands busy. "Why?"

He smooths his big hands along the silky fabric of my midnight blue dress and settles them on my hips. "Pete gets on my fucking nerves," he growls. "I wish we could celebrate Christmas together, just the three of us, away from all the drama."

My heart swells at the fact that he always includes me in his plans, those involving Maddie as well. It's such a contrast to the Cal who was terrified of having me in his life because he has his little sister to worry about.

"I understand how you're feeling," I tell him softly, my

fingers playing with the short strands of his hair. "But try to keep it together tonight, yeah? For Maddie."

"If I'm doing this in the first place, it's for her." He shuts his eyes and presses his forehead against mine. "I know you wanted to go home for the holidays, but I'm so fucking happy you're here with me, sunshine. I need you."

"I need you, too." Our lips meet in a brief, soft kiss. "Although our plans for New Year's might have to be postponed."

"Don't care. All that matters is that you're here, and we have now." He presses a soft kiss on my lips, so tender it leaves my knees shaking. When he pulls away, there's a new resolve in his eyes. "Come on. Let's get this over with."

* * *

I've always prided myself on being an understanding, non-judgmental woman. Knowing better than most that there's always more than what meets the eye, my brain automatically tries to push past those initial barriers and see what might be living underneath the harsh exterior.

I can't do that with Pete Stevens.

Because I can't, for the life of me, stand this sorry excuse of a human.

Cal is a reasonable, laid-back man and he wouldn't make a fuss if the situation didn't call for it, but *shit*. I understand him now, and I wish I didn't.

Because seeing a man, a *father*, ignore his daughter so blatantly is a sight I never want to see again.

I know I'm privileged in the sense that I grew up in a fully functional family, surrounded by love and laughter and, yes, financial stability. I get that. And while being the adopted child of gay parents wasn't always a walk in the park—bullies have mercy on no one—I would rather take the hatred of some insecure kid at school than my own father not giving a shit about me.

To be fair, Cal's mother isn't half as bad as I thought she would be. She gave me a genuine smile and a hug when he introduced me as his girlfriend, and when recognition dawned on her she asked me if we'd met before. I told her I was Maddie's ballet teacher, and we must have seen each other at TDP. Even though she flinched just barely because she rarely picks up Maddie anymore and I bet she feels at least a little guilty about it, she proceeded to ask me about my work there. The woman might have her issues, but she seems pleasant enough.

She went the extra mile with Christmas dinner too, which Cal himself seemed taken aback by. Stuffed turkey with gravy, mashed potatoes and roasted vegetables were already adorning the table by the time we sat down. On top of each of our empty plates, and because my heart was meant to hurt that night, there was a beautiful drawing made by none other than Maddie herself.

"She's been on a drawing frenzy lately," Cal's mom, Larissa, commented with an almost rueful smile as she picked up her own picture.

"This is so pretty and thoughtful, Maddie. Thank you." I pressed a small kiss on top of her head when she came by my side to explain her drawing to me. There were two figures—one small with dark hair and the other taller with a blond bun, dancing ballet on a stage. We both had crowns on our heads.

"Because we are princess-ballerinas," she explained. It took all my willpower and then some not to start crying right there.

Then she moved on to her brother, climbing onto his lap and stealing the drawing from his hands. "This is you." She pointed at the tallest stick figure. "And this is me, and this is Grace, and we are in your new house with a pretty garden with flowers."

Larissa gasped. "You're moving in together?"

"No," Cal said quickly, and for some reason my stupid stomach sank at that. It is true, though. We aren't moving in together any time soon and haven't even discussed it. Still, I felt a tang of disappointment coating my tongue. "This little one here has a very vivid imagination. Don't you, munchkin?"

Maddie nodded and pressed her back to Cal's chest like a silkworm on its cocoon, safe and warm. "Will you buy a house like this after you have a wedding, Sammy?"

We looked at each other, briefly, but enough for something charged to pass between us. His eyes twinkled, and he said, "Of course, Mads. And you'll be invited to stay over any time you want."

That was the last heartwarming, happy moment of our dinner.

Now, with the turkey and the cheesecake for dessert long gone, I fight the anger boiling up in my stomach as I watch the most infuriating and equally heartbreaking scene unfold before my very eyes.

Pete has long abandoned the dining table for the couch after having barely engaged in conversation with any of us at all. He grunted a "Hello" when Cal introduced us and that was the last and only thing he said to me. Not that I have a problem with it, to be honest.

He is balding, has a perpetual scowl on his face, and was hunched over the table during dinner as if he were avoiding eye contact with everyone. He's tall, but not as tall as Cal, and lacks all the muscle and strong build his stepson has. However, Pete's objectively unappealing looks are the least of his problems.

Maddie—my sweet, innocent Maddie—has ditched us too and is now climbing onto the couch next to her dad, whose eyes never leave the TV. Not once. He doesn't acknowledge her as she cuddles her little body against him, splaying her arm across his stomach and snuggling closer to his chest. She tells him something, but I can't hear her over the sound of whatever show Pete is watching.

He doesn't reply.

Over to my right, both of Cal's hands are curled into tight fists under the table, tension radiating off his huge body, and I know he's watching them. Larissa isn't.

Cal's mother is nursing a glass of some kind of strong alcohol, judging by the pungent smell of it, and she's not drunk but she isn't sober either. I know that's making Cal angry too, even if his attention is somewhere else for the time being.

Several minutes pass by, and if it weren't for Pete's wide-open eyes, I would think he's asleep. Why else would a father ignore his own daughter?

I've just grabbed Cal's hand in mine, my thumb caressing his rough skin in soothing circles, when hell breaks loose.

"For fuck's sake, Maddie! Can't you keep quiet for a goddamn second?" Pete roars, startling her. Maddie falls back on the couch, and before I can fully understand what's going on, the beast strikes.

Cal is on Pete in seconds. I didn't even feel his hand leaving mine.

He holds the smaller man by the collar of his shirt, pressing their foreheads together in an intimate gesture that screams violence. "Say that again," my boyfriend growls, baring his teeth like a rabid animal. "I fucking dare you, you worthless piece of shit."

Long gone is the man with a calming aura, always unbothered and level-headed, and I can't bring myself to care. I'm not scared of this new, violent side of Cal.

But I have to think of Maddie.

His mom jumps into action, almost knocking her glass over as she stands to pull the two men away from each other. "Samuel, let him go," she orders. Cal doesn't.

"Listen to me, motherfucker," he spits into Pete's still too-close face. It's like the whole room, the whole *world*, vanishes for him and only anger remains. "You talk to my sister like that one more time, I'm gonna make sure you don't utter a single word again. You know why? 'Cause I'll tear your tongue right out of your fucking mouth."

I don't know what it says about me that the violence pouring off of him is turning me on so freaking much right now.

I push all that away, though, when I notice Maddie on the opposite end of the couch, eyes wide with hurt and confusion. I don't think twice before rushing out to her and cradling her in my arms. "Hey, Maddie," I whisper softly into her ear. "You haven't shown me your room in this house yet. Would you like to give me a tour?"

She nods, still unsure, but it's enough. Cal's mother gives me half panicked, half grateful look before I disappear down the hall with her daughter.

Once in her bedroom, which isn't as nice as the one in Cal's apartment but it's still super cute, she proceeds to show me all her favorite toys one by one. We're on the tenth one, a mermaid doll with a glittery tail, and I can still hear their muffled voices in the living room.

I got it when he first explained it to me, but I see it even clearer now—why Cal is so disgusted by Pete, why he thinks Maddie would be better off with him, why that could still be a harmful choice to her. She's a kid, seemingly oblivious to the tension and the neglect, and to strip her off everything she's ever known... Her routine, her home, her parents...

Cal may be afraid that all this family drama might push me away, but it does the opposite. If anything, all I feel in this moment is an even stronger resolve to help as much as I can.

"My daddy isn't very nice," Maddie blurts out of nowhere, and I know she can hear their voices too.

Fear grips my heart and refuses to let go. Luckily, I've spent enough time around kids to know how to navigate their minds and make them talk without being too obvious of my intentions.

"Why do you say that?"

She shrugs. I wait, but when she says nothing else, I ask, "Is he mean to you?"

"Sometimes," she mutters, grabbing a plastic comb and passing it through one of her doll's tangled mane. "I don't think he likes me very much."

Now my heart isn't only fearful—it's weeping.

"Maddie," I start, my voice only a little louder than a whisper. "Has your daddy ever... Has he ever hit you?"

A beat of heavy silence passes. Then, "No. But he says mean things."

I breathe a little easier. "Can you give me an example?"

She shrugs again, and I know it pains her to say it as much as it hurts me to hear it. "He says I talk too much, and I move too much."

"Move?"

"Yes, because I like dancing in the house, and he says I don't let him watch TV and that I'm annoying."

If Cal hadn't already threatened to slaughter him, I would. But my rage won't do us any good now, so instead I grab her little hand and make her sit in front of me. "Maddie, sweetie, listen to me," I start softly, a reassuring smile on my face even if happiness is the very last thing I feel right now. "You're the best little dancer I know, and I want you to always remember that, okay? You're so good, Maddie. The best. Dancing makes you happy, doesn't it?"

She nods and lowers her gaze to the ground, but not quickly enough that I don't see that first tear roll down her cheek. "Promise me something. Promise me that you'll always keep dancing as long as it makes you happy. That you'll always do what makes you happy no matter what other people think about it. Can you promise me that, sweetheart?"

She nods. "I promise."

"Can I give you a big bear hug?" I ask, and she instantly

launches herself at my arms as an answer.

Tears dwell at the back of my eyes, and I'm done fighting them. Careful not to let her see my face, I let them fall.

In silence, I cry for the little girl who deserves so much more than what life has given her this far. I vow then and there to always look after her, to keep her happiness and her dreams intact, and help her bloom like I'm learning to do myself.

I vow to keep the monsters at bay even in the darkest corner of her heart.

There's a knock at the door, and I quickly wipe my tears as Maddie pulls away. Cal's deep, strained voice fills the room as second later. "Hey. Everything all right?"

"Yes." I don't even sound convincing. I turn around as Cal picks his sister up. "You?"

"It's sorted." He doesn't elaborate, but I trust him with whatever he's done. He turns to Maddie. "Come on, princess. Time for bed. Santa is coming in the morning, remember?"

Her little face lights up at that. "Yes! Santa! I asked him for a big dollhouse this year."

"I know you did." He kisses her nose. "Let's get changed into your pajamas. Grace and I will tuck you in, yeah?"

I walk out of the room with Cal as Maddie gets changed. Wrapping my arms around myself, suddenly cold, I say, "Please, tell me you didn't do something illegal."

He chuckles. "I wanted to, but no. Don't worry, he left."

"Left?"

"He does that sometimes. Storms off when he's pissed." He sighs and wraps an arm around my shoulders to keep me close. "I can come back tomorrow alone; you don't have to tag along."

"Absolutely not, Cal. I want to see Maddie, you know this." I frown up at him, suddenly worried. "Aren't you afraid Pete will come back and...?"

"No," his voice is so sharp it could cut glass. "He won't do shit. All bark and no bite. He's done this before."

"Okay." I swallow and brace myself for what I have to say next. "I talked to Maddie. She said... She said Pete is mean to her sometimes, and I asked her if he's ever hit her, but she said no."

Cal gulps and pulls me closer. "Thank you for watching out for her, sunshine."

"You know I love her, Cal. I'd do anything for her."

I feel his arm stiffening around my body, and I wonder if I've said the wrong thing.

"You...love her?"

I extract myself from his embrace only so I can properly look at him. There's not a single doubt in my mind, no fear in my heart, as I say the words I've been dying to confess.

"Yes, Cal. I love Maddie, and I love *you*. More than anything in this world." I swallow past the lump in my throat. "This may not be the ideal moment or place to tell you, but—"

His breath hitches before he captures my lips in his, kissing the words right out of me. I feel the calming weight of his hands on my cheeks, and little by little my heart starts healing again. When he pulls away, he's looking at me with bare adoration.

"I love you, sunshine. My heart has loved you since the moment it recognized yours, so akin to mine, so beautiful and selfless. I want to cherish it forever, keep it safe between my hands."

And just right there, in the dark hallway of Cal's childhood home, the sun reaches my growing soul and makes it bloom into a tiny, delicate bud.

"I love you. Forever and always," he whispers before kissing me again.

The bud inside my chest opens, and opens, and opens—

"Ewww. Stop kissing!" a little voice whines behind us, and when we pull away to see Maddie glaring at us with her arms crossed, we both start laughing.

A small trace of light in the darkness.

A happy moment I would've cherished only a tiny bit more if I had known everything would be taken away from me only a few weeks later.

# chapter 39

## CAL

"*FUCK.*"

I'm not being gentle right now. I feel like an unleashed wild animal, giving in to my physical urges and the intoxicating feeling of Grace's body wrapped so tightly around mine.

My strong grip will leave a bruise on her hips, but I can't bring myself to slow down, nor does she tell me to stop. I'm too mesmerized, too captivated by the sight of my erect cock thrusting in and out of her weeping pussy, ripping her in half. She's so damn tight, like she hasn't been fucked in a while, when I took her the day before, and I relish the sound of her desperate moans every time I breach her entrance.

My girl loves being fucked from behind, and I'm nothing but an eager servant, happy to give her what she so desperately needs.

"Oh my god, Cal," she cries out as I shift my hips, thrusting into her even deeper. "It feels so good. Shit."

One of my hands leaves her hip to caress the roundness of her ass before spanking her. She moans. "Shh... I know, babe. I know it feels good." I watch how her lips swallow my cock. "Look at you, taking my cock so well. Such a good girl for me."

Her pussy tightens around my cock, causing me to throw my head back and curse under my breath. This is too much. She is too much, too good.

My impending release grows, and I know I won't last much longer.

I lean down until my chest is pressed against her arched back and slip a hand to her clit. My middle finger starts massaging her sensitive nub as her moans become louder and her breathing heavier. "Yes," she moans. "Cal..."

"That's right. I want you to scream my name as you come."

"Yes, yes. Don't stop, please. Oh god. I'm so close..."

"I know you are." Her walls tighten around me as my finger works faster. "Choke my cock, babe. You're so fucking wet for me."

Grace pants, breathless, as my punishing thrusts build her own release. She's such a sight to behold, my pretty girl, so delicate and fierce she makes my heart beat uncontrollably. Even as I fuck her like a mad animal, my soul can't help but swell at the notion that this incredible woman is mine.

And I'm hers, completely for the taking, for as long as she'll have me.

Her walls squeeze my cock once more, and I know I won't last another minute. I move the hand that was pleasuring her clit and wrap it around her throat. Leaning into her ear, I whisper, "Come on my cock, sunshine."

She explodes, shattering under me like a bomb. As she squeezes me hard, I find my own release between the delicate mounds of her ass. I don't remember a time where I've come this hard, where my mind has gone blank after spilling my load inside of her. If there ever was a person capable of breaking all my inhibitions, it's her.

Breathing raggedly, I press a soft kiss on her shoulder before pulling out and lying next to her as I take off the condom. "You okay, love?"

Breathless, Grace turns her head and the glow in her eyes is enough to make my heart stop. I swear she's never looked this beautiful.

"I'm more than okay." She smiles faintly. "I told you I like it rough."

And wasn't that a pleasant surprise?

The second time we slept together, she gave me permission to fuck her a little harder, and then she begged for more. And more. Insatiable like me.

Sex with Grace is as much a physical relief as it is a way for our hearts to grow closer. To plant seeds of love and trust and watch them grow into a precious thing.

"Cal."

"Mm-hmm..." My mind isn't the most alert after a session of mind-blowing sex, and she giggles at my grogginess because she knows this.

"You know how my dads wanted me to go home for New Year's, right?" she asks, and I nod. "Well, I looked up the weather forecast today and it looks like the storm is pretty much gone, so I'll be able to fly out in a couple of days."

"That's great." Even if my selfish ass would rather be with her every day, she's made it very clear that she wants to see her family after such a long time, and I would never take that away from her.

"I want you to come with me."

That sobers me up *instantly*. "Come again?"

She chuckles. "I said, I want you to come with me to Canada for New Year's."

My heart hammers inside my chest. "To meet your dads?"

"Yep."

"And they're okay with me coming over?"

"Yes." Her smile is nothing short of wicked. "I told them about you before Christmas. Well, I told them you were just a friend then because I wanted to break the news about us in person. I've never had a boyfriend, and this is...a pretty big deal, considering everything."

"Of course." I can't imagine what her fathers would think of her dating some...some dude after twenty-two years of being single and the personal hell she had to endure.

"But I called them earlier today to confirm that I was going in a couple of days and I...confessed everything, I guess." It's dark inside my room, but I know she's blushing like the prettiest of flowers. "I told them you were my boyfriend and that I wanted to introduce you guys, and they said yes."

"They're okay with me staying at your house?" I ask again to double-check because it feels surreal.

She runs her fingernails up and down my tattooed arm. "Yes. They are really excited to meet you, actually. I only told them good things about you, don't worry."

"I'm not worried," I say honestly. "Just a bit intimidated is all."

The little shit—also known as the love of my freaking life— snorts. "Trust me, you've got nothing to worry about. My dads are super chill, both of them. And sure, Dad might be a tad more serious, but Daddy will love you right away."

I arch an amused eyebrow. "You call them Dad and Daddy?"

"How else am I supposed to establish a difference?"

"Touché."

Grace presses a loud kiss on my recently shaved cheek.

"Do you mind if I read for a bit?"

"Not at all." I grin as she reaches for the e-reader on her night table. Yes—one of my bedside tables is now hers. "I wonder who bought you such a thoughtful gift..."

A playful smack lands on my arm, and I throw my head back in laughter. For Christmas, I got her an electronic reader with a subscription for endless free books every month, and she's been over the moon ever since. I know she loves her paperbacks and she'll keep buying them, but this will also save her a shit ton of money and space as well as introduce her to indie authors she wouldn't otherwise see at the store.

She's pretty much ditched me for the gadget, but I don't hold grudges. Making my girl happy is what makes me happy, and knowing that I put that little smile on her face when she discovers a new book makes me realize how in love I really am with her.

Every time I think I couldn't possibly love her more, I fall a little deeper.

She got me one of those decorative skateboards I'm so obsessed with for Christmas, and it's been proudly hanging from my living room wall ever since. I pretty much shat myself when I saw the amazing art of one of my favorite rock bands, a limited edition no less.

The true gift, however, is being able to hold her as she reads beside me. With my arms around her and the familiar and comforting scent of my best friend and girlfriend consuming all my senses, my body relaxes until I gave in to the darkness.

"What should I pack?" I ask Grace from behind the front desk at Inkjection the following afternoon.

She stops typing her book on her laptop, leveling me up with a stare that is both confused and slightly amused. "Cal, babe, we leave tomorrow morning. You *haven't* packed yet?"

I shrug. "Did the laundry this morning, so everything's clean. Are we gonna do something crazy like skiing?"

"Maybe some other time." She closes her laptop, leaves it on the leather couch, and comes to wrap her arms around my waist. "We'll only be there for four days, and I want to see my dads as much as I can. They aren't big on skiing, but they love tennis if that counts."

"Okay, no winter sports. What do you have planned, then?"

"You'll see." She gives me a beautiful, mischievous smirk, and presses her chin against my arm. Her head barely reaches the top of my pecs, and I find that adorable. "It's a surprise."

"You're gonna steal my New Year's date idea, aren't you?"

When she bursts out laughing, I already suspect the answer. "Don't be impatient, Sammy."

"Mm-hmm..." I mumble, wrapping my arm around her shoulders to bring her closer. Trey left five minutes ago, and I'm getting everything ready to close so we can go home and pack our stuff.

Tomorrow morning, we'll be dropping by my mother's house to say goodbye to Maddie and promise her we'll be back soon with gifts. She already knows we'll be gone for a few days and, while she pouted for a bit, the prospect of getting a new toy always cheers her up.

Knowing Grace, though, half of our luggage will end up full of stuff for Maddie. I tend to consider myself an older brother who spoils his baby sister perhaps a bit too much, but Grace is on a whole other level. Every time we go out and she sees something that reminds her of Maddie, she insists on buying it and won't take no for an answer. My stubborn, selfless woman.

Last week, it was some kind of candy with a surprise toy inside. She *had* to get it because it was pink, glittery and had a princess on the wrapper. Duh.

It's those small details that prove Grace cares about my sister way more than I could've ever asked for. Hell, she even told me she loves her the same night she confessed she loved me. And if the way Maddie gushes over Grace every time she sees her is any indication, I'll say my sister loves her just as much.

Life can't get any better than this.

My hand moves to the back of her hair, tangling in her soft blond waves. "I love you," I whisper so only she can hear despite being alone. "You're my life, Grace."

"And you're mine," she whispers back, stars shining in her eyes. "But I love you more."

"No way." I smile.

"Uh-huh."

I shake my head, my nose brushing hers as I lean down with a very clear intent. "I think it might be a tie."

She laughs, and I capture the beautiful sound between my lips. Grace relaxes in my arms, parting my mouth with her tongue and exploring so slowly I suspect she wants to kill me.

I groan, the hand on her hair and the one on the small of her back pulling her so close I wish our bodies could become one and the same. Her eager little fingers grasp the front of my shirt, the one that sticks so much to my chest and arms I know it drives her insane, and she sighs against my lips. I capture that sound as well.

I'm two seconds away from spreading her out on top of this same counter and feast on her sweetness when the door of the shop opens.

And Aaron walks in.

"Well, well, well," he drawls. "If this isn't reason enough to get some bleach for my poor, innocent eyes."

Grace pulls away, eyes bursting with complete horror, and puts a safe distance between our bodies as if I were on fire. "Aaron. W-What are you doing here?"

He holds up a takeout bag. "Came by to drop some new tapas for you guys to try out. Didn't occur to me that your mouths would already be occupied."

Strangely, he doesn't sound as angry as he does amused. Still, I brace my feet on the ground and cross my arms, ready to shield Grace from her cousin if it came to it. "Got a problem with that?"

Aaron isn't a small, meek man by any means, but I still tower over him by a few inches. He does the wise thing and puts his hands up in surrender. "Not really, since I wasn't born yesterday and could smell the tension a mile away." He turns to Grace, and something akin to disappointment crosses his eyes. "Weren't you going to tell me?"

She's quick to round the front desk and stand before her cousin. "I was going to, I promise. I was...scared?"

His lips twitch. "Is that a question, G?"

She rolls her eyes in good nature. "Shut up."

Aaron sets the food on the couch and rubs his palms together. "Okay, well." When he turns to me, an unreasonable sense of apprehension settles in my chest. "Cal, a word?"

"Aaron..." Grace starts.

"It's okay." I put my hand on her shoulder and give it a reassuring squeeze. I would much rather give her a reassuring *kiss*, but I don't think that's the right move right now. To Aaron, I say, "Let's talk in the back."

As we make our way to the back of the shop where we keep a small office, Grace's loud voice drifts over to us. "If either of you go all caveman over this, I'll hate you forever!"

"Doubt it!" Aaron shouts right back.

I open the door, switch on the obnoxiously bright light on the ceiling and wait until Aaron walks in. Leaning my weight against the wooden desk that we rarely use, I tilt my head to the side. "Talk, and make it good."

In true Aaron fashion, he gives me a knowing grin that somehow makes me even more nervous. Don't get me wrong— I'm not intimidated by him. He's been my friend for years and, even if he's temperamental when it comes to defending those he cares about, he isn't a violent man.

I'm not scared his fists will hurt me—but his words might.

"I'm gonna make this quick." He sighs, leaning against the door and crossing his arms. He stares me down, forehead wrinkled, and then blurts out the last thing I expected, "Do you like mushroom lasagna?"

I blink. "What?"

"You heard me." He shrugs like that makes any sense at all. "It's my mother's specialty, and she'll want to make it when you come to our house."

I blink again. "Why would I go to your mother's house?" I mean, I've got nothing against the woman, but what the fuck?

"Because she'd like to meet Grace's boyfriend at some point."

When I keep staring at him like he's speaking in a foreign language, he sighs again and peels his back off the door. Stopping right next to me, he squeezes my shoulder.

"Listen, man, I promised Grace I would stop with the whole overprotective act shit." He hesitates. "It's not my business what she does with her life or who she dates. I care about her and want the best for her, and that's why I'm not freaking the fuck out right now."

He's looking at me with such raw intensity I almost have to look away. "What do you mean?"

"I mean, Cal, brother, that I've seen the way you look at her. I've seen the way you act around her, how her eyes light up at the mention of your name. Yours do, too."

My heart skips a beat hearing about Grace's feelings for me from another person's perspective. We might have said "I love you" to each other, but I treasure his reassurance, nonetheless.

"You make her happy. That's all that matters to me." His voice sounds so firm, I know he isn't lying. "I know you'll never hurt her, and that's a great fucking bonus if you ask me."

I can't help the small smile tugging at my lips. "You know I would never."

"Yeah. That's why I'm okay with this whole thing. Not like anyone gives a shit about my opinion, but..."

"That's not true, Aaron. Your opinion matters to her more than you think. Trust me." He's like a brother to Grace, and for that I feel the need to reassure him back.

"Thanks, man." He steps away, hand falling off my shoulder.

A wave of hesitancy washes over his face. It's so obvious he's biting his tongue right now, it hurts. "Spit it out, Big A."

He winces. "I'm not sure about that."

"Just say it."

"For the record," he squares his shoulders like he's about to get into battle. "I don't want to."

I roll my eyes. "Out with it."

"Did she tell you what happened to her all those years ago?"

My whole body freezes over, the reminder of that difficult conversation burning like a fresh wound in my soul. Aaron doesn't wait for me to say anything—my face tells him enough. "I wanted to make sure you know there are... Ah, online resources available for partners of assault survivors in case you need to... When you guys... You know what I mean."

I do, and this is not a conversation I want to be having with her goddamn cousin. "Everything's under control."

He nods, visibly relieved that he doesn't have to go into details. "Good, good. That's good. I'm just...looking out for her."

"I know you are. All's good."

He swallows, looking hesitant before he adds, "I'm gonna text you the link to a couple of trusted websites I've relied on for the past few years. They're from organizations that deal with this type of trauma, and they teach family and partners how to cope with all kinds of situations. Cal, it's... It's all right if it feels overwhelming sometimes, like you can't help much. I've felt like that before."

So far not many issues have arisen between us in the intimacy department, but I'm not naïve enough to believe things will always run smoothly. Healing isn't linear, I know that much, and all I want is to make Grace feel like she can trust me with anything.

"I appreciate it," I tell him with honesty. "I'll check them out for sure."

With a relaxed smile and a pat on the back from Aaron, the tension dissipates from the room. I'm walking behind him when he turns to me with a look in his eyes I can't quite decipher.

"Do you love her?" he asks.

My voice is loud and clear when I say, "With all I've got."

# chapter 40

## CAL

There are very few things in life that make me break out in a cold sweat.

In fact, I'm pretty sure the thought of something bad happening to Maddie and Grace is the only thing capable of making me feel anxious these days.

Only, that's a lie.

Because as I sit back for the hundredth time on the too-small plane seat while Grace writes her book, I realize with no short amount of panic that there's something else I should add to that panic list—meeting Grace's dads.

Listen, it took me nearly an hour to make up my mind about the clothes I wanted to take on this four-day trip when I usually stuff my suitcase without even looking. That should give you a clear idea of what my head is going through right now.

From our scarce conversations about her dads, I've gathered that the one parent I should worry about is Daniel Allen, who she calls Dad. Apparently, Daddy Marcus is a lot more easygoing and will probably like me the second we shake hands. It doesn't ease my nerves, though. Not one bit.

When I told him I was going to meet his uncles, Aaron only laughed and wished me luck. The fucking bastard.

"Ugh," Grace groans next to me. She rubs her eyes, a tired look on her face, and pulls out her earphones. "My brain's fried."

"You did good today. Come here." I open my arms and she

snuggles against my chest. Looking at the time on my phone, I realize we only have another twenty or so more minutes of flight time and I get anxious again.

"Your heart's beating fast," she points out, frowning as she untangles herself from my arms. I instantly miss her warmth. "You aren't scared of flying, are you?"

I arch an amused eyebrow. "I think you would know by now if I were a nervous flyer."

"What's wrong, then?"

I don't even debate whether to tell her or keep it to myself. This is Grace. "I'm kind of nervous about meeting the dads."

That gets me a teasing smile. "Aw, are you now? That's so cute."

I shift uncomfortably on my seat again. Seriously, I know I'm taller than average, but economy is still a sick joke. "Don't taunt me, sunshine, or I'll have to spank you when we get back home."

Her breath hitches only for a moment before the amusement is back. She lowers her voice until it's only a whisper in my ear. "Don't you want to spank me in my childhood bedroom, Cal?"

My hand finds her leg, my thick fingers covering the entire span of her thigh. I click my tongue. "Such a filthy mouth, sweetheart. Don't make me shut you up with my cock."

The little shit bites my earlobe before pulling away, noticing the effect she has on me and how inconvenient it is at this very moment when we can do nothing about it. "For real, though, I promise you have nothing to worry about. They'll love you, I'm sure of it," she says like she hasn't just given me a massive hard-on in the middle of a flight.

Not being able to resist, I peck her lips. "I know it's worse in my head than it'll be in real life, but I've never done the whole 'meet the parents' thing, so."

Her eyes almost pop out of the sockets. "You haven't?"

"No," I confess. "My last relationship was never serious

enough to ever consider it."

"Oh." She bites down on her lower lip, looking down at my hand still on her thigh. When she glances back at me, I see vulnerability in her beautiful eyes. But I also see a hint of insecurity, and I don't like that.

"What's on your mind?" I press another kiss to her forehead.

"This may sound silly and totally not a conversation we should have on a plane, but..." She bites her lip again. "How serious are we?"

One look at her is enough to see this matters to her. I would admit it's not a conversation we've had yet, not *explicitly* at least, but I thought...

Never mind what I thought.

If my girl needs reassurance, I'll give it to her.

"As serious as it gets, Grace," I tell her in earnest. "I'm in for the long run."

She relaxes at that. "Okay." She smiles. "I am, too."

Just then, the seatbelt signs light up and the pilot announces we're minutes away from landing. As Grace grabs my hand and presses a kiss to my tattooed knuckles, the nerves about meeting her dads come back.

I force myself to remember they're normal people. They can't be worse than Aaron, can they?

In my blinding craze about meeting the parents, I completely forgot Grace told me they would be picking us up from the airport.

Which is why, the moment we cross the arrival gates into the terminal and she jumps into the awaiting arms of a tall, blond man, I freeze on the spot.

"Dad!" she exclaims, ditching her suitcase before I take hold of it. Burying her face in her dad's chest, she mumbles, "I missed you both so much."

"We missed you too, honey," says a tall black man beside her. He presses a quick kiss on her hair before turning to me with an easy smile. "You must be Cal. I'm Marcus, Grace's dad."

When he extends a hand in my direction, it only takes me half a second to shake it and snap out of it. "Nice to meet you, sir. Thanks for having me."

"Pleasure is all ours." His body language seems relaxed, and it manages to put me at ease. Only a tiny bit.

When Grace moves on to hug Marcus, though, and leaves me with Daniel, the air changes and my shoulders become heavy under his scrutinizing gaze. Being a couple of inches shorter than me, lean body, and kind eyes, he doesn't look particularly intimidating at first. Not when Marcus is standing right there, as tall as me and with huge muscles packed under his jacket.

Yet it's Daniel who makes my skin prickle.

I push the anxious feeling in my stomach away as I extend my hand. "Nice you meet you too, sir."

He hesitates only for a second before shaking it, but it's enough to make me want to shit myself. Is it possible that he hates me already? Is it my tattoos?

I'm painfully aware of the way certain people judge men like me, fully covered in ink, thinking we're dangerous criminals or some shit. While most of my tattoos are hidden under the black hoodie I'm wearing, the ones on my knuckles are very much visible. But that can't be. I remember clearly how Grace said her dads encouraged her to get a tattoo. That has to mean they aren't against them, right? Hopefully.

My thoughts aren't making any sense, and that's how I know I'm nervous beyond fucking repair.

"Daniel," is the only thing *Dad* says.

Sensing the tension radiating off my body, Grace links her arm through her Dad's and starts walking ahead, chatting animatedly.

"Let me grab that." Marcus reaches for his daughter's suitcase and, although it's pretty small and I could carry both hers and mine, I don't want to come across as an asshole who thinks he's too strong to accept help.

So instead, I say, "Thank you, sir."

"Please, call me Marcus." He throws me another easy smile as we make our way behind Grace and Daniel. "How was your flight? I hope the remnants of the storm weren't much of a pain in the ass."

I never thought I'd hear the words "pain in the ass" from Grace's very serious-looking corporate lawyer father—not within two minutes of meeting him, anyway—so I can't help a small chuckle.

"There was some turbulence, but nothing too terrible. I don't even think Grace noticed with how furiously she was writing her book."

I don't miss his nostalgic smile. "She used to write a lot when she was a young girl. I'm sure we still have some of her short stories at home somewhere." Then, he surprises me once more by leaning in and whispering conspiratorially, "She'll threaten to kill all three of us if we ever showed you, but I'm willing to take the risk."

I laugh, and I'm about to answer when Grace turns her head abruptly and narrows her eyes at us. "Can't you at least wait until we get home to gang up on me?"

Marcus doesn't miss a beat. "No can do, sweetie. You know I've been waiting forever to embarrass you in front of your boyfriend. Don't take this away from me now."

Grace rolls her eyes, unable to hide her amusement, and Daniel smiles too as he takes the car keys out of his pocket. Half an hour later, we park in front of a three-story house with white bricks and a spacious front yard. "This is where I grew up." Grace leans over to my seat and points to a window in the second story. "That's my room right there."

Once we get the luggage out of the car, Grace grabs my hand

and tugs at me with pure excitement shining on her face. "Come on. I want to show you everything."

I can't help but gape at the interior of the house. It's definitely on the luxurious side, far better than anything I've seen growing up.

The ground floor consists of a small foyer, a half-bath, and a huge open concept kitchen and living room. The TV mounted on the wall right in front of the L shaped couch probably costs more than my rent alone. It smells nice and clean, almost flowery, and from the kitchen and dining area I spot quite a big garden with a bunch of trees.

This is the kind of place I envision Maddie growing up in.

"Do you want anything to eat or drink?" Grace asks me, opening the fridge and scanning every shelf.

"Water's fine." She gets a bottle for her and another for me. When she hands it to me, our fingers brush and I lean in, ready to give her a kiss when I hear her fathers' distant voices behind us.

Grace frowns. "What's wrong?"

I lower my voice in a way that is almost comical. "Can I kiss you here?"

She snorts. "Of course you can, Cal. Why'd you ask?"

"I don't know. Maybe your dads have some kind of 'no kissing under our roof' policy?"

At that, she bursts out laughing and the sound of her unapologetic happiness makes breathing a little easier. "Come here, dumbass."

Before I've got time to react, her small hand comes behind my neck and pulls me towards her until our lips meet. But of course, *of course*, someone clears their throat behind us right on cue, and I die inside.

Grace pulls away, cheeks bright red, and looks over my shoulder. "Um, hi."

"Hi, dear daughter. How's it going?" I recognize Marcus's

voice as he comes into my line of vision, an amused grin on his face. "Are you guys hungry? We were thinking we could have an early dinner."

"S-Sure," she stammers.

"Sounds good to me," I add. My heart is still racing so fast I think I might pass out. Talk about utterly mortifying.

As the next couple of hours go by, the tension slowly unwraps itself from my body. Turns out Grace's dads are some of the most easygoing, welcoming men I've ever come across—yes, even Daniel. I can tell he watches my every move, analyzes my every word, but it doesn't bother me.

I get it. If my daughter had gone through hell and suddenly got a boyfriend and brought him home, I would interrogate the hell out of him FBI-style the second he crossed the threshold.

Both men ask me about myself, my childhood in Warlington, my job, and even my sister. I'm sure Grace has already told them the basics about me, but I appreciate the interest, nonetheless. The moment everything shifts, though, is when Marcus asks his daughter to show them her new tattoo.

"Sometimes I forget I even have it." Grace chuckles as she rolls up her sweater until the ink under her bra strip is visible.

Marcus leans in to soak in every detail. "It's so elegant," he murmurs, almost in awe.

Daniel turns to me. "You did this?"

I swallow. "Yes, sir."

Grace gives me a funny look before turning to her dads again. "It hurt a bit, but he was super quick. And you can't even see it when I'm in my ballet clothes, so that's a bonus."

"You can always cover it up with makeup," I tell her, my eyes fixed on the little two suns on her ribs. "I can recommend you a couple of good brands if you want."

She gives me a small, sheepish smile. "Thank you."

Daniel seems to be focused on the same spot I am, because

he points to his daughter's tattoo and asks, "Why the suns?"

"And the comma?" Marcus adds.

Grace's cheeks turn an adorable shade of red as she explains my thought process behind the design and how it has to do with my nickname for her. Something akin to understanding passes her dads' eyes and that's when Daniel stops looking at me like he's ready to attack at any given moment.

Once we finish having dinner, Grace and I help clean up despite her dads' protests. Both of us carry our luggage upstairs, and I take a look at the second floor. There are three bedrooms here—the master, Grace's, and another for guests, right next to a full bathroom. On the third floor is an attic that used to be Grace's playroom, but when she moved out, they transformed it into some kind of movie room and home gym combined.

I'm about to head to the guest room when Grace's hand on my wrist stops me. "Where are you going?"

"To...my room?"

"Absolutely not. You're sleeping with me."

"Um, are you sure about that?" I scratch the back of my neck. "Did you ask your dads for permission?"

She rolls her eyes at me. "One, I'm an adult woman, and I can do what I want. This is my house too. And two, yes, I told them I wanted you to stay in my room and they said as long as I'm comfortable I can do what I want."

I nod. "All right. I just don't want to make things awkward."

"You won't." She stands on her tiptoes and plants a quick kiss on my lips. "Come on, let me show you my room."

When she opens the door, we're instantly greeted with the smell of fresh flowers. Grace looks confused for a moment before we spot the fresh bouquet on her desk at the same time, and she gasps.

"These are so beautiful." She buries her nose in the white and purple bouquet and smiles at the note. "They're from my dads."

"They love you very much." I hug her from behind and rest my head on top of hers. "Do you want to go downstairs and thank them?"

"Later." She turns around to look at me. "Now, let me give you a room tour."

Grace's childhood bedroom is roughly the same size as my room in my apartment, but hers is far cozier. A queen-sized bed with fresh sheets takes up half the space. There's a nightstand with a lamp, a white rug, an empty-looking desk and a big wardrobe. The walls are decorated with pictures of family holidays, ballet recitals, and even selfies of Grace with her three friends from college. One photo in particular catches my eye.

"Is this who I think it is?" I chuckle at the two kids playing in the snow. Grace, who couldn't have been older than five or six, has her little hands buried on the snow while Aaron, who still has that same playful smile today, sits next to her with a huge snowball on his lap.

"We were on a family trip to Sunshine Village years ago." She smiles fondly at the picture.

"Sunshine Village, huh?" I tease her. "It seems like the nickname has always followed you one way or another."

When she looks at me again, the intensity in her eyes melts me. "Seems like it."

Despite not being particularly late, we decide to call it a day so we don't feel miserably tired tomorrow. Grace goes downstairs to catch up with her dads for a bit while I take a shower and Facetime Maddie before she goes to bed. She comes back in time to say goodnight to my sister and after that we get into bed ourselves.

I open my arms on instinct and she snuggles herself between them. "I love you," she mumbles against my chest, her voice already sounding tired.

"I love you too, sunshine. Sleep well." With one last kiss on her forehead, I close my eyes and sleep finds me in minutes.

# chapter 41

## GRACE

Having Cal stay at my childhood home, in the city I grew up in, and hanging out with my dads feels like a fever dream. In the best way possible, of course, but it's still weird.

On the morning of New Year's Eve, we drive downtown to show Cal some of the most popular tourist spots, and after lunch we browse every toy and book shop we can find.

Even though Cal has already given Maddie her Christmas presents—that enormous doll house she wanted so badly, some dolls to go with it, and her first pair of roller-skates—and I bought a couple of things for her as well, we spot the most adorable princess costume in one of the shops and we simply can't *not* get it.

My dads don't even try to hide their amusement as they watch Cal and I bicker back and forth over the princess costume at the quaint shop and I, for a moment, even forget we aren't alone.

"She likes pink. We should get it in pink," I tell Cal after the charming old lady helping us with our gift comes out of the back with not one dress, but *three*. In different colors.

Cal frowns as he looks at the pink dress I hold in front of me, and then back at the purple one in his hands. The costume is tiny already, but in his massive paws it looks comically microscopic. "She has too much pink stuff, Grace. She'll like the purple one."

I narrow my eyes at him. "The other day she said pink is her favorite color because it makes her feel like a princess. Do you want to be a shit brother, Cal?"

His lips twitch at that, and when one of my fathers coughs behind us, stifling a laugh, I remember we have an audience.

"I'm just saying, a purple dress won't kill her," he argues, eyeing the remaining dress neither of us even bothered to pick up. "What about the yellow one?"

"Does she like yellow?" I ask.

"I think she likes every color."

"But she likes pink the most."

"And I like my sanity the most, so let's agree on one and leave."

Another laugh behind us. I sigh perhaps a tad too dramatically and turn to my dads. "You choose the damn dress."

Daddy smirks. "I like blue. Don't they have a blue one?" he asks, knowing damn well blue isn't a choice.

I groan and turn back to my boyfriend. "All right, enough. Close your eyes." When he does, I hold all three dresses in my arms. "No peeking. Reach out with your hand and we'll buy the one you touch. No backing down."

"Works for me." He wraps his fingers around one of the dresses. "Which one is it?"

I look down. "Yellow."

He opens his eyes again and we look at each other with a mixture of amusement and doubt. "Do you think she'll hate us forever if we don't get her the pink one?" I whisper, lips twitching.

"Nah, let's go for this one. It's a very...sunshiny color." He smirks, grabbing the yellow dress and placing it on the counter.

Once the lady with the patience of a saint comes back—we've been looking at those dresses for nearly twenty minutes—she folds our yellow costume neatly and wraps it in the cutest wrapping paper with little penguins on it. As Cal takes the bag and we say goodbye, the woman's parting words make me want to crawl into a hole and die.

"Thank you for your purchase! Your daughter will look adorable in that dress!"

*Again?!*

That is the second time someone mistakes Maddie for our daughter, and while I don't care that much about it, the fact that it happens right in front of my dads is absolutely mortifying even if they don't comment on it.

Now, a few hours later and back at home, they are getting ready to go to their friends' house for a New Year's party. Although they insist we can tag along if we want, I tell them we already have plans. Plans Cal has no idea about.

"We'll see you guys tomorrow." Daddy kisses my cheek while Dad waits at the door, bottle of wine in hand. "Have fun, and Happy New Year."

The moment the front door closes behind my dads, Cal throws me over a shoulder and smacks my butt. "God, I've been waiting to do that for so long."

I burst out laughing as he lets himself fall on the couch and pulls me onto his lap. "Did you have fun today? I'm sorry they tagged along, I haven't seen them in a while and..."

"Hey, don't apologize." He kisses my forehead. "I didn't mind at all. Your dads are dope. I think they might like me and everything."

I roll my eyes. "Please, they *adore* you. I swear they talked to you more than they talked to me." I chuckle, thinking about their super serious, super long conversation about lawyers and tattoos in the car earlier. "And Dad likes you too, believe me. He's just more reserved."

He looks doubtful. "You think?"

"Absolutely." I reassure him with a kiss for good measure. Glancing at the clock in the kitchen wall, I tell him, "Time to get ready for my surprise. And you'd better look sexy or else."

"Or else..."

"I won't eat you for dessert."

Cal buries his face in my neck and starts blowing raspberries on my skin. I squeal loudly, trying to get out of his grip, but he doesn't bulge. He lays me on my back and climbs on top of me, now tickling my sides, and suddenly I can barely breathe.

And it's not from laughter.

The walls start closing in on me. His weight, always so warm and welcoming, now feels like a crushing rock. I stop laughing and squealing, my hands anchoring my body to his arms when my mind starts drifting far away.

"Grace?"

I'm not sure if that's his voice or just a product of my imagination.

My eyes are wide open, yet I can't see a thing.

Nothing beyond feeling trapped, of someone much stronger overpowering me, submitting me, while I lay there unable to save myself.

"Grace."

Two heavy hands are holding my head now, and my eyes are looking right into dark irises. But my brain doesn't respond, and my throat is dry, incapable of uttering a single word—

"Hey, it's all right. You're safe. Come back to me, my love."

I blink once, twice, and the walls go back to their usual spot.

"C-Cal?"

When my sight finally focuses, I'm met with my boyfriend's distraught face. "Where did you go, sunshine?" I blink again and a single tear falls. "Talk to me, please."

"I got overwhelmed," I blurt out as another tear rolls down my cheek, and then another. "I'm s-sorry."

"*I'm* sorry. Was it because I tickled you?" He looks so distressed, his whole face masked in panic, that I almost don't tell him.

But this is Cal. He's my best friend, my boyfriend, my future, and I can't keep this stuff from him. So, slowly, I manage to nod. "I couldn't breathe properly and...and your body crushed me and... I'm sorry Cal, this has nothing to do with you. I don't want you to feel bad."

He sits back on the couch before he says, "Don't worry about me. Are you okay? Tell me what I can do to help."

Shaking my head, I tell him the truth. "I need a moment."

"Whatever you need, baby. *Fuck.* I'm sorry." His gaze doesn't leave mine. I can almost see the million thoughts racing through his head right now.

A silent minute passes, and my heart rate goes back to normal. I had no idea being tickled like that would trigger me, and I hate that he's feeling bad about it. Because it's not his fault. So once I'm feeling like myself again, I shift closer and grab his hand in mine. "Cal... No matter who had done that to me, I would've freaked out. Aaron, Em, you... It wouldn't have made a difference, okay? I love you. I promise I'm okay. It was just a momentary thing. I didn't even know tickles triggered me," I admit. "But now that I do, we'll work on it like we do with everything else. Okay?"

It takes him a moment, but eventually he gives me the tiniest of nods. "Okay. Are you sure you're fine?"

I wrap my arms around him and give the rose on his neck a kiss. "I promise."

His arms wrap around my middle, holding me against his chest. "I love you, Grace. So fucking much. I'm so sorry I scared you."

"Stop apologizing." My lips find his neck again. "We're a team, aren't we?"

He holds me closer, as if he never wanted to let me go. And I would never want to leave, either.

"The best team, sunshine."

* * *

An hour later, I think most of the tension has dissipated from Cal's body. Whatever remains, I hope I can make it go away with my surprise.

It's nothing special, but I think he'll like it anyway.

Once I finish curling my hair, I emerge from the bathroom and go back to my room where Cal is waiting for me. He's sitting on the bed, looking at something on his phone, but when his eyes move up to me and he takes in what I'm wearing his mouth literally falls open.

Ever since my assault, I've avoided wearing tight, revealing clothes that would make me look sexy for fear of being sexualized. And while I know clothes aren't to blame for something like what happened to me, I couldn't stand drawing men's attention in any way.

With Cal, though, everything's different.

When I put on this short, thin-strapped red dress that hugs all my curves I didn't feel like a piece of meat—I felt sexy, yes, but also confident and excited about the ways he was going to worship my body while taking it off later.

Judging by the way he's devouring me with his eyes, I know my fantasies aren't far-fetched at all.

"Fucking hell, sunshine. You look breathtaking."

I lick my lips. "So do you."

And he does, all right. He's wearing a white shirt with the sleeves rolled up to his tattooed forearms, and my core clenches involuntarily. With his dress pants and fancy shoes, he really is a sight to behold.

I almost feel bad for what I'm about to tell him.

"I, um." I walk towards him until his hands are on my hips and I'm standing between his legs. "I called a few restaurants after I scheduled our flight, but they were all booked, so... We aren't going out tonight."

His thumbs move in circles against my ribs. "Why the fancy outfits, then?"

I bite my lip, guilt written all over my face. "I kind of wanted to see you looking like a walking Armani ad."

Cal blinks, and then he throws his head back and explodes with laughter. "Are you for real right now?"

"Yeah?" My hand finds the rose tattoo on his neck and caresses it softly. "I mean, I also wanted this to be kind of a fancy date even though we'll stay at home."

He smiles. "It's all worth it, since I get to see you looking like an angel."

"My dress is red, though. Don't you think it makes me look a little devilish instead?"

His grip on my hips tightens and he pulls me closer.

"You're right. You look like my favorite sin tonight."

I never thought I would want to climb a man like a tree, in my childhood bedroom of all places, but now I need it more than my next breath.

*Nope. You can do that later, you filthy animal.*

Forcing myself to snap out of my lust-filled craze, I take a step back. "Don't make me ruin my lipstick before the night even starts."

He laughs. "Let's go downstairs."

In the kitchen, we grab some of Dad's famous meat pie, a couple of slices of carrot cake, and some baked potatoes along with two bottles of water and napkins.

After that, I take him to the small terrace in the attic where my dads keep a small table and two chairs. Luckily, they aren't wet from the storm. Our terrace isn't too big, but it couldn't be cozier and overlooks the garden.

Once the food and drinks are safely on the table, I go back inside to grab some blankets. We both have our coats on, but my legs are bare, and I know how rough winter nights can get around here.

I glance at the time on my phone—less than an hour until midnight. Perfect.

"We'll see the fireworks from here," I tell Cal as we start our dinner.

"Wow." His eyes widen as he bites into the meat pie. "This is *good*. Is it homemade?"

"Yep." I grin proudly. "Dad made all of this. He's quite the chef."

"I can see that. Holy shit."

"I'm glad you like it." I hesitate as I take another bite of my own slice of pie. My heart races just thinking about it, but my lips move before I give myself enough time to think this through. "These are my comfort dishes, all three of them. They were all I would eat after my assault. I rarely had an appetite, but when Dad made any of these I couldn't resist."

Cal kisses the side of my temple, and I keep talking. "I would sit right here for hours and read or watch movies, and I would always eat these three things. It was kind of a ritual, I guess. It felt safe and cozy. And I didn't want to go outside, so being here allowed me to get some fresh air too."

He's moved his chair closer to mine, and I don't notice until his arm comes around my shoulders. "Thank you for sharing this with me." He kisses me again. "I love you, sunshine, but I also admire you more than you'll ever know."

His sweet words squeeze my heart and refuse to let it go. "I love and admire you too, you know? You're the best big brother in the world, and the best boyfriend too."

"I try."

The sad way in which he says it has me turning my head and searching for his gaze. "Well, you are. You're my rock, Cal, and Maddie looks at you like you could hand her the entire world on a silver platter, and I know you would. What's going on in that worrisome head of yours, love?"

A tired sigh escapes his lips. "Same old, same old. I worry I'm not doing enough for my sister. That I can't help you in the way you need."

I put my food on the table, and he does the same. I place my hand against his freshly shaved cheek and turn his head towards me. "There will be hard times ahead, Cal. That's part of life. But you're the most incredible, selfless, and caring man I could ever share mine with. I love you, and so does Maddie. That will never change no matter what happens."

*Boom.*

A firework goes off in the distance, tinting the sky red. Cal's eyes never once leave mine, looking right into my soul with a such a raw intensity it should feel overwhelming.

But all I feel is undying love for the man in front of me. Another firework booms over our heads, its blue light illuminating Cal's tanned skin. He swallows, I swallow, my words hanging between us until he speaks again and my world shifts.

"Marry me."

*Boom.*

Was that another firework, or my heart?

My whole body starts shaking, and it's not from the cold. "W-What? Now?"

His gentle hand cradles my face, and I lean into his touch, seeking its comfort. "Now, next year, in five years... Whenever you wish, sunshine. Whether you want a big wedding or just the two of us, I don't care. All I need is to know that one day you'll be my wife and I'll be your husband, because I can't stomach the thought of a life without you, Grace. I want it all with you, everything, and I will wait an eternity for you if that's what it takes to get our happy ending."

*Oh my god.*

I'm not aware I'm crying until his thumb wipes away one of my tears. He presses a soft kiss to my lips before continuing. "I don't have a ring on me right now," he says almost sheepishly. I'm about to say I don't care about that when he cuts me off with a knowing smirk. "You don't care about that, I know. But I do. I want to make this right, and I will one day. I'll get on one knee and pop the question..."

"Yes."

He blinks. "Yes?"

"I will marry you, Cal."

"But I haven't even gotten down on one knee..."

"I don't care. When you do, my answer will be yes. A million times yes. Nothing would make me happier."

Before I can take my next breath, Cal's lips are on mine. Judging by the way he was looking at me, I expected him to devour me—instead, he holds me gently as his tongue meets mine, stroking it so softly it shatters all my inhibitions. Suddenly I'm sitting sideways on his lap, his hands firmly planted on the small of my back as I circle his neck with my arms, never wanting to let go.

More fireworks explode above our heads, mirroring what I'm feeling inside, but all my senses are focused on the raw emotions he's drawing out from me. Pleasure, comfort, safety, love. It hits me then, like a brutal tidal wave, that the man holding and kissing me so tenderly right now is my *future husband*.

*Holy shit.*

A warm feeling blooms inside my chest, spreading a calm sense of pure bliss all over me. It feels like homecoming, like this is exactly where I'm meant to be. In Cal's arms, now and always. In the arms of my future husband.

It's not a realization I'm going to get used to quickly, that's for sure.

To be honest, I've never cared that much about marriage.

Unlike other little girls, I never dreamed of a fairytale wedding, nor did I have the perfect bridal dress designed to a tee in my mind.

Perhaps I never saw the point in such a thing because my dads hadn't been able to get legally married until I was older, despite having been together for years. And when they finally tied the knot, it was us three and our immediate family and closest friends. The ceremony was nothing too extravagant because they didn't care about that.

It was my dads who taught me that marriage wasn't the ultimate goal. Because when true love is *right there*, right at your fingertips and wrapping you in its sweet embrace, only your two souls matter. Only that unique, genuine, and everlasting connection.

But I want to marry Cal. Damn right, I do.

Not anytime soon, obviously, since this thing between us is still new although it feels like I've known him forever, but it feels *right* to have the reassurance that it will happen one day. That, someday, I'll be able to call him my husband and I'll be his wife.

And how crazy is that?

We pull away after what feels like hours, yet Cal's lips don't roam too far. He trails the goosebumps on my neck with open-mouthed, lazy kisses, and I throw my head back against his shoulder so he has better access. As I bask in the feeling of his hot mouth against my skin, the question is out of my lips before I can stop myself. "You said you wanted everything with me. What do you mean by that?"

He doesn't answer right away. One of his big hands plays with the hem of my short dress under the blanket, driving me insane, and he continues to kiss my neck as if I'm not about to pass out from sheer desire until he finally says, "It means I'll give you whatever you want, whenever you want, because I'll do anything to protect the happiness shining on your face right now, sunshine."

"What about what you want?" I ask quietly, the sweetness of his words clogging up my throat with raw emotions I'm not sure I'm even able to process right now.

"I want to marry you," he says, giving me a single kiss behind my ear. "I want us to move in together after you finish college." Another kiss as my breath hitches at his confession. "And some day, I would love to be a father."

Yep, it's official. I'm not breathing anymore.

How could I, when he's doing wicked things to me while being such a sweetheart?

My mouth opens, but no words come out. I don't even know where to start.

"Y-You want us to move in together?" Admittedly, the thought had crossed my mind more than once in the past few days, but knowing he shares the sentiment sends a hard jolt of electricity and hope through me.

He presses a kiss to my jaw. "I do. I'd love nothing else than to come home from work and find you there. You're my safe haven, sunshine."

"And you're mine," I whisper against his lips, tears threatening to spill. "I'll need a new place to live after I graduate, so..."

Cal smiles against my neck. "We'll talk about it again when the time comes, yeah?"

I nod, but I can't get the second half of his confession out of my mind. My voice comes out in a shy whisper, "You want us to have a baby someday?"

He chuckles in such a low, manly way it makes my thighs clench. "Why do you sound so surprised?"

A deep blush spreads on my cheeks, and I'm grateful for the darkness that manages to conceal it. "I'm not surprised, I'm... I don't know, excited?"

He blinks. "Really?"

"Who sounds surprised now, huh?" I tease him.

He squeezes my hip. "Are you truly excited about having a baby with me?" There's genuine amazement in his voice, making him sound vulnerable.

"Yes, really." I press a soft kiss on the tip of his nose. "You would be the most amazing dad, just like you're the most amazing brother."

"I love you." His whisper sends a shiver down my spine. "You're my everything, sunshine, and I can't wait for the rest of our lives."

He kisses me again, and our food ends up forgotten on the table. Fireworks go off outside, my quiet childhood street suddenly bustling with neighbors welcoming the new year as I welcome each of his slow, passionate thrusts inside of me. Each gentle kiss, each deep moan.

And after our bodies tremble with pleasure and we come down from our high together, Cal cocoons me in his big arms and a sense of safety and pure love wraps around me in a way that makes nothing else matter.

# chapter 42

## CAL

The night before our flight back to Warlington, Grace gets a sudden boost of inspiration, and I don't hesitate—I get her laptop from her bag and leave her room with the promise of getting her snacks downstairs.

So that's where I find myself five minutes later, scanning the packed fridge, when a voice behind me almost makes me drop the water bottle I've just grabbed.

"Hey, Cal."

"*Shit.*" My hand goes to my heart as I turn around to see Daniel staring at me with camouflaged amusement. "*Fuck.* I mean, *crap.* Sorry, I didn't hear you."

"It's all right. Sorry I scared you." His lips curve into the tiniest of smiles, but that's a sight so rare on the serious man I think I might be imagining it.

"No worries," I say quickly. Closing the fridge after finding only water, I muster all my courage and ask him, "Do you have any snacks around? I wanted to take some upstairs for Grace since she's writing, but I couldn't find anything in here."

"Sure. They're over here." He walks over to one of the cabinets above the counter and, sure enough, it's full of goodies. Daniel grabs a box of Cheez-Its and hands it to me. "She was obsessed with these as a kid."

My lips curl with amusement. I didn't know that particular fact about her, and it feels all the more special that I've learned it from her hard-ass Dad of all people. "Thank you."

I manage a small smile his way and a half-turn towards the stairs before he speaks again. "Can I speak to you for a moment?"

*Well, fuck me.*

I do my best to mask the utter dread I'm feeling and say as nonchalantly as I can manage, "Sure."

As I follow Daniel to the living room, I wonder if he hates me so much he's going to demand I stay away from his daughter. I don't think I would, not if Grace wants us to be together, but the possibility of her father not seeing me as the right man for her would devastate me.

He takes a seat on the gigantic couch, so I place the snacks on the coffee table and do the same. I should've suspected that, being a kickass lawyer and all, Daniel would be a straight-forward, no-bullshit kind of man. Still, I haven't fully braced myself for impact when he blurts out, "Do you love Grace?"

Despite the brutal way my heart is pounding right now, I don't hesitate. "I do, sir."

Silence stretches between us as he sits back on the couch. It only lasts a couple of seconds, five tops, but my brain is on overdrive, and it feels like a damn eternity before he finally says, "I believe you."

*What?*

"Y-You do?"

His intense stare pins me down and I fight every instinct not to cower under it. I might be a six-foot-three wall of pure muscle, but I can recognize a threat when I see it.

Slowly, Daniel nods and puts me out of my misery. "It's in the little things," he starts, eyes sweeping across the living room. "She told us about the sketches."

I gulp, not sure why. He's just told me he thinks my feelings for his daughter are sincere, but that doesn't mean he *likes* me.

I'm thankful that he keeps talking, because I don't think

I could utter a single word right now even if I tried. My stupid throat is clogged up.

"She told us everything," Daniel continues. "How you picked her up from that party and took her to some food truck. How you always support her choices and lift her up. All those times you were there when she needed a friend."

I swallow past the lump in my throat. "I'd do anything for her."

Now, I'm not imagining the smug smirk on his face. "Aaron told me as much."

*Hold on—*

"You talked to Aaron about me?"

"Sure did." He shifts on the couch, his gaze meeting mine. "When Grace told us she was going to spend Christmas with a friend, and that friend also happened to be a friend of Aaron's, I called him for details. It's my duty as a father to make sure my daughter is always safe and cared for no matter who she's with."

"I understand."

"Good." By the intense way he's staring at me, one would think he's trying to see right into my soul. He probably can, to be honest. "You know what my nephew told me?" He doesn't wait for my response. "He laughed and told me you were, and I quote, 'Totally her boyfriend. Those two aren't subtle at all,' but that I shouldn't worry about it."

*That little shit—*

"He said you are a good man," Daniel continues. "And that he trusted you with her. So, in a way, I trusted you too. And then I met you, and I'm relieved to know my gut feeling wasn't wrong." He shifts until his elbows rest on his knees. Grace's dad looks directly at me as he says, "I'm assuming she told you what happened to her."

"She did."

"How is she?"

His question takes me by surprise, and he must notice because he adds, "We ask her about her mental health all the time, but I'm not naïve enough to believe she tells us everything. Parents aren't supposed to know every little detail about their children's lives, and that's all right. But she's never been in a relationship before, serious or not, and I can't help but feel worried about how this change might be affecting her."

"I can assure you that she's fine, sir," I tell him with honesty. "There are times where she feels a little more...insecure, I would say. But we work through it. She's still seeing her therapist, and I think that helps a lot. She very rarely gets uncomfortable about something, and when she does, we talk about it and work it out. I would never, ever dare to disrespect her boundaries."

He nods, seemingly deep in thought and my head starts spinning again. Maybe that was the wrong thing to say? But that's the truth. That's *our* truth. Grace isn't uncomfortable around me—I know she'd tell me if she were because that's our number one rule.

However, it hits me that I might not be seeing the full picture. It's possible that her father sees something that I don't, that he knows better than I do what Grace needs and—

"You don't have to call me sir." Wait, what? "Daniel is fine. We're family now, after all."

Am I dreaming right now?

"Don't look so stunned." He smirks.

I blink. "I'm sorry, si... *Daniel*. Shit, sorry. Sorry. I thought..." I scratch the back of my neck like a nervous young boy. "I thought maybe you didn't like me very much."

He chuckles. "Oh, I like you Cal. Don't even worry about it." His eyes light up as they focus somewhere behind me. "See, darling? I can still pull off the Scary Dad act."

Marcus comes down the stairs towards us, rolling his eyes affectionately at his husband. A few seconds later, a hand clamps my shoulder as he sits next to me on the couch.

"I tried to stop him from having the Scary Dad talk with you, but he wouldn't listen," Marcus tells me, the smile never leaving his face. Blood related or not, he's all sunshine like his daughter. Now I see where she gets it from. "He wanted to be a dramatic ass."

Now it's Daniel's turn to roll his eyes. "Well, it worked. Cal here thought I hated him."

Marcus's booming laughter fills the room. "Don't trust this guy, Cal. We liked you from the start. Where's Gracie, by the way?"

As the minutes go by, the snacks sit forgotten on the coffee table as I talk to Grace's dads about anything and everything. They ask me some more about Maddie, and after they insist on seeing pictures of her, they think it's only fair to bring out the family albums so they can embarrass their daughter some more.

A shit-eating grin dominates my face the whole time we browse through the pictures of baby and toddler Grace.

"We took that one on her first day of school," Marcus says.

Indeed, a miniature version of Grace is smiling widely in front of a school, wearing a blue uniform and her blond hair in two braids. But, for some reason, what catches my eye is the pink backpack she's holding with both of her little hands.

Images of Maddie flood my head, mixing with all the baby pictures of Grace I wish I could embed in my mind forever, because suddenly it hits me out of the blue with the force of a thousand explosions.

*It* being baby fever. And it's hitting *hard*.

A warm feeling grows inside my chest as I imagine, and not for the first time, a perfect future in which I get to have my sunshine, my princess, and another little sunshine who will look so much like her mom she would steal my heart right away.

I realize then and there that nothing would make me happier

than spending the rest of my life with my girls. And maybe a dog or two.

The mere thought of being a dad should probably scare me, given how I never had any father figure worth looking up to when I was younger. But Grace is right—I'm a kickass older brother and, as long as she's by my side, I'm going to be the best dad I can be.

"I know you didn't just bring out the photo albums," a sharp voice starts behind us. "I know it."

I laugh, looking over my shoulder where Grace is currently sending death glares to her dads. "Aw, sunshine, come on. Look at those chubby cheeks."

She snatches the album right out of my grip and snaps it shut. "Took you two long enough to embarrass me *again*."

Marcus chuckles. "There's nothing embarrassing about your baby pictures, you drama queen. We were showing Cal how adorable you looked as a baby."

"And here I thought you were getting me snacks." She sits on the coffee table and opens her box of Cheez-Its. "I should've known you were going to gang up on me sooner than later."

Daniel throws an arm around the back of the couch and gives his daughter a smug smile. "You poor thing."

Grace sticks her tongue out at him. "Not fair. There's too much testosterone in this house. I need Maddie."

Her words wrap around my heart and *squeeze*. "Nuh-uh. You two gang up on me all the time. Give me a break," I say casually even though my heart couldn't be beating any faster.

"Sucks to suck." She smirks.

Despite her aversion to me seeing her baby pictures, she ends up snuggling next to me as the four of us browse through the family albums. After my conversation with Daniel, the air in the room becomes lighter and I feel...at home, like I belong. I always feel at home when I'm with Grace, but this time it's different. Now, just like she does with Maddie, I feel like her family is also part of mine. When I wrap her in my arms hours later, I fall asleep to the thought of starting our own someday.

# chapter 43

## GRACE

My hands wrap around the steaming hot chocolate mug, seeking any kind warmth, while my feet tap nervously on the wooden floor. Luke closes the laptop moments later and brings his own mug to his lips, smirking smugly as he takes a sip.

"Don't be an ass." I narrow my eyes at him, anxiously waiting for his feedback. "What did you think? It's only the first draft, so..."

"Relax." He sets his coffee down and taps his knuckles on my laptop. "I like it a lot, Grace. The storyline makes sense, and the characters are well-crafted. The dog is definitely a plus. I left a couple of comments, but I really don't see any major issues with it."

My feet stop their obnoxious tapping, and I manage to breathe a little easier. "For real?"

"Of course. I wouldn't lie to you. You're my friend," he reassures me, and I believe him.

Luke has been nothing but that for the past few weeks. It says a lot about him that he remained such a good sport after I turned him down. He knows about Cal, and even told me that he'd seen it coming. That we made sense together.

He still comes by The Teal Rose every other Saturday morning, and he was excited to be a beta reader for my first draft, which I couldn't be more grateful for.

"It would be a good idea if you read it to a couple of children and see if they'd enjoy it," he adds. "Someone from your family, maybe?"

My mind drifts to Maddie and her love for books. Sure, this is no princess or mermaid story, but there is a Sammy. It should be enough to grab her attention. "I can do that."

We stay at the café for nearly another hour, catching up until he has to leave for lacrosse practice. I'm free for the rest of the day, and I know Em is too, so I send her a quick text to see what she's up to. When I got to our dorm this morning after spending the night at Cal's, she wasn't there. Now that I think about it, I haven't heard from her since yesterday.

It's probably nothing. If something bad had happened, I'm sure our friends would've let me know by now...right?

I'm about to start for our doom when, to my relief, my phone buzzes with a text from Emily.

> **Hey hon. Sorry I've been MIA. I'm busy rn, but I'll see you later? x**

A busy Emily isn't out of the ordinary so, with a calm heart, I leave campus.

My stomach rumbling is indicative enough that I need to fill it with something before I get cranky, hence why I find myself at The Spoon twenty minutes later, waiting for my order.

One of the waitresses tells me Aaron isn't coming until tonight, so I decide to grab something for him too and leave for his apartment. On his days off, he's either at the gym, lounging in front of the TV or playing some random game—with Cal, sometimes—so looking for him at his home is a no-brainer.

After knocking on his apartment door ten minutes later, though, I realize my mistake.

I always text him when I'm about to come over, but this time I totally forgot about it. And that is a *huge* mistake because as much as I wish I was, I'm not imagining the female voice on the other side of the door right now.

"I got it, babe," Aaron tells this mysterious woman as he rustles around with the lock.

*Babe?!* Who the hell is b—

"Grace?" A second later, my eyes collide with my cousin's bare chest and panicked expression. "What the fuck are you doing here?"

As it turns out, I'm not the only one too stunned to move right now.

Because right behind Aaron, wearing the same panicked expression and one of his t-shirts with nothing else underneath, is my best friend.

Emily.

\* \* \*

"This is exactly what it looks like," is the first thing Emily says to me when she comes back from Aaron's room after *thankfully* putting her leggings back on.

She's my best friend and I've seen her in her underwear before, but it doesn't mean I'm comfortable with her nakedness now that I know exactly why she was half-naked before I walked in.

Ew. Mental image, please go away.

The food I brought from The Spoon sits on the coffee table next to a couple of pizza boxes the delivery guy dropped off not even five minutes ago, looking less appealing than ever. Apparently, Aaron thought I was him and that's why he didn't bother to check who was on the other side of his door before he opened it.

My cousin is currently munching on an extra bacon-y slice, and for a second, I wish he choked on it just to see him suffer a little.

Because I'm suffering *a lot* right now.

"Are either of you going to give me a real explanation like, today?" I glare at the traitors, who look like they don't have a care in the world despite me essentially walking in on them doing... whatever it was they were doing.

"There's not much to explain," Aaron says with his mouth full. Gross.

"I thought you didn't like each other?" I arch an eyebrow towards my friend, who I very vividly remember pushing my cousin's buttons not long ago, and not in the nicest way.

She shrugs and opens the pizza box, taking a slice for herself. "We fight sometimes, but it's like foreplay."

"For fuck's sake," I mutter in disbelief, hiding my face behind my hands so I don't have to look at these two disgusting idiots. She did *not* say that.

Aaron claps me on my shoulder like I'm one of his bro-dudes and they haven't just scarred me for life. "Chill, G. Everything's cool. We're having fun."

I look at my friend again only because she's the one with the most brain cells between these two. "So, what, you're like, friends with benefits now? How long have you been hooking up?"

"A month? Maybe two?" Aaron replies instead.

I snap my head in his direction. "That long?! Why didn't you tell me that you were fooling around with *my best friend*?"

He glares at me. "Like you told me *right away* that you were dating Cal?"

"Touché," Emily chimes in.

"Okay, whatever." I let myself fall against the back of the couch with a defeated sigh. "So what's the plan?"

"The plan is to keep doing what we're doing," Emily says as she takes another slice and gestures to the box. "Help yourself, babe. There's enough for everyone."

"I'm not hungry anymore," I murmur.

My brain doesn't have enough time to process this life-altering information before Aaron wraps an arm around my neck and pulls me towards him. "Let me go, you animal!" I try pushing him away as he starts attacking my forehead with kisses, but it's pretty obvious that he has no plans to stop until he wants to.

Defeated, I sigh against his chest and admit after a few seconds of contemplative, dramatic silence, "I just don't want to take sides if you guys fall out and it gets ugly."

"We would never put you in that position," Emily assures me.

"Plus, if you and Cal ever break up, you'll put me in that position as well," Aaron reasons. Then, he quickly adds, "I don't think you'll ever break up, that's not what I mean. What I'm trying to say is that every situation has the potential to become a mess if we don't face it with understanding and the right attitude. And I know you're capable of those things, so I'm not worried."

"Me neither." Emily smiles. "See, Grace, we're all adults here. I know this thing between us may feel weird to you for a while, but this...arrangement we have going on is what we both want now, and we would really appreciate your support."

"Of course you have my support. Not that you need it anyway, but you have it," I reassure them. "It feels...new, nothing else. I'll get used to it."

And I know I will. If two of the most important people in my life find happiness together, who am I to stand in the way?

"Wait." I turn to Em as a sudden understanding washes over me. "All those times you told me you were with a friend... You were with *him*?"

My best friend puts her hands up in mock surrender.

"Guilty as charged, babe."

"I can't believe you." I glare at her for what feels like the hundredth time today, but I can't hide my smile. I shake my head and reach for the takeout bag I brought. The food is probably cold by now. "Well, now that's out of the way, would either of you be interested in reading the children's book I wrote for class?"

For the next two hours, the three of us sit in Aaron's living room with some action movie playing in the background, even though none of us are paying attention. They ask me about our trip to my hometown, what my dads think of Cal, and how I'm feeling about my new relationship status. Since they both know about my assault, I'm free to talk openly about it. Not that there's much to tell in the first place.

I don't think I've ever felt happier or more alive in...well, ever. Being with Cal not only makes me feel loved and safe, it makes me feel valid, valuable, and confident, like what I do and say matters.

Before him, I already knew those things thanks to years of therapy and my amazing support system—of which the two people in front of me are and will always be part of.

But being with him, knowing that he's mine and I'm his, knowing that I make him as happy as he makes me... It's truly an indescribable feeling.

Every time we are together feels like an energy boost, like nothing could ever stop or hurt me. Like, with his love and support, I can do *anything*.

I know it's silly. I knew I could be an unstoppable force before I met him, but now it all comes easier. Natural, like a new part of me I planted within myself years ago is finally blooming.

They say love cannot save you, that you must save yourself first. I don't think that's always true. I think you have to be the one to plant that first seed of salvation and allow love to water it until it grows into the most beautiful, strong flower capable of surviving it all.

It's a team effort, and Cal and I are one hell of a team.

Maybe that's why, after two hours and three unread texts, I start to worry a little.

He's working, I know this, but he always takes time between appointments to text me back even if it's only one word or some laughing emojis. An "I love you."

But because he's not answering and he still has a couple of hours more to go, I stay with Aaron and Emily and submit myself to the torturous story of how this whole arrangement between them started.

"I didn't like him at first, that much is true." Emily has her feet draped across his lap as she munches on a bag of caramel popcorn. "But one night we ended up at the same party, and when some random guy wouldn't leave me alone your cousin here threatened to beat him up. It kinda turned me on, not gonna lie."

"Too much information."

"Don't be a baby." Aaron grabs my ankle and squeezes it. When I smack his hand away, the dumbass only laughs.

"And the rest is pretty much history," Emily says and pops a single popcorn into her mouth.

"Thank you for sparing me the traumatic details," I deadpan.

"Hey! I literally walked in on Cal and you sucking face the other day, so shut your mouth, young lady." Aaron points an accusing finger in my direction. "That was *traumatic*."

I roll my eyes. "Live with it, loser."

He's about to reply when my phone goes off with a call. One look at the caller ID and my stomach sinks, a sick feeling settling in. "It's Cal."

Don't ask me how I know everything's gone to shit. I just do. I don't need to take this call to find out my instincts were right, but of course I do anyway.

"Hey. Is everything okay?" I ask, chewing on my thumb nail.

For a few seconds, only loud breathing meets me from the other line. There's background noise I'm too nervous to make out right now.

"Cal?" I ask again because he's not saying anything and I'm

about to have a heart attack. From the corner of my eye, Aaron and Emily sit up straight on the couch, paying attention.

When Cal finally lets out the words, his voice husky and pained, my whole world stops and crumbles at my feet.

"It's Maddie. There's been an accident. She's... *Fuck*. She's at the hospital."

# chapter 44

## CAL

There's a black hole inside my chest, eating me alive from the inside and consuming every inch of my bleeding soul little by little.

I can't bring myself to feel, to care, to stop it.

My phone shakes between my trembling hands, and not even Grace's calming words as she tells me she's coming right away manage to wake me up from this fucking nightmare.

It's funny how I knew this was going to happen eventually. Maybe *not* this, exactly, but I've always suspected the ticking bomb that was our family life was going to explode sooner rather than later.

This is my fault. By doing nothing to fix the situation, I allowed it to get this far.

Once again, my family has failed Maddie. Only, this time, it's *my* neglect that put her in the ER.

I was in the middle of tattooing Oscar when my mother called. I rarely pick up the phone while I'm working, but she never, *ever* calls, so the moment I saw her caller ID I knew. I fucking knew.

She had gotten into a fight with Pete, which ended with him packing his bags and leaving. For good, she'd said. Good-fucking-riddance and all that. At least that was my immediate thought when she told me, thinking that was it. Pete walking out of our lives and never coming back was more a blessing than a curse, even if my mother couldn't see it as such at the time. But there was more.

He wasn't out of the door for five minutes before my mom opened her liquor cabinet and chugged down her whiskey straight from the damn bottle. And then went for another. I know this because she'd confessed everything between broken sobs.

My sister was in the house while all of this went down. When she spotted our mom on the couch, drunk and crying her eyes out, she sprinted towards her. Probably because she thought she was dying. And in her way, she tripped over a bottle my mother had left lying around on the floor and hit her head on the sharp corner of the coffee table.

I'll give it to my mom—despite her pathetic state, she sobered up enough to understand she needed to call an ambulance. I can only imagine how badly Maddie was bleeding for her to come to her goddamn senses while being two bottles deep into oblivion.

And now I'm sitting alone in the waiting room outside of the ER, where they're stitching up Maddie's head, and I have no fucking clue what kind of damage has been done. I don't know if there's brain trauma, if she's hurt somewhere else too, or if it's so bad she'll have to stay the night, maybe even a few days.

Images of her small, fragile body choke me up until I can barely breathe. She might not be strong enough to sustain a head injury... She might have lost too much blood already... My mother might have called the ambulance too late...

I hide my face between my trembling hands, and I break down.

This is all my fault. My head hasn't been in the right place. I've been distracted with...other things, when all my focus should've been on my sister. For the longest time I refused to see the signs, blinded by wishful thinking that our mother would get her shit together and we would avoid this dumpster fire. Of course not, and now my sister is in the fucking ER for it.

If she doesn't make it... If something happens to her... "*Fuck.*"

I feel my whole body shaking with fear as my head spirals, down and down and...

"Cal."

Grace's soft, worried voice drifts over towards me like a gust of fresh wind in the suffocating desert, and for a moment this nightmare turns into a short-lived dream.

"Cal..." Her hands engulf mine and peel them away from my face.

I can't look at her right now. Not when I have to fight back this magnetic pull towards her. Her gentle lips kiss away my tears, making me feel guilty for feeling so fucking loved when Maddie is alone and afraid in the ER right now. Grace tangles one of her hands on the back of my hair, trying to sooth me with the gentle scratch of her fingernails on my scalp. "Tell me what happened, love."

When I muster the courage to lift my eyes to look at her, I wish I hadn't.

Her eyes are red and puffy from all her tears, and seeing her so utterly distraught over my sister breaks me down again. She doesn't speak. Silently, she wraps her arms around me, and I pull her onto my lap. Her sweet, familiar scent wraps around my heart to the point where I want to break something just thinking of what I have to do next.

"Please," she whimpers against my neck as she holds me so tightly her grip might leave a bruise. I couldn't fucking care less. "Please, tell me what happened. Don't leave me in the dark."

I hold her against me, wishing things would be different, longing for that future I was so sure was in the cards for us, and I tell her.

How I should've done something. How it's too late now. How selfish I have been, ignoring the signs, and what it cost my sister.

By the time my throat clogs up and I can't get any more

words out no matter how hard I try, we're both crying. "Where's your mother now?" Grace asks me in a whisper once she calms down.

"In custody." My voice trembles as I speak. "Grace, I'm... I'm gonna file for Maddie's guardianship."

If my confession shocks her, she doesn't show it. "How can I help?" she asks instead, making my fucking heart tighten again.

"You can't." I swallow past the lump in my throat. "You... I can't do this to you, Grace."

Luckily for my sanity, because I can't bear to have this conversation right now, a doctor enters the waiting room. "Samuel Callaghan?"

I stand up in a rush, pulling Grace up with me as I go.

"How is she?"

The doctor eyes Grace briefly, tucked under my arm, and slowly turns to me again, "She's awake and recovering. She had a mild cut on her hairline that required stitches, but fortunately she didn't lose a lot of blood. Would you like to see her?"

Nothing could've prepared me for the heartbreaking sight of my sister lying on a hospital bed. Grace squeezes my hand as we step inside, both of us wearing our fakest smiles to avoid freaking her out even more.

"Hey, princess." I kneel next to her bed and take her small, cold hand between my shaky one. "How are you feeling?"

To my surprise, Maddie smiles. "My head hurts a little, but the doctor said I was very brave, so I think now I feel better." When her eyes move behind me, her smile widens. "Grace!"

"Hi, sweetie." She comes to stand next to me and rubs Maddie's covered leg in a comforting gesture.

I'm so fucking anxious I barely notice the bright yellow walls full of animal stickers and other kiddy props before the same doctor comes back again with an easy smile on his face. "You are her brother, correct?" I nod. "Will she be going home with you today?"

"Yes," I say without hesitation.

He proceeds to explain the care instructions for the cut, and I start breathing normally again when, after a quick check-up, he confirms she's ready to go home.

Little did I know the nightmare was far from over.

## GRACE

Cal isn't talking to me.

Not more than strictly necessary, anyway, which is freaking me out.

After we got confirmation that Maddie was all right and ready to go home, I texted Aaron with the update and he and Emily stopped by Cal's apartment to drop off some takeout and new toys for Maddie, as well as an obnoxiously big "Get Well Soon" pink balloon that the little girl loved and immediately took to her bedroom.

But they left an hour ago to let us rest, and it's been fifteen minutes since Cal and I finished our food, and he still hasn't uttered a single word to me. He put Maddie to bed as soon as Aaron and Em left, and the apartment is eerily silent.

In some capacity, I understand he's still in shock.

Right as we were leaving the hospital, he got a call from his mom saying social services will be getting in touch, and that she was voluntarily signing up to rehab as soon as she was able to. Cal barely said a few words to her before he hung up.

His words from the hospital flood my head as we sit in silence, not really looking at each other.

*I can't do this to you, Grace.*

And while I have a fair idea of what he meant by that, I wish he had just ripped off the bandage and told me.

I wish he had the courage to tell me he wants to break up with me.

"Do you want to talk?" I ask him when I can't take the deafening silence anymore.

Without looking at me, he nods.

I take a deep breath. It's clear that Cal isn't okay right now, which is understandable—and it's also why I need to be a little stronger and a little more compassionate than usual, for the both of us. Because he can't right now.

"Tell me what's on your mind," I start with something simple enough.

Still, it takes him a good five minutes to get the words out. But I can be patient. For him. For the both of us.

"I should have seen this coming," he finally mutters, his eyes never leaving the table. "I put too much trust in my mom getting her shit together when I shouldn't have. The signs were right under my nose, and I ignored them."

"There's no way you could've predicted what happened, Cal." I search his eyes, but there's no use. "Please, don't punish yourself for this."

"Too late," he mumbles.

Gathering all my inner strength, I count to ten in my head before speaking again. "Doing so is pointless now. It happened, and it sucks, but we should focus on moving forward. For Maddie."

Slowly, too slowly, he lifts his head until our gazes collide. What I see is absolute devastation. "We?" A whisper.

"I'm not leaving you, Cal." I reach out my hand and brush my pinky against his tattooed knuckles. I'm not sure he wants to be touched right now, so I keep our contact to a minimum when he doesn't pull away. "When I said I understood that Maddie will always be your priority, I wasn't lying."

I can see the storm raging inside his head, and for the first time since I've met him, I don't think he's doing anything to stop it. "I..." he starts, and in my heart, I somehow know the rest before he says it. "I can't do this."

Still, I swallow down my nerves and focus on keeping a cool exterior and a steady voice. "You can't do what?"

He shakes his head as if I don't understand a thing. "This... This thing, Grace. I can't put you through this nightmare too."

"Hey." This time, all my fingers wrap around his unmoving hand. "I'm choosing to put myself through this because I love you, all right? Both of you. I'm not going anywhere, and I refuse to let you push me away. I know this is your panic talking and not what you really want."

But he shakes his head again and when he releases himself from my grip, my stomach sinks with dread. "It's not my panic talking."

I wet my lips, which are suddenly as dry as my throat. "What do you mean?"

He rubs his eyes with the heels of his palms and refuses to meet my gaze once again. "I need time."

*Time.*

Do you ever hear a word so many times that it stops making sense in your head? Well, that's exactly what's currently going on in mine. Not because someone is physically saying "time" over and over again, but because it's echoing inside my head until there isn't room for anything else.

*Time. Time. Time.*

Anxiety grips at my chest and refuses to let go. "Time," I repeat. It sounds foreign on my tongue, tastes too sour.

"I'm filing for permanent custody tomorrow," he says. "I'll become Maddie's legal guardian until she's of age which means... Which means there is no life for you and me alone, Grace. It's not just the two of us anymore. We've only known each other for a few months, been together as a couple for even less and I can't... I can't take your freedom away from you."

"I'm going to stop you right there." I hate the way my voice becomes more agitated with each passing second. "One, we've already been through this. I already knew this could happen before I agreed to be your girlfriend, Cal, so don't act like this is news to me. And two, what freedom are you even talking about right now? Do you seriously think I'd feel shackled to you because of Maddie?"

He quickly meets my gaze. "That's not what I meant—"

"Well, that's what you said." *Deep breaths, Grace. Deep breaths.* Forcing my voice to its usual soft tone, I ask him, "Are you still afraid of what could happen to Maddie if we ever break up?"

He gulps. "Yeah."

"Okay." Another deep, useless breath. "I understand. But I'm not going to let you push me away, Cal. Not when there's a possibility we might never break up. Because I don't think we ever will. You're it for me."

"It's not just that." He runs his fingers through his already messy hair in a nervous gesture. "I don't think you understand the seriousness of this situation, and I get that because this isn't your family issue to worry about."

"You are my family."

He ignores me. "But you must think long-term now. Maddie is moving in with me and won't leave at least until she's eighteen. That's *fourteen* years. It will feel as if I have a kid, Grace. It's not temporary, and it will change our relationship forever."

"I know that," I whisper between gritted teeth. His condescending attitude and the way he's treating me like *I'm* the child rubs me the wrong way, and I try my hardest not to lash out at him. It won't help anything if I do.

"We won't have much alone time," he continues, oblivious to the helplessness consuming me from the inside. "Maddie will be glued to our side most of the time, and it's not just that. I have to raise her. I have to cover all her expenses and take care of everything that concerns her. That's a lot of pressure for...for our relationship. For you. We haven't been together long."

"I know." It's too late now to stop the anger from lacing my every word. "Do you think I'm playing house here? I don't know how else to put it, Cal—*I love you*. I love you with everything I've got. You're the freaking love of my life, and *this* is the kind of thing people do for love."

"Grace..."

"I'm not done." I stand up from my chair, suddenly feeling like a caged bird. Bracing my hands on the wooden table, I tell him in a low but firm tone, "I love Maddie as if she were my own sister, and I'd do anything and everything for the both of you. I thought you knew by now, but I guess I have to make myself even clearer. Well, here it goes."

I take a deep breath, bracing myself.

"I'm moving in with you as soon as I graduate. I've already talked to Adelaide about going full-time at the studio, and between that and all the money I've been saving these past few years I've got enough pay rent and help you cover Maddie's expenses. No—I don't want to hear it, Cal. If we're together, if I'm ever going to be your wife and the mother of your children, this is what you'll have to put up with. My stubborn ass, yes. If Maddie is living under my roof, you better believe I'm going to help you pay for her food, her toys, her clothes, and everything else because that's what family does."

My palms are sweating, my heart is racing, and my head is spinning as I press a lingering kiss to Cal's forehead and say, "You wanted time, so I'm giving it to you. Just please remember that I love you more than anything in this world. I'll respect whatever decision you come to as long as you believe every word I said, because I meant them, Cal. We are in this together. Always."

And without waiting for a response, I grab my things and leave his apartment with unshed tears in my eyes.

# chapter 45

## CAL

The next few days are hectic, a whirlwind of events and emotions I'm not sure how I get through in one piece.

As promised, I get a call from Child Protective Services the morning after the accident only to find out that my mother has been fined for child neglect, but that she's also signed a temporary guardianship agreement stating her wish for me to become Maddie's legal guardian until she comes out of rehab.

I already know that's code for "forever."

The lady I talk to assures me that a written consent from our mother helps speed up the process and makes it easier for me to be granted Maddie's custody. Because, apparently, there's a slim chance I can be denied. Imagine that.

Since Pete is gone and unreachable and my mother's an only child whose parents died when I was a boy, I'm the only family member left. It's more than enough.

Maddie can't go back to school for at least another week since it would be too risky for her stitches if she engaged in any demanding physical activity. Which means I have to cut my appointments at the parlor in half and take Maddie with me to each of them.

Trey has been nothing but a great friend and a loyal co-worker for the past few days, and it helps that my clients are so understanding too. They all but coo at my little sister when she comes to either draw or watch something on my iPad while

I work. It's not ideal, but Inkjection is a two-man show and I can't leave Trey hanging for a whole week. We'd lose a shit ton of money, and now I need it more than ever.

Grace stops by the parlor every day to play with Maddie or take her for a walk. She hasn't slept at my place since the accident, and we have barely talked at all. I needed time—I still do—and the fact that she respects that without allowing it to affect her relationship with Maddie speaks volumes.

I love Grace. There isn't even a shred of a doubt in my heart about my feelings for her. She's it for me. My present, my future, my everything.

But I need to come to terms with our new situation first. I want to give her enough time to think things through. The last thing I want is for her to agree to all of this only to come to me in a couple of months and say, "Hey. I changed my mind, by the way. Fuck this co-parenting shit, I'm out." Granted, she would never say anything even remotely close to that, but the sentiment still stands. She could regret her decision if we rush into this, and I'd rather lose her now than in a few months when I fall even more in love with her.

Because I know I will. It's impossible not to.

Aaron also stops by the shop every other day to help me with Maddie, and it's obvious how hard he tries not to bring up Grace to me. She probably warned him against it, which I'm thankful for. Grace-talk is something I can't handle right now, even if she occupies my thoughts all day every day.

There's something else taking over my mind these days, though.

Three weeks after the accident and already in talks with my lawyer about filing for Maddie's permanent guardianship, I started looking for a bigger place to live. My apartment is cool and all that, but it's not the place I see myself raising my sister in from now on. She needs a backyard to run around and play in, a bigger bedroom she can organize sleepovers in, and overall, a *home* to grow up in. This two-bedroom apartment isn't it.

However, no matter how many nice houses I see online, I can't bring myself to sign a lease yet. And I know exactly what is holding me back. *Who* is.

That's why, exactly forty-six days after the accident that turned the wheel of our fate forever, I find myself in front of an empty TDP with a bouquet of flowers in my hand and a single question on my lips.

# GRACE

Life for the past month and a half has been...quite miserable, actually.

Cal asked for time, and that's what I've been giving him. Still, I saw Maddie every day after the accident because how could I not? I wasn't joking when I told him I think of her as my own little sister, as every bit of my family as he is.

Other not-so-miserable things have happened in the meantime, of course. For example, I wrapped up my final draft of *Gracie and Sammy: Undercover Detectives* and Céline is helping me with the formatting because, despite my age, I can't figure out technology to save my life. This means I'll be able to turn in my final project way before it's due, which takes a heavy weight off my shoulders—the biggest, since the rest of my college work is pretty much a walk in the park compared to fighting off my impostor syndrome demons. Those little shits.

It didn't really register how much time Cal and I spent together until we didn't see each other as often anymore. Now my days feel emptier, duller.

Don't get me wrong—I've lived my whole life without a man by my side and I can keep doing it, no problem. The thing is I don't want to.

Cal is everything to me, and these past few weeks without

seeing much of him only have solidified my feelings. He's my best friend, my rock, my safe haven, my home. I feel our bond withering away like a flower without rain and too much sunshine, and sometimes it hurts to exist.

When my head becomes too loud and thoughts that aren't really mine threaten my peace of mind, I turn to the only thing that has always managed to bring me back to earth.

The studio is empty after our last class of the day. I dim the lights and turn on the soft music, allowing the familiar notes of Pachelbel to take the reins instead. And I dance.

Without a routine in mind, I simply let my feet lead the way. I don't want to think—I just need to feel.

My eyes close on their own accord as the music flows through me. Dancing has helped through every storm, every fog, and every landslide I've been through since I was a small girl. It is how my soul and heart grow, how I nurture every part of me that I normally don't have access to. No matter whether I seek it or not, dancing heals me.

Adelaide has always told me that dancing is another way to speak. And as the song ends, I hear my body talk loud and clear.

"Beautiful."

Only that it's not my body talking.

I turn in the direction of the deep voice, a hand pressed over my heart as it jumps out of my chest, and I gasp, "What are you doing here?"

Both hands behind his back, Cal steps into the classroom and walks up to me, stopping only when a few inches separate us. "I wanted to see you."

He is... He is here. For *me*.

"These are for you," he says, and a second later his hand comes forward holding a stunning bouquet of pink azaleas that immediately makes my eyes water. "Don't cry, sunshine."

"I'm not crying," I deny like an idiot while wiping away my

very obvious tears.

He chuckles. *Chuckles.* I haven't heard a more beautiful sound in forty-six days. "Come here."

Erasing the painful distance between our bodies, I throw my arms around his neck and hold him tightly in case he ever wants me to let go again—because I won't allow it. And that's a threat.

"I love you so much," he whispers against my neck, his arms coming around my body to hug me closer. "I love you. I love you. I love you."

"I love you too, Cal. More than anything." I squeeze him, and he squeezes me right back. "I don't want to be away from you ever again, you hear me?"

"I hear you, sunshine." When we pull away, he cups my cheek with his free hand and promises me, "Never again." His mouth is warm when it finally meets mine, and I sigh into his kiss. All the tension leaves my body at once. Cal is gentle as he licks my bottom lip, nipping softly at it before the tip of his tongue parts the seam of my lips and, with a groan, slides it into my mouth. I whimper with need as our tongues meet, his hand holding my cheek and my arms still wrapped around his neck.

He tastes like the rain our flower needs to bloom again.

Breathing heavily, he pulls away in the same gentle way our lips came together. "Come back home to me."

*Home.*

I hold his face, the pads of my thumbs caressing the short stubble on his cheeks. "I hope you want me to stay, because I'm not going anywhere."

He kisses me again, gentle and quick, before pulling away once more and saying, "Don't worry, I intend to keep you forever."

He hands me the azaleas, and I almost whimper at the loss of his warm body against mine until it registers what he's doing.

Without saying another word, Cal gets down on one knee

and reaches for his back pocket.

My whole body stops responding all at once, except for the hand that flies to my mouth to hide my shock.

"It's not what it looks like." He smirks as he brings a small, shiny object forward. It's a key. "No matter how badly I want to marry the fuck out of you, I know it's still soon and we have the rest of our lives ahead of us. But I do have one question for you, sunshine, if you want to hear it."

I give him a silent, shocked nod.

Cal holds up the small key between his fingers. "For the past few weeks, I've been looking at houses in the suburbs. *Family* neighborhoods. And since that's what you are to me, Grace, and that's what I want to build with you, will you do me the honor of moving in with me? And with Maddie, of course."

My fingers shake around the bouquet. "D-Do you have a new house?"

"Not yet," he says. "I have looked at a bunch of nice rentals, but I haven't made up my mind about any of them because I want us to choose one together. For us, for our family. So, Grace, will you—"

"Yes!"

I throw myself into his arms, tackling him to the ground, and he laughs as he hugs me against his chest. "Thank God."

"You really thought I was going to say no?" I arch a playful eyebrow.

He gives me a quick peck on the lips. "Not really, but it still feels good to hear it."

I kiss him again for good measure. "So... When are we moving in?"

"You finish your classes in a couple of months, right? We could do it then."

I nod. "It sounds perfect." However, I don't allow the bliss to blind me for too long. "We haven't talked much in the past several weeks. How is Maddie holding up?"

Cal sobers up instantly, but the tension from a month ago is long gone from his handsome features. "I told her Mom wasn't feeling well, and that she needed to live somewhere else for a while to get better. It wasn't easy for the first week. She cried a lot, but since she loves living with me, I guess she's getting used to the idea more easily. She can still visit my mom, so that's good."

"What about Pete?" I smooth a hand through his dark hair, and he leans into my touch. "Has she asked about him?"

"Yes, and it was more complicated to tell her about him since... Well, since he's probably never coming back." He swallows. "I found a therapist last week. She's gone twice so far, and she likes it."

"That's amazing, Cal." I press a kiss to the tip of his nose, making him smile. "You're doing all the right things. It won't be easy, but Maddie is a strong little girl, and she has the most amazing older brother in the universe taking care of her."

His eyes sparkle under the dim lights of the studio. "And she has you."

"And she has me. She has *us*." I give him a soft smile. "She has a family who loves her more than anything. Everything will be all right, Cal. I promise."

He presses his forehead against mine and whispers, "I love you, sunshine. And I'll love you until my last breath, until I'm nothing but a whisper in the wind."

My eyes fill with tears as I say, "You're the best thing that's ever happened to me. I can't wait for our future together."

"Our future is already here, love."

And when he kisses me with that gentleness again, I can feel the truth in the way my universe shifts and pauses on my destination.

Because this is where I belong. I'm finally here.

# chapter 46

## GRACE

The next few months are full of big changes and conflicting emotions.

Two weeks before my college graduation, Cal officially became Maddie's permanent guardian. His lawyer explained that guardianship isn't the same thing as adoption—which I had thought at first—but that Cal would take care of his sister from now on like a parent would.

The whole process turned out to be a lot more tedious than expected, particularly because we had to update the school, the medical center, the dentist, and literally everything else. Cal asked me if I would be okay with being Maddie's emergency contact, and of course I said yes.

However, the toughest part of all was to make Maddie understand her new living situation. For weeks, she didn't understand why she had to visit her mother at some strange building that worked like a hospital but didn't really look like one. She kept asking why she couldn't live with her mom again. If it was because she didn't love her anymore.

"Mommy loves you, princess," Cal would tell her every time she asked, which happened less frequently as the weeks went by. "She's sick right now, and she needs the help of doctors and nurses to get well again."

Weirdly enough, she rarely asked about Pete. The "official" explanation (we weren't going to tell a four-year-old that her father had abandoned her) was that he had found a new job very far away, and he didn't know when he would be able to come back for a visit. I always suspected Maddie wasn't too attached to her dad—thank God—and time only proved me right.

Just like he had done before, Cal attended another Daddy-Daughter event at her school, not before complaining about how unnecessary and insensitive those could be. Many kids don't have a father for whatever reason, and there's no point in reminding them that they're not like their classmates.

Surprisingly, months after Maddie left for her "big girl school"—as we call primary school now—we learned they had changed the dreaded events into Parent-Daughter and Parent-Son gatherings, which sounded much better.

As for *Gracie and Sammy: Undercover Detectives*, not only did I end up getting a big, fat A, but I also got the tremendous opportunity of having an agent look at my manuscript during the summer. Professor Danner thought it was worth sending out to a few publishing houses and that's precisely what I did.

If impostor syndrome is a bitch, then I'm the Bitch Supreme.

A month before graduation, Aaron dragged me out of a ballet lesson I'd just finished teaching because one of his clients told him she had finished renovations in one of the old houses near the river and she wanted to rent it out. We picked up Cal and Maddie on our way, and the second we stepped foot into the three-bedroom, two-bathroom, two-story house, we knew it was the one.

It sits in one of the nicest areas of Warlington, right next to a park with a pond and a lot of ducks Maddie loves to feed. There was no way I could walk from the house to TDP as it was too far away, but luckily that stopped being an issue the day after graduation, when my dads came all the way here to drop off my new car.

I literally cried for hours. Not only because of my first and new vehicle—which is a beauty, by the way—but because both of my dads fell in love with Maddie *the second* she went up to them with her yellow princess costume and ballerina bun to introduce herself.

She got a bit confused when she found out I had two dads instead of one mom and one dad like she did, but a simple explanation from Cal was enough to make the confusion go away.

"Some families have a mommy and a daddy, but others can have two mommies or two daddies," he'd told her.

"Or one big brother?" she'd asked, a hopeful gleam in her eyes.

He'd kissed her little forehead and said, "That too, pumpkin."

That was a year ago.

Now, in the middle of a hot July afternoon, I'm about to lose my shit.

"Maddie! Dinner's ready!" I shout from the kitchen, knowing she's probably watching something on Cal's tablet upstairs and won't hear a thing. "Maddie!"

"I'm coming, Gracie!" she finally shouts back, right before I hear her loud footsteps on the staircase. A moment later the five-year-old appears in the open-concept kitchen, dressed in a little orange dress with flowers all over it—she's in an orange craze these days. Don't let her fool you, though, because the flowers are still pink. "Where's Sammy?"

"That's what I'd like to know," I mutter more to myself than to her as I take the big bowl of salad and pass it to Maddie so she can bring it to the table. She always wants to help around the house, and it makes me melt every time.

Cal is raising her well, and I hope I'm doing a good job, too. Trying to calm down, I set the chicken on the wooden table where we have breakfast and dinner as a family every day—Cal and I usually eat lunch together at the parlor or at The Spoon when Maddie's at school—and I press a kiss on Maddie's head. She's gotten slightly taller in the past year, and although she's still a cute little thing, by the time she's my age she'll probably be taller than me. Which isn't too difficult to begin with.

Oh, but don't broach the "Maddie is growing up so fast" subject to Cal because he'd have a literal meltdown, and then I'd have to cuddle him and remind him that she'll always be his little princess. Such a man-baby, that one.

Speaking of my over-the-top dramatic boyfriend...

Where the hell is he?

Nearly an hour ago he left the house after saying we'd run out of milk and butter. Mind you, there's a supermarket five minutes away. I wouldn't mind his delay so much if the chicken wasn't getting cold. Or if he replied to my texts.

"I'm so hungry," Maddie whines, plopping down on the couch with a dramatic sigh. I smile to myself. Like brother, like sister.

"I'm sure he'll be here shortly. Do you want to have some crackers? Just a couple, though. You know the rule." The rule being don't stuff your face with snacks right before dinner.

"Yay! You're the best, Gracie!"

It isn't until ten minutes later that we *finally* hear Cal's car pulling into the driveway. I hold out my hand to Maddie. "Come on. Let's see what took your brother so long."

Hand in hand, we walk to the front of the house and are immediately met with an overwhelming wave of heat when I open the front door.

And a very smiley Cal getting out of the driver's seat, going back to the trunk of the car, and getting out...

"Is that a dog?!" Maddie screams as I spot the biggest, cutest black Labrador I've ever seen.

"Surprise." Cal smiles sheepishly, taking the dog by the leash and coming towards the front of the house. "Sit," he instructs the animal, and my mouth hangs open when the dog doesn't even hesitate to do as it's told.

"What... Cal?" I'm speechless right now. We've talked about getting Maddie a dog sometime soon, but I had no clue he had gone ahead and sorted everything out already. "Explain."

He chuckles. "Sorry about the supermarket thing, I actually didn't go there."

"I figured." I roll my eyes, unable to stop a smile as I watch Maddie bouncing up and down with excitement and the dog wagging its tail in response.

"This big guy is Rocket," he explains under his sister's astonished gaze. "He was born in the local shelter four years ago, is fully trained, and good with kids and other dogs despite his size. Do you want to pet him, princess?"

"Yes!"

"Okay, but do it gently."

Maddie makes her way towards the newest member of our family and extends her hand at him, which Rocket wastes no time sniffing and licking. Maddie laughs. "He likes me."

"Of course he does, baby. He's a really good boy." Cal scratches him behind the ears. "Come here, sunshine. Say hi to our son."

"Our son, huh?" Kneeling before Rocket, I wait until he too licks my hand in approval. "Aw, he's such a cutie."

"He's a big teddy bear," Cal agrees. "I've also brought some food, toys, and a doghouse with me in the car."

Once Rocket is settled in our big backyard, busy running and sniffing around, we finally dig into our—now cold—dinner.

"We'll have to walk him every day," Cal tells Maddie, who immediately nods.

"Yes, Sammy, I will walk him. He's my best friend," she says around a mouthful of chicken. She turns to me, "He looks a little like Poe."

"You're right, he does," I agree with a smile.

Rocket looks exactly like Poe, Gracie and Sammy's fur-buddy. That's how Cal imagined him more than a year ago, and that's how he'll be hitting the shelves in a little over a month.

That's right—the first installment of *Gracie and Sammy: Undercover Detectives* is being published by one of my favorite publishing houses from when I was a kid. And I say first installment because, according to the juicy contract I signed a few months ago, there will be at least another two coming out in the following years.

No matter what happens with that, though, I've already told Adelaide she won't get rid of me. I owe ballet—and TDP—too much to quit. It's not in my plans.

The afternoon summer breeze filters through the open window facing the backyard, where Rocket is busy chasing a butterfly, already feeling at home.

A warm sense of calm settles inside me. As I steal a look at Maddie and Cal, who are laughing and watching Rocket with heart eyes, I wonder if life could get any better than this.

The short answer is yes. Yes, it can.

# epilogue

## GRACE

*Five years later...*

"GENTLE, MADDIE."

"I know, Sammy. Stop pestering me."

"Oops. Someone's grumpy," Aaron quips.

Emily swats at his arm. "Don't tease her. She's nervous."

"I'm *not* nervous." Maddie glares at both of them before turning to me. "Tell them I'm not nervous, Gracie."

"She's totally not nervous." I smirk, sending a knowing glance to my best friend and cousin who, by the way, have been married for a year now. So much for "we're having fun." They're an incorrigible pair of idiots, but I love them all the same.

"See? I'm not," the ten-year-old insists, extending her short arms towards her brother. "Give her to me, please?"

"Yes, princess, but remember—"

"Gentle, I know." She shifts nervously on the couch, because our girl is totally freaking out right now despite her cool exterior. A trait she's inherited from her brother, no doubt.

"All right, here we go." Carefully, Cal sits down next to her and even more slowly, places the small bundle in her awaiting arms.

The four of us hold our breaths as Maddie gapes at the tiny baby in her arms, mouth wide open with an expression of utter bewilderment and indescribable love. I recognize it because that's exactly what I felt—and I'm still feeling—two days ago when I gave birth to our daughter.

Our own little flower, our beautiful Lila.

"Hi, baby," Maddie whispers as she carefully touches a finger to Lila's forehead, brushing away some blond fuzz that has fallen from her pink hat. I steal a glance at Cal, who has never looked more in love. And that's saying something, since he all but broke down the day we got married three years ago. "I'm your Auntie Maddie. You're very tiny."

"You'll have to take good care of her now that she's here," Cal tells her softly, one hand brushing his sister's long brown hair. "She's going to look up to you and will want to be like her auntie."

Maddie smiles, not taking her eyes off the newest member of our family. "She's my new best friend," she says. "I hope Rocket doesn't get jealous."

I chuckle. "I'm sure Rocket won't mind sharing. Now there'll be two of you to drive him nuts."

Aaron watches his nieces with loving eyes—yes, he's a self-proclaimed Cool Uncle of both girls despite not being my brother and Maddie not being my daughter for that matter. "Em, I want one," he blurts out.

I expect one of my best friend's usual snarky comebacks, but instead she says, "Okay. We'll order one when we get home, if you know what I mean."

"Gross," Cal mutters, throwing them an amused glance. "Thank you for watching Maddie for the past couple of days, by the way."

"No biggie." Aaron smiles. "She's a gem, and I'm sure this little one will be too."

"I hope so, because I already miss all the sleep I won't get for the next few years." I sigh, which makes everyone laugh.

As Aaron and Emily go back to drooling over Lila, Cal wraps me in his arms and kisses my forehead. "She's finally here, and she's perfect."

I press a gentle kiss to the side of his jaw. "I love you so much, Cal. Thank you for giving me our beautiful family." He pulls me even closer as he whispers, "I love you, sunshine. Forever."

A sudden blast of love and happiness crashes into me like a wave that's been waiting far too long to get back to the shore. *Finally*, my heart sings as I drown in pure bliss.

When my dads arrive in Warlington the following day to meet their newborn granddaughter, I take a moment to just... look. To look at the family I love, the one I've always longed for, and in that moment, I realize the single most important truth of all.

No matter how many obstacles were thrown my way, no matter how many times I felt I would never be enough, no matter where life planted me...

I bloomed with grace.

## THE END

# bonus chapter

## Cal and Lila's
## Great Adventure

"Daddy?"

"Yes, baby?"

"Am I a grown-up?"

I peek over my shoulder at the five-year-old firecracker currently licking tiny cookie crumbs off her fingertips. She'd been pretty quiet since I told her she was allowed to have one after lunch, so I'm surprised by her sudden question.

"Not until you're a bit older, no," I tell her.

Her face falls a little, but she doesn't let the brief disappointment get to her. "When I'm a grown-up can I touch a knife?"

I face the sink again and rinse the last pasta bowl before I put it away to dry. "Only when Mommy or Daddy are around."

She stays quiet for a moment before she asks, "Can Maddsy touch a knife?"

She's referring to Maddie, my little sister and her fifteen-year-old aunt, who's been living with us since before Lila was born. And I couldn't be happier that they're growing up as close as sisters.

I dry my hands on a tea towel, my back still turned to her. "Depends on the knife. She can use smaller ones to cut her food."

But my daughter is still not done with her interrogation about knives. Should I be worried she finds them so fascinating all of a sudden?

"Daddy."

"Lila."

"Do you do your tattoos with a knife?"

I resist the urge to laugh out loud, not because I think she's being ridiculous but because I love her so damn much, my heart can't take the cute things she says. Her curiosity is never-ending. Grace and I are never too busy or too tired to give her all the answers she seeks.

"I don't do my tattoos with a knife," I explain wiping the countertops spotless. "I use a tattoo machine with a needle."

"What's a tattoo machine?" She uses her little finger to pick up another cookie crumb and brings it to her mouth. Why am I mesmerized by every little thing she does?

"I'll show you."

I pull out my phone, find a picture online, and hand it to her. As she looks at the screen with attentive eyes, I take the chance to redo her pigtails.

It's during these small moments that I can't believe I was lucky enough to marry the love of my life, and this little person I love with every fiber of my being and who I'd give my life for is the result of that.

Grace insists that Lila looks just like me—minus the blond hair—but I don't see it. She has the same eyes as Maddie—kind, attentive, curious—but the rest is all Grace. Lila is my little sunshine for a reason.

"And all the colors are inside here?" she asks next, glancing between the few colored pieces on my right arm and the phone screen.

"Yep."

She continues her careful perusal of the photo. "But this is small, and you have so many tattoos."

"That's because I've had them done over the years, not all in one day."

"You had tattoos when I was a baby in Mommy's belly?"

"Yes."

"And when you met Mommy?"

My lips twitch with the beginning of a smile, remembering the first time I saw Grace through the windows at Inkjection. How unsure she looked. How damn adorable she was, which explains Lila's own cuteness. See? She's all Grace.

"Yes, even back then I had tattoos."

That has her gasping. "You're so old!"

I chuckle. "Well, yeah. Dads are supposed to be old."

She gives me back my phone and locks her eyes with mine, a determined glint in them I'm very familiar with because my sister has it too.

"Daddy, I want to draw a tattoo on your arm," she declares.

Her words stop me on my tracks.

Just like Maddie, Lila's expressed curiosity in my tattoos before. She always traces them with her finger when I hold her, especially the rose on my neck. But she's never shown any interest in inking me until right now.

And frankly... Grace might kill me for this, but that doesn't stop me from asking, "Really?" like I'm truly considering it.

Because why not? My body is so covered in ink, one more wouldn't hurt. Especially when that tattoo would automatically become my favorite one.

Lila nods firmly. "Yes." She holds out her hand until she's touching the tiniest patch of bare skin on my wrist. "Here," she decides.

I'm more convinced by the second.

But I can't forget that she's still five, so she might change her mind in about two seconds. My hopes are already sky-high when I ask her, "What would you tattoo on me, baby?"

She chews on her chubby cheek as she considers it. "I want to draw a heart here," she declares, her fingers still on my wrist. "Because I love you so much, Daddy, so I have to tattoo a heart on you so you never forget because tattoos don't go away."

My heart stops functioning altogether.

With just a few words, I'm gone.

I crouch down so we're at eye level, my hand caressing her soft hair, and it's impossible to hide the adoration in my voice not that I'd ever want to—as I tell her, "I will never forget that you love me, Lila. That's impossible. Will you ever forget that I love you more than anything in this world?"

She shakes her head, blond pigtails flying everywhere. "Never, Daddy. I love Mommy and Maddsy too."

"And we all love you," I reassure her with a soft smile.

"But I want to draw a heart," she insists, like she thinks I'm trying to talk her out of it. "Can I, please?"

How am I supposed to say no to those doe eyes?

To her?

I pretend that I haven't already made up my mind as I stand back up and ponder all the ways in which my wife could kill me when I tell I let our five-year-old handle a working tattoo machine. Maybe it's not the most responsible thing a father could do but...I pretty much raised Maddie since she was born, and she's turning out just fine.

My sister is pretty keen on pursuing a ballet degree, and the spark in her eyes along with her sheer determination to go after her dream career make us insanely proud. She's clearly found her passion, and since she's as stubborn as her dear older brother, I know she won't stop until she gets exactly what she wants.

Both Grace and she are spending the day at the dance studio, rehearsing for their summer show. If I'm remembering correctly, after their rehearsal Maddie wanted to shop for some clothes, so they'll be heading to the mall and won't be back for a few hours.

It's Daddy and Lila Day today, which means Daddy calls the shots.

I look at Lila.

She looks at me.

She gives me one of those toothy smiles I'm so damn weak for.

And I'm sold.

"Fine. Let's go."

She squeals with excitement when I pick her up and carry her to the mud room, where I set her on the small bench as I get her shoes. And once she's wearing her favorite white and green sneakers, she takes a big jump from the bench and hurries to hold my hand and drag me to the car. "Come on, Daddy! We'll be late!"

I chuckle. "I own the shop, Li. We can go whenever we want."

That doesn't deter her. In fact, she doesn't calm down at any point during our drive, bouncing with bubbling excitement until I park behind Inkjection.

She can't unbuckle herself from her seat fast enough, so she's frustrated when she has to wait for me to set her down on the ground because the car is too high for her little legs. Her pediatrician says she still has a lot of growing to do, but for now it looks like she hasn't inherited a single one of my tall genes. She's a bit shorter than the average five-year-old, not that it's ever been a problem for her. Again, Lila is a carbon copy of Grace whether she sees it or not.

I'm surprised when Lila doesn't immediately run to Inkjection's backdoor while I lock the car, but instead grabs two of my fingers as she jumps up and down. "Tattoo! Tattoo!" she chants.

I can't help but laugh. "All right, all right." I take a moment to kneel in front of her so we're eye-to-eye. "You know Daddy is taking the day off today, but Uncle Trey is working in there with clients. That means you can't jump around or talk very loudly, okay? You understand?"

Her nod is nothing short of enthusiastic. She's such a good kid, it doesn't surprise me that she doesn't lose her smile as she lowers her voice to a whisper and asks, "Do you think Uncle Trey will give me a hug?"

"Uncle Trey always wants to give you a hug."

And indeed, after we enter the shop through the front, since the back door turns out to be locked, we're immediately met by my best friend's big smile. The fucker doesn't even glance in my direction—and I get it—because as soon as Lila realizes the shop is empty, she darts toward him. He leaves his spot behind the counter and scoops my daughter into his arms.

"Uncle Trey!" she beams as she wraps her arms around his neck.

He laughs as he hugs her back. "What are you doing here, pipsqueak?"

"Daddy said I could draw a tattoo on his hand, so I'm doing it now."

"Is that right?" Trey looks at me with a knowing smirk. "You want to be a tattoo artist like your dad?"

Lila shrugs. "I don't know." She looks back at me, and I throw her a wink. "I think I want to be a teacher better."

"Oh?" It's the first time I'm hearing about this, and I'm pretty sure it'll be news to Grace too or she would've brought it up at some point. "Is that right?"

"I don't know. I don't want to work right now," she ends up saying. "Work sounds pretty boring."

Trey throws his head back in laughter. "Fair enough. Come on then, my next client won't be here for another twenty minutes so you'll have plenty of time to work your magic."

Lila beams at that and grabs my hand again to drag me toward the back. Trey helps me set everything up as my daughter sits impatiently on the tattooing chair.

"Okay, Lila, you need to listen very carefully now," I start, suddenly wondering if this has been my worst idea yet. *Sunshine, please don't kill me for this.*

"Yes, Daddy."

I let out a deep, nervous sigh. Here we go.

"Do you want to practice your hearts first? I can give you a pen and some paper."

But she shakes her head. "I got it."

I grab a pair of latex gloves next. "Let me help you put these on first." Once she's ready, I hold out the tattoo machine in front of her. "Pay attention now, yeah? I don't want you to hurt yourself."

"I won't." She eyes the needle with interest. "This doesn't look like a knife."

Trey, who's gone to the front again, snorts in amusement as he glances at us over his shoulder.

"That's because it's a tattoo machine, baby, not a knife." I smile gently at her. "I want you to hold it in your hands first so you can see how it moves. If you don't like it, we can just leave and go do something else, all right?"

She makes grabby hands, unfazed. "All right, but I want to draw a heart."

"This isn't like your pencils at home," I warn her one last time. "It moves a lot, and you need to be careful."

She sends me one of those serious glares that makes her look so much like my sister it's both adorable and kind of spooky. "I'm a grown-up, Daddy. I can do this."

"I know you can, little sunshine. I just want you to be safe," I tell her gently as I pass her one of the smallest tattoo guns we have. And I swear the sparkle in her eyes only brightens as she inspects every inch of it. "I'm going to plug it in now."

Once I've got her nod of approval, I plug it in and watch as it starts buzzing in Lila's tiny hand. Much to my surprise, she doesn't even flinch. Instead, a slow smile takes up her whole face.

"Gimme your wrist," she orders in such a firm tone I can't help but chuckle.

"Hold your horses, boss baby. Let me explain how it works first."

We spend the next few minutes going over the whole process. Although she's pretty confident, I still make her practice an invisible heart on my skin while the machine is unplugged so she can get used to the weight. When I ask her if she wants Trey to help her hold it, she says no.

As I get everything ready for the real deal, I become very aware of the fact that her tattoo might not end up looking like a heart at all, and I don't want her to be upset about it. Because I couldn't care less about how perfect or imperfect it looks. She could tattoo a straight line on me and it'd still be my favorite tattoo on my whole damn body only because my little sunshine did it.

And I tell her just that.

"Okay, but I got this," she insists once more. Her shining confidence makes me immensely proud of her. "Are you ready?"

"Whenever you are. Remember to go slowly and do it gently. You won't hurt me, but you might hurt yourself, and we don't want that."

Wordlessly, Trey moves closer to our booth so he can step in if she gets overwhelmed, but none of that happens. With an impressive, adult-level of concentration and her tongue peeking out of her mouth, my daughter is careful as she inks one of her signature hearts on my skin forever.

When it's done, she says it doesn't look as good as the ones she draws on paper, but to me it's perfect. It's way more than that—it's everything.

"I love it, Li," I tell her with honesty.

I'm sure every parent thinks this about their child, but she's so damn brilliant. I already know she will go far. Whatever she'll want, wherever she'll wish to go, she'll make it happen. Because she's Lila—as simple as that.

When she beams at me, I pick her up and place her on my lap so I can give her a big kiss. "You're a very talented tattoo artist."

She shrugs, a blush covering her cheeks. "I'm just okay."

Trey whistles as he looks at my new tattoo and starts

assembling everything to clean the excess of ink and wrap up the heart so it can heal. "Looks good, pipsqueak. It's looking real good."

It does. I'm actually impressed she gripped the machine strongly enough that it didn't slip. Maybe Grace won't kill me after all. A man can only hope.

Once Trey sorts everything out with my new tattoo, I ask her, "What do you want to do now? You did such a good job, we have to celebrate."

She thinks about it for a moment. "I want to have a princess tea party in my room."

I smile. "Am I invited to that princess tea party?"

She stands up on the chair and wraps her tiny arms around my neck, planting a loud kiss on my cheek. "Always, Daddy."

\*\*\*

Two hours later, I have a sparkly crown on top of my head and the tiniest plastic tea cup in my hand when I hear the door opening and then shutting downstairs.

"Lila!" My sister calls, loud enough to wake up the dead.

My daughter forgets all about the fake tea she was pretend-pouring into my cup. She feels such raw admiration for Maddie, she drops everything at once the second she sees or hears her.

"I got you something at the mall!"

Lila lets out the loudest squeal known to humankind and rushes out of her room without so much as a goodbye to our guests (aka her many plushies, all set in a circle around us). After taking off the crown—so that Maddie and Grace don't make fun of me *again*—I follow her downstairs.

"Whatcha doing?" I ask my girls, who are both sitting on the last step of the staircase.

My sister glances up at me. "I got her one of those animal Lego sets she wanted. We're going to build it together later," she explains.

Indeed, Lila is struggling to open the sturdy cardboard box, but Maddie doesn't interfere. She always gives her a chance to do things by herself so she can see that, even if she's little, she's still very capable.

"Sounds fun." I ruffle both of their hair as I reach the bottom of the stairs. "Wash your hands before dinner."

"Yes, Dad." Maddie rolls her eyes at me, giving me that moody teenage attitude she's been displaying for a couple years now. But there's no hiding her smirk when I stick out my tongue at her.

Our interaction makes Lila laugh. "Yes, Dad," she repeats, mimicking her aunt.

These two will be the reason for my gray hairs one day. I'm calling it now.

I hear Lila asking Maddie about her day at the studio as I enter the kitchen and find Grace putting a bag of groceries away in the fridge. She's humming some song with her back turned to me, and I don't miss the chance—I wrap my arms around her middle and lean into her ear. The goosebumps along her arms and her slight intake of breath draw a smirk on my face as I whisper, "Daddy did a bad thing today."

The blush on her cheeks is unmistakable. "Cal," she hisses, swatting my arm to no avail because I don't stop hugging her. "You're a menace."

I might be, but she can't deny that she loves it.

We've been calling each other "daddy" and "mommy" around Lila since she was born and it's become kind of a joke between us. Something silly and not at all sexual, but can you blame me for messing with my wife from time to time?

One of my hands leaves her waist to cradle the back of her neck as I guide her lips to mine. She melts against my body, and I have to remind myself where we are.

She pouts when I pull away, and I throw her a wink. "Later," I promise her. The heat in her eyes tells me I'd better keep it—and I will.

For the sake of my balls, I decide to change the topic. "How did Maddie do today? Is she nervous?"

I start helping Grace with the rest of the groceries as she says, "She'll nail the summer show." The pride in her voice makes me fall in love with her all over again. "She's totally serious about going away for college, too. The school counselor is helping her look for ballet degrees and it looks like the one in Norcastle is her favorite. She's pretty set on passing the audition for The Norcastle Ballet after she graduates, too."

Norcastle. That's a big city. Five hours away, in a completely different state. Panic rises in my chest at the thought of my little sister moving away, so far from us and everything she knows. The fact that she'll be eighteen by then brings me no relief.

As always, Grace picks up on my incoming meltdown.

"We'll cross that bridge when we get to it." She closes the fridge and pins me down with one of her no-nonsense stares. "It wouldn't be fair to keep her here forever if she wants to leave— and she does. Not because she doesn't love us, but because she thinks her future is somewhere else. I left my dads to go to college too, remember? Jeez, I left the country. And it turned out pretty well."

I nod, but my mind is still spiraling. We're talking about my princess. "I won't keep her here," I assure Grace as much as I'm reassuring myself. "As difficult as it's going to be to watch her go, she's her own person. I would never take her freedom away."

Grace gives me a nostalgic smile before wrapping her arms around my waist, her head tilted back so she's looking at me. "I know you wouldn't. That's why she's looking at so many options, because she knows we'd never force her to do something she doesn't want."

I cradle the back of her neck, my fingers massaging her scalp. "Not many people her age know what they want to do after high school, so I'm not going to interfere."

A stomach-turning thought fills my mind then, and before I can stop, I blurt out, "What if she meets someone in Norcastle?"

Grace snorts. "I'm sure she'll meet lots of people."

"I mean someone as in...*someone*."

I'm very aware that Maddie's had a crush or two on boys at her school, but I never paid them any mind because it's harmless. Moody teenage attitude and all, she's a responsible girl. Plus, she knows she's too young to date anyway. But if she moves away for college...

"I'll kill him," I decide then and there. "I won't care who he is. I'll just kill him."

Because that's the most logical and reasonable thing to do to my sister's future boyfriend.

"You won't do such a thing." Grace rolls her eyes. "Because we taught her well, and she's already setting strong boundaries for herself. Whoever she chooses to be with when the time comes will be the best person for her."

I let out a loud sigh because, all right, that's true. We couldn't be prouder of the young woman she's becoming, and she's more than earned our trust over the years.

I guess I'll just need to get over myself.

Grace plants a soft kiss on my stubbled cheek. "Don't think I've forgotten about that one bad thing Daddy did today."

Right, that.

I give her a sheepish smile, which earns me an arched eyebrow in response. "Before I tell you, you should know that everything went well and no tears were shed."

"Okay..." she says, slowly. "Did something happen to Lila?"

"No, nothing like that," I assure her before she gets any ideas. She might not be as overdramatic as I am, but Grace is a big mama bear.

Slowly, I disentangle my hand from her hair and bring it between us. Her eyes immediately land on the transparent wrap in my hand, and her face relaxes. "Oh. You got a new tattoo? That's it?" She sounds calmer now. "What's the fuss about, then? You've taken Lila to the shop before."

"Look closer, sunshine."

She frowns, but takes my hand between both of hers and does as I say.

I can tell the exact moment it dawns on her, because her whole face softens and her eyes turn glassy. "Did she...?"

"Yeah." My voice comes out rougher than before. I hate seeing Grace cry, even if they're happy tears. "She randomly asked if she could tattoo me today, and I said we could try. She was so confident I almost couldn't believe my eyes."

"She was?" Her voice sounds small, emotional.

I press a soft kiss on her forehead. "Trey was supervising, but he didn't need to step in. It looks good, doesn't it?"

"It's my favorite tattoo of yours," she says before she goes on her tiptoes and kisses my lips. "You're the best dad in the world, Cal. I knew you were going to be from the very first time I saw you with Maddie."

My heart soars as I press another gentle, brief kiss to her lips.

Both of our eyes land back on the tattoo and I admit, "I was afraid you'd make me sleep on the couch for this, honestly."

I'm met with another eye roll. "I trust you, Cal. I wouldn't have had kids with you if I didn't."

"Kids? In plural?" I arch a questioning eyebrow.

She shrugs. "Fine, we didn't have her, but Maddie counts too."

That she does. But...

"I almost had a heart attack just now thinking you were pregnant again," I confess, which makes her shake her head in amusement.

"No worries, I'm not."

It wouldn't be the end of the world by any means, but after Lila was born we decided we had our hands full with just two girls. Our family is complete.

"Are you guys done smooching?" comes the unmistakable voice of my little sister from the hallway, followed by Lila's sweet giggle. "Can we come in, or will we be traumatized for life?"

"The drama," I say.

At the same time Grace laughs and tells them the kitchen is now a smooching-free zone.

"Mads, look at this," Grace tells her as she holds out my hand for her to see.

My sister frowns, looking at the small tattoo that she knows hasn't been done by Trey or me because she's familiar with our styles. Her eyes widen in realization. "She did it?" she asks, mouth agape as she throws her thumb back, pointing in Lila's direction.

"Yep."

"Holy moly, Li, this is amazing!" My sister beams before she gets down on her knees to hug her niece. "I was never brave enough to tattoo anything when I was your age, but you did it. It's so good!"

Lila shrugs, cheeks flushed. "It's just okay."

Maddie puts both of her hands on Lila's shoulders and squeezes them just a tiny bit. "No, Li, it's amazing. It's the best tattoo your dad has, and he has many."

My daughter looks at my sister with a question in her eyes, like she doesn't really believe her words. "Really?" Lila tends to do that, thinking the amazing things she accomplishes aren't that great, and we haven't figured out why yet.

Maddie gives her a firm nod. "I'd never lie to you."

Grace and I exchange a soft look. We didn't know how Maddie was going to react after Lila was born—if she was going to feel jealous or neglected because we had to split our attention between them. Or if she was suddenly going to feel like she didn't belong in our family because she's not our daughter.

What happened with our mother and Pete left a darkness in her heart that therapy is slowly trying to clear out. She sees our mother sometimes now that Mom's clean, but Pete...

Well, that's a story for another day.

Instead, Maddie welcomed her niece with open arms and has been nothing but a sisterly figure to her since. Needless to say, Lila adores her right back.

We watch as Lila's smile and confidence come back to her little face. She turns to Grace. "Do you like it, Mommy?"

Grace kneels too and gives her a kiss on her temple. "Don't tell Daddy, but you're a better tattoo artist than he is," she whispers conspiratorially, loud enough for all of us to hear.

When Lila giggles and slides her playful gaze to me, I throw her a wink.

It's my turn to make dinner tonight, but Grace decides to help me as Maddie and Lila start building her new Lego set in the living room.

Grace starts telling me about her day as I get on with my cooking. Our girls' laughter fills the kitchen from the other room. And just like that, I know that no matter what life throws at them, they will bloom, just like the incredible woman beside me.

# acknowledgements

You are holding this book in your hands right now thanks to years of therapy. Not a single part of me would have been confident enough to even entertain the idea of publishing Grace and Cal's story a few years ago if I hadn't asked for the help I so badly needed.

I suppose it is true what they say about things happening when and how they are supposed to.

If you are reading this, I hope you take it as a sign to get the help you need. I promise it will get better. Much, much better. You are not alone.

This book is for that little girl who dared to pick up a pen and a notebook and write her first story more than ten years ago (and never let a single soul read it because she felt too self-conscious—look at you now. Ha!).

This book is for everyone who has ever believed in my purpose, even when I still hadn't found it myself. Your faith in me has led me here, and words to describe how thankful I am will never be enough.

This book is for you, Abue. I feel your love from the other side of the veil—I hope you feel mine, too.

# about the author

Lisina Coney is a New Adult and contemporary romance author with a weakness for heartfelt love connections and happy endings. She believes in creating complex and relatable characters that will make her readers feel less alone in their journeys.

Besides putting her daydreams into words when the sun comes down, Lisina is an avid reader who is obsessed with French fries and tends to force kisses on her very patient cats.

For more information about Lisina's books (as well as some good ol' bonus content), you can visit her Instagram page @lisinaconeyauthor and her website www.lisinaconeyauthor.com